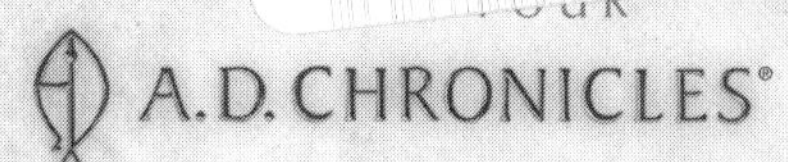

Fourth Dawn

Tyndale House Publishers, Inc.
Carol Stream, Illinois

BODIE & BROCK
THOENE

the middle east
FIRST CENTURY A.D.
Sidon
ITUREA
PHOENICIA
Tyre
Caesarea Philippi
TRACONITIS
GALILEE
Korazin
Capernaum
Gennesaret
Bethsaida
Mediterranean Sea
Magdala
Sea of Galilee
Nazareth
Gadara
DECAPOLIS
(Region of Ten Towns)
Caesarea Maritima
SAMARIA
Jordan River
PEREA
Jericho
Jerusalem
+Mount of Olives
Bethany
to EGYPT
Bethlehem
Herodium
Dead Sea
Machaerus
JUDEA
IDUMEA
N

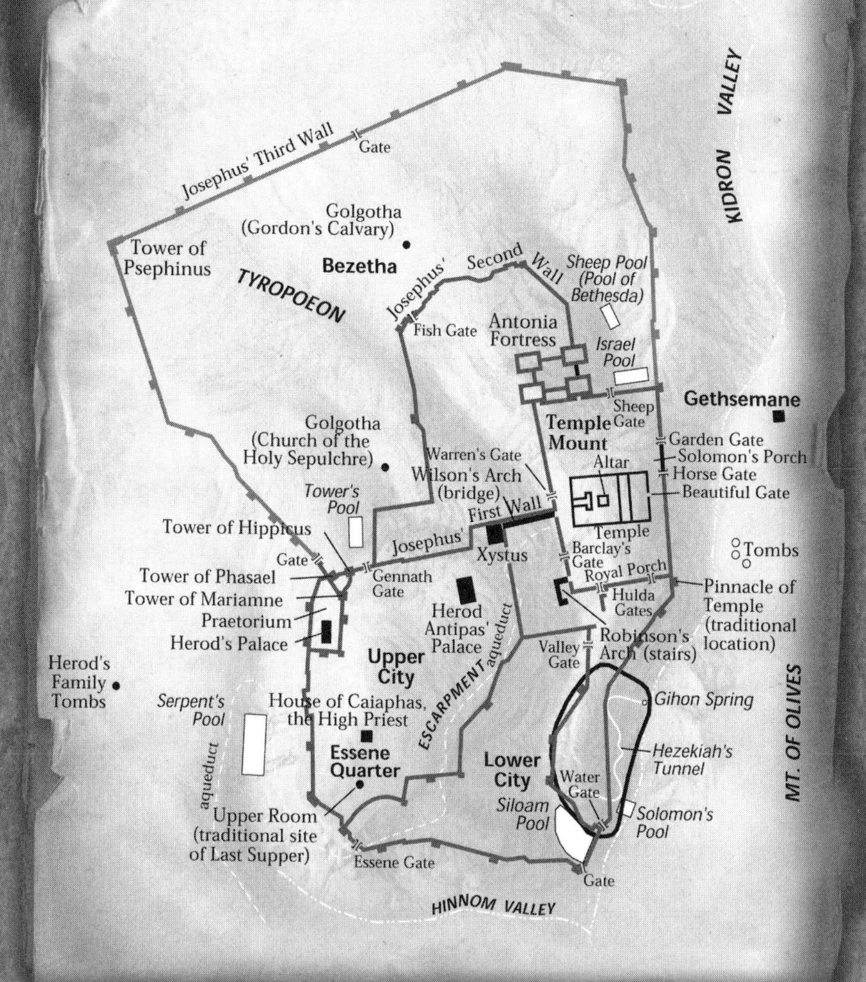
Jerusalem
FIRST CENTURY A.D.
Josephus' Third Wall
Gate
KIDRON VALLEY
Golgotha
(Gordon's Calvary)
Tower of
Psephinus
Bezetha
TYROPOEON
Josephus' Second Wall
Sheep Pool
(Pool of
Bethesda)
Fish Gate
Antonia
Fortress
Israel
Pool
Gethsemane
Sheep
Gate
Temple
Mount
Golgotha
(Church of the
Holy Sepulchre)
Warren's Gate
Garden Gate
Solomon's Porch
Horse Gate
Beautiful Gate
Altar
Wilson's Arch
(bridge)
Tower's
Pool
First Wall
Temple
Tower of Hippicus
Josephus'
Xystus
Barclay's
Gate
Tombs
Gate
Tower of Phasael
Gennath
Gate
Royal Porch
Hulda
Gates
Pinnacle of
Temple
(traditional
location)
Tower of Mariamne
Praetorium
Herod's Palace
Herod
Antipas'
Palace
aqueduct
Robinson's
Arch (stairs)
Valley
Gate
Herod's
Family
Tombs
Upper
City
ESCARPMENT
MT. OF OLIVES
Serpent's
Pool
House of Caiaphas,
the High Priest
Gihon Spring
Hezekiah's
Tunnel
Essene
Quarter
Lower
City
aqueduct
Water
Gate
Siloam
Pool
Solomon's
Pool
Upper Room
(traditional site
of Last Supper)
Essene Gate
Gate
HINNOM VALLEY

Visit Tyndale online at www.tyndale.com.

TYNDALE and Tyndale's quill logo are registered trademarks of Tyndale House Publishers, Inc. *A.D. Chronicles*, the A.D. Chronicles logo, and the fish design logo are registered trademarks of Bodie Thoene.

Fourth Dawn

A.D. Chronicles series designed by Rule 29, www.rule29.com

Designed by Dean H. Renninger

Edited by Ramona Cramer Tucker

Published in association with the literary agency of Alive Communications, Inc., 7680 Goddard Street, Suite 200, Colorado Springs, CO 80920.

Library of Congress Cataloging-in-Publication Data

Thoene, Bodie, date.
Fourth dawn / Bodie & Brock Thoene.
p. cm. — (A.D. chronicles ; bk. 4)
ISBN 978-0-8423-7515-3
ISBN 978-0-8423-7516-0 (pbk.)
1. Jesus Christ—Fiction. 2. Bible. N.T.—History of Biblical events—Fiction. I. Thoene, Brock, date. II. Title.
PS3570.H46F68 2005
813′.6—dc22 2005010858

Printed in the United States of America

19 18 17 16 15 14 13
11 10 9 8 7 6 5

For Laurie Potratz, with love . . .

and ten pounds of See's chocolate!

God said, "Let there be lights in the expanse of the sky to separate the day from the night, and let them serve as signs to mark seasons and days and years, and let them be lights in the expanse of the sky to give light on the earth." And it was so. God made two great lights—the greater light to govern the day and the lesser light to govern the night. He also made the stars. God set them in the expanse of the sky to give light on the earth, to govern the day and the night, and to separate light from darkness. And God saw that it was good. And there was evening, and there was morning—the FOURTH DAWN.

GENESIS 1:14-19

Prologue

Dawn. A sky the color of a crimson apple ripening above the world.

"Get up. Don't be afraid," said the Incarnate One who had by His word created the rising sun and the heavens and the earth.

Yeshua was Himself again. Or . . . no. Rather, He was the human part of Himself again. He was—or rather, He seemed—ordinary. Mary's son. Like any mother's son.

But the three talmidim trembling before Him had witnessed His transfiguration from mere human to something beyond their understanding. The thunderous voice of the Almighty had silenced their foolish comments. The booming words of the Almighty Father had rattled their bones and flattened them on the ground: **This is my beloved Son! I am well pleased with him! Listen to him!**[1]

Peter, Ya'acov, and John had seen Yeshua's true identity revealed: Who He always was before time. Who He is now. Who He will be when time ceases to exist.

Yeshua, Messiah, had stood face-to-face talking with Mosheh, the lawgiver, and Elijah, the prophet, who never died. The three had discussed Yeshua's exodus from the world of men and time. His terrified talmidim had witnessed something amazing: They had seen Yeshua transformed! No longer ordinary human flesh, He shone like molten silver, eternally alive, shimmering like the sun upon a vast sea!

And then afterwards Yeshua said, "Don't be afraid."

"Don't be afraid?" He must have been joking.

Their knees were weak as they followed Him. They dared not speak as He led them down toward the plain. The earth, hidden beneath a layer of clouds, seemed as though it was covered in water.

A hawk cried and spiraled above their heads. A covey of quail, startled by footsteps, burst from the brush.

Yeshua looked over His shoulder at their ashen faces. Were they still too shaken to notice the beauty of the sunrise?

His eyes twinkled with amusement.

He could have been every man's son.

Any man's brother.

The son of Mary.

The events of last night left no doubt that He was also the only Son of The One who had thundered from the cloud.

Gravel clattered from the narrow path into the ravine below. Yeshua instructed them, "Don't tell anyone what you have seen, until the Son of Man has been raised from the dead."[2]

"Raised from the dead?" Why did that phrase not elicit a flood of questions?

Ah, well. Like the covey of quail, Peter's thoughts scattered, and the minds of his companions flew after.

Curiosity turned to Mosheh and Elijah, the two men who had coalesced from thin air to converse with Yeshua.

Mosheh, the lawgiver. Elijah, the prophet. In the flesh?

Peter skipped over the part Yeshua had mentioned about Himself being raised from the dead, which implied Yeshua would actually die. Peter ignored the part when the voice of Yahweh had spoken, interrupting his prattle. Peter asked, "Why then do the teachers of the law say that Elijah must come first?"[3]

Yeshua replied, "They are right. True. To be sure, it is written by the prophet Malachi that Elijah will come first and will restore all things. But pay attention to what I am telling you. Elijah has already come, only they did not recognize him. They have done to him everything they wished. In the same way, the Son of Man is going to suffer at their hands."[4]

It seemed that Peter had momentarily learned his lesson not to contradict Yeshua. There was no follow-up query on that subject. *You? Suffer like Yochanan? You? First Light of Dawn? Gleaming Daybreak? Shining Star of Righteousness? You? Who illuminates the dark night of men's souls? You? Suffer at the hands of the same dissipated, ignorant louts who silenced Yochanan the Baptizer for the sake of a dancing girl's whim?*

These were not questions Yeshua's disciples asked Him. Perhaps because they could not fathom the possibility that the Messiah, Son of the Most High God, Lord of all the Angel Armies, could be injured by a drunken, lecherous tyrant like Herod Antipas. Perhaps now they understood and believed that Yochanan the Baptizer truly was the Elijah—the long-awaited fulfillment in the very last two verses of the scroll of Malachi.[5] Yochanan the Baptizer was indeed the subject of the Malachi prophecy.

Yeshua often told them that no man ever born of woman was greater than Yochanan.[6] "*And yet,* tsaowr, *the youngest child, in the kingdom of* olam haba *is greater than Yochanan.*"

A child? The least? The smallest? The youngest? The most vulnerable? *Tsaowr?* So near to the word *tsara*, the word for leper. So, an infant without value to the world was greater than Yochanan? And Yochanan, the Elijah, was Yeshua's second-in-command, the messenger sent ahead to announce the coming of Messiah?[7]

The disciples as yet did not understand how a little child could be greater than Yochanan if Yochanan was the greatest man ever born of woman. How could a baby be as exalted as Elijah or Mosheh on the mountain? They had no real answers that first dawn as they paused to pick Peniel, the man born blind who now could see, off the ground and collected the others who had spent the night waiting for Yeshua to return with an army to conquer the world.

And later that day, when Yeshua pointed at Mount Hermon and explained to them that faith could move a mountain of evil and dump it into the sea, they did not understand what He meant.[8] Several among them spent the morning summoning their faith and then commanding stones to fly in the name of Yeshua. The stones were not impressed.

The talmidim longed for the kind of clarity that would support their ideas. *Their* ideas of how things should be. Not God's ideas. They did not really want to know the truth. Not really. They wanted Herod Antipas deposed. They wanted their own king. They wanted the

Romans soundly beaten and Rome leveled by fire from heaven. Therefore they did not ask questions that, if answered, would have made a different kind of sense out of the purpose of the birth and incarnation of Messiah.

"Suffer," He said. *Hmm.*

You? First Dawn rising on eternity? You? Messiah! Son of Man! Suffer at the hands of men? But WHY?

No, they did not ask this question. Nobody asked WHY He had to suffer. And they secretly wished Yeshua would stop talking about the suffering part of it.

A few weeks had passed since the transfiguration of Yeshua from mortal to immortal, then back to mortal again. But Peniel had not stopped dreaming of the thunder. It made him sweat. Often he awoke with his heart beating like a drum at the thought of his own unholiness.

For a time, the three disciples who had been with Yeshua on the mountain—Peter, Ya'acov, and John—were more quiet than usual. And, as Yeshua instructed, they did not speak of what they had seen to anyone.

On occasion they discussed it among themselves. Peniel saw them, heads together, whispering. Always whispering.

Peniel, who had witnessed the revelation uninvited and from a distance, did not reveal what he had seen and heard and felt. He carried the knowledge of it, the terror of it, alone.

Now Peter was again as blustery as ever. Ya'acov and John appeared to have forgotten the event.

But Peniel's hands still shook when Yeshua came near. He bowed in nervous bobs and backed away from Yeshua, like a court jester leaving a king's throne room.

Peniel had not heard Yeshua's command not to be afraid. And how well he remembered what awesome power was locked inside Yeshua's seemingly ordinary flesh.

Hidden behind hands and feet and a face and skin was the very One whose first word had commanded *LIGHT*![9]

His second word had been *GOOD*![10]

Too soon he had spoken the word *MAN*![11]

And after the word *man*, things had become difficult and complicated because every man secretly wanted to be God. Every man wanted to give the orders.

Peniel lay down in terror each night and stared up at the stars. He wondered what great command the Incarnate Word would issue when He stripped off His disguise and once again revealed His glory to all men.

Don't speak the next word yet, Yeshua. I'm not ready for it! Please. Call me to you with a smile and the crook of a finger. Don't speak! I am afraid of the fourth word!

At last Yeshua took notice of Peniel's strange behavior. It was back in Caesarea Philippi at the wedding of Alexander the Flute Maker to Zahav, daughter of Rabbi Eliyahu.

Old friends of the family had come from as far away as Alexandria to attend.

Alexander sat in a chair and played his flute. Peniel and several other strong fellows lifted him up, chair and all, and passed him around above them.

The women danced on one side of the partition while all the men danced on the other side. Yeshua, spinning in circles, laughing, danced with four-year-old Hero, son of Alexander, high upon His shoulders.

It was plain that Yeshua liked weddings. Peniel wondered, *Did Yeshua dance at the first wedding ever? The one in the Garden?*

Yeshua looked so ordinary, Peniel thought, stepping out of the line of dancers when Yeshua came near. How could the King of Heaven continue to live among men and pretend that He was not the creator of mankind and the inventor of weddings?

The dancing continued, joyful. No one in a hurry to stop.

Peniel staggered back to the table to find his cup of wine amidst the clutter of the banquet. He was hot. Someone had pinched his cup, so he chose another full one and quaffed deeply. Good wine. Very good. Peniel scanned the table, spotted another full cup, and drained it dry. He wiped his lips with the back of his hand and was near to picking up a third.

Suddenly he felt a hand on his shoulder.

A voice spoke his name. "Peniel?"

It was The Voice! Yeshua!

Peniel flinched and knocked over a bottle, which fell into a plate of hummus, which splashed on his clothes.

Peniel began to bow and bob. "Yes. Yes . . . yes . . . Lord."

Yeshua threw back His head and laughed a huge laugh. Why did the stars not spin like tops at such a laugh?

"Peniel." Yeshua cupped Peniel's face in both hands. "You knew who I was before you saw me on the mountain."

Peniel closed his eyes. "Yes, but . . . I hadn't seen you as you really are!"

"Open your eyes," Yeshua said gently.

Peniel obeyed.

Yeshua was still grinning as if He might burst into laughter again. "Peniel, do not be afraid. This is who I am for the present. Do not be afraid."

"I can't help it."

"Why are you afraid?"

"Because you're not at all what you seem. I saw you as you are."

"Peniel. Have you forgotten? I was a baby born just like you." He put a hand on Peniel's brow. "There, now, do not be afraid. I was born just like any man."

At His words it was as though warm oil poured over Peniel's head, soothing his spirit all the way to his toes. No, it was not the wine. It was the Word that calmed him.

Peniel said, "Heh. Well, all right. If you say so. I won't be afraid."

"Good." Yeshua patted his back. "I have a job for you, eh?"

"A job?"

"Only for you, my friend. You see, gathered here at this wedding are some who remember what happened. They recall the birth of my cousin Yochanan. Zadok is somewhere; I saw him dancing. Yes, there he is. And his elder brother, Onias, just arrived from Alexandria, is in the house now. A very important part of the story. Onias' daughter is speaking to my mother, telling her they have finally made it. Oh yes, they all remember the details of the last days of old Herod. Thirty years it has been and a little more. And they will be ready to sit and talk awhile. Someone needs to collect the stories. Can you do that?"

"Oh, Lord, you know me! I'm Peniel! I love a good story!"

"And I love a good wedding."

For just a moment Peniel imagined Yeshua, the great and glorious

Yeshua of the shining Mountain, standing as Rabbi before the first couple. Peniel blurted, "Lord, please tell me, then. I must know! Was there a wedding canopy in Eden?"

His laugh! Oh, such a laugh. Did the stars shine more brightly when Yeshua laughed?

He answered Peniel softly, "Such a good question. You always ask such good questions. The first wedding canopy? Yes, there was a chuppah in the first wedding." Yeshua spread His arms wide and stood on His tiptoes to demonstrate a very tall chuppah. "The canopy was the outstretched wings of the groomsmen. You see, the archangels Michael and Gabriel stood as witnesses to the first marriage. One on one side, one on the other side. Very tall. Their wing tips touched above the heads of the bride and groom. Yes, like that. You see, I'm not the only one who likes a good wedding. Now go tell Zadok that his brother has arrived." Yeshua gave Peniel a little nudge.

Peniel, calm for the first time in weeks, hailed Zadok, the old shepherd of Beth-lehem. A giant of a man, with a patch on his left eye and arms like the branches of an oak, waved at Peniel as he sat and chatted amiably with a man half his size and half his age.

Beads of perspiration stood out on Zadok's brow. "I'm not the dancer I used to be! But my boys! My boys!" He waved toward the three little boys who played a game of tag in the midst of the whirling dancers. "They'll not give in till the sun peeps up in the mornin'."

Peniel broke in. "Zadok, sorry. Sorry. Yeshua told me I should tell you your brother's arrived."

Zadok sprang to his feet. "My brother? Here?"

"Inside, Yeshua said. I'd rather listen than dance. I can't dance anyway. So if you don't mind—"

"Praise be to the Eternal. I sent word to Onias months ago. Thirty years it's been! Thirty years and more since I laid eyes on him! I'd almost given up hope."

"And Yeshua told me to ask you questions about what happened in the last days of old Herod the Butcher."

"No need to ask questions! We'll be talking all night! Aye! Thirty years to make up for." Zadok dashed into the house. "Brother! Brother!"

"We're in here," the mother of Yeshua called to them from a bedchamber. "Me and Menorah too! They've come a long way!"

Zadok grasped the door frame of the room where his brother lay. Half in and half out of the room, Zadok seemed to take in the pitiful sight, as though he did not recognize the person who was his brother.

"Zadok?" The word was feeble.

The familiar voice broke through. Zadok burst into tears. "Onias! Onias!" Weeping, Zadok fell to his knees beside the bed, where an old man lay propped up on pillows. The two brothers were a sharp contrast: Zadok, strong and hearty; Onias, like a brittle leaf that might crumble and blow away at any moment. His hands were clawlike and bore terrible scars through the centers of his palms. His skin was yellowed parchment. Cheeks sunken and eyes blue-white with cataracts.

The brothers embraced. Menorah began to weep as her uncle pulled her into their circle. "Menorah! Your aunt Rachel is gone these two years past. Ah, that she could have lived to see the both of you!"

Mary, eyes shining, looked on, drinking it in.

Thirty years was a long time to be apart.

Peniel, not wanting to intrude, backed away and lingered outside in the corridor while the two men, Mary, and Onias' daughter, Menorah, related the news of recent months. Onias and Menorah told how long it had taken to travel by ship from Alexandria and where they had stayed on the way to Caesarea Philippi.

Zadok spoke of Herod Antipas, the death of Yochanan the Baptizer, and the corruption that had once again soiled Jerusalem and swept across Eretz-Israel.

"Like in the days of the old butcher king, eh, Zadok?" Onias wheezed.

"Aye. Very like. Thirty-some years. A snap of the fingers."

Just then Mary said to the brothers, "There is one who will hear and remember." She popped her head out the door. "Peniel! Yeshua says you are a fellow who knows how to ask good questions."

"I listen better than I dance. That's true," Peniel said.

Zadok shouted that Peniel should enter and not stand outside like a ninny when Yeshua had commanded him to record the story of his brother and Mary and himself.

Peniel tried not to stare at the disfigured hands of the old man in the bed when he came into the room.

"Honored sir." Peniel bowed slightly. Then, to the daughter, who was a pear-shaped, golden-haired woman in her midthirties, "And you, honored daughter of Zadok's brother."

Zadok leaned close to his brother. "Never mind that y' cannot see him. He's a scrap of a lad. A good fellow. Used to be a blind beggar at Nicanor Gate but can see like a hawk now. And what a head for stories he has."

Onias chuckled. "Well now, well. So you are the one. We heard about you even in Alexandria."

"Yes, sir. I'm Peniel. I was blind, but now I see."

Mary showed Peniel to a desk in the corner.

Zadok growled, "You'll have to listen at top speed, boy, if you want to get all the details. We have a lot to catch up on."

After that, Peniel's presence was hardly noticed. The brothers took up their conversation where they had left off thirty years before.

"As I was sayin'"—Zadok scowled—"very little changed after thirty-odd years. It was a time, that was! Oh, it was a time! Only difference is, now the sons of the butcher king are even more corrupt than their father, Herod, was."

Onias wagged his head slowly. "Not possible, Zadok. In all the history of Israel, there's not been a king so corrupt as Herod the Great."

Peniel, who knew the treachery of Antipas, old Herod's son, frowned at that assertion.

Zadok scoffed. "Never any as bad as old Herod? I may differ on that point! Ahab, in the days of the first Elijah! Now Ahab, there was a devil in man's skin."

"No, not even Ahab can match Herod the Butcher King! In the days the second Elijah was born, not even Ahab could match the devil." Onias held his claw up to the light. "What do you say, Mary?"

Mary raised her eyebrows slightly before she spoke. "I agree. Hmm, I do. Not even Ahab. I remember it well, that year. Though I was only a girl. David's tomb. The genealogy records in the Temple. What a time it was."

"Aye, I'll concede to it." Zadok stuck out his lower lip and glowered at Peniel. "Herod the Great was tyrant over our people. It was the year our Elijah came. Elijah. Have you got that, boy?"

PART I

See, I will send you the prophet Elijah before that great and dreadful day of the LORD comes. He will turn the hearts of the fathers to their children, and the hearts of the children to their fathers; or else I will come and strike the land with a curse.

MALACHI 4:5-6

CHAPTER 1

Tovah found the baby early one morning in a ravine beside the road as she traveled home to Jerusalem. With her was her husband, Onias, a young rabbi who made his living teaching Torah school.

A thin, bleating cry emanated from beneath the seven-branched sage.

"Onias? What's that?" Tovah stopped and peered over the embankment. Other travelers surged past, not hearing or noticing what Tovah had plainly heard.

"Just a baby goat." Onias took her arm and urged her to press along. "The mother's nearby, no doubt. They never leave the kids for long. Come on then, Tovah! I have a meeting with Simeon and Zachariah before our course begins in the morning."

A reedy cry, so human, drifted up.

"I have to see." Tovah started down the faint track.

Onias shrugged impatiently and planted himself on the verge of the highway as she picked her way down the ravine.

The rustling of brush. Where was the creature? Had the mother hidden it?

"Tovah?" Onias called.

She waited, held her breath, listening. Pilgrims' voices, laughter, and feet crunching on gravel nearly drowned out the weak mewing of the thing.

Then, beside the boulder, the low branches of the sagebush trembled. As Tovah crooned, "Where are you, then?" the timid cry erupted into a bellow of infant rage.

This was no goat! Tovah knelt and pulled back the brush to reveal a baby girl, kicking and squirming in the dirt.

She was only hours old. The cord was uncut and still attached to the afterbirth. She was unwashed and caked with blood. She had not been rubbed with salt, anointed with oil, or swaddled in cloth.

"Onias!" Tovah cried. "Hurry!"

He scrambled down the path to her side, knelt, and gasped at the sight. Missing, for once, was his usual crooked smile. Plain enough, the infant had been abandoned, meant to die of exposure to the elements. Such barbarity was common in Rome among the poor or prostitutes. It was more unusual here in Judea, but rumor was that east of the Jordan unwanted infants were still sacrificed to the fires of Molech.

"Poor thing! Poor little thing! Who would do such a thing? Where is your mother?" Tovah unlaced her sandal. "Onias, your knife!" First tying the cord, Tovah cut it and scooped the infant up in her shawl. She cradled her.

Tiny fists flailed angrily. The back of the child's head fit perfectly in the palm of Tovah's hand. Ten toes. Ten fingers. Perfect! Perfect! And Tovah knew. She was certain. This was the child she had prayed for daily through seven years of miscarriages and stillborn sons!

Somehow the infant knew as well. She fell silent, calmed by Tovah's touch.

"A beautiful child," Tovah said in awe. "Look, Onias! She turns her face to my breast. She's hungry."

"How will she eat?"

"There's a woman on Tinsmith Street whose son is nearly weaned. She let it be known she would like work as a wet nurse."

"Yes. Zadok will be coming to Yerushalayim today also. I'll tell him we need a good milk goat, eh?" Onias put his hand on Tovah's back and gazed down at the child. "She will be fair. Look there! Her eyes are blue—like yours, Tovah. And her hair. Tovah! Golden, like yours."

So Onias and Tovah took the foundling home. They named her

Menorah, because they had found her under the seven-branched sage that resembled the candlestick in the Temple.

Onias and Tovah raised Menorah as their own daughter. She thrived and grew until, by the age of four, she was reading Hebrew as well as any student among Onias' eight-year-old Torah schoolboys.

Everyone in the neighborhood forgot that Menorah had been found beneath a seven-branched sagebush. Her name took on the meaning of the golden candlestick—light and warmth and holiness before the Lord. Her hair was like finely spun gold; her eyes innocent and as blue as the sky.

"Tovah! Your little girl looks just like you," the women in synagogue remarked. "Have you ever seen a child so much like her mother?"

And, like her father, Menorah had a heart for God. She made up songs about angels and heaven as she played at her papa's feet. She spoke often and out loud to the Almighty about every concern and joy. Quick to make friends, Menorah was her father's pride and her mother's comfort.

"Such a gift," Onias remarked to Tovah on the fourth anniversary of her birth and the discovery. It was the day before Onias began his priestly duty serving at the Temple as part of the course of Abijah.

That morning Tovah counted out four new silver temple shekels that she had earned washing the linen clothes of priests. She slid the coins across the table to Onias. "Please, Onias. Take these today for the treasury for the poor . . . as a thank offering to the Merciful One for every year of Menorah's life with us."

Onias and Tovah laid hands upon the head of their sleeping child and prayed, "Blessed are you, O Adonai, who heard our prayers and remembered to have mercy on us when we had no children. Blessed are you who sent us Menorah to lighten our days! Omaine!"

It was the darkest part of a moonless autumn night in this, the thirtieth year of the Roman-backed reign of Herod the Idumean over the Jewish nation of Judea. In Jerusalem there remained at least an hour until cockcrow.

It was the watch when men's souls remained connected to their bodies by the slenderest of threads. It was the season when courage often failed.

In the depths of the Kidron Valley, hundreds of feet below the Temple's pinnacle, a dog barked once, then yowled. Its wail stopped abruptly.

Absolute stillness settled again over Jerusalem.

The aroma of hot blood and charred meat from the day's sacrifices hovered about the armed men like an unseen cloud. The platform of the Temple had long since been sluiced clean and the paving stones scrubbed, but here on a platform, below the brow of the Mount, the thick odor lingered.

The charged air hung heavy around the thirteen watchers, making it difficult for them to breathe. Like the atmosphere, the quiet was oppressive. But no one spoke. Their silence was ordered by the tall, lean figure commanding the nocturnal foray.

Herod, aging king of the Jews and friend of the Roman emperor Caesar Augustus, stood wrapped in a hooded cloak, concealing him from ears to ankles. He was flanked by two of his personal bodyguards, Odus and Silus. These companions-in-arms were supplemented by a troop of ten soldiers from Herod's Idumean homeland.

The monarch's keen, black eyes peered into the west. Saturn had just set—one less witness to Herod's nocturnal undertaking.

The king was not superstitious. Besides, after a reign of nearly thirty years, he was powerful enough to carry out his plan in broad daylight. Both statements were lies.

Lately Herod had been troubled by dreams. In some he saw again the ghost of his wife Mariamme, whose execution Herod had ordered twenty years ago. In his sleep he heard again her ignored protests of innocence, her disregarded pleas for mercy. In some nightmares Herod himself was the target of assassination attempts. He woke panting for breath and drenched in sweat.

He shook off the memories.

Herod was glad neither Jupiter nor Saturn, or any of the gods, remained in the sky to observe him. He was also relieved that the God of the Jews, the occupant of the marble-and-gold-covered sanctuary on the hilltop, had apparently gone to sleep for the night.

Herod reckoned if he offended either the gods of the Romans or the One God of the Jews, he would just make it up by additional sacrifices.

Soon there would be plenty of gold with which to buy the lambs and the bullocks . . . and the compliance of the priests.

There was another reason for the secretive nature of this expedition. It was not that Herod cared a fig for public opinion. His was an absolute monarchy, subject only to the approval of Rome.

But therein lay the rub: Herod did not want a repeat of the riots and mass crucifixions and the possibility of armed intervention by the Romans. Public outrage was certain to follow this night's proceedings. But if nothing was actually seen happening, then the reports could be ascribed to rumor.

Intimidation would take care of the rest.

However, Herod's air of satisfaction was disturbed when he turned eastward. There, newly risen over the mountains of Moab, hovered Sirius, the star the Hebrews called The Guardian.

Hundreds of years earlier the blind Greek poet Homer had written of Sirius: "Whose burning breath taints the red air with fevers, plagues and death."

Herod shivered inside his cloak, straightened his creaking back, then growled to Odus, "It is late enough. We go now."

Torches were produced from inside a guard tower, melting the mass of men and shadows into a molten pool flowing down the Temple steps. Five heavily armed men preceding and five following, flanked on either side by attendants of undoubted loyalty, Herod was at the center of an entourage of protection.

But he did not feel secure even so. Innuendo and scandal were rife around Herod's palace: half brothers at each other's throats, plots being hatched, poisonings contrived. Betrayal and suspicion were the coin of the realm.

Herod swayed briefly, experiencing that momentary dizziness from which he suffered more and more frequently as he neared his sixty-fifth birthday.

Who would succeed him when he was dead? One of his sons: Antipater? Alexander? Aristobulus? One of the others?

How many of them would willingly slit another's throat to clear the line of succession?

And would the heir be willing to wait for Herod . . . or would he try to hurry things along?

And among the common people? More mutterings about their longed-for Messiah, their liberator, their heir of King David, who would set the world right.

The recent years had been lean in Judea. Roman demands for tribute grew ever heavier; so did the requirements of Herod's ambitious building projects. More payments flowed out than taxes and customs duties brought in.

Gold was necessary to purchase security. More gold than remained in the treasury. More than could be extorted from High Priest Boethus and his cadre of Temple officials. More than could be wrung out of the *am ha aretz*, the impoverished people of the land.

Gold would pay more Syrian archers, more Samaritan swordsmen. More gold crossing more palms would uncover more plots, purchase more allegiance.

And Herod knew where to find it.

Partway along the curving, cobbled path skirting the eastern wall of the Ophel Quarter the street climbed again, ascending the hill identifying the ancient City of David.

Halfway down the stretch of King David's capital was the shepherd-king's tomb.

Set into the side of the eastward-facing slope, fronted by granite columns, the bronze door of the crypt displayed the royal seals of both David and his successor-son, Solomon.

At a peremptory gesture from the king, four of the guards shucked their cloaks, revealing stout iron bars slung alongside their short swords. They went to work, prying out the bronze rods that sealed the tomb's entrance from their masonry settings.

Chipping and cracking sounds splintered the night. The other guards scrutinized the deserted streets, ready to challenge and disperse anyone roused by the noise.

Herod broke his own rule of silence by muttering to Silus, "Nothing to be afraid of. Hyrcanus helped himself to some of the gold a hundred years ago. Scribes claim he saw much more than he removed. Much more!"

The last rod clanged to the pavement.

Odus stepped forward. With a single heave of his shoulder he levered open the catch holding the bolt and shot it back.

The way in was open.

Herod impatiently gestured Odus and Silus onward.

The two soldiers exchanged a glance before Silus thrust his torch into the antechamber of the tomb. Fine dust covered the floor. Except for a pair of stone benches, the room was empty.

Silus moved to the next vault. Over his shoulder he said, "I see a gold-covered chair. A throne? Silver bowls. The walls are hung with bronze shields."

"And coins? Chests of coins?" Herod demanded.

"No, nothing like that."

"Go farther in!" Herod stepped past the entry to urge his bodyguards to hurry their search.

Odus drew himself shoulder to shoulder with Silus. The flames of their torches flickered in the draft coming from the outside.

The combined light revealed another inner room. Over the doorway hung a round golden shield inscribed with the six-pointed Mogen David. Around this artifact were carved representations of a shepherd's crook crossed with a scepter. On the other side was inscribed the figure of a lyre supporting a crown.

The view through the portal displayed a pair of raised platforms. On one was a bronze coffin; on the other, a marble sarcophagus.

"Burial chamber of the kings," Silus murmured.

Four narrow openings branched off from the tomb. The fitful gleams of the torches did not penetrate any of the side cavities.

"Go on!" Herod hissed. "What are you waiting for?"

Odus put his foot on the sill.

The torch flames reversed direction as a wispy breeze from inside the grave whispered out. Fiery fingers reached toward Odus' face, making him duck his head aside.

Silus stuck out his hand, thrusting his light past the doorway and into the chamber.

From floor and ceiling, from both sides of the portal, sheets of brilliant white fire, dazzling the eyes, leapt across the opening. Curtains of flames enveloped Odus and Silus. Their robes blazed upward in an instant. So did their hair and beards.

Their screams were cut off by the sound of a furnace's roar.

The inferno's heat drove the horrified onlookers back.

The two lifeless bodies fell to the floor, and the flames were snuffed out as quickly as they had appeared.

Herod screamed, then whimpered, clawing his way out of the crypt. "Drag them out! Seal it up!" he shrieked. "Marble! I will build a marble monument!" Facing the Temple, he cried, "Do you hear? A marble monument!"

There was no reply. Over his shoulder the accusing eye of The Guardian star followed Herod all the way back to his palace, where he drank himself to sleep.

Ecbatana, Kingdom of Parthia
29th year of King Phraates IV
Journal of Court Astronomer Melchior
New Moon Observation
First New Moon after the Fall Equinox
Weather cold, but not unseasonable

Tonight I celebrate the 25th anniversary of my birth and the 5th anniversary of my appointment to serve as Chief Observer here in the capital of this northernmost province of Parthia. This is a special mark of favor for me since the court astrologers are all Zoroastrians, while I am a God-fearer—a Gentile follower of the Jewish faith. The astrologers prefer interpreting signs in warmth and comfort and daylight, so leave the long night watches to me.

With me tonight, as he is every New Moon night, is Balthasar, a venerable Jewish scholar of some seventy years, and his lone granddaughter, Esther.

Because of my personal studies, I will list the names of the wandering stars in both their common form and as they are known to the Jews.

Mercury, called in Hebrew The Messenger, remained visible for almost an hour after sunset.

It is unusual for Mercury to stay aloft for so long. Balthasar says this is significant—a portent of a message about to be delivered.

The thinnest sliver of the New Moon, which is referred to as The Holy, descended behind Mount Alvand in the west some three-quarters of an hour later.

By this time the southwest was aglow with the flame of The Milky Way.

Jupiter, The Righteous, was already well placed for viewing, being almost due south in the constellation of The Water Bearer. Balthasar commented that this was a reminder of baptism, the righteous Jewish practice of religious bathing, but did not elaborate further.

Saturn, called by the Jews The Sabbath, was southeast, in the sign of The Fish. Since ancient times The Fish has represented the nation of Israel. Balthasar says it means there is great longing in the hearts of the Jews for their Sabbath rest—the true rest that can only come with the advent of Messiah. He says nowhere is this more true than in the homeland of the Jews, anguished by the long reign of Herod the Idumean, puppet of Rome. (This I believe Balthasar got from caravan news and not from reading the sky!)

I studied the revolving wheel of night for the rest of the dark hours, till Sirius rose in the east, heralding the dawn. Balthasar noted that its Hebrew name is The Guardian, or in its compound form, Naz-Zer, as in the ones who take the Nazarite vow of separation.

Nothing further suggesting itself and sleep overtaking us, we descended the seven levels of the city to our homes in the White Ring and so to bed.

Will cast up my accounts after some hours' rest.

And Peniel wrote:

It all begins with a Jewish priest, Zachariah, who lived when Herod was king of Judea. Zachariah was a member of the priestly order of Abijah. His wife, Elisheba, was from the priestly line of Aaron. Zachariah and Elisheba were righteous in God's eyes, careful to obey all of the Lord's commandments and regulations. They had no children because Elisheba was barren, and they were both very old. One day Zachariah was serving God in the Temple, for his order was on duty that week.

CHAPTER 2

Zachariah the Levite hunched his bony shoulders within his white robe and cinched the colored sash tighter around his narrow waist. The fall morning was chilly, especially to one who had already completed three score of his hoped-for three score and ten years.

Even here, inside the Temple assembly hall called the Chamber of Hewn Stone, the air had a decided bite to it. Zachariah's knees ached, as did his back. Though his glance through the portal showed the pink light of dawn just beginning to thaw the icy white marble, it seemed an age since the watcher on the pinnacle had cried out day's approach. Surely hours had passed since the triple blast of silver trumpets rang across Jerusalem to announce the beginning of another day's worship of Adonai Elohim, the Lord God of Israel.

The massive gates of the Temple Mount compound swung silently open. Wide-eyed pilgrims assembled in the courts alongside pompous scribes and pinch-faced money changers.

Zachariah ignored his discomfort and prepared his mind for duty and his heart for reverence by mentally replaying what he had earlier recited in unison with the other priests: *"Hear, O Israel! The LORD is our*

God, the LORD *alone! And you must love the* LORD *your God with all your heart, all your soul, and all your strength.*"[12]

Two of the lots for the morning's duties had already been drawn. Those chosen Levites were going about their duties or perhaps had finished. The preparation for the third casting of lots, the one to determine who would enter the Holy Place to burn incense before the Lord, dragged on.

Unable to keep his attention fully focused, Zachariah dreamed of home: his stone cottage in Judea's hill country and his wife, Elisheba. One more day of service he owed the Almighty; then it was home again for at least half a year. Zachariah loved that he had been born a Levite, loved performing his appointed obligations for the Master of the Universe.

Since his bar mitzvah Zachariah had been coming twice each year with others of his division of the priesthood. Over ninety weeks of his life had been dedicated to aiding in performing the sacrifices for HaShem, The Name of the Most High.

Looking around the room, Zachariah could see only one Levite who had a longer term of service: Old Simeon, whose years were beyond counting but whose mind was still quick. Simeon's tongue was even quicker to speak of his longing for Messiah's coming.

Unlike other Levites, whose grandfathers had returned from the Babylonian captivity ignorant of their proper heritage, Zachariah actually knew his lineage. He knew he was truly of the course of Abijah—perhaps the only surviving descendant of Abijah to serve in the correct course.

For many years, when he was younger, that knowledge had been a source of pride for Zachariah. Abijah was the Eighth Course of Levites out of the rotation of twenty-four courses, honored at least in superstition because eight was the number next beyond the completion of the continual Sabbath cycle of seven. Eight as a number was beyond the routines of this world; eight was the number of *olam haba*—the sign of the world to come.

Zachariah sniffed. Long ago he had given up any sense of self-importance. It had disappeared entirely at the same time he and Elisheba despaired of ever having children. If he was the last true heir of Abijah, well then, he was the last. That was all the Almighty's doing and not to be questioned.

Shifting position, Zachariah eased his creaking joints. He was not a scholar, nor did he possess political influence. He was respected and well liked in his village for his piety and his humility and his kindheartedness, but forty childless years of marriage had long since convinced him his lot in life was forever to be a humble one, unnoticed by men or the Almighty either, apparently. Despite the fact that his parents had given him the name meaning "Yahweh has remembered," Zachariah's life was one of humble charity and good counsel, not one celebrated for mighty deeds or acts of faith.

How many times over the early years of their marriage had Elisheba dispatched him to the Holy City with an urgent request for the Lord to remember her? to give her a child as He had done for Abraham's wife, Sarah? to take away her reproach the way He had remembered the patriarch Jacob's barren wife, Rachel? like He had blessed Samu'el the prophet's mother? as He had miraculously quickened the womb of Samson's mother?

All to no avail.

How long had it been since Elisheba had stopped asking?

Zachariah pondered the recollection. Try as he might, he could not recall when they had given up hoping for a child. Fifteen years now? More?

His friend Eliyahu nudged his elbow. "It's you! They've called your name!"

Zachariah blinked, shaking his head as if just awakened from sleep. He? Called to enter the sanctuary?

Astounding! Zachariah had never been selected for the most singular honor a Levite could receive. So great was the distinction that a man was only permitted to receive it once in his lifetime.

Zachariah's head spun. Enter the Holy Place? Rekindle the fire on the Altar of Incense? Stand a heartbeat away from the presence of the Almighty, just beyond the veil?

Dimly Zachariah was aware of being asked to name two other Levites to act as his assistants. Distantly, as if listening to someone else's voice heard from far off, Zachariah requested Onias the Tutor and Simeon the Elder.

The three men were brought to the front of the chamber to receive instruction from the officiating priest. But Zachariah scarcely heard a word. It was to be his privilege to reignite the coals on the altar in front of the veiled Holy of Holies. It was his responsibility to sprinkle the incense there, entreating the Almighty to hear the prayers of His people. It was his obligation to inaugurate the blessings of the Almighty on the day's worship. His alone was the sacred task without which none of the day's sacrifices could begin.

Nor would the charge leave Zachariah unchanged. Forever afterward the men of his village would call him Zachariah the Blessed!

Not Zachariah the Elderly, nor Zachariah the Childless, nor yet Zachariah the Unnoticed by God.

According to the traditional interpretation of Mosheh's promises to the tribe of Levi in Deuteronomy chapter 33, he would always be called Zachariah the Enviable.

His mind swirled with awe and praise and anticipation as Zachariah and his two companions moved toward the sanctuary's entrance.

Zachariah the Richly Remembered!

Ceremonially washed a second time that morning and dressed anew in white robes, Zachariah was now inside the Temple proper. God's house, built by Solomon, rebuilt after the return from captivity, and still undergoing King Herod's expansion, begun over ten years earlier.

Every fragment of his senses stood at attention. While fully reverential in each motion, each action of his duty, Zachariah nevertheless instructed his soul to faithfully record every nuance of this once-in-a-lifetime experience.

The air was dense, hard to draw into the lungs. But did the difficulty lay with the atmosphere or in himself? Zachariah wondered. The Holy Place was redolent with the sweetness of years of burnt incense: balsam and frankincense, galbanum and onycha root. Thirteen spices in all, to which salt was added, according to a formula handed down since Mosheh first issued Yahweh's instructions after Sinai.

Simeon stood to his left, Onias to his right. They faced the square top of the three-foot-tall golden Altar of Incense. It stood immediately in front of the handbreadth-thick brocade curtain screening them from the awesome presence of the Living God.

The gleaming light from the seven-branched menorah lit the scene from the south wall of the Holy Place. Behind Zachariah's right shoulder, on the north wall, was the Table of Shewbread.

Music filtered through the curtained entry that separated them from the outside world.

It was the signal to begin.

Simeon stepped forward, bowed, and approached the altar. With bare hands he carefully brushed the ashes of the previous evening's incense away from the rim of the altar so that none would fall on the floor. Yesterday's prayers were heaped into a golden bowl. Retreating to Zachariah's side, he bowed again and prayed silently.

When Simeon raised his head, his eyes were glistening with tears and his head tilted to one side, as if he had been listening to a soft voice directed to him alone.

Onias advanced, biting his lower lip in concentration. By his side, hanging from golden chains, was a censer containing live coals. These had been retrieved from the Altar of Sacrifice immediately outside the sanctuary, around which other priests gathered, waiting. The fire of the sacrifice provided continuity from one day's worship to the next.

Onias spread the coals across the top of the Altar of Incense, spacing them so they evenly filled the square. They flickered fitfully, orange and black against the gleam of precious metal.

The overlapping light of the menorah's flames cast multiple shadows on the Veil. The silhouettes of many more than three men appeared to Zachariah's eyes, entwined on the embroidered image of the sky.

Onias likewise bowed and withdrew.

When Onias had prayed, both assistants looked to Zachariah, who nodded. Then Onias and Simeon bowed again and backed toward the entry. Their shadows dwindled and disappeared.

Zachariah was left alone in the Holy Place.

The music outside swelled and increased in tempo, in anticipation. When Zachariah applied the incense—a mixture of spices and herbs—to the coals, one of the herbs would give off a profuse cloud of black smoke. This was purposeful since the vapor emerging from the roof of the Temple would signal that the offering of incense had been completed.

There was no longer time for reflection. Any delay would cause consternation and anxiety to the onlookers. It would delay the morning sacrifices, disrupt the routine.

Zachariah raised the lid from the golden bowl nestling in its basket of silver filigree, preparing to ladle a half pound of spices onto the embers.

To Zachariah's left something moved against the backdrop of the curtain. It was not a black shape but the reverse. A glowing patch of light increased in size until, though manlike in form, it was larger.

Much larger.

Zachariah's head prickled. His legs weakened. His right hand reached toward one of the horns of the altar to steady himself but stopped short of touching it.

Do not be afraid, Zachariah, boomed a voice that seemed to resonate within Zachariah's chest as much as it rang in his ears. *God has heard your prayer. He has remembered you . . . and your wife, Elisheba, will bear you a son. You are to name him Yochanan. You will have great joy and gladness, and many will rejoice with you at his birth, for he will be great in the eyes of the Lord. He must never touch wine or hard liquor, and he will be filled with the Holy Spirit, even before his birth. And he will persuade many Israelites to turn to the Lord their God.*[13]

Zachariah's eyes bulged. His lungs felt near to bursting as he held his breath, trying to take it all in. A child? A son? His and Elisheba's? Now, after all this time?

In spite of his confusion, every word, every inflection, imprinted itself on Zachariah's mind.

The angel—for Zachariah knew what the being was—continued at length, then finally paused.

Unbidden, unrehearsed, almost like the involuntary gasp of a drowning man inhaling water instead of air, Zachariah babbled, "How can I know this will happen? I'm an old man now, and my wife is also well along in years."[14]

The music outside swelled to a climax, then stopped. This usually occurred the instant the cloud of black smoke billowed over the sanctuary.

Now the void was awash with murmurs of consternation.

The angel increased in size, swelling the way a full moon appears greater when near the horizon than when overhead.

Zachariah, for his part, shrunk.

The angel said, *I am Gabriel, warrior of the I AM! I stand in the very presence of Elohim. It was He who sent me to bring you this good news. And now, since you didn't believe what I said, you won't be able to speak until the child is born. For my words will certainly come true at the proper time.*[15]

Zachariah sank to his knees at last, holding the bowl of incense in front of him like a supplication. As he watched, Gabriel's form diminished to a point of light, then vanished altogether.

Minutes passed before Zachariah was able to regain his feet. Mechanically he spread the incense over the coals, which blazed with renewed vigor. A wave of smoke billowed upwards, filling the space and overflowing toward heaven.

Zachariah escaped into broad daylight, only to find himself trapped inside a circle of dumbfounded and apprehensive onlookers. He tried to speak, to explain, to praise, to offer any verbal reassurance, but he could not.

He could not utter a word.[16]

Daylight still picked out the topmost spires of the Temple, suffusing the gold-leaf-trimmed facade with the even-more-golden glow of sunset. It was as if burnished tongues of flame leapt up from the House of the Almighty. The Tyropoean Valley, between the Temple Mount and the Western Hill, was already buried in shadow.

From the rooftop of his modest home in the valley, north of the Gennath Gate, Onias the Tutor studied the gleaming elevation of the Temple. With him were his taller brother, Zadok the Shepherd, and his smaller brother-in-law, Eliyahu the Rabbi.

"And y' both questioned him directly? This is not the embellished report of some gossiper?" Zadok inquired bluntly.

"No!" Onias responded firmly with a shake of his thick, brown hair. "I was the first to reach him afterwards. He was straining to speak. His eyes bulged like he had something caught in his throat. When Eliyahu suggested a writing tablet, Zachariah nearly jumped on the Levite who fetched it!"

"But you yourself saw nothin' *unusual* within the sanctuary?"

Onias shook his head vigorously. "Old Simeon and I had already gone out. It seemed like forever before Zachariah staggered out."

"He couldn't speak, yet he remembered everythin' that had happened to him?" Zadok queried doubtfully.

Eliyahu, dwarfed alongside the towering form of the shepherd, affirmed this fact in a voice that squeaked with excitement. "Every detail! Every word! Here is a true copy of what the angel spoke." Eliyahu waved a folded wooden case containing a pair of wax tablets under Zadok's nose.

Resuming his narrative where Zadok had previously interrupted, Eliyahu read:

> *"He will persuade many Israelites to turn to the Lord their God. He will be a man with the spirit and power of Elijah, the prophet of old. He will precede the coming of the Lord, preparing the people for His arrival. He will turn the hearts of the fathers to their children, and he will change disobedient minds to accept godly wisdom."*[17]

"Exactly as the prophet Malachi wrote four centuries ago,"[18] Onias noted, pondering. "And now this. Coming on the heels of the rumor that Herod has desecrated David's tomb."

"No possibility of trickery?" Zadok asked.

Onias gazed firmly into the shepherd's challenging eyes. "Zachariah? Blot out that notion, Brother." His crooked smile crept across his thin features. "There is no more honorable, more worthy soul than Zachariah! Besides, to what purpose? He's no Sadducee seeking to advance in Temple hierarchy, currying favor with High Priest Boethus. He's not a scribe hoping to increase his reputation and thereby his fees! Day after tomorrow he goes back to his home. It means more to him that he's to have a son! I truly believe the rest of the message will take longer to sink in, if you follow me."

With lowered voice Zadok inquired, "And the Temple officials? The high priest's cadre? What of them?"

Onias waved a dismissive hand. "There's to be an 'inquiry.' The word has already been sent around not to speak of this at all. The Temple officials told Zachariah that to his face. Not to speak of it. He cannot speak at all, but who can stop him from telling it!"

Zadok nodded, his jet-black braids of hair and beard swinging solemnly. "Politics. High Priest Boethus needs to consult with King Herod before he responds, y' know, to see how the king wants this to be handled. Anything related to the comin' of Messiah makes Herod nervous . . . and anything makin' Herod nervous has twice that effect on Boethus!"

"It'll be hard to keep this under wraps." Eliyahu stared at the first stars popping out in the eastern heavens. "Old Simeon says he saw no angel, but he did hear a voice! It told him he'd not die before he saw the Lord's Messiah!"[19]

"So, what's to be done?" Zadok asked. "For our part, I mean?"

Onias shrugged. "We watch. We wait. We study. Zachariah stays with Old Simeon while here in Yerushalayim. I'll see what else I can learn from them. Meanwhile, you go back to your duties with the flocks, Eliyahu to his flock, and I to my students. And most of all, we pray." He gestured toward a bright star hovering over the Temple, directly above where the golden eagle carved into Agrippa's Gate was swallowed in deep blackness. "*A star will come out of Jacob*,"[20] Onias said, quoting the prophecy in the book of Numbers. "What if it happens in our lifetime? What if?"

CHAPTER 3

Panting, snarling, glaring about like a wolf at bay, Herod the king stood in the corner of his bedchamber in the Jericho palace. His feet were bare. The hem of his nightdress hung to his knees. This much was as it should be, but nothing else was in order. Over the silk robe Herod wore, hammered bronze armor covered him from his shoulders to below his waist.

While Talmai, Herod's chief steward, looked on, the Judean monarch seized a bronze helmet shaped like a pointed Phrygian hat and plopped it on his head. He also grasped a sword from a cache of weapons displayed beside the royal bed.

Whirling suddenly, he confronted Talmai. "Is it a judgment, do you think?" the king babbled.

The present fit had begun when Herod heard the news that something *unusual* had supposedly happened at this morning's sacrifice. Herod had ranted and raved for about an hour, then calmed down.

The aging monarch, after being dosed by his physicians for a variety of ailments, had eaten his supper as usual. Then he drank himself into a stupor and was dragged off to bed.

But this time the drug-and-alcohol-induced rest had not lasted.

A quarter hour ago Herod had awakened, screaming that someone was in his room trying to kill him.

Finding no intruders, the baffled and frightened guards had summoned Talmai.

The king snatched the long, slender Nabatean sword free of its scabbard and flashed it around his head. "It is because of the tomb! The tomb! Spirits are preaching rebellion!"

The chief steward did not want the blade slashing about his own ears. He shook his head. "You've done all due penance, paid for countless guilt and sin offerings, been absolved by High Priest Boethus himself. This is not about the tomb of David. The Levite involved in this wild tale about an angel and a prophetic message is a frail old man, a nobody pretending to be dumbstruck, trying to make himself seem important. Nobody else saw anything. Besides, what possible significance does a crazy man's imaginary vision hold for the king of the Jews?"

"That is it, then? The fabricated story of an old man?"

"Certainly, Majesty. Nothing more."

Herod nodded slowly; then a crafty expression crept over his face. "But what if it is part of a plot? a deliberate attempt to spread rumors about how Messiah might come soon, eh? Coming to replace me! Inflame the people against me!"

Talmai, in his turn, displayed a brief wily gleam in his squinted eyes. This reaction by the king was promising. It might give Talmai the very opening he had been seeking to launch a plot of his own. "High Priest Boethus will make certain the tale spreads no further. And I will see to the rest, Majesty; I promise you that. No spirits, but if there is a real conspiracy, I'll root it out and destroy it."

An edge of hysteria crept back into Herod's voice. "But will Boethus stay controlled? What if he is involved?"

Talmai reassured him. "I'll double my spies in Yerushalayim, Highness. I'll trust no one."

From the wall-mounted trophies, Talmai plucked a rectangular Jewish shield. It was leather over wood but embossed with gold leaf. On it was engraved a stylized shape called the Tree of Life. "You are the only king of the Jews, Majesty. No one can take that from you. Rest now. Rest."

All of Jerusalem was asleep yet the air crackled with danger and rumor since Zachariah's vision.

From the city walls the night watchman called out the beginning of the third watch. Wise men did not speak openly of signs and portents in a city ruled by Herod.

Ashen, Zachariah sat before the lamp in a windowless basement room of Simeon's house and with gestures attempted to explain to Onias and Old Simeon what he had seen and heard inside the Holy Place.

"A vision?" Onias pressed him.

Zachariah shook his head and spread his hands to say that it was much, much more.

"A dream?" Simeon asked as smoke rose in a haze before him.

Zachariah waved away the suggestion that he might have imagined something. *Bigger! Bigger!* his hands seemed to say.

Old Simeon twirled his right earlock. "Not a dream . . . more than a vision . . . for many of us have dreamed dreams and seen visions these days." Simeon leaned forward and grasped Zachariah's arm. "An angel, true? An angel was sent?"

Zachariah nodded vigorously.

"Of course true. An angel has come to you . . . been sent . . . and has spoken to you. Told you things that are to come."

Zachariah mopped his brow in relief. Simeon understood. Zachariah pantomimed rocking a baby in his arms, then pointed to himself.

Simeon interpreted for Onias. "Zachariah will father a child . . . hold his own child in his arms."

Zachariah pointed to his throat and then his mouth. He mouthed a word without a sound: *EL-LI-JAH.*

Simeon closed his eyes. "Elijah. The one who is to come . . . to prepare the way for Messiah." The old man smiled. "So I will see him. I will see The One who will wear the crown!"

Onias stuck out his lower lip thoughtfully. "I am a teacher and one of your talmidim, Rebbe Simeon. But when it comes to something as miraculous as this, I feel as dim as Zachariah is dumb. Help me understand."

"Onias, you're descended from Levi as I am. As is Zachariah.

Priests before the Lord. Among the few who can trace our lineage back to Aaron. You witnessed something—"

Onias raised a hand in correction. "Hold on. No, I saw nothing. Heard nothing. But there I stood, with hundreds there as well, waiting in the court for Zachariah to come out. I thought maybe he'd been struck dead, but it never entered my head he was in there communicating with something—someone—who struck him dumb. But you were as much a part of the scene as I was, Rebbe Simeon. Did you hear anything?"

Simeon nodded slowly, then nodded again. "Aye."

"Well, one of the two of you must speak up and tell me what. And since it isn't likely to be our friend Zachariah who'll speak, why don't you, Rebbe Simeon, explain to me what this all means?"

Simeon tapped the side of his nose, stood, and rechecked the bolt on the door, lest servants enter. Beckoning Onias and Zachariah to follow, he inclined his head to a stone seat built into the wall. It was covered with cushions for sleeping and a brown wool blanket. "Young man, Zachariah *will* soon speak to us. Though not this Zachariah, but the *prophet* Zechariah who long ago wrote of this very hour and what was to come." The old rabbi passed the tattered covering to Onias and, pressing between the cracks, pushed back the top slab, which disappeared into the wall. A shallow tray, cluttered with spoons and plates and cups, was revealed.

Onias blinked down at it.

"Take out the tray," Simeon instructed.

Onias obeyed, revealing neatly folded linens and a fine prayer shawl and ornate phylacteries on top. Onias scratched his beard. "Clever storage, but still no clearer to me."

Simeon stooped and removed the second layer of contents, placing everything on the table. "Zachariah! Lift the lamp higher."

The interior of the stone hollow was illuminated. Simeon slid his hand along the lowest joint, then pressed inward. The stone bottom groaned and slid open with a *whoosh*, revealing steep, almost vertical steps vanishing into darkness.

Simeon seemed to take delight in the expressions of surprise on the faces of Onias and Zachariah. "An ancient cistern. From the days of Solomon. Nothing out of the ordinary . . . yet. Here." He took the lamp from Zachariah, swung his leg over the ledge, and descended into the hole. "So? You are coming?"

Zachariah followed without hesitation.

Onias hung back a moment before he plunged in. He shuddered, his emotions a stew of terror, curiosity, and excitement as his shoulders brushed the narrow passageway that led twenty-two steps into the empty water cistern.

The shadows cast by the lamplight deepened the lines of Simeon's face. He held the lamp to reveal the raised carving of a seven-branched menorah at eye level on the far wall.

"A menorah? In a cistern?" Onias asked curiously.

"Each of its seven branches represents one of the visible lights in the heavens and the seven eyes of the Eternal. Even here, where all is darkness, the radiance of the Lord's creation shines. The pagans have made false gods of what the One God has created, but here, in the stones of Yerushalayim, Truth will shine."

Simeon touched the flame of each branch from right to left and spoke the meaning of their Hebrew names.

MOON-MERCURY-VENUS-SUN-MARS-JUPITER-SATURN

Holy Spirit ***Sabbath***

Messenger Star ***Righteous***

Splendor ***The Adam***

Holy Fire

The wall yawned open. The space filled with a rushing wind that blew out the light.

Onias gasped at the absolute blackness and the sweet fragrance of incense. "It's very dark." He groped at the cold stone.

"You're afraid, Onias? Remember the song your mother sang when you were a boy? Afraid of the dark, eh?" In a croaking voice Simeon began to sing a child's song about Messiah, in which each of the seven visible lights was mentioned:

"Shabbatai, Sabbath Lord, we rest in you.
Tzadik, Righteous One, we long for you.

Ma'Adim, The Adam, perfect, coming soon.
Shammesh, Holy Fire, to purify iniquity.
Nogah, Splendor of Heaven, descend to men.
Cokhabh, Star, ascend out of Jacob.
HaKodesh, Holy Spirit, illuminate our hearts!"

An echo like many ancient voices resounded beyond the cistern.

Onias waited until the song died away. "My mother never sang that song. And it's still dark. How do we get on?"

Simeon instructed, "Raise two fingers and touch the ceiling. You'll find three patterns. Grooves. One as wide as one finger. Another as wide as two fingers. A third as wide as three fingers."

Onias found the patterns directly above his head. His heart raced. Fear evaporated. "Which one is our road?"

Simeon directed, "Zachariah, you! Between Onias and me. That's right. Come on. In line. Each holds to the back of the other. I lead. Onias in the rear. Two fingers fit into the groove two fingers wide. Don't step to the right or left, eh?"

"Why not?"

"If you knew, you'd worry. Why worry? Better you shouldn't worry. Trust me."

"Rebbe Simeon? The other slots?"

"Lead to other places. Places we aren't going."

Onias hooked his left index finger in the back of Zachariah's belt. Right hand aloft, Onias thrust two fingers up like a raised torch in the blackness and slid them along the map in the roof of the passageway. He was aware when walls opened and the path forked. The three tracks diverged. Staying on course, the three men shuffled through the darkness. Their track wound down and down until at last the trail became level.

Onias knew they had traveled far beneath the Temple Mount in the labyrinth of secret chambers constructed hundreds of years before by Solomon as the first Temple rose to crown Jerusalem. Some now claimed that the prophet Elijah was still living. And that he knew of a passage by which he entered the Temple grounds on special days to stand among the citizens of Israel and worship, his true identity unknown to anyone.

Legend said that just before the last exile, when Babylon laid siege to Jerusalem, the prophet Jeremiah and his secretary, Baruch, had hidden the Ark of the Covenant in a secret chamber directly beneath the Temple. The location of the Ark and other holy artifacts remained concealed. After the return from exile, the Ark was never returned to the Holy of Holies. Knowledge of the location was lost forever as lines of guardians died out. But in some cases, knowledge of the exact hiding places of certain artifacts had been passed from father to son as the ancient pact of guardianship continued.[21]

Was old Simeon among those entrusted with such a secret?

The groove in the low ceiling ended abruptly.

Simeon was hoarse as he halted. One decisive syllable announced they had arrived: "So."

"We're here?" Onias queried. "What is 'here'?"

"The chamber of the prophet Zechariah."

Onias heard the sound of fingers brushing stone and then the grinding of a portal opening slowly.

"Hear, O Israel: The LORD our God is One LORD."[22]

Onias joined Simeon in repeating the Shema:

> *"The LORD our God is One! And you shall love the LORD your God with all your heart, and with all your soul, and with all your might. And these words, which I command you this day, shall be engraved upon your heart."*[23]

They moved forward once again. The frame of the entrance brushed Onias' head.

> *"You shall teach them assiduously to your children, and speak thereof when you sit in your house, and when you go on your way."*[24]

The *click, click, click* of flint against iron punctuated each phrase as Simeon sparked a flame and lit an oil lamp in a niche just inside the door.

Onias shielded his eyes as the room was illuminated. The light reflected off polished marble surfaces, making them glow like the interior of a lamp's globe. The space was twelve feet by twelve feet by twelve feet—a perfect cube not much bigger than the cistern where they had begun their journey. Something like a bema, a lectern for reading, stood in the exact center. It was overlaid with black onyx and had two doors in the lower portion, as though a storage area lay inside. The floor of the chamber was inlaid with blue lapis and white marble, the pattern similar to that of a prayer shawl. Every available inch of the four walls was inscribed with the Hebrew text of the book of the prophet Zechariah, and every letter inlaid with gold. The ceiling was smooth blue lapis set with golden stars in the precise pattern Onias had seen on the veil of the Holy of Holies. It portrayed, Onias observed, a sky like that of an autumn night around the time of Rosh Hoshanah and Yom Kippur. All seven visible lights of the heavens as represented on the menorah were portrayed there.

Astonished, Zachariah spread his fingers and stretched upward as though to embrace the beauty of the craftsmanship. He touched his lips in a gesture that declared unspoken praise. He inhaled deeply.

Onias followed suit, aware of the strong aroma of cinnamon.

Simeon gazed at the words and turned slowly around, as if drinking in the entire text of the scroll.

"What is this place?" Onias said at last. His voice intruded on a silence broken only by heartbeats and breaths.

"In Solomon's day it was one of the spice storage rooms. Cinnamon. Smell it?"

"Plainly."

"The stone absorbed the aroma. The scent of cinnamon lingers to this day."

"But this . . ." Onias spread his arms and gestured at column after column of writing.

"The scroll of Zechariah. The entire scroll carved in stone," Simeon explained. "It was commanded by Zerubbabel and the High Priest Yeshua after the return from the Babylonian exile when the Temple was being rebuilt. It is rumored there are many such rooms beneath the Temple Mount—one secret chamber for every scroll in the Holy Scriptures. So I was told when I was very young. The Temple above our heads is built upon the foundation of the Eternal Word. Truth. Yahweh's promise to Israel. Even while those in this present day who rule the Temple above us profane what is visible . . . even so, that which is beneath, and within the heart of the mountain, unseen by human eyes and locked beneath this Holy Mountain, remains eternal and true, built on the solid rock of God's truth."

"Will you show us?" Onias asked. "All of the rooms!"

Simeon's hands trembled as he caressed the bema. "This is the only room I know how to find. I am its guardian. Members of my family have inherited the duty for over four hundred years. Perhaps I'm the last of my line, since my son has allied himself with the false high priests appointed by Herod."

"So you brought us here. To show us."

"I brought you to show you . . . something." Simeon's eyes lingered on the bema, as though he was still hesitant to reveal everything.

Zachariah, in awe, leaned his forehead against the words in the wall and traced the letters with his fingers as his lips moved silently.

"Onias, come." Simeon took his arm and placed him beside Zachariah. "*Zachar* means 'remember.' What was prophesied will come to pass. Remember. Read the words written on the wall. No scroll speaks more about the coming of Messiah than Zechariah. Remember. It is no accident that our friend here—Zachariah, who shares the name of the prophet now in our own day—has been visited by an angel. His name points us back to the scroll of the prophet. Remember. But why Zachariah has been struck dumb, I can't say. So you and I will read."

With his finger Simeon underlined the beginning place.

Onias read the words of the prophet Zechariah:

> *"'Shout and be glad, O Daughter of Zion. For I am coming, and I will live among you,' declares the LORD. 'Many nations will be joined with the LORD in that day and will become My people. I will live among you and you will know that the LORD Almighty, El Shaddai, has sent Me to you. The LORD will inherit Judah as His portion in the holy land and will again choose Yerushalayim. Be still before the LORD, all mankind, because He has roused Himself from His holy dwelling!'"*[25]

Simeon explained, "The *Ruach HaKodesh*, The Spirit of the Lord, has told me I will not die until I have seen The One about whom this is written. I heard his voice again in the Temple. The Lord has shown me. I know his name. What Messiah's name will be. It's written here. Plainly in Zechariah. Though this story was written about the high priest who presided here in the day of Zechariah, it reveals the name of The One who is coming to deliver his people." Then Simeon directed Onias and Zachariah to another column. "Begin here."

Onias cleared his throat and stepped nearer to the inscription:

> *"The angel of the* Lord *gave this charge to Yeshua. . . . 'Listen, O high priest Yeshua and your associates seated before you, who are men symbolic of things to come: I am going to bring my servant, the Branch.'"*[26]

Onias paused. "Yeshua? The Branch. The name of Messiah?"

"Yes. The name of the *cohen hagadol* at the time of the return from exile was Yeshua. Jesus, the Greeks call him. And this high priest was the symbol of Messiah. The righteous High Priest coming to cleanse and restore the Temple after years of defilement. It's no mistake that the fellow who was visited by an angel has the same name as the prophet Zechariah, whose name means 'The Lord Remembers.' The Lord has not forgotten what is inscribed upon these walls. Read on, Onias."

> "'*See, the stone I have set in front of Yeshua! There are seven eyes on that one stone, and I will engrave an inscription on it,' says the* Lord *Almighty, 'And I will remove the sin of this land in a single day.'*" [27]

Onias tugged his beard. "One day? All the sins of this land? That'll take more lambs than Zadok's got in his whole flock. Such is the sin of Herod and the pretenders he's put in place to run the Temple."

"I've read this passage a thousand times," Simeon said, "and never understood how it will happen. Not with Herod and his kin on the throne. Not in one day." Then Simeon began to read: "'*Not by might nor by power, but by my Spirit,' says the* Lord *Almighty.*"[28]

Simeon took the arm of Zachariah and led him to the eastern wall. He pointed up to another section. "Here is the key! Here is the name of The One, the Messiah! Here is the name of the Branch we are waiting for!"

Onias continued:

> *"The word of the* Lord *came to me: 'Take silver and gold from the exiles Heldai, Tobijah, and Jedaiah. . . . Go the same day to the house of Josiah son of Zephaniah. Take the silver and gold and make a crown,*

and set it on the head of the high priest, Yeshua, whose name means "Salvation," the son of Jehozadak, whose name means "Yaweh's Righteousness."

"'Tell him this is what the LORD Almighty says: "Here is the man whose name is the Branch, and Yeshua will branch out from this place and build the temple of the LORD. It is Yeshua who will build the temple of the LORD, and He will be clothed in majesty and will sit and rule on His throne. And He will be a priest on His throne. And there will be harmony between the two." The crown will be given to Heldai, Tobijah, Jedaiah, and Hen, whose name means "Grace," the son of Zephaniah, as a memorial in the temple of the LORD.'"[29]

Simeon raised a hand to stop the reading. "The crown of Yeshua, the first high priest of the restored Temple, has been hidden, kept safe within these walls as a memorial to the Lord's promise to bring a Messiah to rule Israel in righteousness. For over four hundred years the crown of Yeshua has been waiting for The One, our Messiah. Messiah's name will be Yeshua. And I'm certain now that I'll see him with my own eyes!"

Simeon pulled a key from his pocket, wagged it at Onias, then knelt to unlock the top door of the bema. He reverently bowed and removed an object swaddled in purple silk and placed it on the bema. Fold by fold he unwrapped it until a crown of gold, interlocked with a crown of silver, was revealed, gleaming in the center of the room. The two parts—silver and gold—formed one piece.

On the silver crown were inscribed seven Hebrew words:

Nezer, crown
Yeshua, salvation
Netzer, branch
Nazir, consecrated
Notzeri, guardian of the truth
Notzer, watcher
Ha Adam, The Adam.

Simeon spoke each word reverently. "As it is written by the prophets, '*He shall be called a Nazarene.*'[30] I am convinced the title of Nazarene for Messiah refers to all the qualities engraved on this crown—truths about him which are yet hidden to us. In Isaiah the Lord said, '*From this time forth I make you hear new things, hidden things,* netzourot, *which you have not known!'* "[31]

On the golden crown were the words *TZITIZ NEZER HA KODESH-KODESH LA YHWH,* which means "HOLY and set apart TO YAHWEH."

Blinking in amazement, Onias hovered over the ancient double diadem that symbolized the coming reign of Messiah in Jerusalem.

Zachariah's eyes brimmed with emotion.

"I thought it was lost." Onias almost touched the crown. Then he drew back and bowed slightly, as though he could already see it on Messiah's brow. "Everyone knows the three crowns on display in the sanctuary are replicas. Everyone thinks Messiah's crown, the true crown spoken of in the scroll of Zechariah, was lost."

Simeon replied tenderly, "Not lost. Hidden. Waiting for the second Yeshua, the true High Priest and King, to come and claim it. The first Yeshua to wear the crown was only a symbol of The One yet to come. Every word inscribed on this crown is found in a prophecy about Messiah. And now the true Branch, *the Netzer* whose name is Yeshua, is coming.[32] I'll know when I hear his name spoken. When I behold his face, I'll know him. Today in the Temple I heard his name. I will not die . . . the Holy Spirit has told me. I'll know."

CHAPTER 4

W Zachariah finished his course of service, he returned to his home among the vineyards of Beth Karem, which means "House of the Vine."

A thousand joyful possibilities spun webs in his mind. He wanted Elisheba!

Zachariah was a winegrower who produced special sweet wines for Holy Days and Shabbat meals. His wine was known as Womb of Beth Karem Holy Wine because of the cave in which it was stored.

He was far from wealthy, but now, since his lot had been drawn in the priestly duty, he would be called Zachariah the Rich.

He was smiling as he rode his reliable old gelding through the leafless vineyard and past the storage cavern, where his wine was kept in sealed jars. Ironic that if Zachariah sired a son as the angel predicted, the boy could never be allowed to taste the sacred wine or eat the fruit of his own vineyards. The vow of a Nazarite, such as the angel had commanded for the child, forbade such joys.

All right then, Zachariah decided, as Elisheba stepped out of the house and hailed him from the top of the lane. *All right!* So the Almighty did not intend that the son of Zachariah the Winegrower would tend the vineyards of his father. This was not the miracle Zachariah had envisioned. *A son and heir to take over the vineyard,* he had prayed. *A boy to learn his father's trade!* Forty years he had prayed and hoped and waited for such a miracle. But, as Elisheba would say, hoping and waiting make fools out of clever people! So who was he to question an angel?

"Zachariah!" Elisheba waved her arms in enthusiasm.

He returned the wave. No matter he could not speak, he thought. Elisheba always talked enough for both of them. It might even take her a while to figure out he had no voice.

Barefoot, she plodded down the hill towards his horse. In her youth Elisheba had been like a luscious cluster of ripe grapes. As tall as his shoulder, slim, red-haired, fair-skinned, eyes a shade between blue and green, she had turned the heads of all who saw her. Now, at age fifty-five, she had gained weight enough to give her curves. She had once remarked that she had begun to feel past ripe; she was moving toward raisin status. But to Zachariah, she was a fine vintage wine that had grown more complex and delicious over the years.

A life without children had been Elisheba's public shame and her private sorrow, but she had borne it well. Without bitterness she had become every child's Aunt Elisheba. She poured all the untapped mothering skills into loving Zachariah. And he spoiled her as he would have spoiled a daughter. He had never stopped loving her, praying for her, hoping. As Elisheba often said, "Stuff yourself with hope and you can go crazy."

Years had passed since hope that she might yet bear a child had died. Still he desired her, found comfort and pleasure in her arms. He missed her voice and longed for her touch when he was gone from her. He hated sleeping alone. He was glad today to see her coming down the path toward him.

"Zachariah!" The same bright smile. The same eyes that always set him on fire.

He waved again, pulled back on the reins, and dismounted.

She ran to him. Embraced him. Kissed him. "How's my boy?" She patted his cheek and smoothed his tunic. "Hmm? Did you bring me the perfume?"

He held up one finger commanding her to wait. Then, rummaging in the saddlebag, he took out an alabaster bottle of a delicious oil he had smelled in Jerusalem, wafting from the perfumer's.

She squealed with delight. "You! You!" Another peck on the cheek. "Expensive! For a little love you pay all your life!" She uncorked the bottle and inhaled the aroma. "So, you must have missed me. The gift is not half as precious as the thought."

He put his arm around her, and they strolled toward the house. The horse, a good, calm fellow of sixteen, trailed behind them.

Zachariah threw off the saddle and turned the gelding into its pen, then followed her into the house. It was not a large house, though they could have afforded better. Elisheba said early on that room enough for a few guests and themselves was room enough.

After washing their feet in the courtyard, he followed her into the dining room, where she had laid out all his favorite foods: cold lamb shashlik, chicken, flatbread, lentils, apples and honey, wine.

As he reclined on cushions to eat, Elisheba talked about what had happened while he had been away. "The rabbi's son said this and that about Boethus, Herod's pet high priest. He's right, but the truth doesn't die. It just lives like a poor man. He needs to watch his tongue or his father will be the one to pay."

Zachariah nodded in solemn agreement. Dangerous business, criticizing Herod's high priest. Better to ignore him. He would be replaced by someone worse in time. Zachariah chewed as she talked.

"Lem's daughter had a baby boy on Shabbat. An easy delivery. Her husband is away working in Bethsaida and doesn't know he has a son. Love is sweet, but it's nice to have bread with it. Can you find the lad some work in the vineyard?"

Zachariah plucked a chicken leg, took a bite, and nodded. He ate and listened. Nodded. Smiled. Listened. Pondered her words as he chewed. Listened.

"Good! He's such a polite fellow. They're so poor. And now to have to be away while his wife has a new baby! I'll send word tomorrow. Ah! The last of the grape harvest for the sweetest wine has been put up in the cavern. And the great synagogue of Alexandria has sent an order for three hundred gallons from the Womb of Beth Karem!"

She still had not noticed he had not spoken a word. It became a game to him. How long could he keep the secret from her?

Nearly an hour passed. The meal finished. The sun began to sink in the west.

At last Elisheba looked at him strangely. "Zachariah? You haven't said a word about your meal. You didn't like the lamb? You hated the chicken?"

So, at last he was caught. If he wagged his head no, meaning he didn't hate the chicken, she would think he did not like the lamb. And if he nodded yes, meaning he liked the lamb, she would think he hated the chicken.

He put a hand to his throat, indicating that something was not working.

She sat forward. "Are you ill?"

The shake of his head reassured her.

"Lost your voice?"

The nod placated her worry.

"Yerushalayim! The air! Would you like something sweet after supper? Look. Apples and honey. Sweet. And sweet wine if you like."

He smiled and put out his arms, beckoning her to him. She was the only sweet thing he had an appetite for tonight. She sighed happily and leaned against him. He kissed her head and lifted her chin, kissing her mouth.

She rubbed her cheek against his tenderly. "Zachariah. How I missed you. Oh, a whole week without you! No one to talk to me. Kiss me. Hmm?"

He obeyed willingly.

She smiled up at him. "Love is like butter, eh? It's better with bread."

Onias the Tutor lay quietly with his wife, Tovah, in his arms. He had been awake for hours, unmoving, afraid to disturb her with his concerns.

She stirred. "You're not sleeping?"

"No."

"Worried about something?"

"Worried? No, not worried."

"Then what?" She gave him a quick squeeze and propped herself on her elbow.

"Since I was in the sanctuary with Zachariah yesterday, you know how anxious—even apprehensive—everyone connected with that has been. Well, today I was approached by certain . . . officials."

"Herodians?"

"Not exactly. At first I thought they were Herod's men, coming to arrest me, interrogate me. But they were emissaries of the King of Cappadocia, Archaelaus, the father of Princess Glaphyra. They want me to give up my duties at the Torah school and tutor only Herod's grandson Alexander."

"Only Alexander?"

"Yes, that's it. No other students. I suppose I should be flattered. They say the young prince likes me well enough. And his mother approves of my teaching."

"But?"

"Tovah, I don't know. It's more money. And I've already made it clear I won't ever enter the palace of Herod."

"They agree to this?"

"All of it."

"But?"

Onias thought through what he wanted to say. He spoke carefully, lest he frighten her. It occurred to him that perhaps Glaphyra and her father were setting him up as a channel of communication outside Herod's reach. The word *conspiracy* ran over and over again in his mind. But he dared not tell Tovah. What good would it do to worry her? "I don't know. I suppose this is not something I can refuse to do. And that's what bothers me, Tovah. I don't really have a choice. I'm already marked just for having been in the Temple with Zachariah. And with all the politics swirling around Herod's court, I just . . . you and Menorah . . . I'm concerned. That's all."

The soft, even breathing of little Menorah told them the four-year-old was asleep.

Tovah said in a matter-of-fact way, "It's best if Menorah and I aren't here when the Herodian prince comes."

Onias sighed with relief. "That was the very thing—the very thing—I wanted to talk with you about. I sense there could be danger. Not that there *is* danger, mind you. But that there *could be*—to us. To anyone who ever comes near his family. Herod is growing more insane every day. He sees plots where there are no plots. Even in children as young as Menorah. You see, Tovah, I wish I could refuse the commission, but I can't."

Tovah twirled his beard with her fingers. "When they come for lessons, Menorah and I will go to my cousin Adena's house to visit, eh? An easy solution. We'll be away when the Herodian royals come for lessons. Though I had hoped to have a good look at such rich and beautiful people. Princess Glaphyra."

Onias kissed her. "Look in the mirror. You are all the princess any man could desire. My treasure. You and Menorah. I am a rich man for having you as my wife. And you are more beautiful than . . ."

She kissed him back. "Don't be afraid, Onias. I'm not. What can they do to us?"

It was early morning after prayers when Zachariah sat down to write out the details for Elisheba of his encounter with Gabriel in the sanctuary. He had just finished when Elisheba arrived home following a meeting at synagogue to arrange cast-off clothing to distribute to the orphans of Jerusalem.

Her expression was troubled, almost hurt, as she stood over his writing desk, tapping her fingers impatiently.

He smiled. What was troubling her?

She pressed her lips together as if choosing her words carefully. Her eyes swam behind tears. "Well, you know what they say. When you go to your neighbors, you find out what is happening at home."

She was angry? hurt? By what? He spread his hands in innocence.

"It was you, wasn't it? We heard the rumor last week about something . . . a vision. An old priest, they said, had seen a vision in the Temple sanctuary. And they thought he had died because he took so long. But he came out and something had happened to him. He couldn't speak. Everyone's talking about it. And there I was, listening to them talk, and it came to me that you were there all last week. You! You're not old, as the last seven nights and mornings and afternoons have proved, but . . . Zachariah? Something happened. And you're either not talking because you don't want to, or you're not talking because you can't. Either way you're not saying a word. Haven't said a word. You're just acting like a bridegroom, all week. Very nice. But at our age, Zachariah! I don't know what this is about. And you're not telling me. Do I have to hear this from the neighbors?"

He would have laughed if he could have laughed. Instead he stood, and Elisheba took the chair he offered her. He tapped the parchment upon which he had written every detail, every word. Everything, lest the account of the promise be forgotten and remain untold.

"After forty years of marriage you can't confide in me?"

He was unable to tell Elisheba to read it. Could not explain that he had longed to tell her everything. That he had been too busy acting on the angel's good advice to write it down. That he believed something incredible was about to change their lives.

Zachariah pointed. Tapped. She should look at the heading at the top of the sheet.

She read, then gasped and covered her mouth with her hand:

The True Account of Zachariah, priest of the Course of Abijah,
who was visited by the angel Gabriel
while on duty in the sanctuary of The Most High
in the first week of autumn following Yom Kippur
at which time the birth of a son was promised
to Zachariah and his wife, Elisheba, of Beth Karem.

It was not the response he had hoped for. Elisheba read all of it and began to cry. Only one or two tears at first. Then she read it again, and a fountain within broke loose. Her shoulders shook as she wept quietly. She read the document a third time and began to weep more loudly. The ink ran away from her tears.

She did not look up at Zachariah as he hovered over her, worrying, hoping this would bring her joy.

What? What? Why did she not speak to him? More tears. Elisheba had never cried so hard in all the years of their marriage.

She, who always had a proverb for everything, had no words. She wagged her head. Wiped her eyes. Blew her nose on her kerchief. Reached out to grasp his hand. Kissed his fingers. Read again. Finally she stood and wrapped her arms around his middle, pressed herself tightly against him, and sobbed.

He stroked her hair, wiping away copious tears with his hand in an attempt to comfort her. Could such good news break her heart when they had both prayed for such an answer all their married life?

He gave up trying to understand and let her sob. Leading her to their bed, he lay down next to her.

"With God, nothing is impossible," she finally managed. And then she kissed him with startling fierceness and once again . . .

He would have asked her if he could have spoken. He would have written down the question if there had been time and if the paper and ink had not been in the other room.

So, maybe Elisheba was crying because she was really very happy?

CHAPTER 5

Tovah told Onias the news before their little girl was awake. Before the sky was light.

She got up and was suddenly sick. She washed and rinsed her mouth and came back to bed. And she told him. She was certain of the news now.

A dull amber glow illuminated the belly of the clouds that hung in the predawn sky above Jerusalem. Onias walked slightly behind Tovah and little Menorah. He was on his way to teach Torah school, and they on their way to the souk to buy vegetables from the Galil before the crowd packed the market.

The Temple gates had not yet opened. The palace of Herod stood out ominously against the sky. The butcher king was in residence. His banner snapped from the highest tower, and Herodian guards paced the parapet.

But Onias was not thinking of politics.

Tovah walked in front of him, her head and shoulders erect. He briefly considered running up and grabbing her, spinning her around, and demanding that they return home and go back to bed so she could tell him again.

His blood surged through his veins. He felt ridiculous. Happy. Joyful. Brave. Tender. Honorable.

Another baby!

Memories of their secret moments together lit up his brain like torchbearers illuminated the dark streets. Things no one else knew about her were his treasured secrets. Her breath on his cheek. Her lips moving against his with almost inaudible words of love.

Another baby!

He looked at Menorah's neat braids. Tovah was such a good mother. Never was any woman as careful and loving a mother as Tovah. And now!

One more in the family!

Menorah would have a baby brother or sister sometime in early summer. Still a long way off.

Months of anticipation. *Boy or girl?*

Months of pride. *Yes, Tovah is mine, and yes, my Tovah is expecting a child!*

He was grinning stupidly when they came to the gates of the Torah school. She turned to kiss him good-bye.

She looked a little pale, he thought. "Are you all right?"

"Fine." She patted his cheek. "As long as I get my shopping done and get home before the smells hit." By this she meant the confusion of foul odors that flooded the marketplace before midmorning. She inhaled deeply. "I'll be all right."

He patted Menorah's cheek. "What do you think? A baby brother or sister?"

"I'd like a sister." Menorah shook her golden braids for emphasis. "Boys!" Much disdain in the word.

"All right, then." Tovah's eyes shone with adoration for him. Their secret! "I'll see you after class." Then, "Are they coming today?"

"Oh, I forgot. The prince. Alex. Yes." He was disappointed. He would have to wait awhile longer to exult with Tovah in their good news.

She sighed. "We'll be at my cousin's until you call for us."

Standing by the gate of the Torah school like a child looks after his departing mother, Onias watched Tovah and Menorah until they rounded the corner.

Another baby!

How could he contain his joy until he saw her again? Surely everyone he met would see the news written on his face: Onias' lopsided grin would be more pronounced than ever!

Ecbatana, Kingdom of Parthia
29th year of King Phraates IV
Journal of Court Astronomer Melchior
New Moon Observation
Last New Moon before Spring Equinox
Weather unseasonably warm and dry[33]

Carried out this night's observations from a new location: the top of the tomb of Queen Esther of ancient Persia. It was Balthasar who suggested the alternate site. Ecbatana is the final resting place of King Xerxes' Jewish wife (despite the claims of the city of Hamadan to the contrary).

Queen Esther is justly renowned as the woman who saved her people from the plots of Haman. Balthasar's granddaughter, who accompanied us this night, is named in her honor.

All this historical connection was entirely appropriate since this New Moon marks the month of Adar, when the Jews celebrate Purim, the annual memorial of Esther's courage.

King Xerxes chose a spurlike ridge of Mount Alvand to erect a beehive-shaped tomb surmounted by a central tower for Esther's final resting place. It is from the top of this tower that we observed.

The descent of the New Moon into sunset, vital for my records, was not observable, since the west was shrouded in cloud. At sunset none of the wandering stars were visible either. Much later I made note of Mars, The Adam, riding near the hand of Virgo, The Virgin.

Balthasar directed me to pay particular attention to the star Regulus in the constellation of Leo. Leo, or as the Jews say, Aryeh, means "The Lion." In many languages and cultures Regulus represents a king. Balthasar instructed me that Jews believe the future Messiah must be of the tribe of

Judah in order to fulfill prophecy. The symbol of Judah has always been a lion, so the king star always passes through the night sky in company with a lion, just as the prophecy in the first book of the lawgiver Mosheh insists.[34] *Unfortunately the constellation gives no clue as to when Messiah will come.*

The night proceeded pleasantly, with Esther telling me all the stories of her namesake, including how the queen was the most beautiful woman in all Persia.

I asked Balthasar's granddaughter if Queen Esther had gleaming dark hair, dancing dark eyes, and a pert nose like hers, but I think I embarrassed the girl because she changed the subject.

I have known seventeen-year-old Esther since she was twelve and she has changed a lot, but I had not noticed how significant were the changes until recently.

Just before dawn Mercury, The Messenger, rose in the sign of The Water Bearer. According to Balthasar, this signifies a message or messenger connected to the Jewish baptism ceremonies.

Finally, I received the briefest glimpse of Jupiter, The Righteous, appearing in the Jewish sign of The Fish just before the sun's glare washed the sky clear of stars.

A messenger having to do with water baptism precedes one who represents Righteousness to the Jews. As we walked back to Ecbatana, I asked Balthasar what this connection might mean. He referred me to the prophecies of Malachi, who writes of a "forerunner"—that is to say, one who precedes the Messiah and is connected with the prophet Elijah in some way.[35] *Balthasar reminded me that Elijah was the prophet whose prayers shut up or loosened rain from the heavens.*[36] *That certainly provides a connection between Elijah and The Water Bearer. Beyond that, Balthasar said, the next New Moon would give us still more vital information.*

Almost dawn. Everyone asleep but Zachariah, who searched the scrolls of Isaias, Malachi, Dani'el, and Zechariah. His head ached. He was exhausted, but the fascination kept him riveted to his desk. So much he did not understand. So much. Layer by layer he examined the prophecies, inwardly rehearsing the words the angel had spoken to him.

He got up and stood by the window to watch as Mercury, The Messenger star, rose before the sun in the constellation of The Water Bearer. Were the heavens not filled with such signs in these last few months?

Was it not stated clearly in the book of Malachi?

> *"See, I will send My messenger, who will prepare the way before Me. Then suddenly the Lord you are seeking will come to His Temple; the messenger of the covenant, whom you desire, will come," says the* LORD *Almighty!*[37]

Zachariah studied the notes he had made after the vision. The words of Gabriel had sounded so familiar: *Many of the people of Israel will he bring back to the Lord their God. And he will go on before the Lord, in the spirit and power of Elijah, to turn the hearts of the fathers to their children and the disobedient to the wisdom of the righteous—to make ready a people prepared for the* LORD.[38]

The angel had used the word *teshuvah*, "to turn one's heart," to repent. The acts of repentance required the outward sign of ritual cleansing known as baptism. The constellation of The Water Bearer represented Elijah. Many had commented on the fact that The Righteous had first risen in The Water Bearer the night before Zachariah's vision in the sanctuary. And now, as if announcing Elijah's coming, The Messenger star burned brightly within The Water Bearer.

Zachariah sighed and returned to his desk. He opened the scroll of Malachi, the final book written in the compilation of the Scriptures, and turned to the last two verses:

> *See, I will send you the prophet Elijah before that great and dreadful day of the* LORD *comes. He will turn the hearts of the fathers to their children, and the hearts of the children to their fathers; or else I will come and strike the land with a curse.*[39]

They were, Zachariah observed, almost the exact words the angel had used to explain to him the purpose of his child's life. The immediate fulfillment of the final prophecy in Scripture had been announced to Zachariah in the Temple. Over four hundred years had passed since this ending prophecy had been recorded, yet to the angel it was as though no time had passed. Gabriel proclaimed that God had remembered, and now Elijah was coming. The old blended seamlessly with that which was brand-new. The coming of the Lord was very near!

Zachariah put a hand to his throat. How foolish he had been to question the angel on a point of Scripture: *How can I be sure of this? I am an old man and my wife is well along in years.*[40]

Zachariah slapped his forehead and blushed again at the memory of his challenge. As if the promise made in Malachi's prophecy depended on the age of Zachariah and Elisheba and not upon the ageless promise of the Lord!

He wagged his head slowly in regret that he had not instantly recognized the verse. Malachi! Elijah! It was repeated at every Passover seder, every circumcision, every High Holy Day! What household did not set an extra plate at the Passover table and open the door in hopes Elijah would enter and share a meal with the family!

And now, the promised Elijah, he who prayed for the cleansing rains to heal the land, was coming as a baby to share Zachariah's life!

The candle on the desk burned low. Outside an owl hooted. Zachariah rolled up the scroll of Malachi, wrapped it securely, and replaced it within the chest.

So, Zachariah thought, he had been the worst kind of doubter. The Lord had sent him the best news of his life, and he had said he was too old!

"Zachariah?" Elisheba called to him. "Are you ever coming back to bed?"

So, good for Malachi! He was a true prophet.

There was Elisheba, lying in the next room, belly round as a melon! "Zachariah?"

Nothing is impossible for God!

"The Lord has done this for me." Elisheba placed Zachariah's hand on the place where the baby tapped elbows and knees.

Zachariah closed his eyes and felt the drumming of life within her. Was there ever a miracle so great as this? And with it came boundless joy as the angel had promised him.

Elisheba said quietly, "In these days he has shown his favor. He has taken away my disgrace, and no one can call me barren ever again."[41]

It had been five months since Zachariah's homecoming. Elisheba's pregnancy had blossomed into reality during those months. And so had their love. Youthful energy and feelings almost forgotten were renewed between them. Zachariah thought she had never been more beautiful than now. He pampered her and cared for her every need as she remained in quiet seclusion in their home.

There was no doubt now that the vision he had seen and heard in the Temple and written down was true. Nothing was too hard for God!

So where was the second half of the equation to be found? If the miracle child Elisheba carried was to be the forerunner of Messiah, then where was Messiah?

Zachariah spent his hours poring over the Scriptures, making notes, quietly studying the prophecies about the coming of the Son of David. On clear nights he climbed onto the roof and gazed into the heavens and saw the certain sign of Messiah as Mars, the star called The Adam in Hebrew, moved nearer and nearer to the constellation of The Virgin. The branch lifted high in her right hand, the shock of wheat in the other, the constellation of The Virgin told a story to anyone with eyes to see and a mind to ask the questions.

As the eternal plan quietly unfolded on earth, the heavens proclaimed the glory of God! Great wonders were transpiring above the nations. Yet except for a handful of men, no one on earth took note of the signs of the times.

Like a spider waiting in a lightless corner for the next victim to blunder in, Herod, king of the Jews, preferred darkened rooms and shadowed chambers. A lifetime spent practicing cruelty and ruthlessness left thousands of bodies in his past . . . and thousands of ghosts in his thoughts. Waking or sleeping, Herod never seemed to be free of their cries. His tormented mind and universal suspicion turned anyone nearby into a potential casualty of his insanity.

Of all Herod's courtiers, only one sought to turn Herod's madness to his own profit: Talmai, Herod's chief steward.

The colonnade surrounding Herod's private bath at his Jericho palace presented a forest of marble enclosing the spacious blue-and-gold, mosaic-tiled pool. The outer ring of pillars was carved to resemble date palms. The inner enclosure portrayed the precious balsam trees that furnished much of Herod's private wealth.

The aging monarch was not in the swimming area; he never was these days. He took no pleasure in beauty, exercise, or fresh air. He said the cold water made his bones ache, and he no longer had the energy for swimming.

Instead Herod preferred one of the chambers branching off the main room: the caldarium, or hot room. Both bathwater and floor were warmed from beneath by heated air forced through the pottery ducting of a hypocaust.

Out of sight, on a balcony inside one of the other rooms, a small ensemble of musicians played on harp, flute, and panpipes. Music pleased Herod. These days its calming influence was more necessary but less effective than ever.

A single lamp glowed in a wall sconce. Herod hated bright light but panicked in full darkness. Two living figures occupied the gloomy chamber: Herod and his barber and body servant, Trypho. Trypho was responsible for a state secret: maintaining the king's jet-black hair and beard with dye.

As one of the more trusted of Herod's devotees, he was permitted to attend the monarch without a guard. Despite the length of his service, however, no safety came with the position.

King Herod, swathed in toweling, lay on his stomach on a couch while Trypho massaged the king's shoulders and back. The music was punctuated by Herod's grunts as Trypho's fingers dug into knotted muscles.

A guard cautiously poked his head into the room. "Pardon, Majesty. Chief Steward Talmai wishes a word with you."

Herod growled a reply, which the guard took as consent.

Just as Talmai entered, Trypho's vigorous kneading made the king snap, "Stop! Enough, Trypho! You have lost what little skill you ever had!"

Nervously murmuring many apologies and casting equally as many worried looks toward the steward, Trypho bowed and stepped away from the couch. He stood waiting, uncertain if he was dismissed or not.

"You see?" Herod addressed Talmai in a tone of aggrieved complaint. "I am surrounded by incompetents! And any who are capable of proper service are capable of villainy as well. Well? What do you want? I left word I was not to be disturbed."

Talmai, who had the build of a wrestler long out of training, was undeterred. "I understood that, Majesty, but the matter is urgent . . . and for your ears only."

Herod levered himself into an upright seated position and waved Trypho away. The barber backed out of the room but secretly remained within earshot, concealed in the corridor between colonnade and caldarium.

"What is so urgent that you bother me tonight? You know my headaches . . . my stomach. I have not been sleeping well."

Talmai offered words of sympathy, then stated, "The matter could not wait. One of my informants brought me this." The steward displayed a torn scrap of parchment, scorched on two edges and discolored by smoke and heat. On it appeared a few words in Hebrew. "My spy found it on the grate of the servants' gathering hall. Someone had attempted to burn the document completely, but this fragment escaped."

Herod's eyes darted about the room; then his extended clawlike hand demanded the writing. On it he read: *. . . must be soon. He can't last much longer.*

"Conspiracy! I knew it! Haul them all into the dungeons! Get at the truth! Spare no one!"

"I suggest . . . let me pursue the matter quietly. We don't want the plotters to be warned and flee. In the meantime, double your guards, but let me see where this leads."

The king agreed, but added, "No matter where this leads . . . even if to my own sons, Talmai. Root them out!"

Herod did not see the smile that played briefly over Talmai's lips as he tucked the parchment into a fold of his robes before exiting the chamber. The "conspiracy" existed only as a scheme in Talmai's head, but Herod's innate brutality and colossal mistrust of everyone would provide the motive force.

Concealed in the shadows behind a row of potted ferns, Trypho listened to every word between Talmai and the king. The barber returned to Herod's massage when the king bellowed for him, but he rubbed with less vigor. An anxious frown remained imprinted on his round, sweaty face.

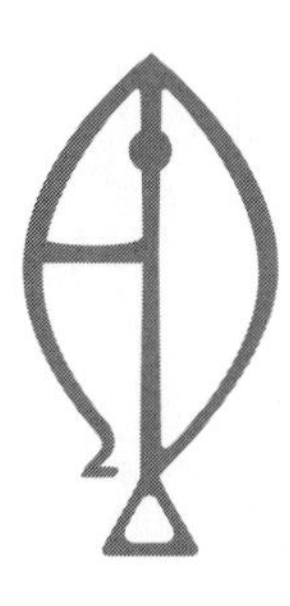

PART II

Therefore the Lord Himself will give you a sign: The virgin will be with child and will give birth to a son, and will call Him Immanuel.

ISAIAH 7:14

6 CHAPTER

Ecbatana, Kingdom of Parthia
29th year of King Phraates IV
Journal of Court Astronomer Melchior
New Moon Observation
First New Moon after Spring Equinox[42]

This was a particularly important observing session. The last two New Moon observations have been obscured by cloud. (In both cases resulting in snow, since Ecbatana is a mile above the level of the distant sea.) Those months were thus only tentatively calculated, pending a more exact confirmation, which occurred tonight.

I was late arriving at my post, and by the time we arrived at our station on top of the palace at the gold level of the city, the sun had set and only the tip of the New Moon's remaining horn was visible on the head of Aries, The Ram. (This designation is, Balthasar tells me, a bad metaphor, since that constellation is called by the Jews The Lamb.)

But most of our attention in the early evening was directed toward Mars, then rising in the east. The planet is called The Adam, because it is red, just as the first man was named for the red clay from which he was formed. As soon as it was full dark, we saw The Adam very near the heart of Virgo, The Virgin. Balthasar studied this for a great time . . . long enough for Esther to grow cold and enter our poor observing hut to huddle under furs next to the barely glowing coals.

Balthasar was excited by what he saw. He explained that Porrima, the star at the heart of The Virgin, is called in Hebrew The Star of Atonement. When Messiah comes, His purpose will be atonement for mankind, just as The Adam was very near The Atonement star tonight. I asked him what it meant that atonement dwelt beneath the virgin's heart, and he told me about a prophecy delivered by the renowned Isaias, in which the prophet says a virgin will conceive and bear a son[43] and that this miraculous child will be the Messiah. Furthermore, there is an even more ancient prophecy, in the Book of Beginnings, that the seed of the woman will conquer the serpent, the enemy of mankind.[44]

I confess that this is very confusing to me.

Balthasar also says we must never run ahead of Adonai Elohim, but wait for confirmation.

And so we waited. The night being crystalline in its clarity, I used the opportunity to take detailed observations of the figure called The Sheepfold. The Sheepfold always circles The Tent Pole of the Sky.

Just as my eyes, aching already, were blurred for want of sleep, Balthasar grew very excited. He raced from the west parapet where he pointed to The Adam and The Virgin finally disappearing, to the eastern brink of the height. With quavering voice, he showed me both bright planets—Saturn, The Sabbath, and Jupiter, The Righteous—now appearing together in The Fish, the constellation known to designate the Jews. With clasped hands he begged me to understand. If this sign continued in the months ahead, it portended a time of Sabbath righteousness coming to the people of Judea. I asked if that meant a new king to replace Herod the Butcher, but yet again he told me to wait on the Lord.

Shortly after this, the sun peeked over the rim of the world. We woke Esther and descended through the still-sleeping town.

In the sixth month of Elisheba's pregnancy, God sent the angel Gabriel to Nazareth, a village in Galilee, to a virgin named Mary. She was engaged to be married to a man named Yosef, a descendant of King David.[45]

The season had turned at last, bringing an end to the coldest winter anyone in Galilee remembered.

Snow had fallen four times on Nazareth. In all the sixteen years of Mary's life, she had never touched snow until this year. She had seen it gleaming on the distant peaks on the border of Lebanon even into the summer months, but she had not imagined anything could be so cold.

It had been a delight the first morning when she had tumbled through white powder with her two younger sisters and thrown snowballs and caught snowflakes on her tongue.

Childish behavior, Papa said, from a young woman who would be married by her next birthday.

The novelty had worn off after a week of mucking out ice, mud, and manure from the pens on the south side of the barn, where Mama kept four fine milk cows—one for each unmarried daughter, and one for herself. Selling the cheese and butter and cream supplemented Papa's income as a carpenter, and a portion of the money was saved to provide a dowry for the girls.

Over the years each of Papa's five daughters had been assigned a cow that was her own to care for and which would eventually be a part of her marriage contract. Two cows were gone with Mary's two older sisters. Mary was the next in line.

This evening, as Mary filled the grain bucket, a warm southern breeze stirred the branches of the orchards. Crickets chirped. Somewhere a dog barked. The air smelled like new grass, earth turned for cultivation, and blooming wildflowers. Spring was well and truly here.

Each day at dawn, midday, and twilight Mary milked her cow, a placid two-year-old roan heifer named Rose, whose first calf had been stillborn two weeks before. The death of the calf was a disappointment after so many months of looking forward to the arrival. It had been a beautiful, perfect little thing—red roan like its mother. Mary had slept in the barn for a week before Rose had calved. She had cried for a week afterwards.

This was more than the loss of a calf. Mary had raised Rose as a pet. Papa always said that if Rose had been a dog instead of a cow, she would have slept at the foot of Mary's bed. The heifer was indeed as gentle as an old dog and followed her young mistress to and from the far pasture without a rope. After a day of languidly pulling tufts of grass, Rose would raise her head and bawl greetings when Mary came to lead the little herd home to the old stone barn each afternoon.

At the age of sixteen, Mary's figure was still boyish. She was slight of build, with large, gold-flecked, brown eyes; an abundance of curly brown hair; and a cheerful disposition. Of all the girls, Mary was most like Mama. She had a knack with animals. People in the village noticed and remarked on it. Such comments about his future bride pleased Yosef, the fellow she was betrothed to, because it was generally believed that a woman who was good with dumb creatures would also be good with children.

The marriage had been arranged some years before, and the date for the union was fast approaching. With two more daughters to marry off after Mary, Papa was anxious that each transaction go smoothly and that his daughters' husbands be pleased with the bargains.

Last year Papa had paid old man Menna in carpentry work to have the roan heifer bred to his black Lebanese bull so Mary would have a gift of extraordinary value to present to her husband on their wedding day. A calf could have provided the couple with a fine start on building their own small herd of milk cows.

But it was not to be.

So Mary and Mama set to work converting Rose's abundance of milk into cheeses and tubs of butter to sell at market. Extra cash would be part of the dowry terms set down in the final contract—a legal protection for the bride. The money and material goods she brought with her into a marriage were to be returned to her in the event her husband divorced her.

Not much chance of that, Papa said. Yosef was smitten with Mary. For two months Yosef had been away from Nazareth, working with several thousand of his countrymen on the construction of the Temple in Jerusalem. At every opportunity Yosef sent small gifts home to his future bride. The latest offering had been a blue-glazed, clay pilgrim lamp stamped with the picture of a seven-branched candlestick. He had purchased it at the Temple bazaar and sent it to her by way of a returning family who had made aliyah. Yosef's note read:

Beloved Mary,
I send this light from Zion to you. Keep your lamp burning for me.
I will be home soon.
Your bridegroom,
Yosef

A good gift. Practical but romantic.

Mary liked Yosef. He was a strong fellow, neither handsome nor ugly, not too tall or too short. Mama noted that his black hair was thick and his teeth good. He had good skin, clear eyes, a nicely shaped head, and thus would age well and produce strong, healthy children.

Papa often remarked on Yosef's amiable disposition and knowledge of Torah. He was a descendant of David, as was Mary. He was a zadiyk, a righteous man, who kept the laws of Torah and prayed daily for the coming of Messiah. He was honest to a fault and a man of his word. At twenty-seven, Yosef had served out his apprenticeship. Now he was a journeyman carpenter, out on his own. As an offering before the Lord, he had joined several thousand volunteers working on the expansion of the Temple. As a skilled craftsman, he was chosen to carve the vines that adorned the beams of Solomon's Portico. When his sabbatical service ended, he would be ready for marriage.

He and Mary would never be rich, but neither would they be poor. Everyone needed a carpenter sometime. A door hung. A beam leveled. Papa had chosen well for her.

Tonight would be a very dark night. The New Moon had set right after the sun, and daylight was rapidly fading. Stars began to appear in the blue dome of sky above her head. Mary did not carry Yosef's lamp for fear of breaking it. No need to waste the oil, she told herself. She knew the path by heart and could find her way to and from the pens with her eyes closed.

Mary entered the barn, grabbed the three-legged stool from its peg, opened the gate of the stall, and called for Rose. The heifer bawled a grateful welcome to her mistress and ambled out.

Rose butted Mary more forcefully than usual, lowering her broad head and pushing her mistress. Rose was trembling.

"So now, what's all this? I'm late?"

Mary placed the grain bucket on the ground beneath Rose's nose, positioned the stool, and slid the empty milk pail in place. Rose did not munch the grain as usual. The creature turned her great face toward Mary and bellowed mournfully.

Practiced hands grasped the near teats in the circle of thumb and forefinger and slid them downward, releasing a steady stream of milk.

Rose stomped her hind foot three times, as though she was impatient.

"What? What? Rose girl, what?"

Then Mary touched the back side of the udder and discovered the left-rear teat was rock hard, hot to the touch, and distended. Even without light Mary knew this was very bad. "What's this? So! Between midday and now? *Oy!* Poor girl. Sweet, sweet girl!"

The roan bawled at her mistress.

Summer bag! Infection had blocked the teat and extended into the left-rear quarter of the udder! What could be done?

Shadows closed in. Mary regretted now that she had not brought the lamp. Resting her cheek against Rose's flank, she deftly milked the healthy quarters until only the infected portion remained full and rigid.

Gently, cautiously, Mary began to massage the infected tissue and strip the fluid as she had seen her mother do when summer bag had struck an old cow three years before.

That cow had died in spite of all their efforts.

It was certain that Rose's milk would dry up. And it was also sure that she would lose at least this one quarter. If the rest of her udder was permanently damaged, Rose would be fit only for slaughter. "There now, Rose. There, there." The putrid odor of infection was strong. "I know. I know it hurts. But you must let me try. Oh! Sweet Rose."

At the anguish in Mary's voice, the beast stood trembling all over, patiently bearing the pain, as though she knew Mary was attempting to relieve the pressure.

Mary prayed as she rested her cheek against Rose's side and slid her fingers downward with little result. "Blessed are you, O Adonai, who gave me strong hands . . . very strong hands. Blessed are you, O Adonai, who made Rose with such a sweet and patient heart to bear this agony. Blessed are you, even though Rose's calf did not live. Blessed are you, O Adonai. You, who own the cattle on a thousand hills. So maybe you can heal my one sweet cow to give to my husband on our wedding day. Blessed are you . . . blessed. Please send Mama out."

Mary, whispered a voice.

Mary turned her head and peered about.

Mary, it called again.

No, even *whispered* was too emphatic a word. *Sighed?*

It was as if Mary heard her name called within the recesses of her own heart.

Nearly an hour passed. Darkness pressed in. At last a glimmer of light shone on the path from the house to the stone barn on the hill.

Mama called, "Mary?"

"In here, Mama!"

"Are you coming in, girl?"

"Rose is sick."

"What is it?"

Mary did not stop working until the circle of light touched her. "Summer bag."

"*Oy.*" Mama put a hand on Rose's rump. "I smell it."

By lamplight, Rose's eyes looked glassy.

"I was afraid to leave her. Left-rear quarter. Only one. I've been working on it, Mama. Stripping it out. Rubbing her bag. Like you taught me."

"Good girl."

"Doesn't feel any softer to me."

Mama studied Rose for a long moment before answering, running her hand from the crown of Rose's head, along her spine, then down her back leg. "We'll be at it all night if we hope to save her."

"There was plenty of milk from the other three quarters."

"We'll have to throw it out. No good to drink." Mama knelt and held the lamp under Rose's belly. Mother and daughter examined the black, distended teat and the lopsided udder. Rose lifted her hind leg nervously when Mama touched the tender area. A puddle of black, stinking serum was evidence of Mary's effort.

"Bad, eh, Mama?"

Mama winced at Mary's filthy hands in the light. "I'm afraid so." She did not elaborate on what this meant. A cow with summer bag lost its market value and often its life.

"Is it my fault, Mama?" Mary worried aloud.

"Even if she had a calf to suckle her and keep her drained all day, it could still happen. Sweet thing. We'll just have to take turns with her, work on her all night, try to save her. We'll need to strip out the infection, massage the tissue. See if we can't move the stuff out . . . loosen it up."

"I can do it, Mama. Please, she's my dowry. And you know, my little friend too. Let me do it. I want to . . . need to, you know? Couldn't sleep now anyway."

Mama nodded. "Well then, I'll go in and tell Papa and the girls. Fetch you a blanket and trim the lamp. Shall I bring out Yosef's lamp to keep you company? You'll need light. Warm salt water first to wash the teat and a towel, then wine and olive oil to rub into it. It's bad fortune, this. A bad business. First your calf and now this. Poor Rose. Oh, Mary, I am so sorry."

Mary went back to work, crouching on the stool, leaning her cheek against Rose and closing her eyes.

"Blessed are you, O Adonai . . . who gave this little cow such a sweet and trusting heart. Blessed are you! Let me help her, please."

There was a chiming sound on the night wind. Pleasant—too pleasant to be from the belled neck of a wandering goat. More like the patter of soft rain on the tile roof of the synagogue.

Mama had left to fetch the things Mary would need. And when she returned, Papa came with her. Papa was not a stockman, but he hummed and clucked his tongue like a cattle buyer at market. He walked slowly around Rose several times, as though by looking he could change something.

"If she lives . . . a milk cow with three teats." He stuck out his lower lip and shook his head slowly like the cattle buyer would do. "Well, I suppose there's nothing to be done."

Mama cleared her throat as a warning to Papa that he must not say more. Must not say everything he was thinking. Mary recognized the unspoken language of her parents and had learned to understand it.

Papa glanced at Yosef's lamp as if Yosef were present. "Yosef is a fair man. Things happen. He will understand; that's all." Papa was imagining the terms of the marriage *ketubah*: *The daughter of Heli of Nazareth includes in her dowry a dry milk cow with only three teats. Value of said cow: hardly anything.*

Mama instructed, "Heli, you're no use to us here. Go back to the house. Tomorrow, I promise, you'll have troubles enough to worry about. Tonight Mary and I can worry about Rose without your help." Then firmly, "Mary, I'm staying awhile. I'll give your fingers a rest."

Papa, truly useless in all such previous emergencies dealing with livestock, spread his helpless hands. "Anna? Mending a broken gate I can manage."

Mama was gentle as she nudged Papa out the door. "I know. So go, Heli; go to bed."

Mary was grateful to have Mama with her, cleansing the bag in warm salt water, followed by the astringent power of strong red wine. She showed Mary how best to lubricate and massage the tissue.

But Mama had been up since before dawn. After nearly two hours of working on Rose, Mama looked exhausted.

Mary ate a bite of bread and hummus and washed it down with apple juice. "Thank you, Mama. Go in now. I'm grown—almost a married lady. And I am marrying a fellow like Papa, who barely knows one end of a cow from the other. I can do this. Go on now, go to bed. There's only room for one on the milking stool, and it should be me. I'll fetch you if I need you."

Mama straightened up in stages. When she finally stood erect, her back was still crooked. She kissed Mary lightly on the cheek and patted Rose's rump. Mama bit her lip. "Mary, I know how hard this is for you. I do know. Understand, eh? How disappointed you must be and sad. So many happy plans gone wrong. And . . . you're a good girl, Mary. What mother would not be pleased to have such a daughter? Your name means 'bitter,' because of your father's unhappiness that you were not a son. But his bitterness was his own, never yours. And bitterness of any sort never entered your heart. No, I've never seen a drop of bitterness in you—nor rebellion either. Adonai has watched you grow up from the day you were born. He sees how even in every misfortune you keep your heart in tune, trusting. I'm proud of you, Mary. I just wanted to tell you in case you didn't know. You are the joy of my heart. I thought I should tell you tonight."

Mama hugged Mary hard and long. A hug of sympathy for hopes that seemed to be dying one after another.

"Mama, you'll make me cry," Mary said at last. "Don't make me cry. Too much to do."

"Right." Mama wiped her eyes on her sleeve and drew herself up in a businesslike way. Her voice was cheerful, though her eyes were sad. "So I'll rest a bit and come back. We'll pray. The best medicine, eh? I'll pray for you and Rose. And perhaps . . . a miracle. Who knows?"

Mary nodded, took her place on the stool, poured olive oil onto her hands, and began to work the tender tissue, finding the impacted glands and rubbing gentle circles. "Blessed are you, O Adonai, who has given me such strong hands. . . ."

She closed her eyes and, when she opened them again, Mama had gone.

Yosef's lamp burned cheerfully in the gloom of the barn. Rose's head drooped, but still she did not touch the grain under her nose.

Mary, breathed the voice again. *Mary, the Lord is with you.*[46]

CHAPTER 7

Chief Steward Talmai knew that Herod would not rest until his suspicions were pacified with the blood of yet another victim. Anyone would do. And Talmai intended to feed that hunger in a way that would also personally benefit him. In the meantime, affairs of state in Judea continued as always.

In a few days Herod would have to go to Jerusalem for Passover. He sometimes spent the spring months there, but this year the weather remained chilly and the king proclaimed he was not eager to leave the warmth of Jericho. This year he would make his obligatory appearance in the Holy City, then retreat back to Jericho until the end of the dreary rainy season.

Later in the cycle of the seasons, when the sun's warmth changed from pleasant to irritatingly hot in both Jerusalem and Jericho, the royal entourage would move on to Caesarea Maritima on the seacoast.

Every move of the court filled Herod's thoughts with additional dangers, Talmai knew. And every new setting gave Talmai more chances to advance his scheme.

Tonight Herod's Jericho palace hosted the reception for the visiting dignitary, Eurycles of Sparta. The gathering honored the Greek celebrity who had been a comrade-in-arms of Caesar Augustus in the emperor's youth. A vagabond and a scoundrel, little better than a pirate, Eurycles' political connections were significant. Thus Herod maintained every advantage with Augustus that he could.

Though never spoken of openly, Herod's health was failing. The pains in his back and legs increased in intensity. His headaches were more frequent and debilitating. His bowels griped and howled like a demented hyena. His breath had grown as foul as his temper. Physician after physician, magician after magician, was tried and dismissed. Some were lucky to escape with their lives.

Even worse, Herod's madness outstripped his physical complaints. Old friends were dismissed from court without explanation. Everyone was suspect. Men were tortured for the slightest error in speaking or writing.

An air of foreboding and anxiety pervaded the king's household. Supporting the wrong successor could prove fatal eventually. Appearing eager for Herod's death by prematurely favoring any successor at all was likely to be fatal immediately.

Talmai expected to profit by the uncertainty. Instead of trying to guess the winning side in the contest of who would next occupy Herod's throne, Talmai intended to determine the outcome. As kingmaker, he would occupy the most powerful position in the land.

By Talmai's calculations only two possibilities existed.

Antipater was Herod's oldest son by his divorced wife Doris. Antipater was vain and prideful and given to fits of temper.

Alexander and Aristobulus were brothers, sons of the executed—now hallowed—Mariamme the Hasmonean. Both were vain and arrogant but less prone to blistering anger than either their father or half brother Antipater. Moreover, they were sensible enough to support each other and willing to share Judea between them. The brothers hated Antipater, and he returned the sentiment with interest.

All three were gross sinners of first magnitude. The fact that none of the trio deserved to be king bothered Talmai not at all.

There were younger half siblings, like Antipas and Archelaus, but none were old enough to put forward a serious claim to the throne. Talmai concluded that his path to wealth and power lay in securing the throne for either Antipater or the Hasmonean brothers. He didn't care which, except who would pay the most.

The best way for Talmai to accomplish his goal was by means of a lesson learned from the butcher king himself: Completely eliminate the competition, and there is no longer any contest.

Talmai encountered Alexander and Aristobulus walking together among the artificial streams and ponds watering the gardens of the palace grounds. The stars outlining the constellation of Aryeh, The Lion, hung poised in the southwest, as if lunging at a victim hiding in the Judean hills.

When the steward cleared his throat, the brothers jumped apart, as if already guilty of conspiring.

So much the better.

"Shalom, young princes. My pardon for disturbing you. I should withdraw and let you keep your privacy."

Alexander, the older and brighter of the two, shrugged nonchalantly. "Not at all. You interrupt nothing of consequence. We argue about whether the wines of Cyprus are better than those of the Galil."

Talmai nodded. "Sweet wine, whatever its origin, is such a blessing to your honored father. It eases him in mind and body." Talmai sighed heavily. "Your father doesn't look well . . . not at all. His color is a dreadful yellow, and he moves with such evident pain. Surely he can't live out the year."

The meaningful glance the two siblings exchanged was so plain that Talmai struggled to keep from smiling. So they had already been discussing the succession!

The oiled curls of Ari's head bobbed agreement. "He grows worse."

Thirty-year-old Alex broke in smoothly. "Kind of you to express your concern, Steward Talmai."

"There's another matter causing your father great pain," Talmai suggested. "He directed me to track down a conspiracy within the palace. Nothing is certain, but it seems someone has enlisted servants in a plot against your father's life. There are those who even think your brother Antipater may be responsible. Certainly he wants to be king."

"Never!" Ari asserted violently. "He'll never be king. His breeding is as common as his face! *We* are the true stock."

Alex grabbed his brother's arm and wrenched it forcefully enough to be painful. "Thank you for your interest, Steward," Alex concluded, steering his brother back toward the torches gleaming in the reception hall. “If we need your advice, we’ll ask for it.” Not quite far enough away to be out of Talmai’s hearing, Alex hissed, “Won’t you ever learn to keep your mouth shut? Talmai repeats everything he hears when it’s to his advantage. He’ll sell his services to the highest bidder and us along with them!”

Talmai was happy with the outcome of this first encounter. Soon he would approach Antipater with the same proposition of implicating his rivals in a deadly conspiracy. Talmai smiled. Who knew how high the bidding could go?

Even before Onias the Tutor heard footsteps in the chamber overhead, his heart was already racing with excitement. He glanced up from his work, wondering if he was about to be discovered. Leaning forward, he prepared to blow out the flickering oil lamp if the need arose. He held his breath and waited. Padding steps traveled from west to east above him, then faded away in the distance.

Exhaling slowly, Onias laid down his quill pen and scrubbed his aching eyes. So far he remained undetected. There were no guards here in the warren of archives this late at night, and those stationed outside patrolled a regular pattern and were easy to elude.

Only Simeon knew Onias was down here copying the genealogy scrolls. Onias could have sought official permission from the office of High Priest Boethus for his studies. Then he could have come here openly and in the daylight.

The difficulty lay in the fact that official permission also required an official statement of what scrolls Onias wished to examine—what exactly he was researching. The present atmosphere in Jerusalem did not favor anyone who admitted he was investigating the signs of the coming Messiah. Something in the way Zachariah and Simeon had been treated after their encounter with the angel prompted Onias to keep his efforts secret.

Herod’s secret police were everywhere, orchestrated by Chief Steward Talmai. The danger was neither imaginary nor exaggerated. Onias shuddered when he thought about his precious Tovah or little Menorah falling into the hands of Herod’s interrogators. Within the last twelve months some powerful men had tried to start an uprising, based on the public's loathing of Herod and the upwelling of desire for a true king to rule again in Israel. They had persuaded one of Herod's own slaves to announce himself as "the forerunner of Messiah," in expectation that a rebellion would follow.

Fear overrode the desire for liberation.

The infant insurgency had been brutally, thoroughly crushed.

The leaders had been crucified. Their rotting bodies had lined the road from Jericho to Jerusalem.

Onias never believed the claims of the false prophet, nor had he joined the mutiny.

But what Simeon and Zachariah had experienced was something else again.

The scroll in front of Onias had come from the red pottery amphora beside him. It was a two-hundred-year-old list of families living in Jerusalem. From it, and others like it, Onias was assembling a family tree, but not his own. Oh no.

His starting point was simple: Everyone, including Herod, knew that Messiah would be descended from King David.

Here, amidst the dusty shelves and forgotten tomes, Onias believed he was onto something—something significant. Torah schoolboys learned to recite the list of Abraham's descendants through his son, Isaac, then Jacob, then Judah, till they finally arrived at King David.

Fourteen generations later.

Fourteen. Yod-dalet.

The numerical equivalent of David's name.

Also a word suggesting a hand, since there are fourteen knuckles on each hand.

The Hand of God?

Many scholars could also recite the names of the royal offspring of David. Some were pronounced with spitting or with the sign against the evil eye, since some of David's grandchildren had done great evil to Israel.

Still, fourteen again. From King David to the destruction of the Jewish nation by Nebuchadnezzar . . . fourteen layers of lives.

Onias paused to shift the light to a better angle on his reading.

How many generations had it been *since* the Exile?[47]

The trail was not so clearly marked. Many of the records had been lost. Not all those who grew up in Babylon wanted to return to Israel.

Families were divided; histories lost. Of those who did return, few preserved the accounts of their bloodlines. The old tribe and clan allegiances seemed unimportant to many. The kingship had been abolished. What did ancient history matter now, almost five hundred years later?

Many nights Onias had spent piecing the picture together from myriad books and fragments of scrolls. He stitched a patchwork quilt of ancestry: a bit here, a trace there, a letter reporting to a father left behind in Babylon that a new grandson had been born in Jerusalem. The work was all reference and cross-reference, painstakingly built up over many weary, bleary-eyed sessions.

Onias straightened, taking the pressure off his aching back and neck, even as his breathing quickened again.

The conclusion he had reached just tonight lay in front of him: At least twelve generations of David's line had come and gone since the time of the Exile. More likely the thirteenth was grown to manhood.

The fourteenth lineal descendant of King David might already be alive, or at least must be born soon. The times were complete. Messiah would soon be revealed. Perhaps not today or tomorrow. Perhaps not for a number of years yet.

But soon! Soon!

"Come soon, Lord Messiah," Onias spoke aloud. Such words in Herod's kingdom were treasonous.

Herod had reason to be concerned for his throne!

Onias gathered his writing materials. He put away the scrolls and replaced the amphora on its shelf. Soundlessly lifting and moving first table and then chair, he returned the appearance of the chamber to its unused state.

Onias' eagerness to share his discovery was tempered by the realization that this conclusion would endanger the lives of others, including Tovah and Menorah. Whoever repeated the tally of the fourteens might be thrusting nails into their own hands and feet!

Nor was Onias' labor complete. More secret visits would be required to transfer the trail of the information to other scrolls then to be hidden. If anything happened to him, others must be able to re-create his research, reestablish his conclusions.

The back of Onias' neck prickled as he blew out the lamp.

If anything should happen to him!

CHAPTER 8

"Blessed are you, O Adonai, who watches over me."

How many hours had passed?

Mary resisted the urge to sleep. The oil in the lamp ran low. The flame guttered and died, leaving her in darkness.

The wind stirred. Another whisper, barely audible. Her name. *Mary . . .*

Just the wind.

The wind?

In the distance, but moving nearer, came a tinkling—like silver bells on the harness of a rich man's horse. Nearer still. Perhaps broken potsherds tied up as wind chimes beneath someone's eaves?

Mama would surely come soon. She would awaken and see that the lamp had gone out.

Was that her footstep? "Mama? Is that you?"

No reply. Perhaps the livestock, restless in the night?

And then a blast of wind blew the barn door closed with a bang. Rose lowed and shifted nervously.

The chimes again, louder. The whisper: *Mary.*

"Who . . . are . . . you? Who's there?" Mary's heart raced. She stammered loudly, "B-Blessed . . . blessed . . . are you, O Adonai, who is with me . . . with me always, even in darkness. I will not be afraid because you are with me." She turned her eyes to search the absolute blackness. "Is someone there?"

No reply and yet . . . a breath? a sigh? The night wind moaning around the corner of the barn? Again the rustle of fabric, the tinkle of bells.

A sweet aroma, like that of lavender blossoms, crept in among the musty dryness of the barn.

Mary got up, turned her back to Rose, and began to sing softly, as though her song could vanquish her terror:

"Give thanks to the LORD,
For He is good;
His love endures forever.
Let Israel say,
'His love endures forever.'"[48]

Then something remarkable happened. A second voice, a deep and resonant sigh, joined in on the chorus, echoing a beat behind her song: *"His love endures forever."*

"*Let those who fear the LORD say*"[49]—she held up her hands—"who are you?"

The lavender fragrance grew in intensity.

"Let those who fear the LORD say . . ." repeated the hushed sigh.

A translucent glow appeared, like the view of golden dawn breaking through rain clouds.

I am Gabriel.

She tried to sing. "*His love . . .*" Her words faltered and fell away.

The now identified but still mysterious voice replied in song: *"His love endures forever."* With each word the gleam increased in intensity, until something—some*one*—materialized before her.

Mary dropped to her knees and cried out, "Who are you? Who's there? The Lord, Adonai is with me; I will not be afraid! What can man do to me?"[50]

A golden shape—like a man, only not a man—towered over her and the cattle. *I am Gabriel,* came the repeated reply.

His head reached almost to the ceiling. Light and warmth emanated from his presence. Stretching out golden arms, he spoke, yet his lips did not move. *Greetings, you who are highly favored.*[51]

She covered her head with her arms and trembled in terror. Sound and light shook her to the core.

The angel consoled her. *Do not be afraid, Mary, you have found favor with Adonai.*[52]

She hesitated, screwed up her courage, and raised her eyes to look full at his. Perfect, beautiful in form, the radiant being smiled down at her. Eyes—kind, amused, gentle—crinkled at the corners. He nodded. Yes, it was permitted for her to look at him.

"I'm not afraid," she said aloud.

Seemingly pleased by her courage, Gabriel spoke again. *Mary, you will be with child and give birth to a son. And you are to give Him the name Yeshua, Salvation.* The air hummed around them. *He will be great and will be called the Son of the Most High. Adonai Yahweh will give Him the throne of His father David. He will reign over the house of Ya'acov forever. His kingdom will . . . never . . . end.*[53]

Mary exhaled loudly and placed her hands on her thighs. Tilting her head slightly, she asked the angel, "How will this be, since I am a virgin?"[54]

A nod of the massive head sent ripples of illumination into the corners and through the cracks of the stone structure. *The* Ruach HaKodesh, *the Holy Spirit, will overshadow you. So the holy one to be born will be called Bar El Olam, the Son of God.*[55]

Mary remembered other women of Israel who had been granted miraculous births. She thought, *Nothing is too hard for God.*

The angel seemed to hear her thoughts. *Elisheba, your mother's sister, is going to have a child in her old age, and she who was barren is in her sixth month. For nothing . . . nothing . . . is impossible with Adonai.*[56]

Mary smiled at the thought of Aunt Elisheba having a baby. Wonderful news. "I am the servant of Adonai!" She laughed in delight. "May it be to me as you have said."[57]

A moment of joy and comprehension passed between them. The approving eyes of the angel locked on those of the girl. He raised his hand in a blessing of peace over her, glanced once at Rose, then back at Mary. With the tinkling of bells the light of his presence began to fade, leaving only a single flame, the wick of Yosef's lamp, burning.

The soothing echo of Gabriel's voice reverberated in the barn: *Nothing . . . is impossible. . . . Nothing is impossible with Adonai.*

Silence.

Mary cocked an ear to listen. Crickets. The distant barking of old man Menna's dog. Her world had returned to normal.

Rose dipped her nose into the feed bucket and began to munch the grain. Her eyes were clear and alert; the tension that had been evident in every muscle was gone.

"Did you see him, Rose?" Mary patted the cow. "That lovely golden man. An angel. What do you think? Aunt Elisheba. Pregnant, he said. She'll be so happy. And . . . what he said to me . . . I believe him. Nothing is impossible. Nothing."

Still on her knees, Mary probed Rose's udder. All four quarters were perfectly smooth, soft, and supple. No sign of infection. Mary laughed as Rose swiveled her head around, as though she was also surprised. Pain was gone.

Mary locked thumb and forefinger around the affected teat and pulled. Pure white milk streamed out.

"Blessed are you, O Adonai, that you have heard my prayer. I am the servant of Adonai."

The scent of lavender lingered in the air.

The rooster crowed. Morning beamed through the east-facing barn door and onto the haystack where Mary slept. The little milk cow was near, her jaws moving slowly as she happily ground her fodder between her teeth.

"Mary?"

Mary opened her eyes.

Mama stood over her, blocking the sun.

"Mama?" Mary blinked up at Mama, confused. "Did you . . . did you see . . . it?"

"Yes! Such a wonder. All four quarters perfectly healthy. You must have worked on the cow all night through. I've never seen the like, Mary. Not in all my years. You have a way about you." Mama cheerfully rested her elbow on Rose's rump.

"No, not that. I mean . . . Mama, did you see the light?"

"Lovely sky at daybreak."

Didn't Mama understand? Hadn't she seen it—the brilliant illumination that must surely have turned the barn into a glowing lantern?

Details of Gabriel's appearance flooded Mary's consciousness. She sat bolt upright, staring at the place where Gabriel had stood. Sunlight beamed through the thatch on the roof. Motes of silver dust swirled where ethereal angel light had shone. Flecks of straw were trodden in the damp floor where golden feet had touched the earth. Too much to comprehend!

Almost too much. Yet Mary was certain—certain the encounter had been real.

"What is it? Mary? You're pale as a cloud."

"Mama! Last night!"

"I slept right through the night, leaving you to do the work alone. But you managed very well without my help. Well done."

"Not that! Oh, Mama!" Mary grasped her mother round her knees and wept. "Mama!"

Mama's pleasure at the healed heifer turned to consternation. "What is it? Child, what's wrong?"

"Oh, Mama! Last night after you left, something happened. Something wonderful. Wonderful! The light! He was great and tall. His eyes so kind. His lips didn't move, but I heard him speak to me. As clear as your voice it was! He told me . . . and I don't know why he came to me, but he did. A great light! Golden. Bright! Music in the light . . . and . . . the smell of flowers. He looked at Rose, at me, and then he was gone. And look!"

Mama blinked down at Mary. Her voice was a monotone of awe. "An angel."

Mary's head bobbed with excitement. "I was so afraid at first. He knew how frightened I was, and he told me not to be afraid. When I looked at his face, he was smiling, and I wasn't afraid anymore."

Mama sat down hard in the straw beside her, grasping Mary's arms. "A dream?"

"No, Mama! No dream. He was right there! Standing there. There! See? In front of the garden things."

Mama nodded thoughtfully, staring hard at the clutter, almost believing, wanting to believe. "Tell me . . . everything."

Where to start? So much to tell. "He says Aunt Elisheba is six months pregnant!"

"Elisheba? No."

"Oh, Mama! Why would he say such a thing if it wasn't true?"

"Elisheba? Mary! Aunt Elisheba? Not possible."

"He told me. He said, 'Nothing—nothing—is impossible with Adonai.'"

At these words Mama's mouth opened in a silent *O* of amazement. "Father Avraham. The very words . . . the very . . ." Her eyes widened. "Mary?"

"Gabriel. His name. Gabriel. His eyes so kind and yet . . . so very, very sad. If he had stayed even a moment longer, I would have flown away with him."

Mama was silent. She studied a spot in front of the garden tools and then gazed up at the ceiling of the barn. She nodded again, as though comprehending something more. "What . . . else? It wasn't entirely about Elisheba. Why would he? Just to . . . ? Did he say anything else?"

Mary bit her lip and closed her eyes. "Yes. Mama, he said . . . he told me that Adonai . . . was with me." Then, with a rush, "That I would be with child and have a son, and his name would be Yeshua. And that Adonai would give him the throne of his father David and he would rule over Ya'acov's house forever. Mama?"

Mama's head bobbed once. She squeezed her daughter's fingers, urging her to go on.

"I asked him how, since I'm a virgin. He said the power of the Most High would overshadow me, and I would have a son."

Mama tucked her chin. She straightened her shoulders as the meaning of the message seemed to penetrate into her bones. She whispered, "Isaias. It is written, '*And this shall be a sign unto you.*'[58] How did you answer, Daughter?"

"I told him, I am the servant of Adonai. And may it be done to me as he had spoken.[59] Then Rose and I feel asleep. I slept until you woke me."

Mama lifted Mary's hands to her lips and kissed her fingertips. "So . . . it will be as the angel proclaimed to you. My dear, sweet girl." The two women embraced.

"Yes. I don't feel any different—just happy." Mary clung to Mama, comforted that she had believed such a wondrous thing without doubt.

Mary laughed. "I'm hungry. Mama, we should go tell Papa, shouldn't we? Won't he be glad to hear? An angel in his barn?"

Mama hesitated and, in her mother's eyes Mary saw for the first time that there might be some who would not believe her. "Oh, Mary. Papa . . . and Yosef. Let me think. You must . . . let me be the one to tell your father what has happened to you."

The distance from Herod's palace in Jerusalem to the home of Onias the Tutor was not far—no more than a five-minute walk. Of course *walk* would never adequately describe the procession of guards, slaves, and attendants accompanying the young prince Alexander to his Hebrew lessons.

The throngs of pilgrims and other visitors to the Holy City stopped and stared, babbling among themselves about who the exalted personages might be. Every afternoon's lesson provided the opportunity to carry back some choice bit of name-dropping to a village in the remote stretches of the Upper Galil or to another far-off bit of the Empire.

The residents of the Gennath district largely ignored the parade of retainers. It did not pay to show too much interest in matters above one's station. The tales of midnight knocks at the door and common folk who disappeared forever were legendary . . . and terrifying.

Seven-year-old Alexander, grandson of King Herod by his son Alex and Princess Glaphyra, was a bright, eager student. So far he seemed untainted by either his heritage or life in the palace. Partly because his grandfather resented being regarded as not really Jewish, Alexander was being raised as a true son of the covenant.

All Alexander's other schooling took place in the grounds of whatever palace Herod's court was occupying at the time.

Onias came highly recommended, but he also belonged to the sect of the Pharisees. As such he refused to enter the palace grounds because going there would make him ritually unclean. Herod had bristled when told this, but since the boy's other grandfather had engaged Onias' service, Herod relented.

Alexander had been coming to Onias for instruction in reading the Tanakh, the Holy Scriptures, since he was age five. He had left behind the period of childhood known as *taph*, the clinging ones, to join the ranks of the *elem*, the firm and strong.

Few at the court could read the ancient Hebrew texts, though most could read and write Aramaic. Fewer still cared. Study of Holy Scripture was not a high priority at Herod's court. Alexander's father was not very concerned about his son's education, but his mother insisted.

Today was unusual in that Glaphyra and her younger son, Tig, age four, were also present. Glaphyra wanted Onias to examine the smaller boy, to see if Tig was ready to begin instruction also.

Because Onias' house was small—just two rooms behind the front reception area, with a cooking space between the two—most of the royal retinue waited outside in the sun. Only Glaphyra, her two boys, and one guard, an immensely powerful Ethiopian named Selassi, were admitted to the interior.

The day's lesson revolved around words beginning with the Hebrew letter *Sheen*, shaped like a hand with three upraised fingers.

As the young charge painstakingly copied a list of words onto a wax tablet, Onias remarked, "*Sheen* is a very important letter. It is the next to the last letter of the *alef-bet*, and begins words like *Shalom*, peace. *Simcha*, joy. *Shabba*, Sabbath. And *Shanah*, year. So, Prince Alexander, I wish you peace and joy every Sabbath this year and every year. Now pick up a clean tablet and write that sentence five times: 'I wish you peace and joy every Sabbath this year and every year.'"

"What a wonderful sentiment," Glaphyra murmured, eyes downcast, "if it could ever really be true." Her tone was not exactly mournful but expressed doubt.

Onias did not respond but peeked quickly at the guard who stood, arms folded across the tree trunk of his chest, blocking the door.

Glaphyra, Tig on her lap, caught the glance. "You needn't worry about Selassi," the princess reassured Onias. "He is entirely loyal to me and even more so to the boys."

When the copying exercise was complete, Onias asked, "So, young Alexander, you have been to morning prayers in the Temple, yes?"

At seven Alexander could approach no nearer the altar than the Court of Women, but as a pampered princeling he did enjoy a favored spot for viewing the proceedings. He nodded vigorously in answer to his tutor.

"Then you have seen the priests reciting the Shema with hands upraised in this shape?" On each hand Onias crossed first and second fingers together, then third and fourth fingers together. With thumbs left to stick out, the shapes formed were *Sheens*. "This is not by accident. It is full of significance. The letter *Sheen* begins the word *Shema*, hear. '*Hear, O Israel . . . ,*' the great pronouncement of our faith. *Sheen* begins the word *Shem*, Name, as in *HaShem*, The Name—one of the ways we refer to the Holy One, the Almighty, without the danger of actually pronouncing His Holy Name. So we say, *Baruch HaShem*, Blessed be the Name. Now you will write that phrase, please, five times. *Baruch HaShem*."

Glaphyra, showing Tig how to entwine his fingers as described, looked pleased at the information.

"We believe that sign is holy, so please don't make it casually. We believe making the signal is the same as calling on The Name, so it is never to be done frivolously," Onias instructed.

Glaphyra nodded her understanding.

Even while young Alexander continued his writing, Onias mused aloud, "The letter *Sheen* is central to the name of the great lawgiver, Mosheh. It is also key to the title Mashiyah—the Messiah, the Anointed One—because when Messiah comes, he will bring everlasting *Shalom* and *Simcha*. In the power of The Name, the *Shem*, Mashiyah, will right every wrong and correct every injustice."

Now Glaphyra fidgeted as she inspected Selassi's emotionless face. "Messiah . . . is not a topic we are permitted to discuss in the palace."

"Your pardon, Princess," Onias replied.

"Don't apologize!" Glaphyra insisted. "I want Alexander—and Tig, when he's ready—to know it all. Teach them about the great *HaShem*, Tutor Onias. Make certain they learn it well!"

CHAPTER 9

The argument between Mama and Papa in the workshop increased in volume, reaching the ears of the three sisters huddled on the stone wall of the garden. Even the milk cows raised their heads and ruminated as the noise of commotion grew.

Papa's accusation.

Mama's outrage.

Mary, pale and stricken by the unexpected fury of her father's response, could scarcely raise her eyes from the chickens that scavenged for bugs in the furrows of the garden.

How can it be that Papa doesn't believe me? I am your servant, Lord. But what about Papa?

Twelve-year-old Salome grasped Mary's arm in indignation at Papa's words. "I believe you, Mary!"

Nine-year-old Naomi, eyes brimming with tears, said, "Me too. I believe you. But Mary, what did you do? Why is Papa so angry?"

Salome, eyes stony, jaw set, peered around Mary and snapped at Naomi, "She didn't do anything!" Salome gave Mary's arm a squeeze. "Papa doesn't believe her. Doesn't believe an angel would talk to her in our barn, that's all."

Naomi leaned her head against Mary's arm. "An angel came to our house. I believe."

From inside the workshop the conflict between the one who believed and the one who did not believe took a violent turn. Something crashed to the ground. Papa shouted, "What? What's she trying to do? She doesn't want to get married?"

Mama's words were barbed. "What kind of father are you?"

Did Papa not understand how loud he was speaking? "So she makes up such a story?"

"Has she ever lied to us before?"

Naomi covered her ears and crouched down as Papa roared, "Is she pregnant then? Is that what she's saying? A wild story to cover up the truth? Has she been meeting some young fellow without us knowing?"

I am your servant, Lord!

"She hasn't—she wouldn't—dishonor her vow to Yosef or to you!"

"What will I say to Yosef? Eh?"

I am your servant, Adonai. I am yours. Anything. Anything you ask. But Lord, what about Yosef? You know I gave him my heart. My promise that I would always be his. I love him. What will he think?

Mama was staunch in her defense. "You will tell Yosef what happened. What she saw. What she heard."

Papa's words reflected bitter sarcasm. "I can hear it now: 'Yosef, lad, the virgin you pledged to marry is pregnant by the Holy Spirit. An angel spoke to her and told her she was favored by Adonai and would bring forth the one who will sit on David's throne!' Bah! Mary says the Holy Spirit of the Almighty has overshadowed her? Mary says the angel said the *Ruach HaKodesh* would make a virgin pregnant without the help of a man? Ridiculous! Absurd claim on the face of it! Madness, Anna! Never meant to be taken literally. No one in all the world would ever believe such a thing! Who am I? The foolish, doting father? Believe every word of this nonsense—that's what you're saying? The disgrace! We'll all be ruined! I won't be able to hold up my head!"

Mama countered, "And what if . . . what if it is so? As Mary said it was? Think. The holy honor of it! The blessing! Your daughter chosen by the Almighty from all the girls in Israel! But you're too blind to see it."

"Who is Mary? Just a girl. Third daughter of a fellow who prayed for sons. Sons would not have given me such trouble. This girl? Nothing special, I can tell you."

"If you think that, then you don't know her!"

I am your servant, Adonai. But Papa is right. Who am I that you would honor me? Just like everyone else. Small dreams. Yosef to love me. Children of my own. A little life here in the place I grew up. That's all I have ever wanted. Who am I? And am I strong enough to face Papa's anger? certain disgrace? strong enough to maybe even lose Yosef? I am your servant, Lord. I am. But my heart might break for it.

"I follow the laws of Torah," Mary's father continued. "If she has sinned and violated her vows, Yosef can demand she be condemned and stoned. You know that, don't you, Anna? If he is not the father of her child? To be betrothed to Yosef means she cannot lie with another man without the charge of adultery! Stoned! And I, her father, and you, her mother, will have to watch as Yosef throws the first stone!"

Mary's heart beat like the wings of a bird trapped in a snare. In her peripheral vision she caught a movement on the road. Someone was walking toward the house.

Even from a distance, Mary recognized Yosef, unmistakable by his long, cheerful stride, the slope of his shoulders, and mass of black curls and beard.

I am your servant, Lord. But not now, O Lord! Please, not today!

At the sight of Yosef, Salome began to weep. Naomi clung to Mary and asked why Papa was being so cruel. Had Yosef come to arrest her and take her before the council for judgment?

Mary could only shake her head and look away. She could only stare at the barn and wish someone else had been with her when Gabriel had spoken.

So, Yosef is home from Yerushalayim. Coming to visit at the very moment my world is breaking into ten thousand pieces. Oh Lord, let him believe me! Please!

Mama shouted, "I believe her!"

Papa snarled, "Yes, well, you would! Her mother! I believe what's in front of me. Mary's either crazy, or she's a liar. Or she hates me and wants to disgrace me. Maybe all three."

Yosef was smiling broadly as he approached the bottom of the lane. He hesitated, then raised his arm in greeting to the sisters before he hailed them. "Shalom!"

Salome's hands were shaking. "I'll go. I'll tell Mama and Papa he's here."

Mary nodded, feeling queasy as Yosef, grinning, climbed the slight incline of the lane that led to the house. "Mary! Mary! Shalom!" He waved broadly. "Ho! Mary!"

Mary made no move to rise from the stone wall and greet him. Her legs had gone weak. She could not stand or walk, let alone run away, though she longed to vanish. Her voice was barely audible. "Shalom . . . Yosef. Home again."

Yosef came near, saw her expression, heard the loud voices. Consternation knit his brows and slowed his step. "Mary?"

"Oh, Yosef."

Papa's rage resounded from the shop. "You. You are a fool, Anna. A fool! I have married a fool. And my daughter is a harlot!"

Yosef's smile vanished. "What . . ."

Mary did not reply but kept her eyes riveted to his feet and the road-ragged hem of his robe.

Mama's roar turned Yosef's head toward the structure. "Enough, Heli! I'm taking Mary to my sister's house! To Elisheba!"

Salome hesitated at the door.

Oh, why didn't Salome interrupt them? Mary wondered. Why didn't she shout the warning that Yosef was outside at this very minute, and they must not argue anymore?

Salome, though her fist was raised, did not knock. She shifted from one foot to the other, as if waiting for a lull in the altercation.

Papa shouted even louder at Mama, "So, Mary hates Yosef? Eh? Is that it? He'll never marry her if I tell him about this. Never! You think Yosef is a fool?"

Yosef stiffened at the mention of his name. He blinked down at her. "Mary?"

She could not look at him. She managed only a whisper. "Yosef, it isn't like that." How could she tell him about the vision? What if he did not believe her? What if he, like Papa, thought she had made it up?

Papa's words came like hammer blows. "If Mary is pregnant by another man, Yosef can't and won't marry her. Breaking this contract will also ruin the chances for her sisters to marry. Eh? Who would make a marriage contract with me for Salome and Naomi now? Eh? Answer me, Anna! What am I supposed to say to Yosef?"

The blood drained from Yosef's face. His eyes clouded as the avalanche of Mary's betrayal crashed down on him. He turned on his heel and stalked away to join Salome at the door.

O Adonai! I am your servant. May it be as the angel said. I have lost Yosef. His eyes bore through me. I have lost his love.

Mama spat the words, "If you were any kind of a father, you would defend her! You would tell Yosef the truth!"

Papa struck back. "Oh? What is the truth?"

"The truth is . . . the angel offered us proof! A way to know! The angel said . . . Elisheba! If my sister, Elisheba, is six months pregnant—"

"Then I'll believe anything. That barren cow."

Yosef raised his fist and slammed it hard on the door.

For a moment Papa's words seemed to hang in the air. Yosef knocked again.

"I told you girls . . . what do you want?" Papa flung open the door.

At the sight of Yosef's grim face before him, Heli stumbled as though he had been struck.

Salome ducked away and jogged back to Mary.

Yosef faced Papa. Mama, wringing her hands, hovered in the background.

The volume of the conversation dropped low. Mary could not make out all of the words.

Papa, red-faced, sweating, wagged his head over and over, as though someone had died. "Yosef. Yosef! You . . . are . . . home."

Yosef's olive skin had a pale green cast under his beard. Confused, hurt, angry, he gestured toward Mary. "What? What is this . . . what are you saying? I've just come home, and I came to tell you all I am here. Home. And ready to take on my obligation . . . and I walk into this. . . ."

Papa stepped aside. "Yosef, come in."

Yosef's words quavered as though he might weep. "Tell me . . . the truth . . . Heli."

"I don't know the truth, Yosef." Papa took Yosef's arm and led him inside. The door closed slowly. Terrible minutes passed in silence.

Mary trembled as Naomi and Salome linked arms with her in solidarity. The sisters strained to hear.

I am your servant. But Yosef! Have I lost him? Let him believe me. His heart is broken. Such a good heart. Such a good man. Let him believe. Oh, Lord! Broken. Broken!

After a time they heard Mama break into tears.

And Mama too! Broken heart!

Papa shouted at Yosef, "Are you calling my daughter a liar? I tell you that is what she claims to have seen!"

Silence. *Papa believes me? Papa is defending my honor? or his? I am your servant, Lord.*

Papa again. "Mary has never lied to me! You say you love her. Then believe her! This is what Mary says happened!"

Yosef's strident voice replied, "Is she pregnant? Answer me! Is she with child? This girl you promised to me . . . promised as a virgin . . . is pregnant? That is what you are telling me, Heli?"

"I don't know, Yosef! She shows no sign of it. I am telling you what the girl repeated to her mother only this morning!"

Yosef! Husband. I have lost you, Yosef! Our dreams of life together. O Lord, I am your servant, but . . . I will never see Yosef again. He is lost to me now.

Moments passed. Words were indistinct, but the tone conveying Yosef's deep sense of Mary's betrayal was clear enough.

Then Mama pleaded, "Please, Yosef! No! Please! You must not be hasty about this! Only last night . . ."

Papa joined forces with Mama. He had seemingly shifted from unbelief to belief as together they tried to convince Yosef. "Look, Anna will take her to her aunt Elisheba's in Judea this very day. No scandal, no dishonor. Everything will blow over. Give it some time, Yosef, before you make a judgment. A hysterical young girl has a dream. She believes it! A dream and a young girl's imagination. How can we know she's pregnant? Time will tell. A few months away, eh? We don't know what the girl saw for sure. And, Yosef! What if what she told us is true! Yosef?"

The door opened wide. Yosef's back was to the sisters, but every nuance was clear. "What if? What if while I was gone she has been meeting with someone? You understand why I would wonder about it? Eh? Coming home from Yerushalayim? Hoping to greet my bride and her family and coming instead to hear such a far-fetched tale!" Yosef's words were thick with bitterness and sarcasm.

"So, an angel, you say?" Yosef continued. "So, Heli, suppose . . . suppose . . . what you say is true. Just suppose. What am I to do, eh? Tell everyone an angel visited the girl I intended to marry, and now she is pregnant by the power of the Almighty? Without any help from a man? Who would believe this? Who am I—the world's biggest fool? And if it was true that she is the virgin of Isaias' prophecy, how could I ever marry her? How could I? Who am I? Who am I to be chosen with the task of raising . . . the son of . . . David? Was David the name this angel gave the father? Son of David? So, how many Davids do I know in Nazareth? A dozen? At least. I would always ask myself, son of which David?"

Yosef, hand to his brow as if shielding his eyes from seeing something terrible, stepped out into the sunlight. Storming down the gravel walk, he cast a single glance of reproach at Mary, then left without a word.

Yosef! Yosef! You hate me now. Hatred in your eyes. I've broken your fine heart . . . such a good heart. I love you still and remained true to you. Yosef. Who am I that my strength can bear the hatred of such a good man—the man I love? I am only a girl, and not so strong that I can walk away from loving you. He hates me now. Lord, I am your servant. I believe what you say. But . . . Lord, look! I've lost Yosef.

A breeze sighed around the corners of Jerusalem. Its fingers stroked Onias' beard and toyed with the hairs on the back of his neck. Tunics hanging from rooftop clotheslines flapped idly, phantoms beckoning Onias toward his midnight rendezvous with dusty scrolls.

For the third time in as many minutes the tutor looked over his shoulder. Nothing to be seen. Nothing out of the ordinary. A dog barked in the distance. Somewhere a woman's angry voice gave vent to undecipherable displeasure, then subsided.

Onias chided himself for his nervousness. Too many sleepless nights, too much isolation in the catacombs of the archives were taking a toll on him. While his intellect struggled to decipher the meanings of names, the significance of generations, something in the background of his thoughts kept his senses on a knife's edge.

Onias pushed away his apprehension and concentrated on his studies as he walked the dark streets. Rereading the words of the Babylonian captive Dani'el had reconfirmed Onias' conclusion about the imminent arrival of Messiah. The weeks of years spoken of by the prophet were nearly accomplished; that much was clear. The completion of another cycle of fourteen generations matched Dani'el's timeline.

The prophecy given to Dani'el by the angel Gabriel stated:

> *Now listen and understand! Seven sets of seven plus sixty-two sets of seven will pass from the time the command is given to rebuild Yerushalayim until Messiah—the Anointed One—comes.*[60]

The decree issued by the Persian King Artaxerxes authorizing the rebuilding of Jerusalem had been issued about 440 years earlier. The exact time frame of Dani'el's prophecy.

Onias stopped short. Was there a darker shadow lurking within the black outline of the next doorway?

Nothing there. Childish! Foolish!

Onias resumed examining links in the chain of Messiah's advent as he walked. Herod might be king, but he would never be David's heir. Nor was that the end of the story. Herod would not like this role, but Onias believed the Idumean was central to the times: There was a prophecy saying that Messiah would only come after a non-Jewish king sat on the throne.

It was in the *Book of Beginnings*:

> *The scepter will not depart from Judah, nor the ruler's staff from his descendants, until the coming of the one to whom it belongs (until Shiloh, the Sent One, comes), the one whom all nations will honor.*[61]

Judea had been ruled by overlords from Babylon and Persia and Greece and Syria and Egypt and Rome. None had styled themselves king of the Jews . . . until Herod the Great. He was the first non-Jew to claim that particular title. Despite all Herod's pretense to the contrary, he was not—and never could be—of Jewish blood.

He had been born in Ashkelon, a pagan coastal city. Herod's mother was Nabatean. A child of the desert, her home was the Rose Red City of Petra, east of the Jordan. Herod had even lived there for a time in his youth.

Herod's father was a wealthy Idumean, who eventually became governor of Idumea. Throughout the whole history of Jewish existence in Eretz-Israel, the Idumeans were bitter enemies of the children of

Abraham. In the days of the Hasmonean king of Israel, John Hyrcanus, Idumea had been conquered and the males there forcibly circumcised to "make them Jews." However, nothing in that event had made the Idumeans any more Jewish or Jewish-Idumean relations any more cordial.

Onias hastened his pace, his excitement at the prospect of more discoveries increasing.

A cobblestone kicked by an unseen foot clattered softly off a stone wall close behind him. Onias turned sharply. "Who? Who's there?"

No reply, no movement, yet when Onias took another step, so did the pursuer. At least it sounded that way, over the reverberation of Onias' heart surging in his ears.

Abruptly Onias gave up his planned effort for the night. At the next corner he turned, taking a different route back home. If someone was following him, there was no reason to lead them straight to the archives, to divulge the nature of his studies.

Whether this time the hunt was real or not, Herod's spies certainly were. Home and a night's rest were what Onias needed. Tomorrow night he would try again, using a more roundabout route. In the meantime he could not be arrested for his thoughts, could he?

Yosef bar Jacob sat in the middle of his workshop. His elbows rested on the carpentry bench. In his hands he held a woodworking chisel. Though he took no notice of it, the tool was in constant motion, tumbling end over end through his fingers . . . like the thoughts through his head.

What had happened since his return from Jerusalem? since yesterday?

Yosef knew the answer in some intellectual way yet could not fathom the *why* or the *how* of it. When he'd gone away to offer a tithe of his skill to the service of Yahweh, everything about his future had been in order. Very settled, very secure, very satisfying. The sum total of Yosef's expectations involved Mary, his carpentry shop and, someday, children. He'd never thought further than that. Why would he want to?

Yosef's longings were not complex. He was neither ambitious nor vain, not prideful or greedy.

What had happened to his world?

This situation resembled the puzzle box Yosef had once carved: Everything seemed solid and secure until you pulled out one key piece. Then the box fell apart in front of your eyes. And putting it together again was impossible unless you knew the secret pattern. This time there were no instructions on how to reassemble it.

Yosef's head was tilted to the side, the way it naturally posed when he confronted a knot in the midst of a piece of wood. *What do I do with this? How do I work around this problem?*

When facing that issue in regard to a chair or chest, Yosef's inner debate lasted a few minutes at most before a solution presented itself. Then his head would straighten, and a smile would play over his thin lips as he set to work again.

This time he had already been contemplating for hours, and there was no answer in sight.

I love her. That was an easy place to begin: a solid, indisputable fact. It was a choice piece of oak on which to begin to craft.

But nothing stayed simple after that.

She's betrayed me. She's been with someone else. And not just once either. Nobody really thinks that.

She doesn't look pregnant. Is she?

But she doesn't deny it. She and her mother have made up this wild tale.

Could she have been raped? I'd kill him; then I'd marry her.

But she makes no such claim.

From there the hammer strokes driving home the pegs of the depth and breadth of the crisis reverberated ever louder and more painfully.

I can't marry her now. We can never be husband and wife.

That realization made Yosef feel as if someone had plunged the iron chisel's wedge into his chest . . . over and over again. Every time he passed that conclusion the same sharp pain stabbed him. No matter how many times that particular thought came around, the ache never got any less.

Yosef was well liked and well regarded in the village, but he'd never cared much about the public's opinion of him. In fact, he'd never given it any thought at all. He was Yosef, the carpenter, son of the covenant, keeper of the Law. That was all.

I can't marry her now.

Stab!

Can I even live in this village after she has another man's child? What kind of man would that make me? Even if the gossip stops when people meet me, what will I read lurking in their eyes?

And the child? How will he or she be regarded here? How will I *act around the child, knowing it isn't mine?*

Yosef stared at a finishing plane hanging on the wall. *This isn't something I can just smooth away like an uneven joint.* His gaze strayed to the large, sharp-toothed handsaw propped in the corner. *No, this is more like an amputation.*

She could be executed. Yosef shuddered. He'd seen a stoning once, though he'd taken no part in it himself. A man, a murderer, had been proven guilty and was killed with the approval of King Herod's officers. Still, it had been horrible to witness: the cries for mercy; the man's futile attempts to shield his head from the jagged rocks; the misshapen, crushed carcass that remained.

Yosef's shoulders trembled again. *Sweet Mary? Barely more than a child?* Guilty or not, he'd save her himself before it came to that!

Fortunately, it would not go that far.

To save his own reputation, Yosef could have her hauled before the local Sanhedrin. There he'd denounce her. Since they were formally betrothed, the charge would be adultery.

Yosef's mouth had a taste bitter as myrrh as the word *adultery* hammered against his love for her.

Then, so long as she didn't deny the charge, Yosef would be absolved from any wrong, completely justified in the matter. He was the wronged party, liable to receive smirking sympathy but publicly approved for his righteousness.

Of course, Mary's life would never be the same—not here, not in a village as small as Nazareth. She and her family would have to move away. They would have to make up some story about the child's father being dead.

But would they go? What if Heli cast her out? What if he drove her away, as was his right?

Yosef's eyes strayed out through the window to where a stack of sawn lumber leaned against an acacia tree. The carpentry shop was one room. Yosef's living accommodations were only another single room attached to the back.

The boards, which he'd sawn and planed and squared and measured, were all for the additional chamber Yosef had intended to build for Mary before he brought her home with him. Now he could burn them. What did it matter?

What did anything matter?

His view grew blurry with his tears.

If I don't denounce her to the council, what will they think of me? What will all my neighbors think? Will they take all their business somewhere else? How will I live? Will I have to leave here? Where will I go? Back to Yerushalayim?

But I love her.

Yahweh! Yosef's heart cried in anguish. *Help me!*

The chisel, endlessly rolling, was still revolving when night fell again.

CHAPTER 10

Onias blinked and yawned as he stood in the open doorway of his home. He beckoned toward the Herodian soldiers lounging in the shade across the street. Today's lesson was complete. Young Alexander finished copying the text of the first three Sabbath blessings while his mother, Glaphyra, waited for him to be ready to leave.

The fresh air cleared Onias' head. Afternoon light was softened by white clouds drifting overhead. Across the way a pair of shoppers haggled over the price of dates. A coppersmith leading a small donkey hawked his wares. The mild bustle of Onias' neighborhood was so normal, so ordinary.

Could he be imagining the nighttime dangers? Had his thoughts created peril where none really existed? Was he really being followed? spied on? Or was his apprehension without cause?

Onias bowed as the royals left his home. Glaphyra thanked him, as did the boy. The entourage formed, guards before and behind, with the personal bodyguard, Selassi, only two paces behind mother and child.

Onias touched the mezuzah on the doorpost and kissed his fingertips. The tutor stretched his neck and looked idly after the departing procession, now already a block away.

Nearer at hand, two men who were examining the merchandise outside a cobbler's shop abruptly dropped the sandals they were considering. Like bits of sacking blown by the wind, the two figures drifted up the street, following, without seeming to follow, the princess and her son.

Should Onias call out? warn them? The heavily armed guards were more than adequate to a threat posed by two men.

Who or what were they? Rebels? Spies? Assassins?

And who was really their target?

Shabbat morning Papa ordered Mama to stay home from synagogue with the girls while he went alone to services.

When he came back from worship, he would not look at Mary. He did not speak to anyone but brooded in the orchard until Shabbat ended at sunset.

Evening stars shone brightly overhead by the time he came in for supper. His jaw was set, his eyes focusing everywhere but at Mary as he took his place at table and recited the blessings.

Papa! Oh, my poor, dear Papa! What must you think of me? I am the servant of Adonai.

Picking up the bread to break it, he recited the baracha, then said to Mama, "I saw Yosef at synagogue this morning."

"Yosef! Is he well?" Mary blurted eagerly.

Papa's lip curled as though her voice left a bitter taste in his mouth. He addressed Mama. "So far we have escaped disgrace. Yosef has said nothing to anyone about the girl's betrayal. About her madness. He is silent—a man of honor. In two days the family of Joachim is making aliyah to Yerushalayim. I have asked Joachim, and he has agreed. You and the girl will travel with them as far as Beth Karem, where your childless sister, Elisheba, and her husband, Zachariah, live." Papa spoke as though Mary were not his daughter . . . as if she were not in the room.

Mama exhaled in relief and gave Mary a confident nod as if to say that everything would be well. "You won't go with us, Heli?"

He paused, half-torn bread in his hand. "When you reach Beth Karem and see it isn't true that Elisheba is pregnant, that is proof the girl is a liar and a harlot. Then you will leave the girl with Elisheba until it is clear . . . if the girl is pregnant. If the girl has played the harlot, then she'll give birth there in Beth Karem, where our family is not known. If the infant survives, you will give this unwanted child to your sister, Elisheba, to raise as her own."

Mama's eyes flashed. "You've already made up your mind. In your imagination you cast the first stone at your own daughter! But you're wrong, Husband!"

"Mind your tongue, woman! One more word and I'll put you out of this house as well!"

Salome and Naomi clung to one another and began to wail at their father's threat. He ordered them from the table.

Tears welled in Mary's eyes as the gulf between Mama and Papa yawned wider. Mary, ashen-faced and silent, accepted the blows of Papa's disdain.

O Adonai! Papa appears a righteous man, yet secretly he's so cruel and bitter. I have heard Papa pray. Every day of my life he has prayed for the Lord's Anointed to come save Israel. Did he ever believe you would hear his prayers? Or did he only speak the words loud enough and often enough so others would hear him praying and believe he was righteous? O Adonai, help Papa believe you are, and that nothing is impossible for you! O Adonai, I am . . . I am the servant of Adonai. Though my father despises me and the man I have loved believes I am a harlot, I am your servant. Nothing is impossible for you! May it be . . . whatever it may be . . . only as you will it for me.

Mama put her arm protectively around Mary's shoulders as Salome and Naomi fled the house in tears. "All their marriage Elisheba and Zachariah have prayed for a child," Mama told Papa. "I know Elisheba will be made complete by The Eternal. I know the prayers of Zachariah have been heard and remembered. My sister and her husband will have a baby of their own. And all that the angel said to Mary will be proven true. Then you'll know the true meaning of your shame, Heli. You'll know that nothing is impossible with Adonai!"

Papa slammed his fist on the table. "Hear me, woman! If it is proven that the girl is a liar and has played the harlot, leave her."

"Leave her? Where?"

"Does it matter? In the gutter. Let her sell herself for food. She is not welcome in this house. She is dead. Our daughter is dead to us." Only now, as his rage boiled over, did he look at Mary. His eyes were red-rimmed with anger as he shook his finger in her face. "You! See what you've done? What you've done to your family with this . . . this . . . lie? Torn us apart. Don't come back! You are dead to me. Dead to your mother and your sisters. Disgrace! Shame you have heaped on my head. The rocks of Nazareth may not break your bones, though you deserve to be stoned. But you are as dead to me as if Yosef denounced you publicly in the market square and chose the weapon of execution from the rocks of my own field. Now leave me! Both of you. No more words. Go to Beth Karem. That is your only hope of salvation!"

He leapt from the table and stormed out into the night.

Agonized screams echoed throughout the citadel of Herodium, cascading over the battlements like ash from a volcano of torment. Two stonemasons had joked about the king's jaundice. Herod's likeness, they incautiously quipped, should have been done in yellow marble instead of white. They were overheard by one of Talmai's informants. For their offense both craftsmen were being beaten to death with a corax, the bone-pronged whip that ripped skin from flesh and tore at the muscle beneath.

Talmai discovered Herod in the rotunda of the main level of the fortress. Surrounding the king was a phalanx of courtiers, architects, and master masons. All studiously ignored the cries of anguish that funneled past them.

Several floors of battlements and watchtowers, together with barracks for a legion of Herod's soldiers, occupied the space above the central ring. Below this point was the palace, all marble and trimmed with gold. If Herodium ever underwent the siege it was designed to resist, Herod and his court would continue to live in luxury as long as the food and wine held out. The provisions would last two years by Talmai's calculation. As chief steward, he was in a position to know.

Herod's three-decade reign had produced building projects both extensive and costly. He had lavished his attention (and Judea's wealth) on the Jerusalem Temple, but his desire to leave an architectural legacy did not end there.

Judean taxes went into building temples to the Olympian god Zeus in Greece, Pamphylia, and Mysia, as well as to local deities in Syria. Gold restored Herod's birthplace of Ashkelon, enlarged Paneas, and created the purpose-built harbor showpiece now called Caesarea Maritima.

No expense was spared in providing comfort and grandeur for Herod's palaces in Jericho and Jerusalem.

But of all his building projects, the one Herod kept returning to and tinkering with was Herodium, this man-made anthill near Beth-lehem, a few miles south of Jerusalem. Back in his early days, when Herod was on the run from his enemies, he had taken refuge here and used the natural terrain to outfox his pursuers. Ever since that event Herodium never left his thoughts for long, being now part palace, part prison, part fortress, and part monument.

Herodium was part torture chamber as well. A final, high-pitched shriek marked the parting of a stonemason's soul and body.

Herod expected to be buried in the depths of the masonry cone. Glistening white marble carvings, jet-black onyx mirrors, and buffed pink columns all surrounded the crypt Herod planned for his final resting place.

Herod never talked openly about his death. He acted as if the tomb would never have to be fully completed because it would never be occupied.

Talmai knew better. The jaundice in the king's complexion, extending even to his eyes, was more apparent than ever. Dye was no longer enough to hide his advancing age, since his thinning hair was coming out by the handful. The myrrh-and-poppy-juice mixture his Egyptian physician prescribed no longer eased his agony for more than an hour at a time.

Even if Herod was not ready to die, Talmai was more than prepared for the king's departure. Today's step would ensure Talmai's place in the next regime.

Stepping close to the king's side, Talmai whispered, "Majesty, I have more information about the conspiracy in Jericho."

Instantly all the other onlookers were ordered away. Even after demanding the entire floor of the citadel be cleared, Herod still would not permit Talmai to reveal more until they were closeted in a windowless chamber with a single, solid-bronze door. "Speak!" he demanded.

"The origin of the suspicious note is with two servants who remain in Jericho. Their identities aren't yet confirmed, but it appears their initials are *H* and *K*."

Herod staggered sideways, putting out his hand to steady himself. "Hamla and Kendro! Ari's friends. My son's closest attendants. His hunting companions. And if Ari is in the plot, then so must Alex be! Arrest them all!"

The flush that rose into Herod's neck, cheeks, and forehead did not improve his amber color. The combination gave him the appearance of a badly tarnished copper coin. The king's breathing was ragged. He held a clenched fist just below his throat, as if the rage choked him.

"Slowly, Majesty," Talmai cautioned in a solicitous tone. "Nothing is proven as yet. The initials may be a false lead, planted by someone who wants to implicate your sons. Surely Ari and Alex have given you no cause to suspect them! They always speak lovingly of you. They talk quite openly about how completely they've forgiven you for executing their mother. Nor do they ever permit anyone to suggest anything in their presence about restoring the throne to the Hasmonean line, even though they are the chief surviving heirs."

The king's voice was an angry rasp. "Talmai, you are too trusting! You must be more willing to accept reality, no matter how harsh!"

Herod's breathing slowed as he regained his composure. Over the years he had ordered many executions. If this plot led to his own sons, he would not spare them or any of their accomplices.

"Follow this trail," Herod commanded. "Be relentless. Use any means necessary, but get to the bottom of it quickly, before they can put this scheme in motion!"

"As you order, sire," Talmai responded.

Plant a small seed of doubt and soon the fertile ground of Herod's obsessive mistrust would bring in a rich harvest of death and destruction. Antipater had already paid Talmai handsomely to bring about his half brothers' downfall . . . and the campaign had only begun.

It was evident from the look on Zadok's face that he understood why Onias wanted Tovah and Menorah out of Jerusalem. Perhaps Tovah had some sense of the danger as well, but she did not let on.

"Your cousins'll be so glad to have someone new t' wrestle with!" Zadok hefted Menorah up until she brushed the ceiling of Onias' home with her fingertips.

The child squealed with delight and proclaimed that she was bigger than anyone.

Onias gathered the records he had compiled into a satchel as Tovah finished packing. "These as well, Zadok. A few papers. Some mathematical calculations. A safe place, if you please."

"Aye." Zadok lowered his voice. "You'll take care, eh, Brother? There's rumors . . . you'll take care, eh?"

"Papa? When will we be home?"

Zadok returned the child to her father's arms.

"Papa will fetch us home before Pentecost," Tovah replied. "We'll come home with him then. When things are quiet again." She spread her hands, indicating she was ready. "The fresh air will do us good. Until I'm through the morning sickness, I've come to hate waking up to the smells of the city."

"Aye, it's best. It's best, Tovah," Zadok said. "There's half a flock of pregnant women now in Beth-lehem. You'll be in good company, and Rachel will be glad for your presence!"

Tovah's eyes reflected a knowledge she did not voice as she embraced Onias. "Husband, you'll eat well?"

"I will."

"You'll not let your studies . . . harm your health?"

So she knew. He brushed her cheek. "I'll take care of myself. I promise."

CHAPTER 11

So, Yosef—" Tevyah, Yosef's short, portly friend, slapped him hard on the back—"I hear Mary's father is sending her away."

Yosef pretended Tevyah's news was not a surprise. Lifting the plane from the plank and blowing away curls of wood shavings, he did not answer.

"So?" Tevyah probed. His eyes narrowed. One elevated eyebrow propped up his thinning, brown hair. "She and her mother, eh? Leaving in the morning for Beth Karem? What is this, my friend? You come home from Yerushalayim, and your bride's father instantly removes her from temptation? Eh? Eh?"

"She has family in Beth Karem." Yosef eyed the surface of the plank as though this meant nothing at all. Less than nothing.

"You're putting off the wedding then?" Tevyah chewed on a stick and ran his fingers over the unfinished wedding chest. "You rushed home from Yerushalayim because you said not a day longer would you wait to have this girl. And now you let her go?" He snapped his fingers. "Like that?"

"There's a lot to do yet." Yosef straightened up and scowled. "She's still . . . young."

"Ripe for the picking." Tevyah grinned.

A rush of anger consumed Yosef at his words. Did Tevyah know more than he was saying? "*Ripe for the picking*"? Yosef clenched his fists and spun to face Tevyah. "If you think you know something about this, tell me now!"

Tevyah backed up a step. "Me? I'm asking you! She's leaving. That's all. I thought—" he raised his hands as though to ward off a blow—"I take it you didn't know?"

"Of course I know!" Yosef bellowed. "She's going to Beth Karem! She has family in Beth Karem! What business is it of yours?"

"Yosef? Hey! I'm . . . you asked me to be your groomsman. Eh? Sorry. Sorry, Yosef. You didn't tell me . . . didn't say she was leaving. That's all. And I . . . was only curious. As your friend, eh?" He sniffed and gazed uneasily at the wedding chest.

"I have a lot to do. As my friend, my groomsman, I can tell you the wedding won't happen until . . . until everything is as it should be." Yosef, suddenly embarrassed by his outburst, returned to planing the wood.

"Right. And what should I say in case—" Tevyah moved toward the door of the shop.

"In case there is gossip? As my friend, my groomsman, you'll say that she's gone with her mother to visit family and . . . and that Yosef knows this and has much on his mind and work to keep him busy while she is away. Beyond that, is it anyone's business?"

Yosef was still thinking about the news four hours after Tevyah left. *So, Mary is being sent away from Nazareth by her father. Being sent away without informing me.*

It did not bode well for her claim of innocence.

This morning was the end of life as Mary had known it. The end of pleasant childhood and drowsy dreams of a future that would have allowed her to live in the serenity of obscurity.

Mama tucked a new yellow shawl in her things as a gift for Elisheba, and that was the last of it. Mary shouldered her pack that contained food enough for a week of travel by foot.

One last look round to remember how it was.

The little house. Papa's workshop. The barn. The cheese room. Mary drank in the final view of the familiar little farm surrounded by orchards and fields frosted with newly sprouted barley.

When will I see home again, Lord? my little sisters? Papa? Yosef? And where will you lead me between this moment and then? What adventure have you planned? I am your servant.

Even one spring day away from Galilee seemed like too long.

She would never see home again if Papa did not relent. He did not come out to say good-bye.

Salome, red-haired, the beauty of the sisters, was poised on the verge of womanhood. Little Naomi would grow up soon enough. Would they be grown the next time she saw them? Mary would miss them most of all.

She walked backwards for a while, waving and blowing kisses to her unhappy sisters. Papa would not allow them to go to Beth Karem. They were not allowed to be in Mary's company, nor even to speak to her, lest she corrupt them.

It was a punishment too harsh for the sisters to obey.

"Shalom! Shalom! Mary!" Salome, hair glistening in the morning sun, leaned against Mary's milk cow and wept.

Naomi pleaded to come along. Mary could still hear the echo of her voice a half mile down the road. Mama, silent, stoic, seemed firm in her belief that all would come round right in the end.

O Adonai, I am so grateful for Mama! You knew I would need someone, even if it is only one, who believes me and defends me. O Adonai, you haven't left me without comfort. I am your servant!

At last, Mary and Mama climbed the brow of the hill and descended into the swale to meet the couple who would accompany them south to Beth Karem in the hill country of Judea.

Mary spotted the thin and fretful Joachim the Weaver. He was nervously adjusting the load on one of the two donkeys that carried mounds of raw wool cloth bound for the cloth dyer in Jerusalem. Deborah, his broad-hipped, wide-mouthed wife, was busy instructing her husband in the proper way to cinch up the packs. His sullen expression did not brighten at the approach of his traveling companions: two more women!

Deborah, evidently noticing them, broke off bickering. Her lips formed a polite smile, though her eyes remained dark and unwelcoming.

Their heads close together, Mama whispered to Mary, "Five days on the road to Beth Karem with the town gossip. A woman like this, a danger to you and the child. Remember, silence, Mary. Treasure the truth in your heart. On this journey there's safety for you only in silence. Don't cast pearls before swine, eh?"

"Mama, bear witness to my oath! I'll not speak until I see Elisheba."

Greetings were scarcely ended and bags tied onto the donkeys before Deborah began prying for information. "So, Mary, when's the wedding?"

Even such a frontal assault was not difficult to dodge. Eyes straight ahead, Mary did not answer.

Mama replied, "A long, silent journey I'm afraid, Deborah. Mary has taken the bride's vow. The vow of silence and prayer. Not a word until she sees my sister, Elisheba."

Joachim raised both hands in gratitude. "O Lord, that every woman would make such a vow on a long journey!"

Deborah elbowed her husband hard in the ribs. "Well, we'll just have to make up for her stubbornness, won't we, Anna? So, when's the wedding?"

Mama, ever the expert at dodging gossip, shrugged cheerfully. "Yosef is only just home."

"Yes. Yes. Joachim saw him at synagogue. Didn't you, Joachim?"

Joachim answered with a resigned sigh.

Deborah hooked her index finger round the frayed rope on the pack animal and gave it a tug, as if to test its strength. The load held. She chirped, "So, Joachim asked Yosef, 'When is the wedding, Yosef?' And Yosef said, 'I'm just back.' As if that's an answer, eh? Men! I think deep down they're all afraid of marriage. But what's to be afraid of, I ask you?"

Her husband grunted, as though he knew lots of reasons to fear.

And so it went. Mary, protected by her vow, looked up to her right toward the hills where the little houses of Nazareth were scattered among terraced vines.

O Adonai, I believe you are faithful and true. I choose to believe you. And Mama says everything will come right in the end. Be with Yosef. Comfort his heart. Somehow give him peace. Don't hold it against Papa that he doesn't believe your promises. Remember Papa didn't see the glory of the angel or hear the music of the angel's words. He has a daughter who says she is going to have a baby and that an angel said it was your child. No wonder he's so angry. So have mercy. Don't hold it against him. O Adonai, I am excited. And just a bit frightened of what's ahead. This beginning—where will it end? My heart rejoices in your love and mercy! As I start this journey, walk with me; guide my steps and the steps of my beloved. You are Adonai, the Lord who guards my heart . . . my lips . . . from sinning against you. I am your servant.

"So." Deborah smirked and took a bite of apple. She talked as she chewed and studied the fruit. "Was he sorry to see Mary go? Yosef, I mean. Sorry she left him when he's only just back home?"

"Sorry?" Mama spoke and pointed to the rock that jutted above the road like the prow of a ship. "Look there." A man leaned on a walking staff and watched their progress from the boulder. It was Yosef. Mama chuckled. "A lovesick puppy, I would say. Does that look like a bridegroom anxious to say good-bye to his beloved?"

Suddenly cheered by the sight of him, Mary raised her hand in acknowledgment and smiled. He responded with a sad and solemn nod and a hand lifted in peace. He did not call out. Had he also taken a vow of silence, the vow of a mourner? Mary recognized suffering in his eyes. And love? Could he still care for her even though he had reason to believe she was the worst of all women? Such a good man. So easy to love.

Had he come to say good-bye? And was his good-bye forever? Could it be in the character of the Lord to cause her to break her word to him?

Don't be afraid, Yosef! I have always been true to you. You'll know that in the end.

O Adonai! You'll have to let poor Yosef in on the secret. You'll have to tell him what to do. I rejoice that you will not forsake my Yosef! You are the God who keeps your promises. Surely you've seen and remembered the marriage covenant I made with Yosef. Help me honor every vow I made to this righteous man. You are Adonai, who remembers promises.

After several hours of walking, the endless babbling of Deborah was something like the squawk of a magpie in the brush. Mary heard the noise but simply did not understand the meaning of her words anymore. Protected and almost invisible by her inability to speak, Mary was of no more interest to the woman than one of the donkeys.

It was market day in Nazareth. Yosef had eaten very little in days and still had no appetite, and this morning he felt light-headed. There was no food left in the carpentry shop. Even the crusts of bread that had satisfied his wants were now gone.

Dizziness and working around saws and chisels and draw knives were a dangerous combination. Moreover, if Yosef fell ill, he'd get even further behind on his work than he already was.

There was no help for it; he'd have to go out and face his neighbors. The issue disturbing him was this: What did they already know—or suspect—about what had happened between him and Mary? How much of his very private business was the focus of commentary in the little village?

Yosef had been dreading this moment. When the actual time arrived it was, if anything, worse than he'd imagined.

Did the greeting from Hannah, the egg seller's wife, sound a little forced? When she asked how he was feeling, did her words lay extra stress on the casual, commonplace greeting?

After Yosef made his selection from the bread table and walked away, were Yuri the Baker and his wife leaning close together and staring after him?

Yosef wanted to act natural, casual. He also wanted to hurry and get back to the solitude of his shop. As a result, he botched both efforts. He lurched along from stall to stall, grunted in response to pleasantries, and generally evoked the very curiosity from his fellow citizens he'd hoped to avoid.

What is wrong with Yosef today? their expressions said.

When an especially talkative gaggle of housewives filled his path from aisle to aisle, Yosef sought to escape by darting into a side passage . . . and ran directly into Nachman the Butcher.

Nachman was tall and broad-shouldered, with curly hair and beard. He was also a notorious talebearer, considering it a personal responsibility to vend both the choicest cuts of meat and the juiciest bits of hearsay.

"So, Yosef!" Nachman boomed. "Back from Yerushalayim and ready for marriage . . . and your bride runs off to her aunt's house. What's that about? She get cold feet, eh? Young heifer running from the bull, eh? Eh?"

"No, nothing . . . nothing like that. She'll be back. That is, I've got to go. Please excuse me."

Perfect! Yosef scolded himself as he hurried away. By his nervousness, Yosef was sure he had given Nachman something more than crude humor to relay and discuss.

Bread and eggs would have to suffice for this shopping trip. Yosef could not bear to remain on display for the village one moment more.

Besides, if embarrassment wasn't bad enough, another fact swatted him in the head as he watched a pair of teenage boys carrying parcels for their mothers. Apart from Yosef's and Mary's families, there was someone else who knew how matters stood. Yosef could not help examining the young male faces he passed. Did that one turn away abruptly? Did the one with the wispy yellow beard blush under Yosef's glance?

As Yosef inspected the faces of young men for signs of guilt, he blundered headlong into a table of cheeses tended by Mary's sisters, Naomi and Salome.

"Ah, girls," he managed to cough out. "Shalom. So . . . any word from your sister at your aunt's? No, of course not . . . too soon, too soon . . . stupid of me."

Naomi's dark eyes bored resentfully into Yosef's.

"Shhh!" red-haired Salome ordered, shoving her younger sibling hard in the shoulder. "Not a word!"

Yosef sympathized with both sisters. He didn't trust himself to utter a single syllable, though Mary was always in his thoughts.

"So, cheeses, eh? Making a little extra to put by?" he suggested lamely.

Salome's freckles glowed with indignation. "She and Mama made them. The money was to go toward the dowry—*Mary's* dowry."

Flinging down a handful of small copper coins, Yosef grabbed a pair of cheeses. He hurried home, grateful no one called out to him or overtook him on the way. Perhaps leaving Nazareth and moving away permanently was the only answer.

The footsteps came again! The pattering of sandals on cobbles raced forward, but when Onias whirled around, no one was visible.

From the noises there was more than one pursuer, racing from shadow to shadow in his wake. How long had they been behind him?

Onias was on his way home from his night's exertions. Had they been lurking outside the archives all night? He had been aware of the chase only since descending the causeway.

The tutor stopped, listened, then dashed forward to the next cross street and ducked around the corner. Crouching, he fumbled for a loose stone with one hand, then threw it across the intersection as far as he could. It bounced, crashing into a discarded bit of pottery. The clatter echoed along the streets, dying away in the distance.

Two sets of footsteps—one lighter, one heavier—raced along the street. While Onias held his breath, a pair of indistinct hooded figures hesitated mere feet away.

His pulse was so loud Onias could scarcely hear. Would the pounding of his heart give him away?

Just when he thought his lungs would burst, the predators vanished away from him, following the noise of the diversion.

Who were they? Why were they after him? If they were Herod's men, why did they not just arrest him and have done with it? And if not Herod's spies, then whose?

What would happen when the answer was known?

How glad he was that Tovah and Menorah were safe in Bethlehem!

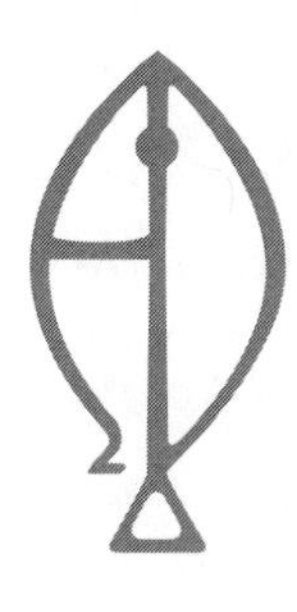

PART III

A shoot will come up from the stump of Jesse;
from his roots a Branch will bear fruit.
The Spirit of the LORD *will rest on him—*
the Spirit of wisdom and of understanding.

ISAIAH 11:1-2

Mary hurried to the hill country of Judea, to the town where Zachariah lived. She entered the house and greeted Elisheba. At the sound of Mary's greeting, Elisheba's child leaped within her.[62]

12 CHAPTER

The village of Beth Karem, House of the Vine, was well named. It was nestled among the terraced vineyards of the Judean hill country. Uncle Zachariah owned a small vineyard of about twenty acres. He and his wife, Elisheba, made and sold sweet kosher wine for Passover celebrations.

Mary and Mama took their leave from their traveling companions at the fork in the highway. To the left was the broad Roman-built road to Jerusalem. Mother and daughter turned onto the narrow dirt lane that led toward the vineyard of Zachariah. Even in the distance across a gorge, Mary recognized the home that always seemed brighter than the rest, as if it had just been whitewashed.

The aroma of cook fires and baking bread mingled with the musty smells of farmyards and new leaves warming in the sun.

From childhood Mary had visited the home of Aunt Elisheba at least once a year when her family made aliyah to the great religious festivals in Jerusalem. Often Mama had let Aunt Elisheba "borrow" Mary for a few weeks of good company during the grape harvest. The girl had helped in the vineyard during harvest and with crushing the grapes. Aunt Elisheba called Mary "her" girl and said that if Adonai had allowed her to have a daughter, she would have asked the Lord for a child like Mary.

It had been a long time since Papa had wanted to travel anywhere close to Jerusalem, however.

The arrests of rabbis and teachers by Herod's secret police had increased in proportion to the king's syphilitic madness. Often innocent men were pulled from the streets, hauled to the torture chambers of Herod's palace, and racked as Herod watched until, in agony, the prisoners confessed to some treasonous plot the king had only imagined.

Three times in four years high priests appointed by Herod had come under suspicion of rebellion and were either arrested or assassinated. Now Herod's Egyptian father-in-law held the office of high priest. Jerusalem had disintegrated into a corrupt and violent place.

For these reasons Papa no longer traveled to the required pilgrim feasts but paid other pilgrims to offer a sacrifice in his name.

Quietly, only within the walls of his own home, Papa would shake his head and say to Mama and daughters, "Where is Elijah, the prophet who will come before Messiah? Why doesn't he come now? It is past time for Messiah to come to us and cleanse the Temple."

And then, in a whisper, as though he feared a spy might be listening beneath the window even in little Nazareth, Papa recited the words of Malachi that Herod had forbidden to be spoken or read or taught in his kingdom.

While the common folk prayed for the coming of the Messenger, those in power feared his coming. In the midst of a host of Herod's political appointees, only a handful of priests in the Temple truly worshipped Yahweh. The most faithful were the peasant priests from the countryside who served for two weeks each year. Looked down upon by the Herodian appointees, very few of these good men were Torah scholars. Fewer still were brave enough to openly discuss the evil times and the prophecies that spoke of Messiah and the great hope that His coming was near. Uncle Zachariah was among the learned and the good. But even Zachariah had told Papa that he was always glad when his priestly course in Jerusalem was finished so he could return to the safety and obscurity of Beth Karem.

Mary knew that the tangled events, the darkness of their age, all had something to do with the timing of Gabriel's message to her. Within

Mary's womb was The One Herod feared more than anyone. Yet Mary was unafraid. The angel had told her nothing was impossible for Adonai to accomplish, and she believed him.

Mary's excitement grew as she and Mama walked up the slope. Just ahead was Elisheba and the confirmation that what the angel had proclaimed to Mary was true: *And you shall bear a son.*[63]

Someday, perhaps, Papa would live to see the prophecies fulfilled through the very child he now rejected. Then there would be no more fear when Papa spoke the prophecies of Malachi aloud!

Mary raised her eyes toward the southern horizon. Sunlight reflected on the gold roof of the Temple of Jerusalem far in the distance. Freshly quarried stone of the structure glistened like the snowcap of Mount Hermon. Beautiful. One of the wonders of the world. Even so, Jerusalem was no longer a place where the glory of the *Ruach HaKodesh*, the Holy Spirit, dwelt among the people of Israel. Mary knew well that under the heel of Herod, the City of David had become as unclean as a whitewashed tomb filled with rotting bodies.

Mama's face was flushed with excitement. "All these years we've prayed for Elisheba! Oh, Mary! To think my sister, after all these years, could be expecting!"

Mary, mindful of her vow of silence, nodded broadly and pointed to the house. Soon enough Mama would see for herself what Mary was certain of. Elisheba, like Sarah and Hannah of days long past, was surely pregnant as the angel had told Mary she would be.

The closing verses of Malachi ran through Mary's mind: *You have spoken, O Lord! See, I will send you the prophet Elijah before that great and dreadful day of the LORD comes. He will turn the hearts of their fathers to their children, and the hearts of the children to their fathers.*[64]

Mary's heart sang out to the Lord:

My soul praises you, Adonai! Can it be that the longed-for baby old Elisheba carries in her womb is the same Elijah you promised would come before the birth of your Anointed, the Son of David? Like Samuel, who was miraculously born to Hannah, so this baby will be a miracle to Elisheba! As the prophet Samuel anointed David, the young shepherd of Beth-lehem, king of Israel, will Elisheba's child anoint the son I carry as king of Israel? Will he mend broken homes, shattered families, and hopeless lives, and bring Israel back to you, O Adonai?

She remembered the words of Malachi's song as they walked.

For you who revere My name, the Sun of Righteousness will rise with healing in its wings. And you will go out and leap like calves released from the stall![65]

Mary loved the image. She knew something about calves kicking up their heels in joy as they were released from pen to pasture. Every morning she would perch on a boulder and watch them play. So would the people rejoice when they were released from the tyranny of Herod's rule and the true Son of the Most High reigned in Jerusalem!

"They will be Mine," says Adonai El Shaddai, "in the day when I make up My treasured possession. I will spare them, just as in compassion a man spares his son who serves him. And you will again see the distinction between the righteous and the wicked, between those who serve Adonai and those who do not."[66]

Mama took her hand. "Oh, Mary. Mary! There is Elisheba! Hanging wash beside the house. Call out to her, Mary. Look! Look at her, Mary! Do you see?"

Her silence at an end at last, Mary cupped her hands around her mouth and called, "Shalom, Elisheba! God who keeps his promises has remembered!"

Elisheba dropped her washing, cried out with joy at the sound of Mary's greeting, and hugged her own rounded stomach in surprise.

Together Mary and Mama sang the song of Malachi as they turned onto the gravel path to the house.

Elisheba threw her hands above her head and danced with joy at the sight of Mary and Mama.

Arms wide, Mary ran to embrace her. Suddenly filled with the *Ruach HaKodesh*, Elisheba gave a joyous cry. "Mary! You are blessed by Adonai above all other women! And blessed, cherished, adored, and longed for is the child you will bear!"[67]

Tears of joy streamed down Mary's cheeks. "Oh! How I praise the Lord! And oh! How my spirit rejoices in Adonai, my Savior!"[68]

Elisheba cupped Mary's face with aged hands. "But who am I, eh? Why am I so favored, that the mother of my Lord and Redeemer should come to me?"[69]

Mary kissed Elisheba on the left cheek and on the right. She laid her head on Elisheba's shoulder and replied, "He took notice of His lowly servant girl. From now on generation after generation will call me blessed! For He, El Shaddai, the Mighty One alone, is holy, and He has done great things for me! Holy, holy, holy is His name!"[70]

Then Elisheba guided Mary's hands to her stomach to feel the joyful thumping of the baby. The two women laughed together. Elisheba, eyes wide with delight, explained, "As soon as you arrived and your voice reached my ears, the baby in my womb began to dance and leap like a little calf for the joy of your coming!"[71]

Mary squeezed her eyelids shut and counted the rhythmic tapping of the baby's kicks beneath her hand. One. One, two, three. Then nine quick knocks followed by one last kick as if to mimic the pattern of the Temple shofar, calling the faithful to worship. A miracle!

Mary searched the lined face of her aunt, then turned her head toward the skyline of Jerusalem. "Adonai's mercy goes on from generation to generation to all who fear Him. The strength of His mighty arm does tremendous things! He scatters people who are proud and haughty. He brings down tyrants from their thrones. But look! See! Oh, how Adonai has lifted up the humble! He fills the hungry with good things but sends the rich away with empty hands. Adonai has remained true to the promise He made to His servant Israel! He has never forgotten His promise to be merciful. This is proof that the covenant with Avraham and his descendants, to be merciful to them forever, is an everlasting covenant!"[72]

Elisheba clung tightly to Mary. "My dear, you are blessed! Blessed, because you believe that Adonai will bring to full completion every word he has spoken to the smallest detail!"

Mary nodded in gratitude that the journey had come to an end. The confirmation promised by Gabriel was here.

Mama stood to one side, weeping quietly. She could hardly speak. "Oh, Sister. Elisheba! You. So pregnant! Such a beautiful sight!"

"Mama! Come." Mary reached out, wiped away Mama's tears, and pulled her into the circle of the embrace. The three women praised God for a long time beside the flapping laundry.

"So, Anna." Elisheba, breathless, addressed her sister at last. "You! A grandmother. But look at your old sister! Just starting. You'll advise me then? After so many years of praying, our prayers are answered."

Mama chuckled. "Only one thing a mother must always remember: All things are possible with Adonai!"

Thirty-year-old Princess Glaphyra hurried through the halls of the Jericho palace. Fear tinged her dark eyes; worry sallowed her olive complexion.

The folded parchment she carried was sealed with red wax but had no identification on the outside. On the inside it was addressed to her father, King Archaelaus of Cappadocia. The same urgency that had driven her to write the letter in her hand, now impelled her to get it out of her possession and off to her father as soon as possible. Afraid to entrust the note to any of the court officials, Alex's wife had decided to give it to Onias the Tutor by the hand of her trusted servant, Selassi.

Onias could be trusted to forward the letter through his connections to the Jewish synagogue in Caesarea of Cappadocia, the capital. The Jews there would, in turn, deliver it to the king.

There was nothing treasonous in the missive, except what the tormented mind of Herod might make of it. Glaphyra's letter expressed her concern that there was a plot under way to implicate her husband in some wrongdoing. She asked her father for his advice and pleaded for him to make a return visit to Herod's kingdom. Once before, when Alex had been out of favor with his father, King Archaelaus had intervened and reconciled the two.

Glaphyra prayed to Yahweh that he might do so again.

Rounding the last corner of the residence hall before the main courtyard, Glaphyra almost collided with Talmai.

"I beg your pardon, my lady." He bowed.

Glaphyra's eyes darted everywhere but at Talmai's face. Her cheeks were flushed and her breathing rapid. She tried to hide the message in the folds of her gown, but Talmai spotted it.

"Why, what's the matter, Lady Glaphyra?" Talmai gestured toward the parchment. "Bad news?"

"No . . . nothing, really. A note to . . . to the boy's tutor. To Onias . . . in Yerushalayim . . . about a new course of study he proposes. I . . . I'm late, that's all."

"May I see to its delivery for you, madam?"

"No, no, thank you. I'll take it myself."

Talmai bowed himself out of her way, but his eyes followed her out into the sunlit courtyard.

She, scurrying, looked very much the hunted rabbit. He, watching from the shadows, gave a perfect impression of a skulking jackal.

"Sit! Sit, Yosef!" Rabbi Mazzar, an elderly man whose back was bent from years of study, offered Yosef the best seat in the little house attached to the back of the Nazareth synagogue. "You are well?"

"I'm fine. Fine," Yosef said dully, though he was not.

"So? What is it? You have not come to speak with me privately since you were looking for a wife and wanted to discuss Heli's daughter Mary. Such a prize, eh?"

Yosef leaned forward. "Just what I wanted to speak with you about, Rabbi."

The old man's toothless grin dissolved. "Am I hearing you are . . . it is not so well with you, Yosef? Eh? What is it?"

"I . . . I'm thinking maybe . . . she is not the woman for me after all."

The rabbi's head snapped back as though Yosef had struck him. "What? What's this?"

"I think we . . . Mary and I . . . may not be compatible. That's all."

"You don't like the girl? I don't know anyone who does not like her, Yosef! What? What is this?"

Yosef spread his hands in an effort to explain but could not speak of the possibility of her infidelity. "I just . . . don't think she's right for me."

The rabbi wagged his head. "You're afraid of marriage. Is that it? Oh, you young men! One wrong thing you notice. Something you don't like about a girl and *psfttt*! Divorce!" He rose and tottered to the chest, where he kept his study scrolls. "Here it is. Here it is! Malachi, the last of the scrolls. Here is your answer, Yosef." The old man unrolled the scroll on the table and, with a crook of his finger, called Yosef to pay attention. "Here. We think we're better than Herod? better than the Romans? Well, perhaps. But pay attention, boy! Read what the Lord says he hates!" He tapped firmly, indicating where Yosef should begin to read aloud.

Yosef parsed out the difficult text:

"You flood the LORD's altar with tears. You weep and wail because He no longer pays attention to your offerings or accepts them with pleasure from your hands. You ask, 'Why?' It is because the LORD is acting as the witness between you and the wife of your youth, because you have broken faith with her, though she is your partner, the wife of your marriage covenant.

"Has not the LORD made them one? In flesh and spirit they are His. And why one? Because He was seeking godly offspring. So guard yourself in your spirit, and do not break faith with the wife of your youth.

"'I hate divorce,' says the LORD God of Israel."[73]

Rabbi Mazzar patted him gently on the back. "There now, Yosef. This is what the Word of the Lord says in regard to what you are contemplating."

"But Rabbi, suppose she was . . . the woman was . . . in love with another."

"Mary loves you, Yosef. Her mother and father have remarked how happy she's been since your betrothal. That's evident!"

"What if she was . . . with . . . someone else while I was away?"

The rabbi snorted. "Nonsense! I would have heard."

Yosef inhaled deeply and contemplated the passage. The rabbi was, in spite of his age, an innocent man who could not believe evil was possible in anyone like Mary.

"Rabbi, what will it be like? I mean, when Messiah comes?"

"Different than any of us imagine, I think. Eh?" Then Mazzar began to read from the last words of Malachi: "*'They will be Mine', says the LORD Almighty, 'in the day when I make up My treasured possession. I will spare them, just as in compassion a man spares his son who serves him. . . . For you who revere My name, the Sun of Righteousness will rise with healing in His wings' . . . in the tassels of His prayer shawl,*" the rabbi interpreted for Yosef. Then he went on, "'And you will go out and leap like calves released from the stall.'" [74]

The old man closed the scroll. "Yosef, my son, be careful not to break faith. The time of the end of wickedness is very near now. We must believe Messiah will come soon to judge unrighteousness or our hope and joy will perish! The last verse of Malachi says, '*See, I will send you the prophet Elijah before the great and terrible day of the* LORD *comes.*'[75] I tell you, Yosef, that this land will not long stand such unrighteousness! Elijah must come first, and after him Messiah will come."

CHAPTER 13

It was nearing dawn when Onias completed another night's work copying the genealogy records.

He crept out of the warren beneath the Temple Mount in time to view Jupiter and Saturn sailing overhead in the constellation of The Fish. After a hasty glance at the sky, Onias drew his cloak close around him and hurried toward home.

The air was very still. Through the dark, vacant streets, Onias felt spied on, as if unseen watchers tracked his progress. He decided his anxiety must be due only to his bone-aching weariness.

At sunset the evening before, when Onias had gathered cloak and satchel, the one-day-old moon had shepherded Mercury and Mars into the sheepfold of night. Those three lights had been watched over in their descent by Regulus, The Little King star, in the paw of Aryeh, The Lion.

From dusk to dawn Onias had pursued this obsession and held his breath at every suspicious sound. No wonder he now felt like an animal being tracked by the hunter.

Had Onias been asked what drove him to labor so long over a list of "begats," he could not have answered with anything like full assurance.

The third set of fourteen generations neared its completion.[76] The first series of men had given rise to King David. The second set was the monarchs who succeeded David, for good or ill.

What would the outcome of the third set bring?

The meaning was as yet unclear, but Onias was certain a critical time was at hand. His studies suggested it; what had happened to Simeon and Zachariah confirmed it. Onias felt driven to write down his conclusions and all the supporting evidence. He hoped he would not run himself into an early grave from scribbling all night and teaching all day. A couple hours' sleep would put things right. Onias would not even stop to eat before tumbling into bed.

Turning the last corner before home brought him a feeling of relief. Rest and security lay just a few paces ahead. Safety was just beyond the dark red of his wood-planked door . . . which, unaccountably, stood partly open, a gaping black maw.

Onias was certain it had not been left that way. Robbers?

He strode toward the entry and paused with his hand on the mezuzah on the doorpost. What if the trespassers remained inside?

Onias called out, "Who's there? Answer quickly before I call the watch. Speak up!" There was no response.

From a heap of sticks at the side of his house Onias grasped a branch. It was scarcely big enough to serve as a weapon, but it would have to do. He thrust it through the door into the darkness of his front room, waving it around as if it were a torch.

Nothing. No response. He kicked the door open the rest of the way, but it bounced off something back toward him. Putting his shoulder against the panel, he shoved it aside, bursting into his own home. He flailed about with the stick but contacted nothing more threatening than his own cloak rack, which fell with a crash.

There was no one there. Onias snorted at his unreasonable panic. Too many wary nights and not enough sleep. He had failed to latch the door properly, and the wind had blown it open. That was all.

Laying the stick across a table, Onias fumbled for and located flint and tinder. In a moment he struck a light to an oil lamp. The cheery glow drove the shadows and fear away.

Until Onias saw that all his papers were strewn across the floor. Wax tablets were broken out of their wooden frames. Scrolls, unrolled at full length and then tossed aside, lay in crumpled heaps like dead bodies.

A thought struck him. He carried the lamp into his bedroom. The upright chest there had also been rifled, his copies of David's family tree scattered everywhere.

But none of them were missing.

Onias had no valuables, and what little he possessed was still here.

What had this been about? What was someone seeking?

Then it came to him. Certain of his conclusion, there was no surprise when he retrieved the leather letter case from beneath his bed and found it empty.

Princess Glaphyra's letter to her father was gone.

Mary and Mama and Aunt Elisheba snapped green beans in the shade of the plane tree.

"God had the right idea making Zachariah mute," Elisheba asserted. "If you can't talk, you can't say anything you regret, true?"

Snap. Snap. Into the bowl with the bean.

Mama agreed. *Snap.* "Of course, true. Now here is the proof. You're big as a cow, Elisheba. No offense intended."

"None taken. I like the new me. Such a profile. My shadow. Two of me standing in the sun. But no one would have believed it. From the day I first heard about it, I spent my days in seclusion. If anyone else would have known, I would have had five miserable months walking around here, waiting to grow big enough to prove that nothing is impossible with God."

Snap. Pop.

Elisheba turned her attention on Mary. "You can stay here as long as you need to stay. Until the baby is born and after. Our sons should know one another. Grow up to be very good friends. High priest and king of Israel. Yes. Very fine friends our boys will be."

Pop. Crack. Into the bowl.

Mary was at peace. She felt little need to discuss her situation. But she had an urgent need, a requirement, to learn everything that the Scriptures had to say about this.

Mama had no real answers for her. But her encouragement was like water on a hot day.

Aunt Elisheba had lots of opinions and a proverb to answer every situation but no explanation for this: Mary was indeed a virgin. And pregnant. There was sure to be talk.

Mary wondered how the Lord would address the problem. What did God have to say about the matter? Uncle Zachariah was a scholar. A descendant of Aaron. A priest who had studied Torah! Surely she could ask him to show her what God's Word had to say about this perilous time and the great One she carried within her!

But Uncle Zachariah could not utter a sound. Therefore he could not teach her. Which left her the wisdom that came from snapping beans with Mama and Aunt Elisheba in the shade.

She spoke one word. One name. Her one concern. "Yosef."

"It's nobody's business, Mary! Take my advice. Lay low. I did. Everybody thought I was dying. Asked Zachariah if I was sick and dying. Nobody's business, I said. Nobody's but God's business! And I stayed inside out of sight. If you lie on the ground, you cannot fall. So, I didn't show myself until I was . . . this . . . big!" *Crack. Snap.* "So, do what I did. If you keep on talking, you'll just end up saying everything you didn't mean to say. They won't believe it anyway."

Snap. Pop. Pop. In the bowl.

Mama said, "God knows, Daughter. If only the Lord would also speak to Yosef. Such a good man, he is. A perfect match. I always said so."

Aunt Elisheba, though she did not know Yosef, agreed with Mama. "Carpenters make good husbands. Wood is warm, living." She shook a bean at the canopy of leaves above them. "Trees are living things. Yes, a carpenter is better than being married to a stonemason. Cold, hard. Treat their wives like blocks of stone."

Mary did not know how to reply. Yosef's heart had turned to stone, it seemed. She loved him. How could she convince him that she had not been unfaithful? that every word of her story was true, and Aunt Elisheba's condition confirmed it?

"This is all too wonderful. Beyond my understanding. But the answers must be in Torah," Mary said.

"A wise woman knows what she says. A foolish woman says what she knows." *Crack. Crack. Pop.* "Say nothing until you know what you're talking about. That's my advice."

"If Uncle Zachariah could teach me . . ." Mary filled her apron with beans.

Elisheba ventured an explanation of all things relating to the recent miracles. "A woman barren who will give birth. A young girl, a virgin, carrying a child. That's what I'm saying. Zachariah could teach you. All his waking hours he spends studying. But he tells me nothing. Not that he wouldn't if he could speak, but since he can't, God must not want him to speak of it."

Crack. Snap.

"So, there's a reason. And the reason—" Elisheba raised an eyebrow and lowered her voice conspiratorially—"let's face it. The reason is that Herod would kill us if he knew the truth that he is not long for the throne. God knows. We know. It's enough. And if God wants your young man, Yosef, to know, he'll let him in on the secret. There's safety in silence. Safety in not knowing everything. And in not saying everything you know. Perhaps that's why the angel made Zachariah mute. He might have forgotten wisdom and talked about the angel to someone who knew Herod."

Elisheba came to the bottom of the beans. "For our sake and the sake of our sons, we must treasure the truth in our hearts silently. What is good news to us may be heard far away in a throne room in Yerushalayim. And our good news is bad news to some." She put a finger to her lips. "If it is God's will, Yosef will hear the truth. But only when he can understand the truth."

Taken suddenly from his Jericho prison cell into the harsh torchlight, Hamla was secured by his wrists to iron rings set in the stone wall higher than he could easily reach. By standing on tiptoe he could take the strain off his arm sockets, but only for a time. Sagging, he moaned with pain, choked by the pressure on his lungs. Struggling upright, he gasped for air.

Most of Herod's Jericho palace was given over to pleasure: bathing pools, shaded gardens, banqueting halls, and the like. This much was widely admired by all the guests who shared Herod's hospitality.

All this opulence existed like a jeweled sheath concealing a poisoned blade—like clean clothes over leprous flesh.

What few visitors were aware of—and what none wished to experience—were the unseen levels beneath Herod's private apartments. Entry to these rooms was by means of a narrow, curving staircase within the guard chamber nearest the king's bedroom, or by way of a secret escape tunnel that ran two hundred yards out from the palace to the banks of a man-made lake. The exit there was camouflaged by a sand-covered trapdoor.

Prisoners of Herod's regime who were not instantly executed for their crimes were kept in a hellhole at the bottom of his desert fortress of Machaerus, or in similar dungeons beneath Herodium. In the case of accused would-be assassins Hamla and Kendro, Herod ordered that they vanish so no warning could be given to any of their coconspirators.

The two men had been dispatched on a bogus night errand to Jerusalem. Just outside Jericho they had been arrested and hauled into prison through the secret entry. Those guards who brought them in were sworn to silence, on pain of their own deaths. The story was put out that Hamla and Kendro had either been set upon by bandits and murdered or captured by Nabatean raiders and were being held for ransom.

Whatever was believed about their fates, there was now plenty of time to interrogate them properly.

The two men had been held for days in separate cells in strict isolation. Given barely enough food and water to keep them alive, they lived in darkness and ignorance. Neither was told with what crime he was charged. Many interesting confessions had been obtained from them in this manner, but not to capital crimes as yet. Hamla had already confessed to debauching Herod's sister's chambermaid. Kendro admitted that his horse had accidentally trampled one of the king's pet greyhounds to death during a hunting expedition. Kendro had sensibly been too afraid to report the accident at the time.

The chief interrogator, a bald Thracian with a scar bisecting his nose and both lips from his time in the gladiatorial arena, carefully followed his instructions. Hamla and Kendro were not to die . . . yet. Every day he told each man he had been indicted by the other as the guilty party and that the other man had already been released.

As far as Talmai knew, neither Hamla nor Kendro was actually guilty of any conspiracy. These preliminaries were merely to soften their resistance before the interrogations began in earnest.

Talmai read over the daily reports with interest but some frustration as well. Herod was anxious to root out the "conspiracy." If Talmai did not produce results soon, Herod was perfectly capable of accusing his steward of complicity. On the other hand, the more difficult this operation appeared, the more money Talmai could milk from the eager, gullible Antipater. The scheme required a fine touch.

Talmai and the interrogator discussed the relative merits of flogging versus branding as a means of eliciting information. Finally the chief interrogator declared his preference for near crucifixion, and Talmai approved.

After three hours of being tormented for breath, Hamla received further torture. Leg irons were clamped around his ankles, making it that much harder for him to fight upward against the weight. Another hour later Talmai nodded, and the Thracian shoved a wooden block under Hamla's heels, lifting the burden and letting him breathe properly. In a soft-spoken, kindly murmur, the interrogator commented, "We already know you planned to kill the king and make it look like an accident. Kendro told us. Oh, yes. He wasn't nearly as brave as you . . . gave you up before we'd hardly started. But we need details, see? Who else was involved? Who ordered it? What was the plan?"

"There was no plan! I'm not guil—"

With a backward sweep of his heel the Thracian knocked the supporting prop from under Hamla's feet. The jerk of his weight dropping on wrists and shoulders made him scream, then pass out from the pain.

When he awoke, Hamla was again left to resist the pull of gravity for a time; then the low step was returned.

"Now we'll try again," the interrogator said. This time his voice was loaded with threat. "What was the plot? To kill the king during a hunting party?"

"There wasn't . . ." When Hamla felt the Thracian shoving the block aside again, he begged, "Wait! Yes, yes! You're right! A hunting accident. But it was all Kendro's doing . . . not mine! His plan . . . not mine."

The Thracian glanced at Talmai, who offered an approving nod in return. "Now about the others?" he demanded of the prisoner. "Was it Alex or Ari who put you up to this?"

"I . . . I don't know. I mean . . . neither? What do you want me to say?"

"That won't do," the Thracian corrected, jiggling the block so that Hamla swayed and cried out in fear. "We want the truth, see? Now we know you didn't make this scheme yourself . . . no, no. Someone put you up to it, eh? Alex is the older. Was it him?"

When the tormented man remained mute, the interrogator let him drop full length yet again, eliciting another yell of agony and another faint.

When he roused once more, Hamla was asked, "Maybe it was both? Ari and Alex together, yes?"

There was no more fight, no resistance left in Hamla. He would have sold out anyone they named in order to escape the torture. "Yes. Yes! Both! They said they'd pay us. They said the captain of the guard at Alexandrium would take us in and protect us till Ari was on the throne. It's all true; I swear it! Only don't let me drop again, I beg you!"

Talmai was pleased. "Even more than we asked for," he remarked to the Thracian. "Keep this up another hour; then switch to Kendro. Between the two of them, they'll come up with a better yarn than I could ever have concocted myself."

CHAPTER 14

An explosive burst of rapid, scratchy-voiced birdsong from the acacia tree outside his window woke Yosef. He opened one eye and grinned up at the male warbler. The bird flitted from branch to branch, letting the world know everything was good.

There was just enough time for five heartbeats before remembrance and reality crashed in on Yosef.

Everything was not right.

In fact, nothing was right.

Mary! O Yahweh! Mary!

There was still no solution to putting the smashed puzzle box back together.

The stabbing pain in Yosef's chest returned like the abrupt entry of a razor-sharp arrowhead. For a moment he could not draw a deep breath.

Mary!

His eyelids were gritty.

Yosef was still dressed from the day before, having fallen asleep at last across the braided rope bed. Late in the darkness he'd finally collapsed, exhausted from questions with no answers and his unrelieved agony.

Why? What happened to us? I thought she loved me.

And what was the purpose of the elaborate lie? Did she think she could spare his feelings with such a hoax? Was she crazy?

Was there no way out of this tangled mess?

Even as he launched into the same endless cycle of searching for the cure to this emotional plague that felt so much like death, Yosef knew it was hopeless. Like cutting a crucial board too short, some things had no remedy except to discard the ruined piece and begin again.

A memory stirred. Something he'd heard talked of while working in Jerusalem. For a time his will opposed pinning down the exact thought. Some rumored miracle? Another story about an angel? Still, how could anything in Jerusalem have any importance compared to the crisis here in Nazareth?

A nagging voice in him persisted: *Think! This means something.*

There had been a yarn making the rounds among the sanctuary craftsmen about an old priest who saw a vision in the Temple. What was the man's name? Yosef couldn't recall it, but the tale had something to do with an angel. That was it: An angel had appeared while the Levite burned incense in the Holy Place. There was a message about a new prophet to be born and . . . about a miraculous birth. Comparisons had been made to the prophet Samu'el's mother . . . and to the expected forerunner of the Messiah.[77]

Of course, the crazier King Herod got, the more Jerusalem buzzed with messianic fervor.

Temple officials discouraged any discussion of the fabled occurrence, labeling it rumor or putting it down to senility on the part of the priest.

Now that Yosef thought on it, he realized that the priests had gone out of their way to suppress the account. Why would they do that unless there was some element of truth to it?

Could Mary have heard the story? Is that what convinced her to cook up such a wild excuse? She was very young, innocent, and sweet . . . before this.

Caught in such a disaster, however much it was her own fault, she was still to be pitied.

Yes, the idea of an angelic visit proved it: Mary was desperately grasping at any excuse to get out of the trap she was in.

In that moment Yosef made up his mind. He sat up, the abrupt motion frightening away the warbler.

He'd spent far too much time feeling sorry for himself and tending his own wounds. Mary was hardly more than a child herself. Was her life to be ruined forever?

Yosef would not haul her before the village council. Instead he'd go to them privately and explain things. The marriage was still impossible, of course, but Mary could be spared the public censure. With a little discussion, the adultery charge could be set aside.

Maybe the other guilty party would then come forward and admit what he'd done. Mary was not the first teenager to break the law against fornication. Other rash couples had married and gone on to lead respectable—even honored—lives.

Yes, that was the answer; Yosef was certain of it.

He drew a deep breath . . . and ignored the piercing grief that still sliced into his heart.

During her visit, Mary came to Zachariah with a thousand questions about what was happening to her.

Bright, she was, and quick to learn. When Mary was only four years old, Zachariah had taught her the twenty-two letters of the *alef-bet* over the course of a one-week visit. By the time she was eight years old she had read the scroll of Esther aloud to him and Elisheba during Purim.

Zachariah always said that if he ever had a daughter, he wanted her to be just like Mary.

Now she had grown into something beautiful. A golden thread woven through the tapestry of their lives.

He listened intently as she repeated again every detail of the visitation of Gabriel. He did not doubt one word of what she said.

By means of his account written down for Elisheba, Zachariah was able to comfort Mary with the fact that the same angel had appeared to him and told him a different part of the story. Beyond that, since he could not speak, he simply comforted her by believing what she told him.

She had come to Beth Karem with a hunger to learn Torah. She wanted to know every messianic prophecy that had taken him a lifetime of study to learn.

Zachariah admitted to himself that, in spite of her youth and a lack of Torah scholarship, Mary, in her instant acceptance of the angel's proclamation, had put men of great wisdom to shame. He included himself in that assessment. Mary had believed the messenger. But he, instead of trusting, had looked at his own weakness and doubted God's ability to use him. Perhaps the young girl had something to teach him about the ways of The Most High.

Still, Mary begged Zachariah to show her where her role in the story was portrayed in the Scriptures. And where in prophecy was this baby boy whom she already loved?

Messiah was everywhere in the Torah. In everything. Once Zachariah had believed that everything in Torah meant something. Now he believed that everything meant *Messiah.* And Messiah meant God's mercy, grace, and atonement for man's sin.

And so Zachariah opened the scroll of Isaias.

> *Nevertheless, there will be no more gloom for those who were in distress. . . . In the future He will honor Galilee of the Gentiles. . . . The people walking in darkness have seen a great light; on those living in the land of the shadow of death a light has dawned.*[78]

Tonight he and Elisheba and Mary and Anna stood on the roof as he pointed out the wandering stars called The Righteous and The Sabbath as they spun around one another within the constellation of The Fish, which symbolized the vast multitude of Abraham's descendants. Zachariah remembered that such a sight had heralded the birth of the lawgiver Mosheh 1,365 years before. He remembered that these same stars had appeared in this exact way above Egypt. Then the frightened Egyptian astrologers had warned Pharaoh that every male Hebrew slave of two years and under must be killed.

Only the infant Mosheh had survived.

At what price was Israel's redemption paid? What would be the cost now?

Zachariah did not write down his belief that the evil king who ruled over Israel now was as much a danger to their unborn sons as Pharaoh had been.

Perhaps Zachariah did not need to warn Mary of hard times ahead.

Instead he tapped his finger on the scroll of Isaias and instructed Mary to read:

> *"For unto us a child is born, to us a child is given, and the government will be upon His shoulders. And He will be called Wonderful Counselor . . . Mighty God . . . Everlasting Father . . . Prince of Peace."*[79]

Then Zachariah unrolled the scroll of the Judges and showed Mary the story of the angel of the Lord who brought word to Samson's parents that they who were childless would soon have a son. And when the couple asked the awesome messenger his name, he replied, *"Why do you ask? For my name is Wonderful."*[80]

Wonderful. The same Hebrew word used in Isaiah to proclaim the name of the Incarnate God who would one day rule upon David's throne.

By Mary's serenity and joy, Zachariah knew that she understood that her son would not be like any son ever born of woman. Her spirit understood all this, though Zachariah had no voice to explain to her.

He deliberately did not show her other verses: glimpses of suffering and rejection and even death for God's Anointed.[81] Zachariah knew most of the atonement prophecies by heart. The scroll of Zechariah, the prophet whose name he bore, was planted thick in the sorrows promised for Mary's son.[82]

It was enough for now, Zachariah thought, that sweet Mary knew only that her child's name was . . . Wonderful.

The idea that Yosef could quietly break his engagement to Mary and avoid a scandal improved the more he thought about it. A dignified solution. Between himself and Heli.

Before he went to the village council, he would broach the plan to Heli. After all, the marriage contract had been negotiated by Mary's father, and he would have to agree to the undoing of it.[83]

Despite Yosef's resolve to hold his head high no matter the gossip, he rose very early and made his way through Nazareth. His mind was full of the things he wanted to say to Heli and his speech rehearsed. The last thing Yosef wanted was to make idle conversation about someone's desire for a new table or the latest outrageous news of Herod's court.

Salome answered his knock. The red-haired girl was growing to be quite a beauty in her own right, but the flashing fire in her eyes would have to be reckoned with by any potential suitor. It was plain by her expression that somehow Salome blamed Yosef for the unpleasantness. Belatedly Yosef remembered that Mary's tragedy could also affect the marriage prospects of her younger sisters.

Salome's eyes bored into his as she waited for Yosef to speak.

He tried smiling at her but got a piercing stare in return. "So, Salome, your father is home?"

"In the garden. Naomi's helping him weed." She did not invite Yosef in. "Mama said the chickpeas survived the snow, so Papa had better not let them die just because she was away."

"So . . . yes . . . the garden? I'll just go round there."

Before Yosef reached the plot of tilled ground where Heli stood knee-deep in the dark green leaves and white blossoms of the chickpea bushes, Salome appeared at the back door of their house. "Naomi!" she snapped. "Come in here! Leave Papa and . . . his visitor to talk alone."

Before Yosef's world had crashed to earth, dark-haired Naomi had always run to him to be swung up around his shoulders, giggling all the while.

Not so now. Averting her gaze, Naomi muttered, "Shalom . . . good morning, sir. Papa, I'll help Salome with the cheeses." The girl's hand flew to her mouth as her thoughts made the sudden connection between cheeses and Mary's dowry. Fear crossed her face, as if she'd already said too much. She hurried away.

Heli straightened up, his hand on his back. He sighed heavily and glowered at the plants, as if whatever he did in their cultivation was certain to be wrong.

"So, Yosef, you've come. Will you tell me it's time to denounce Mary to the council, eh?" Heli had aged since this business began. The worry lines on his forehead appeared permanently etched, and the crease between his eyes was as deep as a scar. As he visibly sagged further, he spoke in a resigned tone. "You're right, of course. I don't dispute that. But she's just a girl. Foolish. But a child."

Yosef said hurriedly, "She won't have to go before the Sanhedrin at all . . . that is, if you agree. You and I will go to them privately. We'll tell them the contract is off—that's all—just called off. Mutual agreement. Then perhaps . . ." Somehow Yosef could not bring himself to say the words that possibly the father of Mary's child would then come forward.

Heli bit his lower lip and stepped closer, as if he was afraid he'd not heard correctly. "No denouncing her publicly?"

Yosef shook his head. "I wouldn't."

"Just a quiet end to the betrothal?"

Yosef nodded. "Heli, I still care about what happens to her." Then, in a deliberately gruffer voice, he added, "You and I can face down the gossips in town, eh?"

Heli's chin lifted, and he stood more upright. "I had hoped to call you Son. You are a good man. No doubt of it. It's your right to be free as soon as you like. But when do you want to do this?"

"I thought . . . as soon as possible. Wouldn't that be best?"

Yosef saw the hint of worry return to Heli's face. Possibly it was the prospect of going before the village council; possibly it was the idea of taking so important a step without Anna's approval. "There's been no word yet from Beth Karem," Heli noted. "About Mary's aunt Elisheba being pregnant, I mean. Not that there's any reason to expect such news. She's well past the age, of course, but still . . . if it were true . . . what if it were?"

Yosef frowned. "I'd thought once we took this step, then you could send word to Mary. She could stay in Beth Karem. As you mentioned."

"Ah . . . as to that, well, Anna and I had a bit of a thought. That what with Aunt Elisheba wanting a child, she could raise it as her own, see? If Mary stayed till after the . . . baby . . . well then, Elisheba could keep it and Mary'd come back and things'd go back to being like before. If you could delay."

But then the town would wonder why Yosef had not married her. If he did not put a definite end to the engagement, his own name would forever be under suspicion. "I'll think on it," he concluded.

Heli took another deep breath and let it out slowly. "That's fair," he agreed. "You're a fine, decent man, Yosef. I've always said so. A good husband for my daughter."

Yosef went back to his shop dissatisfied with himself. Fine and decent did not cure the dull throbbing in his chest. Nothing was resolved yet. There would be more days of avoiding the townsfolk or glaring with suspicion at other young men. This had to get over soon.

This is a record of the ancestors of Yeshua the Messiah, a descendant of King David and of Avraham:

Avraham was the father of Yitzchak. Yitzchak was the father of Ya'acov. . . .

Ya'acov was the father of Yosef, the husband of Mary.

All those listed above include fourteen generations from Avraham to King David, fourteen from David to the Babylonian exile, and fourteen from the Babylonian exile to the Messiah.[84]

CHAPTER

15

Yosef would wait as Heli asked him, yes. But he was certain the marriage *ketubah* must be nullified. It was the best thing for all concerned, Yosef told himself yet again as his eyelids drooped. He tried to pray the words of the seventy-seventh psalm.[85]

Adonai, blessed are you, creator of life. Blessed are you . . . though you don't let me sleep. I'm too sad even to pray. I think of all the hopes I had, over now. When I thought of her, my nights were full of joyful songs. I search my soul and think about the difference. Have you rejected me forever? Will you never again show me favor? Has your unfailing love failed me? Have you slammed the door on your mercy?

Outside his window a night bird sang.

Voices rang in Yosef's head.

The voice of Yosef's mind, telling him what was right, lecturing his heart again that he was betrayed.

The mocking words from his friends and neighbors in the street.

Voices.

His own confusion. His love arguing against Mary's betrayal.

Was there ever a song as lonely as that of the bird outside his window?

To live life alone or to forgive her and take her in. To raise another man's child as his own. The baby she carried was the son of David, she had said. But which David? Who was it in Nazareth that she had yielded to in Yosef's absence?

Voices.

He could not yield to love or mercy! He must do what was just! As for the son or daughter of Mary's unknown David, the child would grow up with Zachariah of Beth Karem for his adopted father.

Nothing Yosef could do would stop the gossip about Mary. After a long time, perhaps, Mary would be able to return home from Beth Karem and live in Nazareth again. More importantly, if she gave the child to her aunt and uncle to raise, she could still have a life, a future. Yosef would remain in Nazareth and see to that. He was a muscular man, known for his powerful hands. He was quiet and unassertive, true, but let his ire get roused, and he could be threatening.

He imagined himself collaring the worst of the gossipers, explaining how their continued prattle about Mary offended him . . . and he was not a man to accept offense. Soon enough they would pick a different, safer target for their whispers.

Yosef was satisfied with his conclusion. In a few weeks he would go back to Mary's father and have another long discussion. Heli was loud and angry sounding, but at the bottom of the bluster, Yosef knew Heli loved Mary and would defend her. Yosef would always love her but never marry her. He would defend her; that was enough. When the two men presented a united front to the village, that would be the end of it.

Yosef tossed and turned. He could not disgrace himself by bringing her into his home.

The night bird fell silent.

Yosef drifted towards sleep, remembering his own father. Old Jacob the Carpenter had manners as coarse as his hands but the heart of a Lamedvov—one of the righteous ones, who by their kindness warded off Yahweh's judgment against a wicked world.

Yosef regretted that the old man had died without ever seeing grandchildren. He had been quite a teacher, that one. When he'd placed his calloused palms over Yosef's young fingers, together grasping chisel and hammer, he'd imparted more than skill. He'd given Yosef a love for wood being worked: the aroma of cedar, the grain of oak, the holiness of acacia. The fashioning of useful and attractive articles from what in another's hands would be no more than firewood—that was true inspiration.

Yosef had wondered if he'd ever have a son to whom he could pass on his abilities. Now he doubted it. Yosef knew he was a man made for loyalty, able to love just one woman. He adored Mary from the core of his being. How could any other ever take her place?

This is my fate. The blessings of The Most High have changed to hatred.

A breeze fluttered the leaves of the acacia tree. The soft rustling was oddly musical, like the tinkling of chimes. The tune swirled in through Yosef's window, increasing in volume as if the musician stood nearby.

The night bird commenced his song again. And in the melody Yosef heard voices.

A shoot will come up . . .
Come up . . .
From the stump . . .
From the stump of Jesse![86]

The message swirled out of silence—ringing like broken shards of pottery in a wind chime.

Was someone there? Yosef spoke aloud the verses of Psalm seventy-seven, which his father, Jacob, had claimed for himself and for Yosef:

"You are the God of miracles and wonders!
You demonstrate Your awesome power
Among the nations!
You have redeemed Your people by Your strength!
The descendants of Jacob and of Yosef
By Your might![87]
Redeem me from this grief, O Adonai!"

Voices!

Singing the verses from the prophet Isaias.

From his roots . . .
Sheresh!
A Branch!

Netzer!
Will bear fruit!
Perach![88]

Voices!

So many voices swirling through the window, singing from each corner of the room until all came together as one voice.

A whisper. *Shalom, Yosef! Son of Jacob! Son of David.*

There was someone standing in the corner of the room. Yosef saw him plainly, despite the lack of lamp or candle: large, shadowy, undefined. There was no instrument in his hands, yet the chiming notes continued.

"Who . . . are you?"

There was an answer in a language Yosef could not comprehend. But a voice speaking, nonetheless.

Yosef was not afraid. He was dreaming; he was sure of that. "You are only a dream," he said to the stranger. "I don't understand your language."

Yosef was only mildly surprised that the dimensions of his cramped room seemed to have expanded. The previously low ceiling was now high overhead; the extraordinarily tall guest did not have to stoop. Also, the spare furnishings appeared richer than Yosef recalled, as if the entry of the visitor enriched the surroundings.

Yosef sat upright. "I know you are only a dream."

The stranger addressed him again in Hebrew. *Shalom, Yosef, son of David.*

"You mock me?" Yosef asked.

Yosef, son of Jacob. Son of David.

What sort of greeting was this? Yosef's name was Yosef bar Jacob. It was true Yosef was a descendant of King David, but that was reaching a long way back on the family tree. "Why speak to me like this? I'm a poor carpenter. Son of Jacob, a poor carpenter. Of David's line, true enough, but far from palaces and kingdoms. And I am descended from the line from which a king of Israel can never be born."

The whisper replied, *Have you forgotten the prophecy your father, Jacob, taught you as a child? the prophecy written in the seventy-seventh psalm?*

"You have redeemed Your people by Your strength!

The descendants of Jacob and Yosef by Your might!"

Yosef considered the question. "I haven't forgotten. My father taught me that our names were part of the redemption prophecies. But he didn't mean . . . he couldn't have meant . . . me? A part of that?" Yosef faltered.

Yosef. Psalm seventy-seven says what it says. Plainly. Everything means something. Your name. Your father's name. The same as the names of the patriarch Ya'acov and his son Yosef, who looked for the coming of the Redeemer. The number of the psalm. Seventy-seven. The number seventy-seven is the same as the word used to declare an eternal covenant. The Lord has sevened Himself, which means He has sworn an oath. You are in the direct line of David but not in the line of those who will bring forth the King, the Redeemer. Still, you are to play a part in the plan of that redemption.

Yosef nodded in his sleep. "You're a dream, but a good dream. I never thought of it in such a light."

Have you not heard? What did the prophet Isaias write?

"A shoot will come up from the stump of Jesse;
From its roots a Branch will bear fruit.
The Ruach HaKodesh of Adonai will rest on him—
The Spirit of wisdom and of understanding—
The Spirit of counsel and of power,
The Spirit of knowledge and the fear of Adonai."[89]

Tell me, Yosef, if you know, of whom is the prophet speaking?

Yosef knew that answer readily enough. "Messiah, our Redeemer King, the Lord's Anointed, David's royal Son who is yet to come. He will be from the root of Jesse, David's father. One of David's descendants, true enough, but surely no connection to a branch as humble as me."

The figure agreed. *Mary is also of the royal line of David. Through David's son Nathan.*[90] *Her line is the lineage from which the Redeemer will be born.*

"Mary? A woman?"

Carpenter. Do not miss the meaning of this writing.

"You are a dream. And I am a poor ignorant man dreaming you. Trying to understand. But I don't understand."

Both of you, Mary and Yosef, descendants of David but through different ancestors. Your ancestor King Jeconiah was cursed for turning from the Lord, and thus Messiah cannot come from your lineage. Mary's line back to David remains blessed. So each of you plays a different roll in redemption. She will bring forth the Redeemer. You are among those in David's lineage who will be redeemed.

"I will take more convincing than a dream. Who am I? An uneducated fellow. A carpenter."

So, Carpenter, consider the number of David's name. Hebrew letters each have a numerical value. In the name David, *the numbers of these letters add up to fourteen. Fourteen is also the number of the word* Yod, *which means "hand of the Lord's might." There are fourteen knuckles on a hand. Count them. Fourteen is double the sacred number seven. Thus we see the Hand of Yahweh moving through history, leading to this very moment. As it is written in the seventy-seventh psalm: "To this I will appeal: the years of the strong right Hand of the Most High!"*[91] *Fourteen, two sevens, is twice the number of completion. The fourteenth of the first month is the day the firstborn of Egypt died while the firstborn of Israel were spared. Everything in Scripture, even such a small detail as a number, means something.*

"All I want is a simple life. I'm no scholar."

The number found in David's name is a prophecy of the generations that will pass from one covenant to another until the coming of Messiah, the Son of David.

"Fourteen?"

Did you not recite the names of your ancestors during your bar mitzvah? There were fourteen generations from Father Avraham to the coming of King David. Fourteen generations from King David to the exile in Babylon and the departure of the Lord from the Temple. And now you, Yosef, son of David, are the thirteenth generation in your line since the day when the Shekinah Glory of the Lord departed from the Temple. The hour has come for completion. In the fourteenth generation after the Exile, the Son of David, Right Hand of Yahweh, Messiah, the Branch, will be born. The year of the Lord is at hand when Ya'acov and Yosef and their descendants will be redeemed, as it is written in the seventy-seventh psalm. Now, in this generation, the Lord will return suddenly to Yerushalayim.

Yosef asked, "But who is his father? Mary doesn't carry a son of mine."

You have spoken correctly. But the child will be yours to care for and nurture, though He is not the son of your body. Mary's name means "bitter rebel-

lion." Her lineage is traced back to Adam . . . back to the first woman's bitter rebellion against the Creator.

"Yes. But . . . I don't understand. Who then . . . who is the father of her baby?"

No reply. Perhaps the being in his dream had run out of patience.

Yosef challenged, "You're a dream. I'll wake up and not remember you. I seldom remember dreams."

You will remember. And more dreams will follow! You will understand and no longer be afraid.

Yosef heard the song of the night bird outside the window. Then, suddenly, voices. So many! Words like bells ringing to a crescendo. The wind! Voices roaring in a mighty wind! Yosef covered his face and trembled in terror in his bed. "Who am I, that a messenger would speak to me?"

Yosef! Son of David! I am Gabriel, who stands in the very presence of the Lord! Humble yourself and remember this! Nothing is too hard for God! The Lord has sevened Himself! He has sworn an oath, and He who is Truth will never go back on His Word! Adonai has sevened *Himself by His eternal covenant with Avraham. Adonai has* sevened *Himself by His everlasting covenant with David. Adonai has* sevened *Himself in a new covenant in this age, promising mercy and salvation to all who call upon Him for forgiveness. As Adonai promised to your fathers—and now swears to you—the babe soon to be born, this son of Mary, whose name means "bitter rebellion," is seed of woman. But, unlike Eve, this woman is no rebel. She is favored by the Lord above all women. He has searched her heart and found no bitterness there. She is found worthy. The seed of this woman is The One of whom it is written that one day He will crush the head of the serpent beneath His heel!*[92] *And though His heel be bruised, He will break the bondage of sin and death over mankind once and forever! He who has spoken these things Was and Is and evermore Will Be! He has sevened Himself!*

Then voices of unseen beings cried out in antiphonal song above Yosef, beneath him, to his right and left:

Your ways, O God, are holy.
What god is as great as our God?
You are the God who performs miracles;
You display Your power among the peoples.
With Your mighty arm You redeemed Your people,

The descendants of Ya'acov and Yosef.
Your thunder was heard in the whirlwind;
Your lightning lit up the world.
The earth trembled and quaked.
Your path led through the sea,
Your way through the mighty waters,
Though Your footprints were not seen.
You led Your people like a flock
By the hand of Mosheh and Aaron![93]
Now You, Immanuel, come to dwell among men!
You will open Your mouth in parables!
You will utter hidden things,
Things from of old![94]
By Your own hand You will lead Your people
By Your own hand
Like a flock
You will lead their hearts back to God.
You are the Shepherd-King!
Son of Avraham, Son of David, Son of The Most High!

Bells rang loudly for a moment longer. Then abruptly the ringing stopped. Yosef opened his eyes. The room was just his room. Gloomy. Small. No one here. No noise. Even the night bird had flown away.

Yosef was sweating. His heart pounded like a drum. He spoke aloud, thankful to hear his own voice. "Only a dream." He wiped perspiration from his brow and trembled as he tried to reconstruct what he had heard. He counted the knuckles on his hand. "Fourteen generations from Avraham to David? Fourteen from David to Exile? Thirteen from Exile to me? One more . . . and then? Fourteen is completed once again. The number of David's name. The number of the strong hand of the Lord. The fulfillment of prophecy. The establishment of David's eternal kingdom."

Yosef rose and lit the small clay lamp. Holding it up, he examined the corner of the room where the being had stood. "Everything means something? Son of The Most High, he said? But who am I to dream such a dream? Who? Who am I to imagine that I could raise and nurture the Lord's Anointed? Just a dream. It was only a dream."

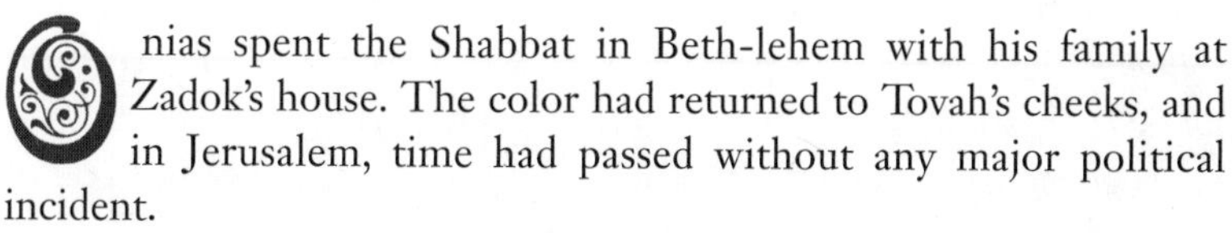

CHAPTER 16

Onias spent the Shabbat in Beth-lehem with his family at Zadok's house. The color had returned to Tovah's cheeks, and in Jerusalem, time had passed without any major political incident.

After weeks in the calm of the village, Tovah's sense of the dangers of the Holy City had diminished. Here was Onias, pale and thin, clearly not eating or sleeping well without her.

She was adamant.

There was no keeping her away from home. The nesting instinct, as Zadok's wife called it, had set in. It was well and truly spring, and Tovah would clean her house and prepare for the birth of the baby! She would feed her underfed husband and see to it that he went to bed and slept normal hours.

Onias could not dissuade her. He did not tell her that all the reasons he had wanted her out of the City of David still existed. There was a hazardous undertow beneath a seemingly calm river.

Zadok laid a hand on his arm as they departed. "You know where we are, Brother," he confided. "If we're needed."

Flickering torchlight cast black shapes onto the walls of Herod's private audience chamber. Wall-mounted spears stretched elongated spikes overhead, like a trap closing around the occupants. Marble bursts of heroes, both mythical and Roman, scowled down accusingly, their deepened eye sockets more terrifyingly alive this way than in full light.

Talmai, crouching at Herod's feet, delivered the latest stroke in his quest for power. "The letter was found in the house of your grandchild's Hebrew tutor, addressed to Glaphyra's father, Majesty."

"Well? Is it conclusive?"

"It is," Talmai temporized, "suggestive. It states that she is afraid for the lives of herself, her husband, and their two sons. It asks King Archaelaus to intervene . . . with you."

"Treason!" Herod snapped. "Bring the tutor in. He is part of the plot. Flog him till he breaks and tells us everything."

"May I suggest . . . not yet, Majesty. We do not know all who are party to an attempt to kill you. We must get them all. Let your son be followed; let Glaphyra be watched. The word will reach them that this letter miscarried. If Alex is truly guilty of plotting against you, he and his coconspirators will be even more desperate. A further betrayal of their schemes will follow. I'm certain of it."

Ecbatana, Kingdom of Parthia
29th year of King Phraates IV
Journal of Court Astonomer Melchior
New Moon Observation
Third New Moon after the Spring Equinox[95]

My observations are required by the king's council only on the nights of the New and the Full moons. Nevertheless, I have been carrying out my studies every clear evening for the past two weeks. The reason will soon be plain enough.

It has been eight months since Balthasar grew excited about seeing The Adam near The Atonement star in The Virgin and seeing The Sabbath in the sign of the nation of Israel, both in the same night.

For all his enthusiasm about linking ancient prophecies to the heavens, he has been the one cautioning me not to run ahead, but to await further developments.

Now I can conclusively say, those further developments have arrived. Every night for the past two weeks of my study, The Sabbath and The Righteous have been drawing closer and closer together. Tonight, an hour after midnight, the nail of my little finger, held at arm's length, covered them both . . . in the very heart of the sign of The Fish! And this on the night of the New Moon!

If my calculations are correct, The Sabbath, which began this month lower than The Righteous in the sky but has now traded places with it, will continue to ascend as the two separate. But Balthasar suggests that the signal of great importance connected with these two heavenly lights is not over yet!

I should also record one other noteworthy occurrence: At midnight one of the brightest stars in the northern skies was directly overhead. It is the one called Vega and named by the Jews The Warrior Triumphant; He Shall Be Exalted. This star is found in the constellation that pictures a harp such as King David played. The constellation is called Lyre for that reason. It is said by the Jews that the celestial music is so enchanting that rivers stop flowing and that lions and lambs lie down together in perfect harmony.

So shall life be after the coming of Messiah.

Onias stretched and rubbed his eyes, then looked out the window for the telltale fading of stars. The Righteous and The Sabbath, conferring together in the constellation of The Fish, were not as brilliant as they had been moments earlier. It must be close to dawn.

The tutor had been up throughout all the dark watches, studying and praying. Such a schedule was not unusual for him of late, but on this night now ending, many other Jews observed the rite as well. At last sunset the counting of the Omer ended, the conclusion of the forty-nine-day cycle begun at Passover.

Today was Pentecost, the celebration of the giving of the Law on Mount Sinai.

Onias heard the distant call from the priest on the pinnacle of the Temple. From that vantage point daylight could be seen gleaming off the walls of Hebron, twenty miles to the south. Day had officially begun. This brought to a close the examination of the lambs of sacrifice that had been going on since midnight.

"Tovah!" Onias called. "Menorah! Wake up! If you want to get there in time for the Hallel, we'll have to hurry."

"Coming, Papa!" Menorah piped.

Onias' family made ready to join the throngs of pilgrims flocking to the Temple Mount. This year the number of visitors to Jerusalem at Pentecost was even greater than at the Passover feast. The season had remained stormy and, with Passover coming early this year, those who traveled by ship from Alexandria or Greece or Rome had sensibly delayed their journeys.

They were certainly all present now. The city was near bursting.

The regular morning sacrifices were over, and the special festive offerings had begun when Onias, Tovah, and Menorah fought their way through the jammed streets. The tutor, with the little girl balanced on his shoulders, led the way so that Tovah's belly was protected in his wake. Slowly they exited the Gennath Quarter, inching toward the heights of the Temple Mount.

"This day we commemorate the marriage of Adonai Elohim and Israel," Onias explained to his daughter. "Torah is the contract of his marriage to his people."

"A wedding? I love weddings, Papa!"

Onias nodded, and Menorah tugged at his curls and giggled. He continued, "They say Adonai loved Israel so much he lifted Sinai right up off the desert. Held the mountain over their heads as a wedding canopy." Here he acted as if he would hold Menorah over his own head, and she squeaked with pretend fright.

"Weren't they afraid, Papa?"

Onias nodded again. "I expect they were, Daughter."

Others also used the occasion of Pentecost to give instruction. Halfway up the broad stairs Onias passed a rabbi teaching a group of his talmidim.

The instructor, thin of face and body, with a thin, pointed beard to match, was not speaking of the love of God for Israel or of weddings. Instead he shook his fist at the golden eagle displayed over the Agrippa Gate two stories above their heads. "Habomination!" he spouted. "Clear violation of the law forbidding graven images. Mounted on the Temple! Hit's a desecration!"

The fellow spoke with the interchanged *hets* and *khets* of a Galilean. His followers responded with the same accent.

In a quiet aside to Tovah, Onias urged, "Let's squeeze through and move a little faster."

"Is there a problem?" Tovah returned.

Onias whispered in her ear, "Rab Zalman of Chorazin is a radical. He speaks without regard for Herod's spies and urges his students to take unsafe chances. I'll just feel better when we're not so close."

"No secrets, Papa," Menorah scolded, kicking her heels against his chest.

"Sorry, Daughter." Onias returned to the story of the giving of the Law on Sinai.

Though already fifty feet away, Onias could not avoid hearing Zalman's inflammatory rhetoric. "Where is the Mattathias for this present age, who despised the pagan altar and slew the hapostate priest? Where? And where is the Phineas who slew the hadulterous son of Ya'acov and his Midianite harlot?"

This was not the message of love and redemption Onias wanted to impress on Menorah, so he spoke still louder. Even so, he could not escape Zalman's clamoring: "How long shall the sanctuary of the Halmighty be fouled with this . . . this thing?!"

Onias did not turn off when they passed one of the inner gates leading to the Court of the Israelites. The plaza was packed almost shoulder to shoulder. Today he would stay nearby, to see that Tovah had the space she needed and also to relieve her of the responsibility of keeping track of Menorah. Tovah gave him a quizzical look, saying nothing to alarm Menorah.

The blond child picked up on the change even so. "Papa? Are you staying with us, 'stead of going with the men?"

"Yes, Daughter. I thought you could see the choir better from your perch."

Menorah gave a delighted laugh and accepted the explanation. She dearly loved songs and singers, and this was a special day for both.

The Levite choir was already assembled on the semicircular platforms fronting Nicanor Gate. On the two bottom steps, forming two wide arcs in front of their fathers, were children of the priests. Today they joined in the Hallel.

A single, quavering flute called the assembly to silence, then introduced the tune for Psalm 113.

"Listen!" Onias urged Menorah. "They say this psalm burst from heaven at the exodus from Egypt, at the crossing of the Red Sea, and at the giving of the Law. Only twice more will that happen: at the resurrection of the dead and when Messiah is crowned!"

"Hallelujah!" sang the priests in resonant baritones and clear, ringing tenors.

"Hallelujah!" echoed the children in high, sweet treble.

"Praise, O servants of the LORD, praise the Name of the LORD!"

"Praise, O servants of the LORD, praise the Name of the LORD," reiterated the sons of the priests.

The antiphonal singing went on to embrace the whole of the psalm, right through the conclusion:

"He settles the barren woman in her home as the happy mother of children.[96] Hallelujah!"

With one hand Onias patted Menorah on the knee, and with the other he reached out and took Tovah's fingers to give them a squeeze.

"Papa!" Menorah whispered emphatically. "I want to sing in the choir too!"

"Of course you do," Onias replied, patting her again.

The Levites began the psalm over. This time they and their children sang the verse together, and the response was sung by the crowd.

It was not until the line demanding, *"Who is like the LORD our God?"* that Onias heard it. A discordant screech, all out of tune with the music, drifted from the far side of the Temple compound. It swelled in volume until it overpowered the Levite choir. Thousands of voices screaming in panic.

"Move!" Onias urged. "I don't know what's happening, but let's get to a side wall at least and out of this mob."

"The eagle! They've torn down the eagle!" The news babbled across the Mount. "The Galilean students! Herod's men are butchering them!" Then: "They're killing everyone!"

With those words, terror became general and the desire for escape universal. But which way to go? There was movement eastward and away from the screams, but no other organization in the terrified flight.

Fights already broke out over the right-of-way.

"Hold my hand!" Onias bellowed to Tovah. "Stay with me!"

Each of the corners of the Court of Women was occupied by a chamber set apart for a particular use. The tutor's family was closest to the southwest chamber—the one used to store oil and wine. It was toward it that Onias shouldered his way.

Halfway there he got shoved sideways. With Menorah's weight on his shoulders he overbalanced and staggered. In doing so, he lost his grip on his wife's hand. "Tovah!" he shouted.

The alarm increased. As he tried to turn back toward her, someone struck him in the back with a fist.

"Go on," Tovah insisted, her voice almost lost amid the shrieking. "Keep Menorah safe! I'll follow!" Her words were as buried in the noise of the mob as if she were standing beside a raging waterfall.

"Move aside for a pregnant woman!" Onias begged. "For pity's sake, clear a path!"

With one hand he reached out and touched the corner formed by two walls. At least that afforded some protection. Peering over his shoulder, he spotted Tovah's shawl, ripped off, floating over the river of the crowd. Her hand reached between desperate faces, frantically waving toward him. Then he saw just her blond hair as she was swept away in the grip of a giant wave of humanity.

Onias lowered Menorah to the ground, making a shield of his body. "Stay here! I'll be back!"

"Papa, don't leave me! Papa! I'm frightened!"

"Your mother needs . . ."

Onias could no longer see Tovah. Not even her golden hair glinting in the sun betrayed her location. He could not move through the mob while carrying Menorah, could not leave her to be trampled.

The panic did not let up. Pushing, shoving, and screaming, women and children swirled around him, threatening at any moment to dislodge his hold on the walls or crush him down on top of his daughter.

His forearms upright on the stones, his face buried in his fists, his knees locked tight against the masonry, Onias kept barely enough space for Menorah to huddle and breathe.

He could do nothing more.

CHAPTER 17

It was the second day after the funeral.

"Papa?" Menorah tapped Onias on his back as he sat in silence on the floor of his house. "Where is Mama?"

The heads of Onias' brother Zadok and Rachel, Zadok's wife, snapped up.

Onias swallowed hard. "Mama is with Father Avraham."

"When will she come home?"

"Oh, Menorah!" Onias embraced the child and wept. She cried too, though she did not seem to comprehend the reason for her father's tears.

After a time Zadok and Rachel approached. Rachel, a small son on each hip, knelt and wiped Menorah's tears with her thumb. "Come out with us, Menorah. The sun is shining. The boys want to get out. Let's take a walk, eh?"

The girl's blue eyes brimmed with fresh tears. "But why is Papa crying, Aunt Rachel? Why?"

"Let's take a walk, eh? Your papa will be better when we get home again."

Menorah's chin quivered. "Papa? Why are you so sad?"

Onias could not reply. Could not make his lips form one word to answer her. He raised his hand and bit his lip. Shaking his head, he pleaded with Rachel to take Menorah out.

"Come on, Menorah." Rachel clasped the reluctant child's hand and led her out of the house.

Zadok sank down beside him. "Brother, come now. She can't hear y'. Let go. Let go." Zadok put an arm around Onias' shoulders. He pulled him close and let him sob for a long time.

Onias said her name again and again: "Tovah! Tovah! I tried to hold on! I wasn't strong enough! I couldn't hold them both!"

"Aye, Brother. I know. I know."

"She was . . . swept away. Like the sea. Like the sea! Oh, Zadok! I couldn't hold on to them both!"

"Aye, but y' saved your daughter, Onias. Tovah would have wanted y' to save Menorah. Y' did what Tovah wanted."

"I tried! I couldn't! Not both!"

At last Onias' sobs diminished. He straightened himself. Exhausted, he looked around the room at all the decorations Tovah had prepared for Pentecost. Everything still just as she had left it that day. Only she wasn't here. Empty! Empty! How could they have known? A moment! Only a moment! And someone else's madness had destroyed their lives forever.

"Menorah can't stay here with me, Zadok. The days of mourning will not be just empty ritual for me. Seven days of Shiva. Then Sheloshim, the thirty days. A year to follow. The rest of my life. How can Menorah's light shine when I am lost in such darkness?"

"Aye. Rachel mentioned it might be good for the child to come visit us in Beth-lehem awhile."

"Yerushalayim! A place of such madness now, Zadok. Not safe! Not safe! And I . . . teaching . . . close enough to the Herodian court through Herod's grandson that I can taste danger."

Zadok patted him clumsily. "Courage, Onias. Bring Menorah out to us when Shiva ends. The sky is as blue as her eyes in Beth-lehem. So many stars. Our flocks and fields are not on Herod's map. She can stay with us until—"

"Until Yerushalayim is safe? When will that be?"

"She can stay with us until you're ready to pick up the broken pieces again, Onias. Lambs and two small cousins to play with. Rachel'll care for her. Rachel sings too, y' know. Menorah'll shine as brightly as ever, and grief won't scar her."

Onias nodded. "Yes, thank you. Thanks, Brother."

Yosef watched from the window of his workshop as seven uniformed Herodian soldiers rode slowly past the house. A prison cart holding three bound and bloodied prisoners and pulled by a team of oxen rattled along in the center of the company.

Who were these men? What had they done to offend the great butcher king? Yosef wondered. He resisted the urge to stare after them. Curiosity about such matters could be deadly. Stepping away from the window, he hovered over the unfinished wedding chest.

The dust had hardly settled before the shrill warning blast of a shofar summoned the citizens of Nazareth to gather at the synagogue. Ominous. Such a call was made only in the most extreme emergencies. Clearly the arrival in Nazareth of Herod's elite bodyguards had some significance.

The shofar sounded a second time. Attendance was thus a requirement.

Yosef ran his fingers through his thick, black hair and pocketed a hammer in case there was trouble. Not much good against a Roman-style short sword, but he was stronger than most of Herod's hired brigands and would go down fighting if it came to that.

Putting on his cloak, he left the shop and joined the hundreds of Nazarene citizens who left shops, fields, flocks, and houses, compelled by law to listen to the latest Herodian outrage.

The soldiers and cart had stopped before the synagogue. Three of the soldiers dismounted. Big bay horses stamped impatiently at the end of their reins.

The elderly Rabbi Mazzar blocked the men from entering the synagogue. "Samaritans. Men of Edom! Moabites! Hirelings of Herod you may be, but you shall not enter our house of worship!"

"Brave talk for an insect I could crush with one blow." The bullies towered over the frail cleric.

The old man refused to move.

Yosef fingered the hammer as he inched forward. He spotted Heli's angry face at the far edge of the crowd. Rebellion already hung in the air, even though the citizens of Nazareth did not yet know the purpose of their visit.

The captain of the guard remained safely atop his horse. He too must have sensed danger. Now the odds were one captain and six Herodian soldiers against hundreds of sullen citizens.

"Stand down," the leader called to his men. His horse, sensing his rider's nervousness, pranced in place.

The three returned to their horses. "Aye, sir. These Nazarene dogs come when they are called. A large pack of them too."

Rabbi Mazzar lifted his chin in challenge. "My people come to the call of the shofar, which declares, '*Hear, O Israel: The LORD your God is One LORD! The LORD your God is One.*' Challenge that if you will, Samaritan!"

The commander unrolled a scroll and shouted, "Hear this, O Nazarenes of the Galil! Your sovereign lord, the great Herod, has this to say to rebels and bandits of the Galil who think they may come south to Yerushalayim to incite rebellion!" He began to read:

> *"Behold these Galilean traitors, caught in an act of conspiracy against the lord Herod the Great. They are condemned to death. For this cause they have been transported to the Galil, which is the nest of vipers and traitors. Here they are to be executed—one in each city here named!"*

He read off a list of twenty villages in the Galil.

Nazareth was third from the end. So the gruesome assignment was near its finish, Yosef realized.

The commander continued:

> *"There the criminals will be crucified before the eyes of all citizens in a township and left to rot as a reminder that the sovereign lord of this land does not tolerate rebellion. Two soldiers will be left in each village to stand guard and see that the execution is carried out. Every citizen of the village is ordered to bear witness and walk by to behold and remember the fate of traitors! Any among you who resist this command will be crucified along with these."*

The crowd stood motionless beneath the sun. Some stared openly at the ragged men behind the bars of the cart. Yosef clasped the hammer and considered how easy it would be to overcome Herod's men and free the prisoners. And the consequences of such an action? No doubt Herod would send a cohort to slaughter every man, woman, and child in the village.

Yosef caught the eye of his friend Tevyah, who shook his head slowly in an unspoken plea. *Don't!*

The commander of the executioners rode forward, urging his muscled bay to the verge of the crowd. He reached down and grabbed the tunic of a ten-year-old boy, hefting him into the air. "You, boy! Where is the carpenter of this village? We have run out of spikes and wood!"

Terrified, the child pointed at Yosef. The soldier flung the boy away and directed his steely gaze to Yosef. "You! Carpenter! Come forward."

Yosef felt his face color with suppressed anger. He clenched his fists and, as the crowd parted for him, walked forward.

"You're the carpenter, eh?"

Yosef jerked his chin down once in reply.

"All right then. You live far?"

Eyes fixed on the condemned men, Yosef shook his head.

"Spikes. Beams. Show my men."

Without waiting, Yosef strode swiftly toward his shop. Repressed rage made him sick to his stomach. What could he do? How could he resist them?

Moments later he heard the sound of hooves approaching behind him. "Hey! You! Carpenter!"

Yosef did not look back but increased his pace and burst through the door of his shop before the executioners caught up.

With trembling hands he pulled out a box from beneath his workbench. What would bear the weight of a man and not further slice through the flesh? *Nothing too thin.* Bile rose in his throat. *Adonai! Merciful! Help me!*

He selected three large iron spikes, the kind he used to secure the rafters of a house. *Adonai! Eternal God! When will you send the promised Deliverer? When will Messiah come? When will Israel be free from this tyranny?*

The soldiers shouted again. "Hey! Carpenter!"

Yosef stared at the spikes. A tear fell onto the iron. He kissed it. *Adonai! Forgive us all that we don't fight! Israel has sold its soul to the devil!*

He slowly exited the house. The soldiers were examining lumber Yosef had cut and planed to construct a barn for Mary's cow.

"This will do." The hobnailed shoe of the soldier kicked at the crossbeam cut to frame the door. "And this." He selected an upright support beam. Then, with a cruel smile, he said to Yosef, "You're a strong fellow, eh? And I see by your face you resent our use of your wood. All right then." He removed a denarius from his purse and tossed it at Yosef.

Yosef inclined his head a fraction, and the coin sailed past him.

The soldier's smile contorted into a scowl. Tapping his fist against the hilt of his sword, he approached Yosef. "You mute?" He slapped him hard across the face. "Eh? You don't talk, Carpenter? Afraid?" He slapped Yosef's opposite cheek. "Or just smart enough to know this could be your cross if you say the wrong thing? Well, then. You're either deaf. Or mute. Or smart. Give me the spikes."

Yosef tasted blood in his mouth. He extended the spikes, placing them into the executioner's hand.

"So you're not deaf." He directed a blow to Yosef's right ear, knocking him to the ground.

Pain shot through Yosef's head. He took a kick to his back. Another in the stomach.

No breath.

The world turned yellow.

One more hard stomp to the head and he blacked out.

It was night when Yosef awoke in a strange place to the sound of some animal howling from the highest brow of the hill.

Heli was in the room. Yosef recognized the location after a moment. Heli's house.

Salome stirred soup over the cook fire. Little Naomi sat cross-legged on the floor, rocking, rocking, with her hands covering her ears.

"Heli?" Yosef's own words sounded distant. He realized something was wrong with his right ear.

Heli whirled around, relief flooding his face. "My son! My boy! I was afraid we would lose you!"

"How . . . long?"

"You've been unconscious since yesterday afternoon."

The racket outside echoed through the valley. What was it? A tortured dog? "That sound?"

"The poor fellow." Heli clasped his hands and raised his eyes heavenward. "All day. On the highest ridge. Ever since last night. Who would think it could last so long? The soldiers fled at nightfall. Everyone is afraid to go up there. Afraid to help him."

It all came back to Yosef. The Herodian guards. The prisoners. Spikes and beams from his own shop. The kicks to his head.

"I . . . remember now." Yosef struggled to sit up. His head throbbed.

Salome whispered hoarsely, "Papa. So . . . horrible. Isn't there anything we can do?"

Heli replied fiercely, "Nothing. Nothing. So, this is our life under sovereign lord Herod. We aren't safe. Even here. Even in the Galil. And there is a whole brood of little vipers who will take Herod's place when he dies."

One long, terrible shriek tore the curtain of night and resounded a hundred times against the mountains. It was as though all of Israel were crying out!

And then . . . at last . . . silence.

After a few minutes, the croaking of frogs and the fiddling of crickets resumed.

"Is it over, Papa?" Naomi raised her face and pleaded.

Heli did not speak for a long time. "Over? It won't end until . . . until . . ."

Salome finished. "Until Messiah comes? Papa! Have we ever needed him more than now?"

CHAPTER 18

"Papa, how long will I stay with Uncle Zadok and Aunt Rachel?" Menorah piped from the back of the borrowed donkey as they approached the village of Beth-lehem.

Onias did not know how to reply. How long? The answer to her question could be given only when Jerusalem was safe again.

When Herod died?

When Messiah came?

When the true hereditary High Priest took His rightful place and drove out the false priests who ruled the Holy City?

"Papa?"

"Not long." He expressed a hope, but hope was no answer.

"Will Mama come visit me?"

Menorah still could not comprehend that Tovah was never coming home. "She is with Father Avraham, Daughter."

"Can't I go with her to visit Father Avraham instead of visiting Uncle Zadok?"

"No . . . besides, there are lambs in Beth-lehem for you to care for. And you must help Aunt Rachel with your little cousins."

"They're only boys."

"Yes, and they need watching, Menorah. Aunt Rachel says you'll be a wonderful helper. A big girl."

Menorah rode in silence for a time as if contemplating such responsibility. Lambs and little boys. "I would still rather be with Mama and Father Avraham. And with you too, Papa. All together. Who will I sing to at night? You like my songs."

Onias swallowed hard, fighting back the grip of grief at his throat. It was good that Menorah could not see his face. "Yes." His voice cracked. "My heart will . . . I will hear you sing . . . in my heart. Teach your cousins to sing, eh?"

"Like Mama taught me?"

"Yes. Like Mama."

Her voice, a silver bell in perfect pitch, rang out:

"Those who live
In the shelter, in the shelter,
Of El Shaddai,
Will find rest, will find rest,
In the shadow,
Of our God, Most High!" [97]

She drew a breath. "There. I'll teach them that one, eh, Papa? My favorite. I'm not afraid when I sing it."

"Then you sing it, Menorah, my love. And every night at bedtime, I'll raise my head and hear your voice all the way from Beth-lehem."

The vast flocks of temple sheep decked the pastures beneath Beth-lehem like a stone floor. White houses shone in the sun.

Was there ever a task more painful? Giving up Menorah, when all he wanted was to hold on to her and watch her grow more like Tovah each day?

Resolute, Onias wiped his eyes with the back of his hand. He would be strong. Surely Beth-lehem was safe from Herod's reach. Evil would not turn its eyes on a village of such serenity. "You will like it here," Onias said to Menorah. "And when Uncle Zadok brings the lambs to Temple, I'll see him and send letters back to you. You must write to me as well. And Beth-lehem is near enough to Yerushalayim that I will come visit you sometimes."

He glanced back to see Menorah's face shining with the possibilities of letters and visits from Jerusalem. "Papa! Can Mama write too? And will you bring Mama here to Beth-lehem with you to visit, Papa? When she gets back from Father Avraham's house?"

Yosef did not speak to anyone about his dream. It was, he convinced himself, only a dream brought on because, waking or sleeping, he could think of little else but Mary.

During the weeks that followed this experience, Yosef was commissioned to build a wedding chest. It was to be a gift for the bride of a wealthy young farmer who had attended Torah school with him.

At his betrothal to Mary, Yosef had begun work on just such a wedding present for her. It was solid oak. Yosef had already carved the pattern of a pomegranate branch blossoming with flowers, which he would later inlay with walnut and cherry wood, on each end. The chest was a lovely thing. Yosef would have given it to Mary on their wedding night . . . if there had been a wedding. Now he considered selling it to the young farmer. What was the use of saving it?

Each evening when he lay down to sleep, Yosef prayed and hoped he would have another dream, hoped he would receive some special revelation for all the questions that rattled around in his head during daylight. But there were no more dreams.

When he was asked by his neighbors when his marriage contract would be celebrated with a wedding, he grinned and shrugged off the questions, as though nothing were wrong. Mary and her mother had gone to visit relatives; that was all. Nothing more.

Perhaps Mary would stay forever in Beth Karem with her aunt and uncle. Yosef's pain would grow dull over time. But not now. It was too soon.

Yosef pondered his dream. He considered again the harsh reality that he was descended from the line of King Jeconiah, whom Yahweh had cursed through the prophet Jeremiah.

Record this man as if childless,
A man who will not prosper in his lifetime,
For none of his offspring will prosper,
None will sit on the throne of David
Or rule anymore in Judah.[98]

Yosef's father, Jacob, a righteous man, had not believed the sins of their evil forebearer had any effect on their present lives. Yosef had always walked uprightly before the Lord, prayed the blessings, paid his tithes, helped those poorer than himself, and lived a quiet life. He had always sensed the approval of God . . . until now.

Though Yosef was the thirteenth generation since that terrible curse of Exile had been pronounced, like his ancestors who had gone before him he unexpectedly felt the sting of the sentence. It was as if the penalty of Jeconiah's sin against the Lord and the subsequent destruction of the nation and the Temple had somehow become his own.

Perhaps, Yosef thought, what had happened to shatter his plans of marrying and raising a family was somehow tied to the curse that declared that the descendants of Jeconiah would never prosper. In a way, Yosef was still in exile. His heritage was stained, as though the ancient curse remained in full effect.

Three stars appeared in the sky above Nazareth as Yosef laid down his tools. It was Shabbat evening. The moment had arrived when wives who had prepared fine Shabbat meals lit the Shabbat candles, and their families gathered round to eat and sing together.

By the Law, which forbade kindling fire on the holy day, it was too late now to light a candle. Yosef groped in the dark. Respecting the command not to work on Shabbat, Yosef did not cook a meal but ate a lonely supper of bread and dried fish. His heart was heavy as he spoke the blessings alone.

After supper he lay down on his bed and stared up into the gloom of his too-quiet house. *I am a simple man, who only ever wanted a wife and a family. Am I to bear the penalty for another man's sin?*

At last he fell asleep.

The breeze from the Great Sea swept up the pass from the west, carrying on it the sweet scent of orchards in bloom. Yosef inhaled deeply and turned his face to the wall.

Outside, the song of a night bird called.

Voices.

Wind chimes stirred.

Voices.

A soft song that had no words.

A dream.

A presence in the room. Warmth on his back. Light penetrating his eyelids. The chiming of tiny silver bells. The sharp tang of cedar blending with the aroma of blossoming trees in a previously unknown incense.

A dream?

A voice. Kind. Sympathetic.

Shabbat Shalom, Yosef, son of David.

"Shabbat Shalom. I am dreaming."

Yes.

"Only a dream."

A dream is enough.

"Well, then, I promise I won't ask you about . . . her . . . if you'll keep me company awhile. And would you please help me sort through some questions? Things have come to my mind as I've been working."

We heard your question. You asked why you must bear the penalty of another man's sin.

"Yes. The curse on my ancestor. Why should I bear the consequences of Jeconiah's sin? Seems unfair to me."

But a fact of life, Yosef. As his descendant, you carry the curse of Jeconiah. But there is an older curse that you bear as well. All mankind is cursed to pay the penalty of another's sin: the rebellion of mankind's first father and mother in Eden. That is how death first entered the world. Because of their sin, all humans who live on earth are condemned to die.

"May I not be judged by my own merits?"

And if you were? Are you perfect? Have you never sinned?

"No one is perfect. Who can live a perfect life?"

That, then, is the answer to your question. Only One is righteous. Only Adonai is righteous. He who walked in the garden with Adam and his wife.

"He's perfect because he's the Lord. Adonai."

Yes, Yosef. He alone is perfect.

"Am I to live forever under an ancient curse and pay for sins I didn't commit?"

No.

"Then tell me how I can be free of it. How can I live the life I want to live? I'd like to marry. Have a family. Serve the Lord and my fellow man."

Listen.

"I am listening."

Obey the Lord. There was a faint drumming sound beneath the words.

"I have obeyed . . . mostly. But look! Look!"

Avraham believed Adonai and that belief was counted as righteousness.[99]

The rhythmic pulse increased in volume.

"Avraham was Avraham. Who am I? An ordinary carpenter."

Elohim is God. Nothing is too hard for Him. Nothing.[100]

"Tell me what I am to believe."

You have forgotten that Adonai uses ordinary men . . . and ordinary women . . . to accomplish His plans. You have forgotten the Lord sevened Himself, promising that He would bless and save His people Israel even at the moment they were carried off into exile and slavery. Believe His promise.

The tapping pattern was recognizable now: the rhythmic pulse of mallet and chisel, removing scraps of unwanted wood.

"Am I an exile?"

Everyone lives in exile. Everyone is lost like sheep who have wandered off. All need a shepherd to lead their hearts back to God.[101]

"I want a shepherd to lead me. I'll follow. Tell me what to do! But I pray the Lord won't make me live here alone! Alone to grieve and rot and wonder if my life is worth anything."

Remember what the Lord said through Jeremiah:

> **The days are coming, when I will raise up to David a Righteous Branch, a King who will reign wisely and do what is just and right in the land. In His days Judah will be saved and Israel will live in safety. This is the name by which He will be called: YAHWEH–TSIDKENU, which means, "The LORD Our Righteousness."**[102]

"I believe God alone is righteous."

Therefore believe . . . only God can atone for the unrighteousness of a man.

Pounding. Refining. Shaping. A pattern of timeless beauty emerged from unformed lumber.

"I know you are only a dream. But tell me, how would God do this for me?"

Yeshua means "salvation."

"Who can save me from my broken life? my loneliness?"

Yeshua alone can make a broken heart whole.

Both the timbre and the tempo of hammering changed. No longer removing obstructions but the softer tapping as perfect joints fitted together according to the plan of the master carpenter.

"Who is Yeshua?"

He is The Lord Our Righteousness.

"What must I do? Tell me. How can I free myself from the curse of a heritage that comes from the unrighteous branch of David's line?"

Free yourself? Yosef! Have you not learned? You can do nothing. It is not your righteousness but God's righteousness that will set you free. The Righteous Branch of David is very near.

"But not for me. I'm born from the branch that is cursed."

The Righteous Branch will not come from *you, Yosef. But He is coming* for *you. You are chosen because you are like all those who live under the curse of exile from the presence of God. You are like every lost lamb who longs to be found by God and forgiven and carried home in the arms of the Good Shepherd.*

"Oh, that he would carry me!"

First you will carry Him.

The smell of the unfamiliar incense intensified. Wood and blossom intermingled. Commonplace and holy entwined, inseparable.

"Me? How am I to carry one so great?"

In your arms. On your shoulders. Sometimes on your back. He will be very small for a while.

"I know I'm dreaming. And sometimes dreams make no sense. But you're Gabriel, the great angel. And so you can explain everything to me so I'm not in suspense. Say it plainly. I'm a plain man, not a scholar. What are you telling me?"

Yosef, son of David, do not be afraid to take Mary home as your wife, because what is conceived in her is from the Holy Spirit. She will give birth to a son, and you are to give Him the name Yeshua, because He will save His people from their sins. It was said through the prophet: "The virgin will be with child and will give birth to a son, and they will call his name Immanu'el, which means 'God-with-us'!"[103]

Mary descends from the branch of David through which the Great Shepherd, Immanu'el, God-with-us, will come. Pay attention! Nawzer *is the Hebrew word for baby.* Netzer *is the Hebrew word for branch. Baby and Branch, the child you name Yeshua, Salvation, will be Adonai, incarnate in human form. Like a perfect lamb of sacrifice, He who is called Our Righteousness will make atonement for all unrighteousness! And as the Good Shepherd, He will lead the exiles home to safe pasture. Those who are lame He will carry on His shoulders. But first you must carry Him on your shoulders. Yahweh declares this to you, Yosef, son of David! Do not be afraid! Hear the command of the Shema: "Hear, O Israel! The* LORD *our God is one* LORD*! You are to love the* LORD *with all your heart, mind, and strength!"*

The sounds of crafting, carving, and fitting reached a crescendo and were sustained there. The scent suffusing the air attained an almost visible aura.

"I say the Shema every day, five times a day. But I have never known how to live it. Not really. Love the Lord with all my heart, mind, and strength?"

To make the meaning of the commandment plain, the Lord enters the world first as a baby. What loving parent does not understand what it means to love his child? This, above all, makes it easy to understand and perform the first commandment to love the Lord. The Shema could be said, "Love this innocent baby as your own son! Love Him with all your heart, mind, and strength." With all the strength of your heart, mind, and body, cherish, guard, and protect the child from the powers of darkness who will seek to destroy Him while He is in your care. For this purpose you were born. Through love of a child you will understand the depth of God's love for you. From the beginning, before time, it was planned: The exiled heart longing for forgiveness will love and nurture and save the Firstborn Lamb of God, who will one day grow up and become his salvation! The plan is written plainly in Torah and will surely come to pass.

"I am the Lord's servant. May all you have said come to pass for me. May the heart of Yahweh fill me with love and the hand of Yahweh give me strength. May the Spirit of Yahweh give me wisdom."

Nothing is too hard for God.

The pile of woman's clothing on the bed appeared pitifully small and sadly unfashionable, though all the garments were neat and serviceable. A couple of shawls, a single cloak. Onias had never known how few gowns Tovah possessed. She had never complained, never once suggested his pitiful teacher's salary did not supply all her wants.

Besides, she had always looked beautiful to him.

Onias gazed down at his own wrinkled robe. The cuffs were frayed. Tovah would never want him to go out in public with either flaw. She said it reflected badly on her reputation as a wife for her husband not to look well-groomed.

The tutor supposed he would have to hire someone to do his mending and darning, just as he had already paid to have Tovah's things washed and folded.

Tovah's great big heart had always reached out to those in need. Onias had been constantly amazed at her ability to connect with people who were hurting. She had been able to get them to open up and speak about troubles Onias had never even guessed at.

"Never draw back from doing any good that is in your hand to perform," she always said. *"There are always those in greater need than you."*

Just one street south and two crossings east, the synagogue of the Persian Jews maintained a cupboard of charitable donations for any of their countrymen who might be in want. Onias had started out his door the day before to give away Tovah's things but had caught himself when he heard her voice in his heart. She scolded him for even thinking of donating clothes still unwashed and untidy.

Onias sighed and gathered up the single armload of garments. There were many things about his life Tovah had kept neat and in working order: Apparel and living conditions were two. And attitudes were an even bigger realm altogether.

CHAPTER 19

"Heli!" Yosef called as he spotted Heli with his daughters near the nut seller's cart in the market square.

Heli raised his head in acknowledgment but did not smile as Yosef, breathless with excitement, cut through the crowds and strode up to him.

"Shalom, Yosef." There was no enthusiasm in Heli's greeting. Yosef noted how Heli had aged years in less than three months since Anna and Mary had been gone.

Once again the two young sisters linked arms and glared, as though Yosef was their common enemy.

"Naomi. Salome." Yosef bowed slightly to the girls, then greeted Levi the Nut Seller.

Levi, hands dripping walnuts, inquired, "So, your son-in-law, Heli! But where is the bride, eh? When's the happy day?"

Heli blinked miserably at the heaps of pistachios.

Levi shrugged and addressed Yosef. "These three aren't talking. So where's your bride, Yosef? Eh? We're in need of a wedding feast. The evenings are growing warm and pleasant, eh? A good time for a wedding, nu?"

"Yes!" Yosef agreed with more enthusiasm than he had intended.

Heli's head jerked upward in surprise. Had he heard correctly? Openmouthed, Naomi and Salome gawked at him as though he were crazy.

Yosef bellowed, "Yes, Levi! Yes, Nazareth! Listen to me! It's time for a wedding!"

He was answered by twitters and calls of laughter from the shoppers:

"Omaine!"

"True!"

"Well spoken!"

Yosef clasped Heli's hand and said quietly, "You see? Everyone agrees. I must fetch her back, Heli. I can't live without her any longer."

"Mary?" Salome breathed her sister's name.

Yosef patted Salome's head. "Who else would I be speaking of?"

Levi butted in. "You see, Heli, the bridegroom grows impatient. For weeks we've all been watching Yosef brood. Barely speaking to anyone. Moody, eh? You know the old saying 'Moody as a bridegroom'? Yosef has made it triple in significance. You can't put this off forever. So where are you hiding your daughter these days?"

Heli regained his composure. "You know well enough. She's in Beth Karem with her mother and aunt, who are your cousins." Then to Yosef, "But . . . we've had no word one way or the other about Elisheba."

"Doesn't matter. It's true. I am certain every word of it is true. At any rate, I'll go to Beth Karem and bring Mary home. Home to a wedding and then to my own house with your permission."

"You're ready then, Yosef? I mean, you're sure you're ready?" Heli cocked his head quizzically.

"Ready in the morning to leave for Beth Karem. I would like to take Naomi and Salome with me to fetch her and Anna back."

The girls squeaked in delight. "Papa! Papa! Papa!"

Heli scowled. "Who will milk the cows?"

"You!" the girls declared in unison.

Heli sighed. "So, I am outnumbered."

Yosef continued. "Mary's sixteen. Old enough. Heli, my father, if you will give your permission, I'll go. And when we come home . . . within the month? Enough time?"

Heli's eyes brimmed. "Blessed are you, O Adonai! You have given my daughter a husband to care for her!"

Levi raised his arms and crowed, "Listen, everyone! It is all decided here. Attention, Nazareth! Right here beside my little nut cart. We've all been wondering when the wedding would take place. We've all wondered if Yosef would survive the separation from his bride. Well, now we know! Right here it was decided!" Levi tossed a walnut to Yosef. "You've been the center of gossip, you know. Everyone wondering when you would crack! Congratulations!"

That evening at Shabbat service, a short, round-faced stranger with a fringe of gray hair entered the synagogue in search of Heli. Yosef and Heli were together in the center of a crowd, accepting congratulations that the details of the match were finally settled. A wedding within the month. The sooner the better as far as Yosef was concerned.

The stranger shouted Heli's name. "I come from Beth Karem in search of Heli, husband of Anna!"

"Make way!"

"Make way!"

"A messenger from Beth Karem!"

Heli broke off from conversation. "I am Heli."

"Sir, my name is Malachi. I come with good news for you. I've come all the way from Beth Karem. I am a vine grower there myself, traveling north to Lebanon on business. I bring you good news, sir, from your wife, Anna, about her elderly sister, Elisheba. Meant only for your ears privately."

Levi the Nut Seller, also the cantor of the congregation, demanded, "Heli has no secrets about his relations! Most of us are his relatives. I myself am second cousin to Anna and Elisheba, her sister. Get on with it, man! Tell Heli his good news about my second cousin Elisheba! We're all waiting. Service will start and be over before you deliver your good news."

Heli motioned that the messenger should continue.

"Yes, well, good news. Delivery . . . the very thing. You see, your wife's sister, Elisheba, whom we have all known for many years, could never bear a child, because she was barren as a stone. Or so we all thought. But now! Elisheba is this big! Big as a cow, I say. Looks to be about twenty months pregnant, though it is only eight and something.

Elisheba is soon to deliver her first child by some heavenly miracle, it is thought by the rabbi."

The rotund Malachi shook his head before he continued. "No, no, not what I meant. The rabbi thinks it is by some miracle that she is pregnant by her husband, Zachariah, who is also elderly. His name is the same as the prophet who wrote about the coming of the Messiah. Though the present Zachariah cannot speak a word because, as he has written to us on a wax tablet, an angel appeared to him in the Temple and struck him dumb because he did not believe. Dumb as a stone. But Elisheba is no longer barren as a stone. Any day now. Any day! By some heavenly miracle, we all suppose, because she is old—though not as old as Sarah was, she is old. And that is the news I was sent to bring to you privately."

For a moment, Heli was as mute as Zachariah; then he sputtered, "Yosef! Levi'll tend the cows. I'm coming with you to Beth Karem!"

Onias sniffed the melon suspiciously. Ripe? Not ripe? Too ripe? Onias had no knack for these things. He had never learned because he had never been required to know. Onias had married Tovah and taken her home to live with his parents until they got their own place. From the home he was raised in through all his wedded life, someone else had done all the shopping and the cooking.

Onias put the melon down. He could have asked someone for assistance, but his pride got in the way. *Please, sir, I'm thirty years old, but I can't tell a ripe melon. Can you help me?*

Not today!

The tutor struggled to recall the rare bits of gossip Tovah had brought home from the souks. Yamin the Grain Merchant was not to be trusted. There was too much grit in his flour, and he gave short measures.

Tobias the Butcher was a good sort. His prices were fair, and the quality of his lamb was excellent.

Or was it the other way around?

Onias was hopeless, tragically hopeless!

He stood in one spot, pivoting slowly, hoping he would see someone he recognized. Maybe someone, remembering he was a recent widower, would take pity on him without his having to ask.

No one did.

Onias stopped beside a display of eggs. Eggs were safe. How could you go wrong choosing eggs?

"How much?" Onias inquired.

"A penny each."

"So much?" He drew back from the table.

"You have an eye for a bargain," said the merchant. "How about only three pennies if you take six of them?" The man reached under the table and displayed a dozen eggs in a loosely woven straw basket.

Onias fumbled with his money pouch.

"Don't do it," warned a female voice at his elbow. "They're rotten. Azara there keeps a crate of two-week-old eggs under his counter. He's always trying that half-price trick on someone."

Angrily Azara crammed the rotten eggs back out of sight and waved for Onias and the woman to go away.

The tutor turned to thank his assistant.

A petite older woman blinked up at him, waiting for him to speak.

Onias' mouth worked, but no sound came out. The woman was wearing Tovah's shawl—her favorite red shawl that she wore the day she was killed. "I . . . where did you . . . that is . . . thank . . ."

The woman stared after Onias as he plunged away without completing a single sentence. Her expression suggested she thought him crazy.

Perhaps he was.

Some of the watchers looked uneasy at their role in the coming execution. Others considered stones for each hand, choosing their favorites for heft and shape.

The sun beat down on the crowd.

Hamla and Kendro stood guilty as accused. They were guilty out of their own mouths and guilty by mutual indictment. Though both defendants were bound and gagged during their appearance before Herod, the facts were attested to by both Talmai and the Thracian interrogator.

If that testimony was not adequate, they were further proven guilty because the likewise tortured captain of the guard at Alexandrium corroborated their story. At the same instant a third glowing poker was applied, hissing, to his ribs, the officer admitted he had known about a plot to assassinate the king and make it appear to be a hunting accident.

Even though the extorted confessions also implicated Herod's sons, Talmai did not push the point with the king. He told Herod the evidence was not conclusive. He said he would investigate further, to be certain this was not some scheme to discredit Alex and Ari. Herod agreed but let his displeasure be known by barring Alex and Ari from private audience with him. Talmai was ordered to keep a strict watch on them for any disloyalty.

As a traitorous soldier, the guard officer received no trial. He was strangled, and his body nailed to the wall of the barracks outside the fortress as a warning to other would-be assassins.

Hamla and Kendro did not get off so easily.

After the testimony was heard, King Herod graciously turned to the assembled crowd and asked for their recommendation. "Stone them! Stone them!" was the public demand, with which Alexander and Aristobulus, of necessity, loudly concurred. Hamla and Kendro were tied by neck, wrists, and ankles to a horizontal pole passed behind their knees. In this position they were loaded into an oxcart for a bone-rattling drive into the hills north of Jericho.

One of the limestone quarries supplying material for the construction of Herod's palaces was in a canyon there.

Even before the condemned arrived at their place of execution, throngs of onlookers had surrounded the pit. Some were curious travelers. Others had been paid by Talmai to attend.

The two prisoners, released from the pole but not from their chains or gags, were barely able to stand. They huddled back-to-back, squinting in the harsh midday light reflecting off the pitiless limestone walls.

Talmai himself read the charge and the sentence. The words *traitors* and *assassins* were barely out of his mouth when the chant began again: "Stone them! Stone them!"

Kendro broke into a shambling run toward the mouth of the canyon. A row of soldiers placed there lowered their javelins and drove him toward the base of the cliff.

The first stone, about fist-sized, struck Kendro behind the ear. He tried to dodge the hail of rocks that followed, till one the shape of a barley loaf hit him in the back of the neck and drove him to his knees.

Hamla had not moved. The flurry of jagged missiles knocked him unconscious in the first salvo. He collapsed without a sound.

Another rock struck Kendro in the cheek, gashing it and tearing the braided leather cord from his mouth. "Not guilty!" he shouted. "Not—" When his denial caused the number of stones to increase and batter him like hail, he bowed his face to the earth and yelled, *"Hear, O Israel, the LORD—"*

He never finished the Shema. He was dead before his body slumped amid the rubble.

The torrent of stones did not cease until both bodies were almost invisible beneath the mounded boulders.

Their heads and hands were cut off for display on the walls of the Jericho military encampment. There they would be visible to all who traveled the pilgrim road between Jericho and Jerusalem.

The bodies were left for the jackals.

Zadok presented Onias with Menorah's latest offering: a letter inscribed on sheepskin with a drawing.

My dearest only Papa,
I miss you very much. Here is a picture of me at Beth-lehem.
Come soon.
Love.
Shalom,
Your daughter, Menorah

Zadok interpreted for Onias. "Here is the sun, eh? And here our house. Those, I think, sheep? Aye. That is the apple tree she climbed. And this—" he pointed to the outline of a hand, her hand, with a round humanlike figure in the palm and another smaller figure beside it—"this is her mama and the baby in Avraham's hand. Rachel said it was good that she draw whatever she wished. I thought you would like to see what is in her mind."

Tears filled Onias' eyes. "She is so young to understand what has happened."

Zadok sniffed. "Aye. I'm a grown man, yet I don't understand it."

"Does she speak of that day?"

"To Rachel. Not me. I think maybe she's beginnin' to understand that Tovah isn't comin' back. And that the baby has gone away to heaven with her. Rachel is helpin'. Every night Rachel sings with her. Talks about angels and tells stories from Torah. Ya'acov's ladder. Heavenly visions. Y' know."

"Rachel has such a gentle way about her." Onias gazed tenderly at the outline of Menorah's hand and the simply drawn figures of Tovah and the baby. "Tovah always loved Rachel."

Zadok was gentle in his question. "Will y' come to Beth-lehem, Onias? The child would love to see y'. And . . . y' would be safe there."

Onias ducked his head slightly. How much did he dare mention to Zadok? "I am . . . I think I may be under suspicion."

Zadok scoffed. "Any creature with two legs is under suspicion in this city."

"It's best, Zadok—truly—if I don't draw attention to any of you."

"What are you involved in?" Zadok demanded. "What is this about, Onias? Haven't I told y' to stay clear of the Herodians and politics?"

"It's Herod's family."

"That's worse. What is it the Roman emperor said about our beloved king? Eh? Better to be Herod's pig than his son. True? Of course true."

"I haven't done anything, Zadok."

"This matters? Guilty. Innocent. Y' don't have to do anything in Herod's world to get crucified. Come with me to Beth-lehem. Disappear for a while."

"I can't."

"Y' mean y' won't."

"Maybe . . . maybe it's best if you don't come round for a while."

The brothers locked eyes.

Zadok's brow creased in a frown. "That serious?"

"Never more so." Onias rolled up a letter written on parchment and tied it with string. "Here. Please, take this to Menorah. Tell her I love her. Tell her I'll come soon. Soon as I can."

PART IV

The heavens declare the glory of God;
the skies proclaim the work of His hands.
Day after day they pour forth speech;
night after night they display knowledge.
There is no speech or language
where their voice is not heard.
Their voice goes out into all the earth,
their words to the ends of the world.

PSALM 19:1-4

CHAPTER 20

Ecbatana, Kingdom of Parthia
29th year of King Phraates IV
Journal of Court Astronomer Melchior
Summer Solstice Observation
Weather hot and dry, south wind[104]

Balthasar and Esther took me to the old palace of King Cyrus of Persia to show me the archive chamber. This is the very spot recorded in the book of Ezra as the place where the original decree permitting the Jews previously held captive by Babylon to rebuild the Jerusalem Temple. It is important, Balthasar says, because that event started some sort of prophetic sands running through an hourglass that pin down the precise time of Messiah's advent.

Balthasar says those sands have nearly elapsed now, in our very day!

That revelation made me pay particular attention to tonight's observations.

The star of Venus, Splendor, started out the twilight very high in the evening sky and remained visible for two hours past sunset. This despite the fact that today is the longest day of the year, and it was light until very late. Venus is in the constellation of Leo—also known as Aryeh, The Lion—near the king star, Regulus. Balthasar says that when Messiah comes, the King, the Lion of the tribe of Judah, will be the most splendid king the world has ever known.

When? I ask. When will He appear?

It cannot be too soon.

Word reached us today here in Ecbatana of the Pentecost riot and panic that resulted in the slaughter and trampling of hundreds of Jewish worshippers in Jerusalem. As if that were not tragedy enough, the travelers from the Holy City report Herod the Butcher has rounded up rebellious students and their teachers and is crucifying them all around the country as examples.

Again I asked Balthasar, when will Messiah appear?

He shook his head sadly and said, "It must be soon. It must be soon."

The Adam remains with Virgo the Virgin.

Of significance is the fact that Jupiter, The Righteous, and Saturn, The Sabbath, rose together at exactly midnight. They remain very close to each other in the sign of the nation of Israel, The Fish.

For long months, The Righteous and The Sabbath were separated in the sky, almost pinned in place, it seemed. Now that they have joined, they are inseparable.

That they appear very close to each other in the sky is rare, but still occurs perhaps three times within the life of a man. Now, Balthasar says, the key is to watch every month and see what happens next.

One more observation of note: Also at midnight, the constellation known as Cygnus, The Swan, was directly overhead. It is always easily identified during the summer months because its body is formed by a clearly seen cross shape of stars. (Ironic that something of such beauty as a celestial swan should be connected to something so evil that carries such shame and torment.)

The Swan's brightest star, known to the Jews as The Judge, gleamed as intensely as a signal fire. The Swan, Balthasar says, has always been regarded as the most regal of birds and prized for bringing celestial beauty down to the earth. Divine Beauty and a Great Judge only connect in the person of Messiah, Balthasar says, as when the prophet Isaias speaks of him as being named both Wonderful and Counselor.[105] And if the sign of The Swan is correct, we may hope that He is already on the wing, coming to put all things right.

In the middle of the noon meal Elisheba stooped to retrieve a spoon. Her water broke, and she went into labor. Mary went to fetch the midwives while Mama put Elisheba to bed.

Uncle Zachariah, who was no help at all, was banished to the house of the rabbi to study Scripture. It was more likely he paced the floor as he awaited the outcome. After nine months of silence, he still had not regained his speech, but his expression displayed both terror and anxious hope by turns. He patted Mary's shoulder as he left and laid a finger on his heart, as if to say she should not be afraid, even if he was. If a woman as old as Elisheba could do this, so could Mary.

It was a warm summer night. The little house of Elisheba and Zachariah was ablaze with light and activity.

On such a night as this, Mary thought of Yosef, wondered what was happening at home. She missed him tonight. Wished he were here to witness the miracle. Had he, being free of her, found someone else? Would Mary hear that the man she loved had married and moved away from Nazareth? What would become of her now that she had no husband to protect her?

The answers to the puzzle of her life were in the hands of Adonai. She believed that. Yes. And yet Mary did not turn from introspection. She resolved to search through to the bottom of her heart and clear the clutter of questions. What was important? What was not? Yosef was important, but Mary would not cling or beg him to believe her. She would not demand he love her. That decision also seemed important. The sky above Beth Karem radiated light. Mary craned her neck to take all the stars in. The path of The Milky Way was so luminous it cast shadows from trees and houses and the stone wall where Mary perched, but her eyes were on the stars, not the shadows.

Creation bathed in star pollen bloomed above her like thrones and great halls and shining spiral stairways leading up and up. Where, she wondered, in all that vastness, did the angel live who had spoken to her in the cowshed? It had not seemed as though he had come from a distant place, but rather as if he had stepped from a hidden room through a secret door into her small world.

The power of the Word that had spoken the universe into existence was beyond her ability to comprehend. And yet she encompassed the Word as it became flesh within her changing body.

Unconsciously she touched her abdomen as she prayed: "Nothing is impossible to you, you who formed me in my mother's womb.[106] Now my one heart beats for us both. It is a mystery, a wonder." Her gaze fixed on the brightest star in the heavens. "A baby is just as much a miracle as a star."

Hours passed. Women neighbors drifted into the yard to stand in knots and gossip. News from Jerusalem and Jericho was grim. There were brief whispers of speculation on the fate of Herod's popular sons, Alex and Ari. But the topic was one that struck terror so deeply in the hearts of even common folks that voices became almost inaudible.

The miracle of Elisheba giving birth—now there was something to consider! Silently Mary allowed herself to agree with a foolish woman who spoke aloud: "Surely this is some portent, some sign that Herod's tyranny will end!"

"Enough!" declared a gray-haired old woman named Hahvah. "Your life is like steam that rises from a hot dish. Say no more! The king has put a spell on the birds." Her finger jabbed the sky. "The birds carry your words and the wishes of the *am ha aretz* into the king's bedchamber. They sing him awake with plots and murders."

"We're only . . . wondering. Can't help but wonder. Elisheba being fifty-six. Who ever heard of a woman giving birth at fifty-six? Has to mean . . . something good."

The old woman scowled. "Sarah was ninety. Aye. And it was indeed a portent of something mighty in the heavens. But speak of it now, tonight, I warn you, and you'll bring death upon this house and upon Elisheba and upon her child!"

Everyone knew she was right. Silence descended. A collective shudder passed through them. Suddenly afraid, some hurried home without looking back. A handful remained, and the conversation sparked again and turned from politics and tyranny to life.

Mary listened as they talked, besting one another with horror stories of what they had endured when they had given birth. How, they inquired, would a woman as old as Elisheba survive when young women frequently died in childbirth?

"She's fifty-six years old by my mother-in-law's calculation! They were girls together!"

"Fifty-six! Think of it! Nursing a child at fifty-six!"

"As Hahvah says, such things do happen. Sarah. Ninety."

"Ninety! Think of it!"

"She's awfully quiet. Do you think she's died, God forbid? But still, it's awfully quiet."

"I remember my last pregnancy. The wee thing was reluctant to arrive. Hours and hours. Almost a full day. From one dawn to another. I shouted so loud they heard me in Egypt and said, 'That's another one of those Hebrew women giving birth, only this one doesn't have it so easy.'"

Contrary to expectation, there were no shouts of anguish from inside the house. Sometimes Mary heard Mama's voice speaking comfort and encouragement to Aunt Elisheba. Other times some instruction was given by one of the midwives.

After a time the chatter fell away. The older women straggled home to sleep in their own beds while Mary and a handful of others lay down to sleep on mats spread out beside the cyprus tree. Among the soft ticking of crickets in the vineyard Mary dozed. And as she did so, it seemed that the whole world and all the stars appeared to be waiting for something . . . longing for a new light to come on the wings of dawn.

A shriek reverberated throughout Herod's Jerusalem palace. Then more high-pitched, agonized cries careened around within the oval of the Hippodrome and bounced off the fan-shaped seating pavilion of the amphitheater. Another torrent of screams rebounded off the bluff west face of the Temple Mount.

Those in the streets of Jerusalem made the sign against the evil eye and hurried indoors. Those safely inside found themselves examining the bolts on their doors before they were fully awake and calling out to each other to check on their children.

Herod—minus wig and false beard, hunched over, panting in terror and trailed by his flapping nightdress—resembled a ninety-year-old crone instead of the monarch of Judea. His night guards, swords at the ready, rushed after him along the corridors, scanning for enemies but finding none.

Finally, out of breath from his screaming, eyes wide with fright, Herod collapsed beside a fountain in his garden. The king crouched next to the marble ring encircling the pool, darting fearful looks in all directions.

That was where Talmai, awakened by the screams and summoned by the captain of the guard, found him.

"Did you see her?" the king demanded of his steward. "Did you?"

"Who, Majesty?"

"Mariamme! Mariamme! My wife! Beside my bed! Calling my name!"

"A bad dream brought on by overwork and the cares of office," Talmai counseled.

Herod peered into the dark water and shuddered. His right hand stirred the smooth surface into agitated motion, as if he had been confronted by a pallid face floating on it. "She was there, I tell you!"

"Of course, Majesty. But let us get you back to bed. This night air . . . very dangerous to your health."

Stifling a whimper, Herod allowed himself to be raised to his feet and escorted back toward the royal apartments. "Her eyes," he moaned, staring into the black, cloud-covered sky in a way that raised the hair on the back of Talmai's neck. "Her eyes bored holes in me! I saw the marks on her neck! I never wanted her killed. You know that, Talmai! It wasn't what I wanted!"

Talmai murmured soothing sounds.

"She . . . she spoke to me, Talmai! She told me he is coming!"

Involuntarily Talmai responded, "Who, Majesty?"

"The rightful King! The true King, she said. The heir of David! When I asked her what I should do, she only stared at me and shook her head. She reproached me! Me, the king!"

The court physician met the entourage at the king's bedchamber. In a wineglass he poured twice the usual dose of myrrh and poppy juice and mixed it with sweet wine.

"Keep the torches lit!" Herod ordered. "And the guards with me in my room, Talmai. Light and guards, do you hear, Talmai?"

Herod, drugged into a stupor, was soon fast asleep.

Not so the rest of Jerusalem's inhabitants, most of whom whispered and shivered in their rooms, eager for daybreak.

CHAPTER 21

Dawn reddened the edges of the world. First light exploded over the mountains of Moab and reflected on the distant spires of the Temple just as a newborn's wail of protest erupted within the house. Asleep beneath the cyprus tree with four women who had come to watch and wait, Mary awoke suddenly. "The baby!"

As the others stirred, Mary clambered to her feet and ran to the open door of the house. Arms extended like wings, she clasped the lintels and drank in the cry like a hummingbird suspended before a blossom.

The child, so angry! The wail increased in volume, making the women who crowded in behind Mary twitter with nervous laughter.

"Such a voice, eh?"

"The bellow of a prophet!"

Mary called, "Mama!" And then again, "Mama! Is everything all right?"

Mama's weary face peered out from the back room. "Bless me! Bless all of us! It's a bright red, angry boy child with jet-black hair and hands like hammers and lungs so big he could shout from Jordan and be heard in Yerushalayim!"

Mary sagged with relief. So long! Eighteen hours of labor! "And Elisheba?"

Mama nodded and wiped her eyes. It had not been an easy delivery for old Elisheba. "Mary." Mama's voice was hoarse with exhaustion. "Run! Run to the rabbi's house! Fetch Zachariah. Tell him his prayers are remembered this dawn, and the Lord has answered. Tell him his wife and son live!"

Voices now continually whispered in Herod's head. Those that did not accuse him of lifelong evil warned him. They spoke of his complicity in so many needless deaths, suggesting his doom was sealed. They also offered him a bargain—the only price being his soul.

And piece by piece he paid his soul into the claws of the whisperers.

Herod believed there were plots against his life, and he would not be dissuaded. He filled his brooding hours with counterschemes—plans to ward off the threats he sensed all around.

Despite the absence of bright lights, the walls of Herod's throne room were garishly decorated with tapestries woven of gold and silver and red thread on black backgrounds. Hangings filling the spaces between jet-black stone columns portrayed lightning bolts flashing out of fiery heavens, striking earth in explosions of incandescence. Around the perimeter of the room, bronze shields surmounted by crossed spears frowned down.

The dais was raised almost head height above the surrounding dark red paving stones. Herod's throne, mounted on the platform, was carved of ebony inlaid with gold filigree. Its high back displayed an interwoven pattern of Jewish symbols: the menorah, the entry to the Temple as viewed through Nicanor Gate, a mysterious winged chest that suggested the Ark of the Covenant without actually copying it.

The setting caused spine-chilling, breath-stealing intimidation. If the Temple on the eastern mount represented the presence of El'Elyon, this chamber on the western hill symbolized the overwhelming presence of Herod, king of the Jews. Client-king of Rome though he might be, few of Herod's decisions were ever called into question by Caesar Augustus. And none of his decisions were *ever* questioned by any lesser being.

The monarch before whom Talmai was summoned in the broad light of day appeared entirely different from the terrified, deathly ill figure of the night before. Seated on his throne, arrayed in robes of gold and scarlet that flouted stiffly protruding shoulders, hair and beard oiled and gleaming, with a circlet of gold on his brow, Herod looked every inch the imperious monarch.

"Approach!" Herod thundered as Talmai entered the room.

The steward prostrated himself and remained on his face until Herod ordered him to rise. Then he stood, head bowed, listening to the king's commands. Though guards maintained their places in the corners of the room, Herod's words were for Talmai's ears alone. "I am king of the Jews—the only one. Any other is an imposter and a traitor. I am the true heir of David. Anyone who speaks otherwise speaks treason. My heirs are the inheritors of the promise. My line will sit on the throne of David forever. There must be no challenge to this and no possibility of challenging this. Like that old fool of a priest with his messianic visions! Take care of him. Him and all his family!"

Talmai's eyes risked a glance upward. He quickly tucked his chin even lower.

The king continued, "You know what is required. There must be no grounds for a dispute. See to it at once."

Dropping to one knee in token of acquiescence, Talmai waited until dismissed, then rose and backed from the room, bowing every ten steps. Once in the corridor outside and away from Herod's vision, the steward shook his head in disbelief.

He knew what the king commanded, knew what the order required him to do. But how to accomplish it without setting off a bloodbath that would cause the Romans to suppress the unrest that would surely follow?

Talmai also knew what he had seen in his momentary glance upward: the king's sickly pallor covered with makeup, the woven substitutes for hair and beard, and the madness in the eyes that not even Herod's drug-induced imperial demeanor could fully disguise.

What demons had Talmai's scheming unleashed?

Insistent knocking woke Onias from a sweet dream of Tovah.

"Onias! Onias!" Zadok's voice, urgent.

Where was Tovah? Where? Then Onias remembered everything.

"Onias! Brother!"

Onias sat bolt upright, shook the sleep from his head and, heart racing, bounded to throw open the door.

Zakok loomed in the portal. Shepherd's staff in hand, clothes filthy from work in the sheep pens, hair untidy, Zadok scowled at Onias. "Aren't y' goin' to let me in?"

"Come in. Yes, sorry."

Zadok pushed past him, kicked the door closed, and whirled around. "Look, Brother. I am myself and you are yourself. Y' never told me what to do—"

"Never dared. Sit down?"

"—and I never told y' what to do."

"Well, mostly." Onias pulled out a chair and offered it to Zadok. "Sit."

Zadok sat but did not let go of his staff. He rummaged in his leather pouch and took out a parchment scroll for Onias. "This is from your daughter. Rachel helped with the letters. She's a smart little sunbeam."

Onias nodded. "But that's not the only reason you came. Straight to it, then. You've awakened me before dawn. Why?"

"Ah, I said I never meddled in your business."

"Zadok." Onias toyed with the scroll. "What?"

Zadok peered over his shoulder, then went to the window and looked out. He lowered his voice. "There's rumors floatin' about."

"Always."

"That maybe Herod's unhappy with his sons."

"Who?"

"The two sons of Mariamme. She who Herod murdered. And now maybe he's suspectin' those two of some conspiracy. The same sons as have a child you're tutorin'."

"I can't help that. I wasn't hired by Herod."

Zadok jabbed the air with his index finger. "My very point! You're in the pay of someone *not* Herodian."

"Zadok, you know how wild this sounds? I'm teaching an eight-year-old boy to read Torah portions correctly."

"And him not even a Jew."

"What's that got to do with it?"

"Everythin', Brother. Here's the word. Herod is now heard to be claimin' that he's a descendant of David. He says he's the true son of David. Sittin' on David's throne. And any who tries to speak otherwise—" Zadok drew his finger across his throat. "Now, someone said you—my own brother—have been seen sneakin' in to the archives at night. That's the rumor."

Onias leaned forward, suddenly alarmed. "Who said such a thing?"

"Is it true?"

"Does it matter?"

"Yes, it matters! I don't want you assassinated. Even for the sake of what's true. Y' die, and the truth dies with you."

"Zadok! You must tell me how you came to hear such a thing."

"In the sheepfold. Fellows talkin'. 'What's this about your brother?' they says. And I ask them, what? And they say they heard some Herodian guards discussin' the brother of Zadok by name. That he's been seen pokin' into things he should not be pokin' into."

Onias rubbed both hands over his face. He tried to think who might have seen him.

"Aha!" Zadok exclaimed. "I see what you're doin'! Scubbin' your face like that! Just like when y' were a boy and guilty of somethin'. Tryin' to figure a way out of it!"

"Yes," Onias admitted, "guilty. But what does it mean? Why should it matter if I trace the records?"

Zadok snorted in derision. "Are y' altogether a fool? Y' know what it means. Herod's grandfather was an Edomite slave. A male priest in the temple of Ba'al. Or some such. The only ancestors Herod has in the archive of the Temple in Yerushalayim are listed under pollutions and desecrations! That's what! He'll kill you for what y' know. He'll kill y' twice if y' can prove what y' know. Onias, y' have a daughter! Will you be so careless when even raisin' your eyes to look at the wrong moment can get a man tortured and crucified?"

Onias steepled his fingers. "You're right. Of course you are. But this lad I tutor, Prince Alex's son, he's also called Alexander. Prince Alex happens to be the son of Mariamme . . . a descendant of Judah Maccabee, who took back the Temple from Antiochus Epiphanes. It's a noble lineage. I thought—"

"Y' thought! Y' didn't think! Do y' want to die?"

Onias smiled faintly. "Yes, sometimes. When I wake up and find Tovah isn't here. When I remember she's not coming back."

Zadok clapped him hard on the back. "You've got a daughter, Onias! Tovah's child she is too. And Tovah would want y' to live for Menorah, not die tryin' to make some point!"

CHAPTER 22

t midmorning Yosef, in the company of Heli and Mary's sisters, topped the rise that overlooked the town and vineyards of Beth Karem.

It was already hot. Heli mopped his brow and squinted into the sun. Raising his hand, he pointed to a small white dwelling surrounded by a crowd of perhaps two hundred people. "There, that's the place."

Yosef did not respond. So many milling about. Such a gathering rarely happened except for a wedding or a deathwatch or a funeral. It was clearly not a wedding.

Salome voiced her worry. "Papa? All the people! Do you think . . . ?"

Heli's lower lip jutted out in consternation. "God forbid, eh? Eh?"

Naomi, her sweet face suddenly a mask of fear, cried, "Oh, Papa! What if it's . . . Mama? or Mary?"

"No, Daughter. There must be some explanation."

Papa passed the water bag round the quartet. Then they pressed on down the swale and onto the rutted road, through the vineyard of Zachariah, until they reached the outer edges of an unusually quiet crowd.

Yosef strained to see over the heads of the people into the open front door. Where was Mary?

Heli, clearly shaken, inquired of a young man with a sparse beard and a sunburned face, "What's happened?"

"You haven't heard?" The fellow gestured toward the house.

Three women turned and shushed them.

Heli whispered, "We've come from the Galil. This is the house of my kinsmen. Tell me quickly. Who's dead?"

"Dead!" Four people spun around at the question. "Why no, sir! It's who's alive!"

"A baby boy!"

"Eight days ago!"

"A miracle, that's what!"

"A son born to old Zachariah and his wife, Elisheba!"

"Elisheba is fifty-six!"

". . . not since Sarah!"

". . . not since Hannah gave birth to the prophet Samu'el!"

"A miracle, that's what!"

A double handful of spectators shushed them to silence.

Heli persisted. "Why's everyone here? Why so solemn?"

The young man muttered, "A holy day, the eighth day. Today is the day of the circumcision. Inside. Rabbi's there. It's about to begin. You're just in time. We've come to see this baby, this wonder. A miracle! Right in our town! A sign from heaven some say! Zachariah, who is the father, and the rabbi will bring him out after the *Bris*, and we'll get to see him for ourselves."

"We're close kin to Zachariah and Elisheba," Heli insisted. "We've been on the road from Nazareth. We heard . . . well . . . we heard Elisheba was due any time. But hadn't heard the child was born. My wife, Anna, and daughter Mary are staying here."

"Mary and Anna! Of course!"

Heli introduced himself. "I'm Heli. This is Yosef, Mary's bridegroom. My daughters. Please, send the word into the household that Heli and Salome and Naomi and Yosef have arrived for the *Bris*."

There was a ripple as the information flowed forward. Only moments passed.

Anna's voice rang out from the entry to the house. "Heli? Yosef? Girls? Are you here?"

"Anna!"

"Mama!"

"Oh, Mama, we're here! Here!"

Anna instructed briskly, "Please . . . my family! Please! Let them pass!"

The crowd stirred and parted.

And there, beside Anna, Yosef saw Mary.

His breath caught at the sight. Beautiful. Beautiful. He had not let himself think of how beautiful she was since she had left for Beth Karem.

Chestnut hair tumbled over her shoulders. Oval face was framed by a pale blue shawl. Gold-flecked brown eyes locked onto Yosef's. Lips parted in a smile that seemed to say, *Well, Yosef, I'm glad you've come. About time!*

She nodded to him. Welcoming. Forgiving his unbelief. Genuinely glad to see him.

He exhaled loudly, ashamed of the anger he had felt toward her and suddenly in awe at the love he saw in her eyes.

She mouthed the words, *Shalom, Yosef!*

Yosef replied in kind. *Shalom.*

They worked their way through the tight human corridor. At the door Anna embraced Heli and her daughters, then turned her attention to Yosef. Eyes shining, Anna confided, "Yosef . . . she always hoped you'd come. That you'd be here to witness this."

Mary gave him an amused sideways smile. "Come on then, Yosef. You're almost late for the *Bris.*" She tugged Yosef's sleeve, pulling him after her into the packed little house.

Mary walked through the crowd gathered in the courtyard of the little house for the *Bris Milah*. Yosef followed close behind. All the old feelings of tenderness—emotions nearly forgotten—awoke again. She was his. Pretty, bright, with a laugh like a song. Everyone liked her. And she was his!

She held her head erect, chin high, smiling, confident in herself. Yosef knew she would have been the same even if he had not come to

Beth Karem. Even without him, even if he had broken off the engagement, Mary would not have seemed alone.

Highly favored. Her joy in that designation was not manifested by arrogance but rather by a kind word for everyone present, a pat on the shoulder, eyes that met another's gaze and connected.

And she is my own to love and protect, Yosef told himself as he noticed admiration in the expressions of other young men when they watched her move. Mary took her place between her mother and the elderly woman Yosef guessed was Elisheba, mother of the infant. Elisheba was pale and frail-looking, as new mothers often were at the circumcisions of their sons. Mary put a hand beneath Elisheba's elbow to support her.

The baby's father, Zachariah, chin tucked, lips curved in a half smile, held the infant in his arms at the side of the rabbi. The chair upon which the circumcision would take place was called The Chair of the Prophet Elijah. It was covered with a wine-colored cloth embroidered with a gold Star of David and the letters of Elijah's name. Flint knife, a cruse of oil, and a cup of wine were laid out on a table. The unsuspecting baby boy, naked, stump of the umbilical cord still attached to his round belly, pedaled the air with scrawny newborn legs.

The rabbi, a venerable, wizened man half the size of Zachariah, raised tremulous hands to silence the whispers of the onlookers. Yosef was unsure he would want a fellow who looked as old as Abraham cutting away the foreskin of his boy!

"So." The voice of the rabbi quaked. "Now are we all here? Eh? All here?" He looked up at the father, who merely nodded his assent to proceed but did not speak.

"All right then. Elisheba, daughter of Avraham. Like Hannah, the mother of Samu'el, the prophet of King David, here is a miracle, eh? A miracle in your life."

"Yes." The old woman's eyes glistened as she stared down at her son. "Praise to the Lord. A miracle."

"Well then. Eight days ago the Lord brought forth a much-desired son to the household of Zachariah, our brother, and Elisheba, our sister. And here is the miracle." He clasped a tiny foot in his hand. "So, baby, what took you so long, eh? Your mama and papa have been waiting for you for forty years. We come to welcome you into the Covenant of Avraham. We are here to give you a name by which you will remember to serve the Lord your God. As we do with every circumcision, we now invite the prophet Elijah to join us."

The baby let out a long, joyful coo as Zachariah placed him in the seat of the chair, as if in the very lap of the prophet Elijah who, it was said, held every child as he was circumcised.

Laughter rippled through the crowd, with those near the back passing on the rabbi's words to those waiting outside the house.

The rabbi waited a beat, then continued, picking up the flint knife. "I think there have never been so many happy people gathered for *Bris Milah* in all my years as rabbi of Beth Karem. Zachariah and Elisheba, when I was a young rabbi, you stood beneath the marriage chuppah before me and took your vows. I hoped with you for many years to see this day. And then when hope died, I counseled you to accept the will of the Most High without bitterness. Now here is the proof that nothing is impossible for God.

"Elisheba, your name means 'El Hears.' Zachariah, your name means 'Yah Remembers.' The Lord has done both those things for you. He has heard. He has remembered. It is said, 'A good name is rather to be chosen than good oil.' One should examine names carefully in order to give his child a name that is worthy so they may become righteous, for sometimes a name is a contributing factor for good or for evil. Zachariah, father of this baby, has been a righteous man for all the years I have known him since his youth. This baby could have no better name to carry on than the name of his father. Since Zachariah no longer has a voice to speak, we shall ask the baby's mother. Elisheba, by what name will this son of Israel be known?"

Elisheba spoke loudly and without hesitation, "We will call him . . . Yochanan."

A splash of surprise spread in a wave throughout the guests.

"Yochanan, did she say?"

"No one in the family is named Yochanan."

"Who was Yochanan?"

Yosef noted the serene look on Mary's face. She leaned in to encourage Elisheba as twitters of disapproval squeaked out the door and into the spectators in the yard.

The rabbi raised both hands. "No, no, Elisheba. You see, my dear, in the naming of a son—especially a firstborn—it is customary he be named after the father. The *shem ledosh*, 'the religious name,' you see, named after a near relative."

Elisheba was adamant. "His name is Yochanan."

The rabbi persisted. "You see . . . tradition, eh? Someone in your line. Yochanan is a fine name, to be sure. Yochanan. 'Yahweh Favored' is the meaning. But neither you nor Zachariah is related to Yochanan, one of David's mighty warriors. Tradition, you see?"

Elisheba insisted. "Yahweh *has* favored. And his name *is* Yochanan."

The corners of the rabbi's mouth turned down. Lower lip jutted out in protest. He looked at the baby's father. "Zachariah, your wife insists the child be called by a name not in your family line. A venerable name, true, but not according to tradition."

Zachariah mimed the act of writing, asking for a wax tablet to communicate his wishes. It was brought to him after a delay of only a moment.

The baby still happily flailed in the air with arms and legs, like a swimmer crossing the river on his back.

Here and there Yosef heard whispered discussion of the inappropriateness of Elisheba's choice of names and the fact that Zachariah was mute.

Zachariah opened the lid of the tablet and pressed the stylus into the wax. With a satisfied nod he passed it to the rabbi, who read the words aloud.

"The father says . . . Zachariah instructs . . . he has written, HIS NAME IS YOCHANAN."[107]

The old cleric passed the tablet on, and it circulated from hand to hand as evidence. As Yosef read the letters pressed into the wax, an unexplained warmth passed through him. It meant something, this name! Yosef passed it on.

"Well? Well then, the word of the father. So, child of the covenant, your name is Yochanan. Yahweh has favored Zachariah and Elisheba with this gift." The rabbi confirmed Yosef's thoughts, announcing to all the witnesses as he took up the flint knife, "Yochanan! Your name is the very name of the one who served in the temple Solomon built in Yerushalayim. He who stood as witness as the Shekinah Glory of the Lord came down from heaven and filled the Temple. Yochanan. May you be worthy of such a great name. In your lifetime may the glory of the Lord fill the Temple once again!"

With deft hands the rabbi circumcised the baby, who opened his mouth and wailed a protest. Elisheba's knees buckled at the sight of her baby's blood. There was a cheer from the onlookers as the rabbi dipped his finger in the wine in order to place it on the child's lips to seal the covenant. Zachariah placed his hand on the rabbi's arm and stopped him. He shook his head vigorously, indicating wine must not touch the infant's lips.

Zachariah lifted his son high into the air to show him to everyone.

And then the most remarkable thing happened. Zachariah, mute for almost ten months, began to sing in a strong baritone voice so beautiful and clear that even those outside heard him plainly:

"Praise! All praise be given to Adonai, the God of Israel,
because He has come and redeemed His people!
He has raised up a horn
of salvation for us
in the house of His servant David,
as He said through His holy prophets long ago!
Salvation from our enemies
and from the hand of all! From all who hate us!
He has done this mighty thing
to show mercy to our fathers
and to remember His holy covenant!
He remembers the oath He swore to our father Avraham:
to rescue us from the hand of our enemies,
and to enable us to serve Him without fear . . . aye!
To serve Him without fear
in holiness and righteousness before Him all our days!"[108]

Zachariah gently kissed the face of the baby, wrapped him in his prayer shawl, then brushed his cheek with his thumb. Instantly the cry of the infant fell silent. Yochanan reached up and grasped his father's beard in two tiny fists.

Zachariah sang gently into the face of the little one who seemed to be earnestly listening to his father's every word—holding on, intent to hear it all:

"And you, my child, will be called a prophet of the Most High;
for you will go on before the Lord to prepare a way for Him,
to give His people the knowledge of salvation
through the forgiveness of their sins.
Because of the tender mercies of our God,
by which the rising sun, our dawn, will come to us from heaven
to shine on those living in darkness
and in the shadow of death,
to guide our feet into the path of peace."[109]

It was sunset. Scarlet plumes spread up from the west and illuminated the eastern mountaintops.

Yosef walked slowly beside Mary. He longed to hold her hand in his like a captive bird, but he did not. Her head reached not quite to his broad shoulder. Her smallness made him seem bigger, somehow, than he had ever thought himself to be.

She said, "It won't be easy."

"I want to take care of you."

"I think . . . there is some danger."

"I want to protect you . . . both of you."

"I don't know what it all means, Yosef. Herod. Those men at the Temple—the men Herod put in power. I'm not afraid of them, not now. But we'll have to be careful, you know?"

Yosef nodded. The sky ripened, bloodred, like banners above a marching army. But there was no army, only the two of them: Yosef and Mary, sharing the deep secrets of dreams and visions and angelic visits.

"I'll take care of you, Mary. I will."

"Everything must seem so . . . ordinary. Even though we both know the truth of it, Yosef."

"A wedding."

"Yes, but—"

Tenderness and knowledge coursed through him. "I understand. You'll come live with me. And I'll . . . take care of you."

"For his sake. Ordinary, as though it's nothing at all. You and I, and soon, our little son. That's what they must believe or . . . you know what they will do."

"Yes. It came to me when I saw you. What would happen to him if . . . if I don't take care of you."

"You're such a good man, Yosef. Easy to love. Good with children. I still don't know why . . . me."

"Can't you see it? I saw it, always. But I didn't know what it meant . . . that I loved you so. Or how big it is. Or that God took notice of you too. I should have believed you."

"Little wonder that you doubted."

"I mean us, you and me. Ordinary, you know."

"I didn't ask the angel why."

"It is what it is." Yosef clasped her hand and placed it over his heart. "I can wait for you. Love you always. Through everything. Anything. My life, that's what I offer you . . . and him. And if it means giving up my life . . . yes. Even then, it's yours."

CHAPTER 23

Talmai and a handpicked squad of Herodian guards marched up the great viaduct leading to the Temple Mount. To the beat of a muffled drum, the ring of armed men carrying torches escorted a score of chained, gagged, and hooded prisoners.

For several days prior to this expedition, the word had gone out that rebels were abroad in the city. A dusk-to-dawn curfew was imposed, with instant imprisonment promised to any who violated the clamp-down.

Much of Herod's reign had been free from banditry in Jerusalem because he imposed crucifixion for even minor offenses. Given the recent civil disturbances over the border in Nabatea and the attacks on Jewish caravans coming through Trachonitis, there was no reason to doubt either the warnings or the threat. Jerusalemites stayed indoors after dark.

All of Jerusalem was afraid of the king of the Jews. But no matter what Herod claimed or how much he blustered, he could not make himself the heir to the promise of a coming Jewish Mashiyah, the Anointed One. Herod, both the supporter and beneficiary of Rome, had never troubled himself over that prophecy . . . until lately.

Now, it seemed, even as the fires of Herod's life burned low, the spark of messianic expectation was everywhere.

Herod's one recourse was clear: If he could not make himself the most fitting heir—one who was born of the tribe of Judah and an offspring of King David—then the only alternative was to eliminate any means by which others could press their claims.

After crossing the causeway, the soldiers prodded their stumbling charges down the steps leading to the archives under the Great Portico at the south end of the Temple Mount platform. A pair of Levite guards was stationed there, but these were easily frightened away. Almost immediately after their departure, alarm bells rang in the night and trumpets sounded.

"No time to waste!" Talmai ordered. "Get on with it."

Half of the contingent of troopers raced through the archives till they reached the section where all the genealogical records were kept. Once there, they pushed over the shelves of clay jars. Pottery crashed down and shattered. Within a space of minutes the aisle was cluttered with scrolls, scraps of parchment, and shredded papyrus. The captain of the squad dumped the contents of an oil lamp over the heap, then thrust in his torch.

The other marauders did the same.

Flames leapt up to the cedar-lined ceiling. The dry sheepskins and desiccated pressed reeds made excellent fodder for the fire. The conflagration required no further urging. It devoured the scrolls, licked walls and ceiling, and roared for more. The intensity forced the soldiers back into the entry corridor, where screams of terror and agony met their ears.

The other body of Herodian troopers was not idle. At Talmai's command they hacked and slashed at the chained prisoners. The members of Herod's specially chosen, Idumean-born force laughed at the antics of the blindfolded Jewish prisoners trying to escape blows coming at them from all sides.

It was over in a matter of minutes. All the "rebels" were dead, slaughtered to a man. Removing hoods and chains took only minutes more, as did scattering a selection of swords and daggers among the bodies.

Frantic priests at last made their appearance. "Rebels," Talmai reported tersely. "We killed them all. But hurry! We'll help you fight the fire!"

With much effort the damage to the Great Portico was confined to the archive chamber. If the fire had spread beyond it or to the floor above it, the entire south end of the Temple complex might have collapsed.

Even so, all the known Jewish genealogy records were destroyed. Every remembered connection since David—every tribe, every clan, every line of descent that had been painstakingly saved from the destruction of Jerusalem back in the days of the Babylonian Nebuchadnezzar—was now lost forever.

When Talmai made his report to Herod, the king had two responses: First he ordered all the soldiers who participated in the night's event marched to the harbor at Ashkelon. There they would board a galley bound for Cyprus. Once on the island they would guard the slaves working Herod's copper mines. It would be difficult for the truth about the "rebels" to get back to Jerusalem anytime soon.

Herod's other comment, overheard by an increasingly alarmed Talmai, was actually directed at King David. "You can keep your tomb now. I will keep your throne."

A week after the circumcision of baby Yochanan, Yosef and Mary's family prepared to return home to Nazareth. There would be a wedding soon, Heli announced during an early supper, and Zachariah, Elisheba, and their new son must come to Nazareth for the celebration.

After supper, as the women cleaned up and Heli dozed, Zachariah asked Yosef to walk with him to check the vines that grew in the valley of Beth Karem.

The sun was still a handbreadth above the western ridge. Plenty of time, Zachariah explained, to share everything that had happened almost ten months ago in the Temple.

Zachariah finished his account as they strolled amid the lush, dark green rows to the far end of the vineyard. "And so I challenged the angel. 'How will I know?' I asked. As if his appearance wasn't enough to convince me. I could not have been more insolent if I had shaken my fist in his face and called him a liar. I suppose he could have struck me dead right then and there. But instead he shut my mouth. Made me mute. I could not speak about the miracle. Until the miracle . . . my son . . . received the name the Almighty had chosen for him."[110]

Yosef, hands clasped behind his back as they strolled, nodded and nodded again. "All of this . . . I'm glad to hear it all. I mean, your part of the story. You confirm everything Mary said."

"And you do believe her." It was not a question. Neither was it a command.

"Not at first. I didn't at first. But now, with all this—you, Elisheba, the baby. And even before, I've had dreams. Dreams of . . . holy things."

"As it's written by the prophet Joel, *'I will pour out My Spirit on all people. Your sons and daughters will prophesy, your old men will dream dreams, your young men will see visions.'*"[111] Zachariah paused and examined a cluster of grapes. Plucking a bunch, he offered them to Yosef. "Now the people of Israel are the ripe fruit hanging on the vine. Sweet and ready for the table. This is the hour Father Avraham longed to see. And we are part of it."

Yosef stared at the orange sun slipping away in the west. "Growing up I heard so many things. Heard my father's prayers morning and night. Messiah was always just a dream, a shadow."

Zachariah gestured toward the lengthening shadow of a tree stretching across the ground. "Shadows are the outline of something solid, something real. The coming of Messiah is more real than the earth beneath our feet. Yosef, you are named for Yosef, dreamer of dreams. Named for the fellow who saved his family when they fled to Egypt.[112] It's right the Lord would speak to you in dreams."

"Perhaps the dreams are a kindness to me. I'm not as courageous as Mary. Or you. If I'd seen the being you described, I would have died from fright, and that would be the end of it."

"And do you trust your dreams? Like Yosef of old, do you believe the Lord speaks to you?"

"I do."

"Good. You must, Yosef. These are dangerous times. You've heard the news from Yerushalayim. I won't speak more than that. Dangerous times. So, for Mary's sake and the sake of the child, you must keep your spirit in trim and listen to your dreams. Believe the warnings when the word of the Lord comes to you. You must act without hesitation."

The two men walked on in silent contemplation beyond the vineyard to heaps of limestone rubble and a cave with a wooden door set within its walls to seal the entrance. Beside the cavern was an ancient quarry. A reservoir of water stood in the deep hole where blocks had been removed. The depths of the pit were already swallowed in pools of shadow.

Streamers of clouds soared out of the sunset, carrying pink and orange fire into the purpling twilight.

"Do you know what this place is?" Zachariah asked, tugging at his beard.

"A tomb?"

"An old quarry. There, in the cavern, is where I store my wine."

Yosef laughed with relief.

"In the Temple the stones of the sloping ascent and of the high altar are from the valley of Beth Karem." Encouraged by Yosef's smile of surprise, Zachariah continued, "Judah Maccabee tore down the original altar after Antiochus offered a swine on it. Those defiled stones were hidden in a place set apart until the Holy One of Israel will come and purify them."

Yosef skimmed a flat pebble across the still water and watched with pleasure as it skipped five times before sinking out of sight. "Stored? Does anyone know where?"

"There may be one of the guardians still alive. Herod has killed so many. So many of the ancient secrets are lost." Zachariah paused and slapped his hand against the oak-planked entry to the wine storage. "They dug into the soil and brought out virgin stones, undamaged, upon which iron had not been lifted, because iron was made to destroy men and the altar was made to save men. A man had his leg crushed by a block in Yerushalayim, so it was abandoned, never used. They dug out another from here. The one chosen as a replacement is now the cornerstone of the altar."

Zachariah patted the smooth surface of the oak-paneled entry. "The boulders from my wine cavern are in the Temple. They are whitened twice a year: once at Passover and once again at the Feast of Tabernacles."

The old man stared down into the dark, muddy water of the quarry pool. A spiral of dust spun off by the departing sun brushed their robes.

"But now this latter altar has likewise been defiled," Zachariah said, "by Herod's priests, who do not know or serve the Lord. They offer sacrifices for heathen kings, and the man on David's throne is not even a son of Israel. It is time for the Deliverer to come and purify the altar stones of the House of the Vine. As Maccabee said, 'One is coming who will cleanse the Temple once and for all and put all things right. He will cleanse the high altar so it will never be defiled again.'"

Taking Yosef's elbow, Zachariah directed their path back toward home, now dimly seen as a single amber glow against a black backdrop.

"Yes," Yosef agreed. "I know the prophecies."

"Listen to me, my friend. This is treacherous business I'm speaking of. Not some fantasy about a golden age. The very existence of an heir to David's throne is high treason against Herod and Rome. Deadly business. Deadly for the boy you will raise as your own. And for the tiny baby who is my son. What a fearsome task they're destined to accomplish for the Lord of Hosts. To purify the altar once and for all."

"I'll protect him. I've thought it through. I'll buy a sword. And you? Have you thought what you might do to protect your son?"

"We'll leave this place. Elisheba and I and the baby. Go over the Jordan with him. To the desert." Zachariah gazed sadly over the darkened vineyards he had worked for a lifetime. "This will be our last harvest here." He spread his hands. "Yosef, the wine in this cellar is famous as the wine created in the womb of the earth where the altar stones were born. I want you and Mary to take this year's vintage . . . for your wedding."

"I . . . I'm not a rich man, Zachariah. Such fine wine for a wedding in Nazareth! It's Temple wine. I . . . I can't—"

"Listen! Yosef, I offer it to The One who is in Mary's womb. Like the stones from this virgin soil were taken to Yerushalayim, Messiah is called the Cornerstone of the Temple.[113] The holy wine from Beth Karem must be my first offering to him."

"Such a blessing! I won't refuse such a blessing!"

"Good. Good. It's settled. Only the best wine for the wedding of Yosef and Mary. We will toast the son yet to come, eh?" Zachariah and Yosef clasped hands on the bargain. "Yes, but there's more. Now hear me, Yosef. From his first breath the son of Mary will be a target. Herod. The high priest. Others, too, will hate him and want him dead. Know this, Yosef. You are a man of great physical strength. Such a grip you have. An oak. A man who can fell a tree or a man with equal ease. So! Listen to your dreams. Believe you are called to be strong in the task which is set before you. Yes. Buy your sword and sharpen it. Wear it even beneath your prayer shawl."

CHAPTER 24

A full moon illuminated the streets of Jerusalem as Onias walked home. Its light was almost enough to use for reading. It would not be possible to travel secretly anywhere tonight.

Onias had dined with his friend, Simeon the Elder, at Simeon's home in the Ophel Quarter. Over a quiet supper of hummus, flatbread, and olives, Onias shared his grief, his loneliness, Zadok's warnings, and the conclusions Onias had reached in his nocturnal research.

Simeon had been full of comfort and reassurance. "I tell you, Onias, Messiah, the Consolation of Israel, is coming soon. My old bones remind me every morning and night of my age, but my heart has the joy of a bridegroom's expectation!"

Onias smiled at the memory. Like one waiting for a royal procession still out of sight but already heard approaching up a grand avenue, Simeon truly had the assurance of one waiting confidently for the King to appear. The old man had no fear of either those who would oppose the Branch, the Son of David, or of reaching the end of his life disappointed.

Simeon had perfect peace.

Onias wished that quality of heart for himself.

A thin spear of high clouds stabbed the moon, fracturing but not diminishing its glow. Shadows of buildings and overhanging terraces were in high relief. The black shapes cast by the moon were as solid seeming as their real counterparts.

A few steps from home Onias turned his face toward the Temple. What changes would happen when the One Who Restores All Things cleansed the priesthood of the paid lackeys of Herod?

The sheen bouncing off the glistening marble was dazzling to see. So bright was the reflection that Onias lost his night vision from the glare. He paused to let his sight clear before proceeding . . . and saw a hooded figure standing directly in his path, where no one had been seconds earlier.

Onias, startled, gasped, "What do you want?"

"Not here," the unknown replied, grabbing Onias by the elbow. "Inside, quickly."

No knife slipped between Onias' ribs. Not an assassin then. Soldiers come to arrest him would not be so mysterious. What was this?

Onias, propelled by the other's urgency, unlatched and pushed open his door. A single lamp flickered on his desk. Onias strode toward it as if it were a weapon to be seized. He heard the door close behind him. The tutor used the flame to ignite another, bigger lamp, then turned. "Again, who are you and what—"

With an imperious jerk of both hands the figure tossed the hood back from his face.

"Prince Alex!"

Outside Onias' house two black-robed figures slipped out of the shadows and approached the small window beside the door. While one kept watch, the other listened intently to the conversation inside.

Alex, heir to the Hasmonean kings, explained, "My wife says you can be trusted, Tutor. Is she right?" His eyes bored into Onias.

The tutor set his jaw and nodded.

Their gazes remained locked for a beat; then Alex likewise nodded. "I believe you. I've had you followed to see if you reported to anyone, but apart from speaking without caution to that old fool Simeon, you seem to be what you appear . . . an honest man."

So that was the source of the shadowy figures! Onias bowed. What was this about?

"My father believes I plan to murder him and usurp his throne, or so my father's barber warns me. I may be arrested at any moment. I have written to Caesar, asking for asylum for my brother and myself in Rome until this can get straightened out. If things don't . . ." The prince drew himself up, squaring his shoulders. He untied a leather pouch from his belt and tossed it to the table, where it landed with a substantial *thud*. "Money. Use it to save my wife and children, if . . ." Alex shrugged. "You'll know when it's needed."

Pulling the hood of his cloak back up, Alex turned toward the door, then pivoted back when Onias said, "Prince Alex, you already know that your wife's letter was stolen from my home. You know that I am suspected of being a rebel. My assistance may harm you . . . and may harm my daughter. She's all I have left."

The eyes Onias now regarded were haggard and without hope. "I also have children," the prince said. "Besides you, there is no one else we can trust."

As Onias' door creaked on its pole hinge and turned outward, the watchers slipped away into the nearest pool of shadow. Alex, emerging cautiously, looked all around before proceeding but did not see them.

After he passed, they followed like wraiths, away into the night, back toward the palace.

Ecbatana, Kingdom of Parthia
29th year of King Phraates IV
Journal of Court Astronomer Melchior
Second New Moon after the Summer Solstice[114]

It has happened! Exactly what Balthasar predicted has come to pass! The wandering star known as The Sabbath has reversed direction and is definitely once again closing the gap between itself and Jupiter, The Righteous.

For the past week I have been in great anxiety because of an enormous, unrelenting dust storm. This great cloud of choking brown sand blew up out of the south. It obscured the sky as badly as the densest clouds and made the air so hard to breathe that it was difficult to walk abroad by either day or night.

Indeed, Balthasar is not with me tonight because the foul dust has been very hard on his lungs. Esther forced him to stay home, much against his wishes.

I fought my way up to my post without any real expectation of success. Then, just at sunset, the wind died away. The heavens cleared in time for me to see the sign of The Virgin descending just as twilight ended.

Between two and three hours later the event I have been hoping for occurred: The two bright lights in the sign representing the nation of Israel are once again heading toward a close conjunction. At midnight they stood due south of me.

United again, true Righteousness and true Sabbath rest for the Jews! It must be significant! It must! I can't wait to tell Balthasar and Esther. Something powerful is happening! The One God, whom I serve, is at last letting His plan unfold.

"Arrest them all, Talmai!" Herod's order reverberated down the halls, accompanied by a high-pitched shriek as Trypho the Barber was dragged away. "Take all the soldiers you need."

Herod's outburst resulted from Talmai's latest and most damning report on his sons' disloyalty. "Appeal to Caesar? I see through their plot! Alex and his brother are trying to usurp my throne, Talmai! Crush their conspiracy! Crush it at once!"

Talmai, trailing after the raging king, jogged to keep up. Now that his plot had reached its climax, Talmai struggled to keep the king's rage confined within limits that would not bring the *am ha aretz* to armed insurrection. Herod would be satisfied, the steward reasoned, if he saw his bloody revenge take effect near at hand.

Then the rest of the kingdom would remain peaceful.

"I'll send word to confine your sons to their wing of the palace," Talmai suggested. "For the rest, there are a hundred who are guilty, including the tutor of your grandson."

A sneer played across Herod's pinched and scowling features. "Don't bother arresting the likes of him! Make an example of him, Talmai! Let Yerushalayim be too afraid to even think of rebelling against me!"

CHAPTER 25

Such a good evening to be married, nu?" Mama smoothed the fabric of Mary's pale blue gown, then clasped her shoulders and kissed her cheek. "He's a fine fellow, Yosef is."

"Oh, Mama! Always. He is . . . Yosef is the best . . . wonderful. Best for me. For us."

Salome piped up, "He's sweating all right. Naomi and I saw him on our way home. Three lambs on the spit. He was worried they would not be cooked through in time for the banquet. And he's pale as death."

Mary laughed. "Poor Yosef."

Mama offered no comment other than a *hmm* as she continued fussing with Mary's wedding clothes. It seemed almost as though this were just any wedding. Mama arranged the veil and placed a woven crown of summer roses on Mary's head. "Now, let us have a look."

Mary spread her arms and turned slowly around for her sisters and mother to peruse the dress. The fabric was fine Egyptian linen bought by Yosef in Jerusalem. Mama and Mary had made four dresses from the material—one for Mama, matching garments for Salome and Naomi, and Mary's wedding gown. A vine of rosebuds was embroidered on the cuffs of Mary's sleeves, her hem, and her neckline.

Salome and Naomi crooned their approval. Was there ever a groom so wonderful as Yosef? To consider wedding clothes also for Mama and the younger sisters! Had any bride ever been so beautiful as Mary? Was any bride ever so beloved by her bridegroom as Mary was by Yosef?

And there was still no outward evidence of pregnancy. Mary unconsciously touched her abdomen. Slim and lithe in her lovely dress, Mary looked the perfect bride. Neither Papa nor Yosef would be ashamed tonight.

The bride's house was thick with the scent of flowers gathered and arranged for two days by Naomi and Salome. Yosef's house was also decked out for the celebration of the wedding feast.

Naomi peeked out the door of Mary's room and hissed, "The musicians are waiting. James and Papa are talking. Papa looks very edgy. He has been practicing his lines for days."

Mama smiled. "He'll know his lines by heart by the time you're wed, Naomi. Five girls. Your papa should know his lines."

Because Yosef's ancestral home was in Judea, the wedding followed the customs of Judea rather than those of the Galil. There were two friends of the groom. During the wedding each waited upon the bride and groom, presenting gifts and making announcements to the guests. Mary's first cousin James, and Yosef's best friend, Tevyah, held the honored positions. Before the wedding James had served as the intermediary between Yosef and Mary, carrying notes back and forth for two weeks.

Now James knocked softly on Mary's door and called, "Mary, virgin daughter of Heli and Anna, I come with word. The papa awaits his daughter. The musicians are at the door. The bridegroom sends me with a message for his beloved bride. Yosef says, 'Mary, everything is made ready for you, my bride. The chuppah, the wedding canopy, is ready.' Yosef, the groom, says, 'The great wedding feast of my beloved is prepared.' The lamb is cooked. *Three* lambs, he cooked. There is plenty of food. Everything. Very nice. Enough for everyone. There is sweet wine from the vineyards of the bride's uncle in Beth Karem. The guests have arrived. There are gifts. The bridegroom, Yosef, says, 'I await my beloved bride.'"

Naomi and Salome were *bene chuppah*, the children of the

bridechamber who would carry the lanterns at the head of the procession through Nazareth, which would end at Yosef's house.

"Well." Salome's eyes shone with excitement. "I guess the lambs are cooked. Are you ready, Sister? Only three days left until Shabbat, and we can all rest!"

The wedding of Mary and Yosef was being held on the customary evening of Wednesday. This gave the families of bride and groom three days after Sabbath to prepare for the ceremony. It further allowed the groom to bring a charge at the Thursday morning meeting of the local Sanhedrin if his bride was found not to be a virgin. If all was well, the celebration would continue for three days more until Sabbath.

Mama gave Mary the bouquet of roses that matched her crown. "I love a good wedding. Nothing like a wedding!"

"Me too. Especially this one." Mary, her full lips curved slightly in a smile of pleasure, nodded.

Naomi opened the door.

At the sight of her a cry of approval rose from Papa, James, and the rabbi. Applause erupted from the rabbi's wife and a crowd of female relatives and friends who had come to escort her through the streets of Nazareth.

The music began. Papa, eyes brimming with pride, kissed her, then offered her back to Mama, who would accompany her on the journey. Naomi and Salome darted out of the house and took up lanterns hung from the end of long poles. And the procession began. Mary and her mother were surrounded by about two hundred women. Musicians—singers and flute and tambourine players—followed.

"You have ravished my heart, my sister, my bride!
You have ravished my heart
with a glance of your eyes!"[115]

Behind the female contingent were the rabbi, the groomsman and his escorts, and Papa, marriage contract clutched in his fist.

"How sweet is your love, my sister, my bride!
How much better is your love than wine,
and the fragrance of your perfume than any spice!"[116]

Lamps burned in every window of Nazareth in honor of the bride. Everyone liked Mary. Everyone liked Yosef. It was a good match! A perfect match! True? Of course true!

"A garden locked is my sister, my bride;
a spring enclosed, a fountain sealed!"[117]

Who had not noticed how Yosef looked at her with such longing and adoration?

Or Mary blushing with pleasure every time he was near?

She was happy and gregarious.

He was silent, strong, solemn—in need of a woman who would make him laugh.

A match made in heaven, the women of Nazareth declared when they had gossiped at the well upon hearing about the betrothal. Something like Jacob and Rachel. A love match.

Little did they know how right they were, Mary thought as she walked slowly through her hometown in a ritual as old as Israel.

The match had indeed been made in heaven!

". . . a garden fountain,
a well of living water,
and flowing streams of Lebanon."[118]

Yosef's hair was damp as he stood fidgeting at the far edge of the market square. The music of the procession advanced through Nazareth with the well as their destination. Four young men, cousins and friends from his guild, carrying the wedding canopy, waited with him as was the custom. Behind the groomsmen the males of Nazareth gathered to await the approach of the bride and her family.

Tevyah, first friend of the groom, clapped Yosef on the back so hard the crown of flowers slipped down on his brow. "You'll survive the night, Yosef," Tevyah teased.

His companions laughed. "It isn't the wedding. It's the forty years that follow."

"Such a beauty he's getting! An angel from heaven is not so beautiful! This is your night!"

Blood rushed in Yosef's ears. Beads of perspiration trickled into his eyes. "Tevyah, please. Stop trying to cheer me up." Only a handful of people close to Mary knew the truth of the circumstances behind this wedding: Mary's parents and siblings, her uncle and aunt. No one else. Not even the rabbi knew about Gabriel speaking to Mary or about Yosef's dreams.

"Yosef! Calm down. Lucky fellow. She's pretty. She's bright. She's worthy of you. She'll live up to all your hopes, eh?"

Yosef did not tell Tevyah he had no fears about Mary's character, but rather about his own. Was he worthy of this awesome task? Was he strong enough to do all that was required of him in such an undertaking? to rear the promised Son of David? to be the sort of father who could teach a prince to be the king of Israel? "She is so wonderful. Who am I? I'm just a carpenter, Tevyah."

"So, a carpenter doesn't deserve happiness?"

Yosef closed his eyes and silently prayed, *O Adonai, if this is wrong, strike me with lightning now where I stand. Don't let me fail! Spare Tevyah, please, who's so near . . . but don't let me marry her if I can't do all you require! I'm not worthy of such a great task. Not strong enough! Who am I that you would appoint me her protector? Who am I that you would appoint me as* his *guardian?*

As the bride's procession approached the corner, Tevyah prompted, "Ready? Ready, Yosef? We go out to meet her, eh? Right. Remember?" Tevyah nudged the groom. "Onward, Yosef. Move your feet. Meet the bride at the well, yes? Like Mosheh met his wife, eh? Like Yacov met Rachel at the well. Almost . . . right! Ready?"

The lamps, swinging on staves held by Naomi and Salome, appeared first at the far end of the market square on the opposite side of the well. The music and clapping seemed almost deafening to Yosef. Tevyah gave him a shove to get him moving. Yosef's heartbeat matched the pulse of the drums as they set out to meet the bride.

Yosef could barely focus his eyes. What was he doing? Was he crazy? How could he ever live up to such a responsibility? Marriage was hard enough, but this! It was a task for a righteous man, a holy man—not a carpenter! It seemed like a mountain too steep to climb! He balked. Tevyah propelled him forward until he stood directly in front of the well.

Suddenly a cheer arose. There was Mary, her large, brown eyes luminous with joy; he could tell she was laughing. She was bracketed by her mother on her right and Aunt Elisheba on the left. And all the married women of Nazareth after them. Then the unmarried girls skipping along. Behind them were Mary's father, the rabbi, and James.

The music fell silent.

Hands clasped before him, Yosef stood erect, chin high, waiting. Mary's eyes were fixed on his. He was lost in her gaze.

The women halted and formed a corridor for Heli and James and the rabbi to come forward. Elisheba stepped to one side. Heli passed the scroll containing the marriage *ketubah* to Anna and took Mary's arm.

He whispered, "Are you ready, Daughter?"

Mary nodded, eyes brimming, never looking away from Yosef's face as they brought her to him.

Was she like Yosef? Breathless at the nearness of God's presence?

The rabbi raised his hands for silence. "The groom and his bride have asked to meet at the well. Like Yacov, our father, met his bride, Rachel, at the well, nu? May Adonai make them fruitful as our fathers." He began to read:

"There Yacov saw a well in the field, with three flocks of sheep lying near it because the flocks were watered from that well. The stone over the mouth of the well was large. When all the flocks were gathered there, the shepherds would roll the stone away from the well's mouth and water the sheep. Then they would return the stone to its place over the mouth of the well.

"Yacov asked the shepherds, 'My brothers, where are you from?'

"'We're from Haran,' they replied.

"He said to them, 'Do you know Laban, Nahor's grandson?'

"'Yes, we know him,' they answered.

"Then Yacov asked them, 'Is he well?'

"'Yes, he is,' they answered, 'and here comes his daughter Rachel with the sheep.'

"'Look,' Yacov said, 'the sun is still high. It is not time for the flocks to be gathered. Water the sheep and take them back to pasture.'

"'We can't,' they replied, 'until all the flocks are gathered, and the stone has been rolled away from the mouth of the well. Then we will water the sheep.'

"While he was still talking to the shepherds, Rachel came with her father's sheep. . . . When Yacov saw Rachel and Laban's sheep, he went over and rolled the stone away from the mouth of the well and watered his uncle's sheep. Then Yacov kissed Rachel and began to weep aloud.[119]

"The word of Adonai."

Then the rabbi crooked his finger, urging Heli and Anna to escort the bride to the canopy.

Even though Mary could not be his tonight, Yosef could not have felt more love for her. Though he could not hold her or take her in his arms as a man takes a wife, a fierce fire of protectiveness burned in him.

See the way she looks at me. Sees my soul. Loves me as I am. Calm my passion for her. Let me be her friend and protector! O Lord, make me worthy of her and the child she carries.

The rabbi offered a benediction, then said, "The formalities have been completed. The *ketubah* is legal and binding, according to the laws of Torah. The dowry provided. The bride is guaranteed to be a virgin of good character. If any here have cause to accuse or know reason this marriage would be unlawful, speak now."

Silence except for the sniffles of little girls and old women who always cried at weddings.

The rabbi continued after the customary moment of waiting, "So, no one objecting, who gives this woman, Mary of Nazareth, to be the wife of Yosef bar Jacob?"

Heli cleared his throat. "I, her father." He extended Mary's hand to Yosef and repeated the benediction from the book of Tobit: "Yosef, receive my daughter as your wedded wife in accordance with the Law, the decree written in the book of Mosheh. Take her and bring her back safely to your house. And may the Eternal of Heaven grant both of you peace and prosperity."

Yosef fought to find his voice. So much he wanted to say to her. He had practiced a speech a hundred times. Words seemed inadequate when he saw himself reflected in her eyes. "I . . . I'll . . . try to say it right. Like Yacov loved Rachel at the well, you all know I've loved Mary from the first time I saw her. So, I, Yosef, take you, Mary, into my home as my wife. I promise I will care for you. With the strength of Yacov I will move any stone in life that covers the well so that you may drink and be satisfied and water your flocks. I pledge my own life to protect you and the children you bear from all danger and harm. I will be your beloved friend first . . . and then your husband. You will be my beloved friend, my wife. I will shelter you and love you as long as I live."

He slid a plain silver band onto her right index finger and kissed her gently.

She clung to him. Grateful. Loving him.

And it was very good.

A cheer rose up, and the music began.

There was great joy in Nazareth that night as everyone accompanied Yosef and Mary to his home.

CHAPTER 26

The curfew was in full effect in Jerusalem again. The report went around that there were rebels in the streets—armed dagger men waiting for the opportunity to strike. Everyone was to remain indoors till morning light.

The tramp of marching feet roused Old Simeon from his narrow bed in the priest's quarter. Despite all Herod's efforts at containment, the stories of what really happened at David's Tomb, of what had really caused the fire in the Temple archives, had been whispered up and down the alleys of Jerusalem. It was now a secret proverb: When the order was given to keep to your houses and then Herod's soldiers violated the stillness, some mischief was under way.

Simeon, trusting in the promise that he would not die until he had seen the Lord's Anointed, was not afraid to follow. Once he saw the soldiers' destination and what they were up to, he would raise the alarm. His age betrayed him; his halting walk could not keep up. He watched the black-cloaked guardsmen march across the causeway. Once they reached the vicinity of the Gennath Gate, the lights they carried knotted into a ball of fire before the guards descended the flight of steps beside a guard tower.

Panting, stretching out his hand toward the wall to steady himself, Simeon followed as fast as he could. He arrived on the crest of the viaduct just in time to see the armed men enter the residential quarter north of the gate. Like a flaming serpent, the file of troopers and their torches wriggled around the corners and up the market street.

Toward Onias' house.

Simeon reached the corner of the street just as they battered in Onias' door. "Rebel! Traitor!" they shouted. Men with drawn swords plunged into the tutor's home.

"Wait!" Simeon croaked from the darkness. "You're making a mistake!" He lunged forward, grabbing a burly guard sergeant by the back of his tunic.

The man swung round, clubbing Simeon on the head with his torch as he did so.

Stunned, Simeon fell to the ground.

The troopers dragged Onias outside.

"Where shall we put him?" one of the captors demanded.

"There . . . the side of his own house . . . Steward Talmai said to make a warning of him. That'll serve!"

"What about the old fool? Him too?"

"He's killed already. Get on with it."

The air resounded with hollow, thunderous blows on countless doors, and muffled screams.

When Simeon managed to regain his senses, he heard shouting and more terrified cries in the distance, way off by the Damascus Road.

Simeon tried to stand, but the world swirled around him. He propped his back against the ledge of a water cistern.

From the darkness around the side of Onias' house Simeon heard shuffling sounds and low moans. On hands and knees he crawled forward, turning his face toward the feeble noises. The moans came as a steady stream of whimpers now, punctuated by gasping gulps.

Simeon rounded the corner.

A blob of white was outlined against the dark wall.

Arms nailed to the roof beams, feet pinned to the block on which they had forced him to stand, Onias had been crucified on the side of his own house.

"Help!" Simeon rasped. "Someone, help me!"

A man appeared in the doorway behind him. After scanning up and down the street for watchers, he and a teenage boy grasped Simeon under the arms, dragging him out of the street.

"No! Help . . . him!" Simeon insisted.

"You're crazy! Anyone helps him'll be served the same way!" the man retorted.

"Then at least send for his brother . . . Zadok. A shepherd in Beth-lehem. Hurry!"

Migdal Eder, the Tower of the Flock, was peaceful. The night was still, the sheep calm.

Breathless, an unknown youth pelted into the ring of sheepfolds gathered around a fire. Zadok, casting up accounts of lambs born and lambs transported to the Temple, was inside the stone structure when he heard the commotion.

"I need . . . to see . . . Zadok!" a voice cracking with both adolescence and emotion demanded.

"What do y' need with him?" growled one of the night herds. The shepherds and the townsfolk did not think well of each other. The men living rough in the hills around Beth-lehem never missed an opportunity to heap scorn on soft city dwellers.

"It's important!" the boy asserted.

"Important, is it? Well, well."

Throwing down his quill with more relief than annoyance, Zadok emerged from the tower into the circle of light cast by the fire basket above the entry. "Enough foolishness," he growled at the watchman. "He didn't come all the way out here in the middle of the night to entertain y', Jared! Here, boy, I'm Zadok. What's this about?"

Doubled over, hands on knees trying to catch his breath, the young man replied, "Simeon . . . sent me! It's about . . . your brother."

"My brother? About Onias? Is he took sick?" As the boy shook his head and came nearer to the burly shepherd, Zadok saw he was trembling all over. "What then?"

"Herod's men! They . . . crucified him!"

"Where?!"

"His . . . house."

Zadok paused only long enough to throw on a cloak and grab his shepherd's staff before pounding off in the darkness toward Jerusalem. Over his shoulder he yelled, "Jared! Give the boy water and food. Send someone to my Rachel but tell no one else. I'll be back!"

With that, he was gone.

It could not be true! Zadok was unable to formulate any plan for dealing with the horrifying news because his brain refused to accept it. If someone had suggested that Zadok might one day get in enough trouble to get himself crucified, the shepherd would have agreed that his temper made it possible.

But not Onias! The gentle, scholarly tutor? Onias was well spoken of by all who met him. He was the personal selection of a king to educate his grandson. He was no criminal, no rebel! How could this be?

At the Gate of the Essenes Zadok was challenged by the guard. When he shouted he was on business for the Chief Shepherd of Israel, he was allowed to pass. Up the street past the Hippodrome and the old Hasmonean Palace he pounded, never stopping for breath.

When he reached the corner of the turning just before Onias' home, Zadok ran into a muttering crowd of people gathered in the lane.

"It's his brother!" someone whispered urgently.

The crowd parted, making room for Zadok to approach the house. He stepped into an expanding ball of light cast by the torches, faced the wall with its obscene ornament.

Onias' face, beaten beyond recognition, was a mask of bruises and agony. His breathing was labored; he was nearly drowning in his own blood. Each wrenching surge upward to catch a sip of air came at the expense of gritted teeth and heart-wrenching moans.

Zadok lunged forward, grasped his brother in a bear hug, and lifted the weight off the tortured feet and hands.

Onias recognized his brother through one eye reduced to a mere slit. "No! Zadok, no! Think of . . . Rachel. Menorah! Your . . . boys!"

Zadok yelled at the crowd, "Why? Why did y' leave him here like this? Get away! Get out of here!"

The crowd melted away, fearful that the next scene of the tragedy would involve more crucifixions. Clearly they didn't want to be available as victims.

Old Simeon shuffled forward. Blood from a head wound outlined the creases in his face. "What can I do?"

"Help me hold him while I pull the spikes!"

Zadok's brawny arms were used to hoisting grown rams. His calloused hands, rough from climbing among rocks and brambles in search of lost lambs, wrenched the spike free from Onias' feet.

Mercifully, Onias fainted.

With Simeon assisting, Zadok took the weight of his brother's body with one hand while yanking at a nail with the other. "God, help me!" Zadok cried. The pin pulled free, and Onias' body swung sideways. "Once more!" he urged Simeon.

Again lifting the deadweight and heaving at the spike with knotted shoulder muscles and bowed back, Zadok screamed and the piercing barb came loose. The three men tumbled to the ground.

"We must get away from here!" Simeon urged. "You can take him to my home!"

Zadok shook his head. "You're in danger enough already. He's fainted. Find me a blanket to throw over him. The Gennath Gate is close. Once outside, no one'll question me. I'll tell the guards my brother died, and I go to bury him. Hurry!"

CHAPTER 27

Lamplight flickered in the bridal chamber.

Mary's hair hung loose in a chestnut cascade, tumbling over her shoulders and down her back. Barefoot in her bridal gown, she stood beside the bed, which had been decorated with garlands of flowers. Rose petals were strewn across the mattress.

Yosef did not look at her. Did not let himself think of what a wedding night was supposed to mean.

Outside the revelry of the banquet continued without them. A wave of laughter rose and fell with the music. Yosef knew what they were laughing at. The bride. The groom. Alone at last.

He exhaled loudly. "They've had too much to drink."

"From the Womb of Beth Karem. The last of Uncle Zachariah's wine. Very good."

"Yes, a fine gift."

"They say there will be no more like it . . . ever. Gabriel warned Uncle that the baby Yochanan must never drink wine. Funny, he was born in Beth Karem. Uncle Zachariah is the last of his family who knows how to make this wine. Now he and Aunt Elisheba are moving away. Taking baby Yochanan to live on the east shore of the Jordan, out of Herod's reach. They have a small house and an almond orchard there on the edge of the desert."

"It's best." Yosef fixed his gaze on the flowers in her hair.

"Everyone likes his wine." She finished with a shrug.

"A good man, your uncle."

Suddenly shy, she babbled. "I . . . I crushed the grapes once to make wine. They put them in a big vat and then . . ." Her smile faltered.

"I made something for you." Yosef glanced toward the wedding chest at the foot of the bed. It was covered with a purple cloth. "I have been working on it ever since . . . since we were betrothed."

Mary uncovered it and gasped with pleasure. What had been intended to be an inlaid oak chest had become a work of art. On the front panel was a seven-branched candlestick, each light topped with a bright star, the Mogen David, the six-pointed shield of David. On each end Yosef had carved a pomegranate branch. On the top of the chest a thin sliver of the New Moon, just like tonight's moon, was set among stars that framed the pattern of the constellation known as The Virgin. The star of Mars, The Adam, touched The Atonement star, which marked the center of the outline.

"The sky was like that the night Gabriel spoke to you."

"Yes." She nodded and ran her fingertips over the smooth surface. "I remember."

"It came to me later, after my dream, that even the heavens proclaimed what you heard from the mouth of an angel. It meant something. Something important, Mary."

"You are an artist. I have no gift to offer you, Yosef."

"You and I. Angels. Mysteries. I'd be awfully ungrateful if I didn't think being part of your life and his is the greatest gift. It's . . . everything."

She sat down hard on the bed. "What shall we do now, Yosef?"

"Do?" Yosef slumped down cross-legged on the floor. Mary had pretty feet, he noted. Small and perfect, like the rest of her. He closed his eyes and leaned his head back on the wall.

"Tired?" she asked.

"Mary. It's been a long . . . day. A long . . . several months, if you want to know the truth."

"Are you all right?"

Yosef clasped his arms around his knees. "I am. I am resolved to it.

You are now my sister, and I am your brother. I . . . I can accept that. Though you know how much I love you."

She searched his face with that straight-on gaze of hers. No escape from her eyes. "Yes. And I . . . love you, Yosef."

His smile was weary. "I believe you do. Yes. And I'm up for the challenge. You know, it's as though I'm not the bridegroom at all. I'm the friend of the groom, eh? I'm the fellow with the sword who stands guard at your door and protects your virginity for the groom."

"Yes, my protector."

"Well then."

She said brightly, "It's very nice. Being protected."

"Thanks."

"No, I mean it. No other man I would trust."

"Should I be flattered?" He laughed softly without bitterness.

There was resolve in her voice. "I think so, Yosef. You should. I'm not the only one who trusts you with . . . with everything. And I think that it really is everything. Bigger than we even know."

Yosef rubbed his forehead. "Yes, that's occurred to me."

Another swell of laughter from the guests penetrated the room. Mary tossed her head. "They don't know what they're really celebrating, do they?"

Yosef shook his head. "They wouldn't believe it. Everyone wants this holy child to be born, so he will call down fire on the heads of Herod and his brood of vipers. But they wouldn't believe it if they knew. And if they knew how near the true King was, well, it would be dangerous for the baby. For you."

"Then I suppose we won't tell them."

His head ached. "How strange it is. How amazing that we . . . two . . . so ordinary. Like any couple in the Galil getting married on a Wednesday night."

"They'll know, I suppose, when they see him. I mean, they'll know he's extraordinary. Do you think?"

Yosef considered how it would be. "I don't know. Maybe his coming will be like this wedding. Very nice. Everyone will have a good time and think they know what is happening in secret. Even though they really haven't got any idea of the truth. Eventually, I suppose the truth of who this baby is will all be revealed. And then everyone will know he never was what he seemed to be. But for now it's our secret."

"Will we know, Yosef? When he's born, I mean. Will we two know how . . . wonderful?"

"I've thought about it. Prayed about it even. No, I think—"

"Tell me!" She leaned forward eagerly, as though relieved to have someone to talk to about it.

"The most wonderful thing about this—for me anyway—is that for a while you and I will be guardians of an eternal secret. You and I . . . does it seem possible?"

"That the Lord of everything will need us? need our help to pull this off? No, not at all."

Yosef nodded. "We're partners then, you and I. I've bought myself a sword, Mary. I can swing an axe as well as any man. No one will hurt you while I'm alive. Or him, either."

"I feel safe with you."

His reply was resolute. "Good."

"Where . . . where shall we sleep tonight?"

"Here. I'll sleep here. On the floor. In front of the door. No one will get past me." He patted the paving stones. "Hot night. The stones are cool. You. On the bed. They expect, you know, that we'll sleep together tonight, so we'll stay together in the room."

She traced the rose pattern on her sleeve. "All right then. But . . ."

"Can you undress in the dark?"

"Can you?" She reached for one of two matching linen nightshirts folded on the mattress. She tossed it to him, along with a pillow and blanket.

Yosef saluted and blew out the lamp.

They undressed, settled into their sleeping places, and lay awake in the dark, listening. The sounds of revelry finally died away. Night sounds, peaceful and almost holy, serenaded them.

Yosef spoke at last. "Mary?"

"I'm awake too."

"I wanted to tell you something before you sleep. I've heard that in the garden at the first wedding of the first man and first woman, the Lord himself acted as rabbi. He made the blessing and gave them the finest wine to seal their vows. And the archangels—our angels, Mary—were the groomsmen. The angel Michael, a strong warrior for The Eternal, stood on one side by the man. And the great messenger angel, Gabriel, stood on the other side by the woman. And their wings stretched out over Adam and Eve to protect them, so their wings made the first wedding canopy."

"Oh! A lovely story, Yosef!"

"Listen, Mary!" A breeze stirred the trees. "Do you hear it?"

"Yes. The rustling of great wings above us too!" she said in awe. "And the ringing of tiny silver bells."

"That's what I heard too."

"Oh, Yosef, it was a lovely wedding."

There was a smile in Mary's voice. Yosef heard her pleasure even in the dark.

"I do love a good wedding!" she continued. "In all heaven and earth almost my favorite thing. Do you think the story's true about the angels in the Garden and their wings making the chuppah?"

"Yes. Yes, I do. And someday when the child's grown, we'll be at someone's wedding and we must remember to ask him about it. He invented weddings, after all."

CHAPTER 28

nias was barely conscious as night began to fade beyond Bethlehem. A syrup of opiate mixed with wine deadened the agony of irreparably shattered hands and feet.

He lay on a cot in the cottage behind Zadok's house. Rachel tended his wounds.

"Where . . . Menorah?" Onias wheezed.

"Sleeping." Rachel struggled to set his fingers, which had already begun to curl into claws.

"Mustn't let her see me . . . like this . . . please." Tears streamed down Onias' cheeks, though he felt no pain. It was not pain that made him weep. It was something else . . . something he knew but could not remember. "What will . . . become of us? What? What will . . . ?"

Rachel worked quickly, disinfecting, setting, wrapping. Zadok, shepherd's staff like a weapon in his hand, glowered in the background.

"The drug is talking," Rachel said quietly. "He's fighting to stay awake."

Zadok asked, "Will he live?"

"Don't know."

Onias groaned. His own voice sounded strange to him. They

thought he did not understand them, but he did. He wanted to tell them he understood, but his tongue was thick in his mouth. "I . . . am . . . the last."

"What's he sayin'?" Zadok asked Rachel.

"I can't make it out. He's hallucinating. The drugs. Loss of blood." Rachel held up Onias' right hand. "How many died last night?"

"We'll never know for certain. The net is cast so wide. Simeon said it was just under one hundred arrested. Herod's own sons by Mariamme—Alex and Ari—too."

Rachel sighed. "So Herod has assured that the descendants of the Maccabees will never cleanse the Temple a second time."

Rachel's face. So angry. Onias had never before seen her angry. A fierce, brave woman she was. Strong. Good. In such a time, mothers needed courage. What had happened to the wife of Alex? to Alex's children?

"Courage," Onias whispered.

Did they hear him?

Zadok stepped to the window and gazed out toward the final fading stars. "We'll have to hide him here. Until he's well enough to travel. Then . . . get him out of the country. No, not Damascus. Not far enough. By ship. Egypt. So many of us in exile in Alexandria, waitin' . . . waitin' for Messiah."

"I . . . am . . . the last . . . who will suffer." Onias knew his words were garbled, but why did they not listen? He wanted to tell them: Messiah would surely come now! Drive out Herod! Drive out the false religious authorities who desecrated all that was holy and set apart for the Lord. Onias would be the last who would ever suffer! Was that not what Scripture foretold? The last! No more suffering! Messiah would come and . . . what was the prophecy? Something about a calf being let out of its pen. Something about running across a pasture and kicking up its heels for joy.[120] Yes. The prophecy went something like that.

Zadok's shadow blocked Onias' view of the approaching dawn. "I fear my brother'll die without ever seein' The One he's longed all his life to see. But if he lives . . . then Alexandria."

Rachel placed her hand on Onias' forehead. "He's burning up, burning with fever. Oh, Zadok, in all our lives was there ever such a dark time as this? What will become of us? How can we live? How? Raise our boys in Judea now? Maybe we should go too. Leave Beth-lehem. Go to Alexandria. What sort of life can our boys have with a monster like Herod on David's throne? Oh, Zadok! So dark. Will dawn ever come?"

Onias turned his face toward the window. He wanted to tell them. Wanted them to understand what he believed.

The Light was coming! There—did they not see it? The bright morning star! Gleaming at dawn! The star, rising out of Jacob![121]

Epilogue

It was almost dawn.

Peniel leaned against Mary's shoulder as Onias and Zadok at last lapsed into thoughtful silence at the memory of that long-ago night.

Their story was burned upon Peniel's brain the way a flash of lightning replayed on his retinas even after he closed his eyes.

Onias, pale and worn in the retelling, wheezed, "I thought I would be among the last to suffer, you see. That Messiah would come, and forever wipe away every tear."[122] The old man turned his face to the approaching light and reached for Zadok's hand. "Hoping for that day made all things possible. I could accept it. But now, my eyes are gone. I can't even read any longer. If only I was the last to suffer before he revealed himself!"

Zadok lifted the contorted fingers of his brother to his lips. "If only it were so, my brother."

Onias coughed and resumed. "My studies. All these years unable to walk more than a few steps. My scrolls open before me. Companions. Teachers." His face turned to Mary. "Everything, everything written about him must be fulfilled."[123]

Mary put a hand to her heart, as though Onias' words had caused her pain. She patted Peniel's arm, then stood and padded from the room.

Menorah, who dozed on a heap of cushions against the wall, sat up. "Papa? Won't you sleep now? It's almost morning."

"Still so much . . . so much of the beginning of it left untold," Onias protested.

"A few more minutes, girl," Zadok said. "Your father's come such a long way. Been waitin' so long."

Peniel heard voices in the courtyard. Footsteps upon the stone floor.

Mary reentered the chamber and stepped to one side. "Onias? He's here."

Yeshua followed immediately behind her. He was washed and dressed, wearing the new prayer shawl, which had been the gift of Zahav—now the bride—some weeks before. Sad brown eyes lingered on the crooked hands of the old man on the bed. Some understanding passed between the two men, as though both heard a voice no one else could hear.

Zadok rose from his brother's side and stepped away to make room for Yeshua. "Onias, he's here." Zadok bowed his head. Lips moved silently in a prayer of thanks.

Onias reached for Yeshua, who grasped both hands. "Lord, you . . . like this . . . grown up."

"You've been waiting a long time," Yeshua said softly. "Faithful friend."

"All my studies. The scroll of Dani'el. This is the Year of Atonement. I had to come. To hear your words for myself. But my eyes. I'm nearly blind now. I see your shadow. I hoped you would remember me."

Yeshua nodded. "Onias. Yes, I haven't forgotten. I heard your cry the night they crucified you for my sake."

Yeshua removed His tallith and spread it over the old man up to his chin. It was almost like a shroud. All the names of God embroidered in the fabric caught the light of the sun rising over the red-rimmed horizon.

Yeshua bent over him, stroked his gray cheek, touched his eyelids, and whispered the words of Malachi. "Onias, faithful friend, here is the promise for the year of the Lord: *For you who revere My name, the Sun of*

Righteousness will rise with healing in its wings . . . in the tassels of His prayer shawl."[124] Yeshua searched the clouded eyes. "And you will go out and leap, Onias, like a calf released from the stall." The room was flooded with sunrise, streaming through the window behind Yeshua.

And Peniel knew. He knew.

Onias spoke softly as the warm oil of Yeshua's words coursed through him. Color returned to his eyes, like clear blue returns to the sky when the sun rises. "Lord! I was afraid you had forgotten. Afraid you wouldn't come. But now, look at you. O Lord, I have been waiting for this day!"

Yeshua, satisfied, straightened up and clasped the restored hands, which had been claws only a moment before. "Onias, get up! Don't be afraid. Onias, walk!"

O LORD, our Lord,

How majestic is Your name in all the earth,

Who have displayed Your splendor above the heavens!

From the mouth of infants and nursing babes

You have established strength

Because of Your adversaries,

To make the enemy and the revengeful cease.

PSALM 8:1-2

Digging Deeper into FOURTH DAWN

Dear Reader,
Imagine living in a country ruled by an evil king. When you see his soldiers brutalize people daily, you wonder, *Who will punish the wicked?* You plead, *When will this world be set right?*

Imagine receiving a visit from an angel while you're milking a cow in your barn. What this angel says is so shocking, your life will never be the same. Would you think you were dreaming? Or would you believe the message? What if the message were true? Would you ask yourself, *If I told others about it, would they believe me?*

Imagine just before you are to be married you hear that your betrothed has been unfaithful. How would you respond?

You have now entered the world of *Fourth Dawn*. Great evil lurks around every corner, waiting to prey upon the innocent. But unbeknownst to many (except those who fervently watch the heavens for signs [like Melchior] or read the ancient prophecies [like Onias]), a great Light is dawning—a Light that will eclipse the darkness of men's plots for all eternity. Yet it will come in a form that few will accept.

Following are six studies. You may wish to delve into them on your own or share them with a friend or a discussion group. They are designed to take you deeper into the answers to questions such as:

What's so troubling about trouble? How will you respond to it?

What are angels—really? Why would they descend from the heavens to appear to a human being?

Why is your heart attitude so important?

How can you deal with life's journeys—and their unexpected detours?

What do the prophecies say regarding the promised Messiah? Why are they so crucial for today's world?

What do the signs in the heavens at different points in history reveal?

Through *Fourth Dawn*, may the promised Messiah come alive to you . . . in more brilliance than ever before.

---

1 THE TROUBLE WITH TROUBLE

> It all begins with a Jewish priest, Zachariah, who lived when Herod was king of Judea. Zachariah was a member of the priestly order of Abijah. His wife, Elisheba, was from the priestly line of Aaron. Zachariah and Elisheba were righteous in God's eyes, careful to obey all of the Lord's commandments and regulations. They had no children because Elisheba was barren, and they were both very old.
>
> —PENIEL (p. 12)

Do you know someone who is "righteous" and yet has trouble—seemingly undeserved—in his or her life? What is the situation? How does that person handle it?

____

____

____

Reflect on any current or past crises in your life. How have you responded to trouble?

____

____

____

Trouble is inevitable. We all face it from time to time—whether on a large or small scale. So why is it so troubling? Perhaps because it has the capacity to change our perspective . . . or even our life path.

Think about it from Zachariah's and Elisheba's perspectives. Both were called "righteous"—they were kind, well-respected, giving, humble folks.

Yet in a period of history where having children (and lots of them) was considered an ultimate blessing and not having children was considered a reproach (others would whisper behind your back about how you must have sinned), they had never conceived a child—not in forty years of a loving marriage.

What were they to make of this trouble? What are we to make of ours?

READ

Zachariah loved that he had been born a Levite, loved performing his appointed obligations for the Master of the Universe.

Since his bar mitzvah Zachariah had been coming twice each year with others of his division of the priesthood. Over ninety weeks of his life had been dedicated to aiding in performing the sacrifices for HaShem, The Name of the Most High. . . .

Unlike other Levites, whose grandfathers had returned from the Babylonian captivity ignorant of their proper heritage, Zachariah actually knew his lineage. He knew he was truly of the course of Abijah—perhaps the only surviving descendant of Abijah to serve in the correct course.

For many years, when he was younger, that knowledge was a source of pride for Zachariah.

—p. 14

ASK

If you had spent over ninety weeks of your life away from home faithfully serving God, would you expect something in return? Why or why not?

____

____

____

Zachariah had an esteemed family name respected in his nation. Generations of his family had served God.

How important is a name to you? What names in our nation do you respect (i.e., the Kennedys, the Billy Graham family, etc.)? Why?

___

___

___

Would belonging to that respected family be a source of pride to you (like the younger Zachariah)? If so, in what ways? If not, why not?

___

___

___

Zachariah's parents had given him the name "Yahweh has remembered" (see p. 15). Perhaps in weak moments Zachariah thought, *Such irony! God has not remembered me, and neither will anyone else since there will be no child to carry on my family.*

READ

As Zachariah grew older, his perspective changed:

Long ago he had given up any sense of self-importance. It had disappeared entirely at the same time he and Elisheba despaired of ever having children. If he was the last true heir of Abijah, well then, he was the last. That was all the Almighty's doing and not to be questioned. . . .

He was not a scholar, nor did he possess political influence. He was respected and well-liked in his village for his piety and his humility and his kindheartedness, but forty childless years of marriage had long since convinced him his lot in life was forever to be a humble one, unnoticed by men or the Almighty either, apparently.

—pp. 14–15

ASK

Zachariah believed his family's state of affairs was "the Almighty's doing and not to be questioned." If you were Zachariah, would you accept easily that your family line would end with you? Why or why not?

When you have troubles, do you accept them as from God and "not to be questioned"? Why or why not?

Have you ever wondered if your lot in life is like Zachariah's: "forever humble, unnoticed by men or the Almighty"? What situation(s) led you to think that?

READ

How many times over the early years of their marriage had Elisheba dispatched him to the Holy City with an urgent request for the Lord to remember her? to give her a child as He had done for Abraham's wife, Sarah? to take away her reproach the way He had remembered the patriarch Jacob's barren wife, Rachel? like He had blessed Samu'el the prophet's mother? as He had miraculously quickened the womb of Samson's mother?

All to no avail.

How long had it been since Elisheba had stopped asking?

Zachariah pondered the recollection. Try as he might, he could not recall when they had given up hoping for a child. Fifteen years now? More?

—p. 15

A life without children had been Elisheba's public shame and her own private sorrow, but she had borne it well. Without bitterness she had become every child's Aunt Elisheba. She poured all the untapped mothering skills into loving Zachariah. And he spoiled her as he would have spoiled a daughter. He had never stopped loving her, praying for her, hoping. As Elisheba often said, "Stuff yourself with hope and you can go crazy."

—p. 36

ASK

Zachariah pored over the promises of Scripture daily, reading of miracles happening again and again. And yet there was no miracle for him and Elisheba. The weight upon them must have been heavy, as they assumed God had forgotten them.

What burden lies heavily on your heart—something you wish God would change in your own or a loved one's life?

____

____

____

If you have prayed asking God for help, have you seen any glimmers of an answer? Or has heaven seemed silent? Explain.

____

____

____

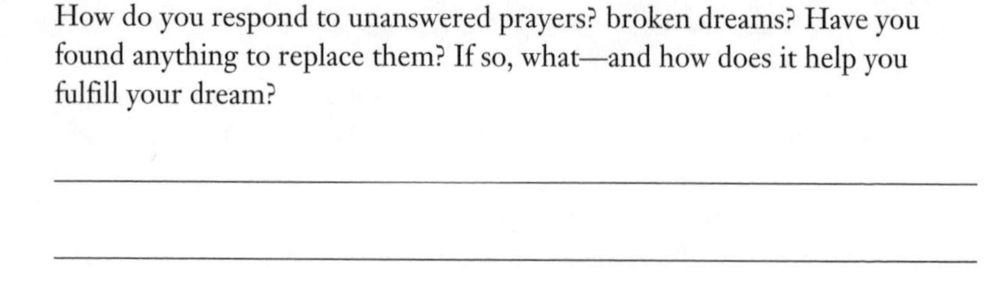

How do you respond to unanswered prayers? broken dreams? Have you found anything to replace them? If so, what—and how does it help you fulfill your dream?

The childless Elisheba became every child's aunt. Instead of becoming bitter or blaming each other for their lack of conception, Elisheba and Zachariah poured their love into each other. Their passion remains: "Still he desired her, found comfort and pleasure in her arms. He missed her voice and longed for her touch when he was gone from her." Even their sense of humor stays keen. To Zachariah, Elisheba was a "fine vintage wine that had grown more complex and delicious over the years," even though she jokes that "she had begun to feel past ripe; she was moving toward raisin status" (p. 36).

After forty years of marriage, Zachariah and Elisheba (now fifty-five) have finally given up hope for their dreams of an heir. Then they are granted a miracle!

READ

Elisheba had never cried so hard in all the years of their marriage.

She, who always had a proverb for everything, had no words. She wagged her head. Wiped her eyes. Blew her nose on her kerchief. Reached out to grasp his hand. Kissed his fingers. Read again. Finally she stood and wrapped her arms around his middle, pressed herself tightly against him, and sobbed. . . .

"With God, nothing is impossible," she finally managed.

—pp. 41–42

It had been five months since Zachariah's homecoming. Elisheba's pregnancy had blossomed into reality during those months. And so had their love. Youthful energy and feelings almost forgotten were renewed between them. Zachariah thought she had never been more beautiful than now. He pampered her and cared for her every need as she remained in quiet seclusion in their home.

There was no doubt now that the vision he had seen and heard in the Temple and written down was true.

—p. 49

> *The Lord has done this for me. In these days He has shown His favor and taken away my disgrace among the people.*
>
> —Elisheba (Luke 1:25)

Elisheba placed Zachariah's hand on the place where the baby tapped elbows and knees.

Zachariah closed his eyes and felt the drumming of life within her. Was there ever a miracle so great as this? And with it came boundless joy.

—p. 48

Zachariah and Elisheba were granted a miracle beyond any proportions they might imagine. They would have an heir, yes. But their son would also be the prophesied forerunner of the longed-for Messiah! This humble couple, who thought they would never go down in history for anything, was part of God's big plan from the very start!

ASK

If you prayed for something for years and finally received the answer, would you respond more like Elisheba (immediately believing) or Zachariah (questioning how it could logically be possible)? Or a little of both? Why?

____

____

____

What is the greatest miracle you could imagine in your life? One that would bring "boundless joy"? Why?

____

____

____

WONDER . . .

He settles the barren woman in her home as a happy mother of children.
—PSALM 113:9

Your ways, O God, are holy.
What god is so great as our God?
You are the God who performs miracles;
You display Your power among the peoples.
—PSALM 77:13-14

If God can give a fifty-five-year-old barren woman a child, what miracle might He grant you? Why not ask—and continue asking?

2 WHAT ARE ANGELS . . . REALLY?

Simeon leaned forward and grasped Zachariah's arm. "An angel, true? An angel was sent."

Zachariah nodded vigorously.

"Of course true. An angel has come to you . . . been sent . . . and has spoken to you. Told you things that are to come."

—p. 25

If you were having lunch with a friend and she leaned close and whispered, "I think I saw an angel in my room last night," what would you think?

___

___

___

Have you ever felt as if an angel were watching over you? trying to tell you something? attempting to keep you from harm? Tell the story.

___

___

___

Angel-on-your-shoulder pins. Portraits of chubby-cheeked angels. Cards that quip "An angel is on your side." Garden statues of white-porcelain-winged angels. . . .

We are surrounded by representations of angels—cute and seemingly harmless. Even people who don't believe in God will say, "Sure, I believe in angels. Everyone has an angel to watch over him."

But is that what angels really are?

In the Old Testament a man named Gideon was visited by an angel (read his story in Judges 6). He lived in a dangerous time, not unlike Mary and Yosef's. Only his bad guys were Midianites instead of the Romans of the A.D. Chronicles series. Gideon was so frightened of his enemies he worked—threshing wheat—down in a winepress so he could hide from them.

Ironically, when the angel of the Lord appears, he says, "The LORD is with you, mighty warrior" (Judges 6:12). Mighty warrior? Gideon certainly didn't feel like a mighty warrior. Mighty coward was more like it.

But God had something great in store for Gideon, just as God had something great in store for the three people in *Fourth Dawn* who receive visits from angels.

READ

To Zachariah's left something moved against the backdrop of the curtain. It was not a black shape but the reverse. A glowing patch of light increased in size until, though manlike in form, it was larger.

Much larger.

Zachariah's head prickled. His legs weakened. His right hand reached toward one of the horns of the altar to steady himself but stopped short of touching it.

Do not be afraid, Zachariah, boomed a voice that seemed to resonate within Zachariah's chest as much as it rang in his ears. *God has heard your prayer. He has remembered you . . . and your wife, Elisheba, will bear you a son. You are to name him Yochanan. You will have great joy and gladness, and many will rejoice with you at his birth, for he will be great in the eyes of the Lord. He must never touch wine or hard liquor, and he will be filled with the Holy Spirit, even before his birth. And he will persuade many Israelites to turn to the Lord their God.*

Zachariah's eyes bulged. His lungs felt near to bursting as he held his breath, trying to take it all in. A child? A son? His and Elisheba's? Now, after all this time? . . .

Unbidden, unrehearsed, almost like the involuntary gasp of a drowning man inhaling water instead of air, Zachariah babbled, "How can I know this will happen? I'm an old man now, and my wife is also well along in years." . . .

The angel said, *Since you didn't believe what I said, you won't be able to speak until the child is born. For my words will certainly come true at the proper time. . . .*

Zachariah escaped into broad daylight, only to find himself trapped inside a circle of dumbfounded and apprehensive onlookers. He tried to speak, to explain, to praise, to offer any verbal reassurance, but he could not.

He could not utter a word.

—pp. 18–19

ASK

When Zachariah encounters the angel in the Temple, what is his response to:

the appearance of the angel?

---

the angel's message?

Why do you think Zachariah was struck dumb? Was this a fitting "punishment" for not believing the message immediately? Why or why not?

Later that day, when Onias the Tutor, Zadok the Shepherd, and Eliyahu the Rabbi discuss what has happened to Zachariah, they are amazed:

"He couldn't speak, yet he remembered everythin' that had happened to him?" Zadok queried doubtfully.

Eliyahu, dwarfed alongside the towering form of the shepherd, affirmed this fact in a voice that squeaked with excitement. "Every detail! Every word!"

—p. 20

Zachariah was struck with awe and fear, yet he remembered every word of his encounter with the angel. Not only would he have a child—the longing of a lifetime fulfilled—but he would be part of God's eternal plan.

READ

In the sixth month, God sent the angel Gabriel to Nazareth, a town in Galilee, to a virgin pledged to be married to a man named Joseph.

—Luke 1:26-27

The . . . mysterious voice replied in song: *"His love endures forever."* With each word the gleam increased in intensity, until something—some*one*—materialized before her.

Mary dropped to her knees and cried out, "Who are you? Who's there? The Lord, Adonai is with me; I will not be afraid! What can man do to me?"

A golden shape—like a man, only not a man—towered over her and the cattle. *I am Gabriel,* came the repeated reply.

His head reached almost to the ceiling. Light and warmth emanated from his presence. Stretching out golden arms, he spoke, yet his lips did not move. *Greetings, you who are highly favored.*

She covered her head with her arms and trembled in terror. Sound and light shook her to the core.

The angel consoled her. *Do not be afraid, Mary, you have found favor with Adonai. . . . Mary, you will be with child and give birth to a son. And you are to give him the name Yeshua, Salvation. . . . He will be great and will be called the Son of the Most High. Adonai Yahweh will give Him the throne of His father David. He will reign over the house of Ya'acov forever. His kingdom will . . . never . . . end.*

Mary exhaled loudly and . . . asked the angel, "How will this be, since I am a virgin?". . .

The Ruach HaKodesh, *the Holy Spirit, will overshadow you. So the holy one to be born will be called Bar El Olam, the Son of God. . . .*

"I am the servant of Adonai!" She laughed in delight. "May it be to me as you have said."

—pp. 72–73

ASK

When Mary encounters the angel in her father's cow barn, what is her response to:

the appearance of the angel?

---

the angel's message?

What one question does Mary ask, and why? How is her response similar to—yet different—from Zachariah's?

In this angelic encounter, a young girl experiences a range of emotions. Not only will she have a child, but this child will be part of God's eternal plan! Because of her joy and trust, the details seem unimportant to her.

READ

There was someone standing in the corner of the room. Yosef saw him plainly, despite the lack of lamp or candle: large, shadowy, undefined. . . .

"Who . . . are you?"

There was an answer in a language Yosef could not comprehend. But a voice, speaking, nonetheless.

Yosef was not afraid. He was dreaming; he was sure of that. . . .

Shalom, Yosef, son of David.

"You mock me?" Yosef asked.

Yosef, son of Jacob. Son of David.

What sort of a greeting was this? Yosef's name was Yosef bar Jacob. It was true Yosef was a descendant of King David, but that was reaching a long way back on the family tree. "Why speak to me like this? I'm a poor carpenter. Son of Jacob, a poor carpenter. Of David's line, true enough, but far from palaces and kingdoms. And I am descended from the line from which a king of Israel can never be born."

The whisper replied, *Have you forgotten the prophecy your father, Jacob, taught you as a child? the prophecy written in the seventy-seventh psalm?*

"You have redeemed your people by your strength!

The descendants of Jacob and Yosef by your might!"

Yosef considered the question. "I haven't forgotten. My father taught me that our names were part of the redemption prophecies. But he didn't mean . . . he couldn't have meant . . . me? A part of that?" Yosef faltered. . . .

The year of the Lord is at hand when Ya'acov and Yosef and their descendants will be redeemed, as it is written in the seventy-seventh psalm. Now, in this generation, the Lord will return suddenly to Yerushalayim.

Yosef asked, "But who is his father? Mary doesn't carry a son of mine."

You have spoken correctly. But the child will be yours to care for and nurture, though He is not the son of your body. Mary's name means "bitter rebellion." Her lineage is traced back to Adam . . . back to the first woman's bitter rebellion against the Creator.

"Yes. But . . . I don't understand. Who then . . . who is the father of her baby?"

No reply. Perhaps the being in his dream had run out of patience.

Yosef challenged, "You're a dream. I'll wake up and not remember you. I seldom remember dreams."

You will remember. And more dreams will follow! You will understand and no longer be afraid.

Yosef heard the song of the night bird outside the window. Then, suddenly, voices. So many! Words like bells ringing to a crescendo. The wind! Voices roaring in a mighty wind! Yosef covered his face and trembled in his bed in terror. "Who am I, that a messenger would speak to me?". . .

Bells rang loudly for a moment longer. Then abruptly the ringing stopped. Yosef opened his eyes. The room was just his room. Gloomy. Small. No one there. No noise. Even the night bird had flown away. . . .

Yosef rose and lit the small clay lamp. Holding it up, he examined the corner of the room where the being had stood. "Everything means something? Son of the Most High, he said? But who am I to dream such a dream? Who? Who am I to imagine that I could raise and nurture the Lord's Anointed? Just a dream. It was only a dream."

—pp. 140–144

ASK

When Yosef awakens from sleep, what is his response to:

the appearance of the angel?

---

the angel's message?

What questions does Yosef ask? In what ways are his responses similar to—yet different—from Zachariah's and Mary's to their angel encounters?

Yosef is from a humble lineage—a family of carpenters. No wonder he thinks he's dreaming when he hears the angel's message! If an angel appeared to you and said, "You are a part of God's wonderful plan to save the entire earth," how would you respond?

____

____

____

READ

Each of the angels had a core message to share.

The angel's core message to Zachariah:

Do not be afraid, Zachariah. . . . God has heard your prayer. He has remembered you . . . and your wife, Elisheba, will bear you a son. You are to name him Yochanan. You will have great joy and gladness, and many will rejoice with you at his birth, for he will be great in the eyes of the Lord. . . . He will be filled with the Holy Spirit, even before his birth. And he will persuade many Israelites to turn to the Lord their God. . . . He will be a man with the spirit and power of Elijah, the prophet of old. He will precede the coming of the Lord, preparing the people for His arrival. He will turn the hearts of the fathers to their children, and he will change disobedient minds to accept godly wisdom.

—pp. 18, 20

The angel's core message to Mary:

Do not be afraid, Mary, you have found favor with Adonai. . . . You will be with child and give birth to a son. And you are to give him the name Yeshua, Salvation. . . . He will be great and will be called the Son of the Most High. Adonai Yahweh will give Him the throne of His father David. He will reign over the house of Ya'acov forever. His kingdom will . . . never . . . end.

—p. 73

The angel's core message to Yosef:

Yosef, son of David, do not be afraid to take Mary home as your wife, because what is conceived in her is from the Holy Spirit. She will give birth to a son, and you are to give Him the name Yeshua, because He will save His people from their sins. It was said through the prophet: "The virgin will be with child and will give birth to a son, and they will call his name Immanu'el, which means 'God-with-us'!"

—p. 167

ASK

What similarities do you see in the three core messages?

Why do you think these messages were so important to deliver *at that very moment* to Zachariah, Mary, and Yosef?

READ

The angel answered, "I am Gabriel. I stand in the presence of God, and I have been sent to speak to you and to tell you this good news."
—Luke 1:19

If you make the Most High your dwelling—
even the LORD, who is my refuge—
then no harm will befall you,
no disaster will come near your tent.
For He will command His angels concerning you
to guard you in all your ways;
they will lift you up in their hands,
so that you will not strike your foot against a stone.
You will tread upon the lion and the cobra;
you will trample the great lion, and the serpent.
—Psalm 91:9-13

ASK

Based on the verses above, what is the purpose(s) of angels?

____

____

____

Considering Zachariah's, Mary's, and Yosef's response to their angel encounters (as well as Gideon's in the Old Testament), has your perspective on angels and today's "angel phenomenon" changed at all? If so, how?

____

____

____

WONDER . . .

> *Are not all angels ministering spirits sent to serve those who will inherit salvation?*
>
> —HEBREWS 1:14

> *Keep on loving each other. . . . Do not forget to entertain strangers, for by so doing some people have entertained angels without knowing it.*
>
> —HEBREWS 13:1-2

Throughout Scripture, angels are God's messengers: pointing the way to Him and to the ancient truths of Scripture. How could you entertain an angel today? or act as a ministering spirit to someone in need?

3 IT'S A MATTER OF HEART

The LORD our God, the LORD is one. Love the LORD your God with all your heart and with all your soul and with all your strength. These commandments that I give you today are to be upon your hearts.
—DEUTERONOMY 6:4-6

"I can't believe my daughter is pregnant," a friend tells you in confidence. After all the years of hopes and dreams for his daughter, he is stunned by this turn of events. What would you say to your friend?

____

____

____

Have you or someone you know experienced pregnancy outside of marriage? How did your life plans change?

____

____

____

Put yourself in Mary's sandals. . . .

You have always dreamed of being married. Because you live in a day when marriages are arranged, you accept that your father will choose your betrothed. You know of the man chosen for you; you think of him at night and wonder what your life will be like together.

Then one night you receive stunning news that could change everything about that future relationship . . . especially if your bethrothed doesn't believe your account.

How would you respond? What would your heart attitude be about your present? your future?

____

____

____

READ

Papa often remarked on Yosef's amiable disposition and knowledge of Torah. He was a descendant of David, as was Mary. He was a zadiyk, a righteous man, who kept the laws of Torah and prayed daily for the coming of Messiah. He was honest to a fault and a man of his word. At twenty-seven, Yosef had served out his apprenticeship. Now he was a journeyman carpenter, out on his own. As an offering before the Lord, he had joined several thousand volunteers working on the expansion of the Temple. As a skilled craftsman, he was chosen to carve the vines that adorned the beams of Solomon's Portico. When his sabbatical service ended, he would be ready for marriage.

He and Mary would never be rich, but neither would they be poor. Everyone needed a carpenter sometime. A door hung. A beam leveled. Papa had chosen well for her.

—p. 59

ASK

What kind of man was Yosef? List his character qualities.

____

____

____

Would Yosef be the kind of person you would want to marry? Why or why not?

____

____

____

Amazingly and wonderfully, in a world where love wasn't necessary between betrothed couples, it was clear to everyone in Nazareth that Yosef was "smitten with Mary" (p. 59)! Seemingly, she had the best of all worlds.

READ

What kind of person was Mary? Perhaps she is best revealed by her mama's words when Rose, Mary's cow (the largest portion of her wedding dowry) gets sick:

"Mary, I know how hard this is for you. I do know. Understand, eh? How disappointed you must be and sad. So many happy plans gone wrong. And . . . you're a good girl, Mary. What mother would not be pleased to have such a daughter? Your name means 'bitter,' because of your father's unhappiness that you were not a son. But his bitterness was his own, never yours. And bitterness of any sort never entered your heart. No, I've never seen a drop of bitterness in you—nor rebellion either. Adonai has watched you grow up from the day you were born. He sees how even in every misfortune you keep your heart in tune, trusting. I'm proud of you, Mary. I just wanted to tell you in case you didn't know. You are the joy of my heart. I thought I should tell you tonight."

Mama hugged Mary hard and long. A hug of sympathy for hopes that seemed to be dying one after another.

—pp. 63–64

Upon hearing the message of the angel—that she, a virgin, would bear a child, Mary responds: "I am the servant of Adonai!" She laughed in delight. "May it be to me as you have said."

—p. 73

ASK

What character qualities does Mary have?

____

____

____

Is Mary the type of person you would want as a friend or a daughter? Why or why not? What about your relationship would be good? What might be disconcerting?

____

____

____

READ

Mary's mother and father responded very differently to Mary's news:

Mary bit her lip and closed her eyes. "Yes. Mama, he said . . . he told me that Adonai . . . was with me." Then, with a rush: "That I would be with child and have a son, and his name would be Yeshua. And that Adonai would give him the throne of his father David and he would rule over Ya'acov's house forever. . . . I asked him how, since I'm a virgin. He said the power of the Most High would overshadow me, and I would have a son."

Mama tucked her chin. She straightened her shoulders as the meaning of the message seemed to penetrate into her bones. She whispered, "Isaias. It is written, '*And this shall be a sign unto you.*' How did you answer, Daughter?"

"I told him, I am the servant of Adonai. And may it be done to me as he had spoken. . . ."

Mama lifted Mary's hands to her lips and kissed her fingertips. "So . . . it will be as the angel proclaimed to you. My dear, sweet girl." The two women embraced.

"Yes. I don't feel any different—just happy." Mary clung to Mama, comforted that she had believed such a wondrous thing without doubt.

—p. 76

From inside the workshop the conflict between the one who believed and the one who did not believe took a violent turn. Something crashed to the ground. Papa shouted, "What? What's she trying to do? She doesn't want to get married? . . . Is she pregnant then? Is that what she's saying? A wild story to cover up the truth? Has she been meeting some young fellow without us knowing?". . .

"She hasn't—she wouldn't—dishonor her vow to Yosef or to you!"

"What will I say to Yosef? Eh?". . .

Mama was staunch in her defense. "You will tell Yosef what happened. What she saw. What she heard."

Papa's words reflected a bitter sarcasm. "I can hear it now, 'Yosef, lad, the virgin you pledged to marry is pregnant by the Holy Spirit. An angel spoke to her and told her she was favored by Adonai and would bring forth the one who will sit on David's throne!' Bah! Mary says the Holy Spirit of the Almighty has overshadowed her? Mary says the angel said the *Ruach HaKodesh* would make a virgin pregnant without the help of a man? Ridiculous! Absurd claim on the face of it! Madness, Anna! Never meant to be taken literally. No one in all the world would ever believe such a thing! Who am I? The foolish, doting father? Believe every word of this nonsense—that's what you're saying? The disgrace! We'll all be ruined! I won't be able to hold up my head!"

Mama countered, "And what if . . . what if it is so? As she said it was? Think. The holy honor of it! The blessing! Your daughter chosen by the Almighty from all the girls in Israel! But you're too blind to see it."

"Who is Mary? Just a girl. Third daughter of a fellow who prayed for sons. Sons would not have given me such trouble. This girl? Nothing special, I can tell you."

"If you think that, then you don't know her!". . .

"I follow the laws of Torah. . . . If she has sinned and violated her vows, Yosef can demand she be condemned and stoned. You know that, don't you, Anna? If he is not the father of her child? To be betrothed to Yosef means she cannot lie with another man without the charge of adultery! Stoned! And I, her father, and you, her mother, will have to watch as Yosef throws the first stone!"

—pp. 82–83

"When you reach Beth Karem and see it isn't true that Elisheba is pregnant, that is proof the girl is a liar and a harlot. Then you will leave the girl with Elisheba until it is clear . . . if the girl is pregnant. If the girl has played the harlot, then she'll give birth there in Beth Karem, where our family is not known. If the infant survives, you will give this unwanted child to your sister, Elisheba, to raise as her own."

Mama's eyes flashed. "You've already made up your mind. In your imagination you cast the first stone at your own daughter! But you're wrong, Husband!"

"Mind your tongue, woman! One more word and I'll put you out of this house as well!". . .

Mama put her arm protectively around Mary's shoulders. . . . "All their marriage Elisheba and Zachariah have prayed for a child. I know Elisheba will be made complete by The Eternal. I know the prayers of Zachariah have been heard and remembered. My sister and her husband will have a baby of their own. And all that the angel said to Mary will be proven true. Then you'll know the true meaning of your shame. You'll know that nothing is impossible with Adonai!"

Papa slammed his fist on the table. "Hear me, woman! If it is proven that the girl is a liar and has played the harlot, leave her."

"Leave her? Where?"

"Does it matter? In the gutter. Let her sell herself for food. She is not welcome in this house. She is dead. Our daughter is dead to us." Only now, as his rage boiled over, did he look at Mary. Eyes were red-rimmed with anger as he shook his finger in her face. "You! See what you've done . . . to your family with this . . . lie? Torn us apart! Don't come back! You are dead to me! Dead to your mother and your sisters! Disgrace! Shame you have heaped on my head! The rocks of Nazareth may not break your bones, though you deserve to be stoned. But you are as dead to me as if Yosef denounced you publicly in the market square and chose the weapon of execution from the rocks of my own field. Now leave me! Both of you. No more words. Go to Beth Karem. That is your only hope of salvation!"

—pp. 94–96

ASK

Contrast Mary's parents' responses. Why do they respond the way they do? What conflicting emotions do you think they have?

____

____

____

If you were Mary's parents (think of the shame and embarrassment brought upon your household to have a pregnant, unwed daughter) how would you respond initially? More like Mary's mama—or her papa? Or a combination of the two?

Notice that although Papa's initial reaction is intense fury, he later defends Mary's honor when Yosef questions it: "Are you calling my daughter a liar? I tell you that is what she claims to have seen! . . . Mary has never lied to me! You say you love her. Then believe her! This is what Mary says happened!" (p. 86).

When there is a gap between belief and disbelief in an incredible story, do you tend to believe (like Mary's mother and her younger sisters—see pp. 81–82) or disbelieve (like Mary's papa)? Give an example from your own life.

READ

I am your servant, Adonai. I am yours. Anything. Anything you ask. But Lord, what about Yosef? You know I gave him my heart. My promise that I would always be his. I love him. What will he think?

—p. 82

I am your servant, Adonai. But Papa is right. Who am I that you would honor me? Just like everyone else. Small dreams. Yosef to love me. Children of my own. A small little life here in the place I grew up. That's all I have ever wanted. Who am I? And am I strong enough to face Papa's anger? certain disgrace? strong enough to maybe even lose Yosef? I am your servant, Lord. I am. But my heart might break for it.

—p. 83

Yosef! Have I lost him? Let him believe me. His heart is broken. Such a good heart. Such a good man.

—p. 85

Husband. I have lost you, Yosef! Our dreams of life together. O, Lord, I am your servant, but . . . I will never see Yosef again.

—p. 86

O Adonai! Papa appears a righteous man, yet secretly he's so cruel and bitter. I have heard Papa pray. Every day of my life he has prayed for the Lord's Anointed to come save Israel. Did he ever believe you would hear his prayers? Or did he only speak the words loud enough and often enough so others would hear him praying and believe he was righteous? O Adonai, help Papa believe you are, and that nothing is impossible for you! . . . Though my father despises me and the man I have loved believes I am a harlot, I am your servant. Nothing is impossible for you! May it be . . . whatever it may be . . . only as you will it for me.

—p. 95

ASK

When Mary is caught in the maelstrom of shouting and anger, what conflicted emotions of her own does she reveal?

___

___

___

If the person you love was walking away from you for good, how would you respond inwardly? outwardly?

___

___

___

READ

She spoke one word. One name. Her one concern. "Yosef."

"It's nobody's business, Mary! Take my advice. Lay low. I did. Everybody thought I was dying. Asked Zachariah if I was sick and dying. Nobody's business, I said. Nobody's but God's business! And I stayed inside out of sight. If you lie on the ground, you cannot fall. So, I didn't show myself until I was . . . this . . . big! . . . So, do what I did. If you keep on talking, you'll just end up saying everything you didn't mean to say. They won't believe it anyway."

—Conversation between Mary and Elisheba (p. 124)

ASK

Why is Yosef Mary's one concern? If you were Mary, would you also be concerned about what other people—especially those in your town—would say as they saw your belly growing? Why or why not?

On a scale of 1 (not important at all) to 10 (crucial), how important is it to you what others think of you? In what ways do you let others' perspectives impact you?

READ

"I say the Shema every day, five times a day. But I have never known how to live it. Not really. Love the Lord with all my heart, mind, and strength? . . . I am the Lord's servant. May all you have said come to pass for me. May the heart of Yahweh fill me with love and the hand of Yahweh give me strength. May the spirit of Yahweh give me wisdom."

—YOSEF (p. 168)

ASK

Whom do you love with all your heart, mind, and strength? If someone was watching your life, how could they tell?

____

____

____

How can you become more like Mary—trusting and accepting what comes your way? In what situation do you need to trust that God knows what He's doing?

____

____

____

WONDER . . .

Onias sighed. . . . There were many things about his life Tovah had kept neat and in working order: Apparel and living conditions were two. And attitudes were an even bigger realm altogether.

—p. 169

Delight yourself in the LORD
and He will give you the desires of your heart.
Commit your way to the LORD;
trust in Him and He will do this:
He will make your righteousness shine like the dawn,
the justice of your case like the noonday sun.
Be still before the LORD and wait patiently for Him.

—PSALM 37:5-7

Mary had a heart for God that overcame great adversity. So did Tovah:

"Tovah's great big heart always reached out to those in need. Onias had been constantly amazed at her ability to connect with people who were hurting. She had been able to get them to open up and speak about troubles Onias had never even guessed at."

"Never draw back from doing any good that is in your hand to perform," she always said. *"There are always those in greater need than you."*

—p. 169

Tovah's daughter, Menorah, also "had a heart for God. She made up songs about angels and heaven as she played at her papa's feet. She spoke often and out loud to the Almighty about every concern and joy" (p. 5).
What is the attitude of your heart today? Do you speak to God about every concern and joy?

Everyone is lost like sheep who have wandered off. All need a shepherd to lead their hearts back to God.

—p. 166

4 UNEXPECTED JOURNEYS

> This morning was the end of life as Mary had known it. The end of pleasant childhood and drowsy dreams of a future that would have allowed her to live in the serenity of obscurity.
>
> —p. 102

When has your life taken an unexpected direction? Share the story.

____

____

____

Have you ever wished for obscurity—only to be thrust into the limelight? How did you feel about the attention? What was the result?

____

____

____

Mary had expected to be married shortly. But all her life's plans were disrupted by her unexpected journey. For her it was an emotional and spiritual, as well as a physical, journey. Because her father didn't believe her, she was forced to leave her home to learn if the angel's message was true or a figment of her imagination.

READ

Mary shouldered her pack that contained food enough for a week of travel by foot.

One last look round to remember how it was.

The little house. Papa's workshop. The barn. The cheese room. Mary drank in the final view of the familiar little farm surrounded by orchards and fields frosted with newly sprouted barley.

When will I see home again, Lord? My little sisters? Papa? Yosef? And where will you lead me between this moment and then? What adventure have you planned? I am your servant.

Even one spring day away from Galilee seemed like too long.

She would never seen home again if Papa did not relent. He did not come out to say good-bye.

—pp. 102–103

O Adonai, I believe you are faithful and true. I choose to believe you. Mama says everything will come right in the end. Be with Yosef. Comfort his heart. Somehow give him peace. Don't hold it against Papa that he doesn't believe your promises. Remember Papa didn't see the glory of the angel or hear the music of the angel's words. He has a daughter who says she is going to have a baby and that an angel said it was your child. No wonder he's so angry. So, have mercy. . . . O Adonai, I am excited. And just a bit frightened of what's ahead. This beginning—where will it end? My heart rejoices in your love and mercy! As I start this journey, walk with me; guide my steps and the steps of my beloved. You are Adonai, the Lord who guards my heart . . . my lips . . . from sinning against you. I am your servant.

—pp. 104–105

Mama whispered to Mary. "Five days on the road to Beth Karem with the town gossip. A woman like this, a danger to you and the child. Remember, silence, Mary. Treasure the truth in your heart. On this journey there's safety for you only in silence. Don't cast pearls before swine, eh?"

—p. 104

O Adonai, I am so grateful for Mama! You knew I would need someone, even if it is only one, who believes me and defends me. O Adonai, you haven't left me without comfort. I am your servant!

—p. 103

ASK

If you were Mary, how would you feel about the journey ahead? Would you be frightened? excited? something else? Why?

____

____

____

When has "only one" believed in you and defended you? How did that event affect your perspective of that person? of yourself?

____

____

____

When have you "cast pearls before swine" (haven't we all at times?!)? What was the result? When do you think it's best to "treasure the truth in your heart," as Mary did?

____

____

____

READ

Mary knew the tangled events, the darkness of their age, all had something to do with the timing of Gabriel's message. Within Mary's womb was the One Herod feared more than anyone. Yet Mary was unafraid. The angel had told her nothing was impossible for Adonai to accomplish, and she believed him.

Mary's excitement grew as she and Mama walked up the slope. Just ahead was Elisheba and the confirmation that what the angel had proclaimed to Mary was true: *And you shall bear a son.*

—pp. 112–113

Mama's face was flushed with excitement. "All these years we've prayed for Elisheba! Oh, Mary! To think my sister, after all these years, could be expecting!"

Mary, mindful of her vow of silence, nodded broadly and pointed to the house. Soon enough Mama would see for herself what Mary was certain of. Elisheba, like Sarah and Hannah of days long past, was surely pregnant as the angel had told Mary she would be.

—p. 113

Mama took her hand. "Oh, Mary. Mary! There is Elisheba! Hanging wash beside the house. Call out to her, Mary. Look! Look at her, Mary! Do you see?"

Her silence at an end at last, Mary cupped her hands around her mouth and called, "Shalom, Elisheba! God who keeps his promises has remembered!"

—p. 114

ASK

Imagine the scene: It's been a long journey (especially with the gossipy Deborah and her scowling husband). Finally Mary and her mother arrive at Beth Karem, the House of the Vine.

What seems to be Mary's frame of mind?

____

____

____

Her mother's frame of mind?

____

____

____

READ

Elisheba gave a joyous cry. "Mary! You are blessed by Adonai above all other women! And blessed, cherished, adored, and longed for is the child you will bear!"

Tears of joy streamed down Mary's cheeks. "Oh! How I praise the Lord! And oh! How my spirit rejoices in Adonai, my Savior!"

Elisheba cupped Mary's face with aged hands. "But who am I, eh? Why am I so favored, that the mother of my Lord and Redeemer should come to me?"

Mary kissed Elisheba on the left cheek and on the right. She laid her head on Elisheba's shoulder and replied, "He took notice of His lowly servant girl. From now on generation after generation will call me blessed! For He, El Shaddai, the Mighty One alone, is holy, and He has done great things for me! Holy, holy, holy is His name!". . .

Mary searched the lined face of her aunt, then turned her head toward the skyline of Jerusalem. "Adonai's mercy goes on from generation to generation to all who fear Him. The strength of His mighty arm does tremendous things! He scatters people who are proud and haughty! He brings down tyrants from their thrones. But look! See! Oh, how Adonai has lifted up the humble! He fills the hungry with good things but sends the rich away with empty hands. Adonai has remained true to the promise He made to His servant Israel! He has never forgotten His promise to be merciful. This is proof that the covenant with Avraham and his descendants, to be merciful to them forever, is an everlasting covenant!"

Elisheba clung tightly to Mary. "My dear, you are blessed! Blessed, because you believe that Adonai will bring to full completion every word he has spoken to the smallest detail!"

Mary nodded in gratitude that the journey had come to an end. The confirmation promised by Gabriel was here.

—pp. 114–115

ASK

Picture this "homecoming" between Elisheba and Mary. Retell the story of their joyful reunion in your own words.

___

___

___

Although Mary's journey was unexpected, because she chose to follow God, the confirmation of His blessing was at the end of it.

Have you ever chosen to follow God in a risky situation—even when doing so didn't logically make sense? What confirmation(s), if any, did you receive at the end of your journey?

___

___

___

Note that Mary believed the "ending," even when she couldn't see it yet.

READ

"Is she pregnant? Answer me! Is she with child? This girl you promised to me . . . promised is a virgin . . . is pregnant?". . . Yosef's words were thick with bitterness and sarcasm. . . .

"Suppose . . . what you say is true. . . . What am I to do, eh? Tell everyone an angel visited the girl I intended to marry, and now she is pregnant by the power of the Almighty? Without any help from a man? Who would believe this? Who am I—the world's biggest fool? And if it was true that she is the virgin of Isaias' prophecy, how could I ever marry her? How could I? . . . Who am I to be chosen with the task of raising . . . the son of . . . David? Was David the name this angel gave the father? Son of David? So, how many Davids do I know in Nazareth? A dozen? At least. I would always ask myself, son of which David?"

—pp. 86–87

Adonai, blessed are you, creator of life. Blessed are you . . . though you don't let me sleep. I'm too sad even to pray. I think of all the hopes I had, over now. When I thought of her, my nights were full of joyful songs. I search my soul and think about the difference. Have you rejected me forever? Will you never again show me favor? Has your unfailing love failed me? Have you slammed the door on your mercy? . . .

Voices rang in Yosef's head.

The voice of Yosef's mind, telling him what was right, lecturing his heart again that he was betrayed.

The mocking words from his friends and neighbors in the street.

Voices.

His own confusion. His love arguing against Mary's betrayal. . . .

To live life alone or to forgive her and take her in. To raise another man's child as his own. . . .

Voices.

He could not yield to love or mercy! He must do what was just! As for the son or daughter of Mary's unknown David, the child would grow up with Zachariah of Beth Karem for his adopted father.

—pp. 137–138

Yosef had wondered if he'd ever have a son to whom he could pass on his abilities. Now he doubted it. Yosef knew he was a man made for loyalty, able to love just one woman. He adored Mary from the core of his being. How could any other ever take her place?

This is my fate. The blessings of The Most High have changed to hatred.

—p. 139

At his betrothal to Mary, Yosef had begun work on just such a wedding present for her. It was solid oak. Yosef had already carved the pattern of a pomegranate branch blossoming with flowers, which he would later inlay with walnut and cherry wood on each end. The chest was a lovely thing. Yosef would have given it to Mary on their wedding night . . . if there had been a wedding. Now he considered selling it to the young farmer. What was the use of saving it?

Each evening when he lay down to sleep, Yosef prayed and hoped he would have another dream, hoped he would receive some special revelation for all the questions that rattled around in his head during daylight. But there were no more dreams.

—p. 163

ASK

Imagine that you are Yosef, arriving home from helping at the Temple in Jerusalem. You arrive at your betrothed's house, longing to see her, and instead hear a far-fetched tale about her being pregnant!
Which of Yosef's thoughts about Mary would you share?

about God's goodness and love?

about your dreams for the future?

What would your plan of action be?

READ

Yosef had always walked uprightly before the Lord, prayed the blessings, paid his tithes, helped those poorer than himself, and lived a quiet life. He had always sensed the approval of God . . . until now.

—p. 164

All mankind is cursed to pay the penalty of another's sin: the rebellion of mankind's first father and mother in Eden. That is how death first entered the world. Because of their sin, all humans who live on earth are condemned to die.

"May I not be judged by my own merits?"

And if you were? Are you perfect? Have you never sinned?

"No one is perfect. Who can live a perfect life?"

That, then, is the answer to your question. Only One is righteous. Only Adonai is righteous. He who walked in the garden with Adam and his wife. . . .

"Am I to live forever under an ancient curse and pay for sins I didn't commit?"

No.

"Then tell me how I can be free of it. How can I live the life I want to live? I'd like to marry. Have a family. Serve the Lord and my fellow man.". . .

Obey the Lord. . . .

"I have obeyed . . . mostly. But look! Look!"

Avraham believed Adonai and that belief was counted as righteousness.

—pp. 165–166

ASK

Do you believe that each person should be judged by his or her own merits? Why or why not?

___

___

___

In what area of life have you "obeyed . . . mostly"?

READ

I love her. That was an easy place to begin: a solid, indisputable fact. . . .

But nothing stayed simple after that.

She's betrayed me. She's been with someone else. . . .

She doesn't look pregnant. Is she?

But she doesn't deny it. She and her mother have made up this wild tale.

Could she have been raped? I'd kill him; then I'd marry her.

But she makes no such claim. . . .

I can't marry her now. We can never be husband and wife. . . .

Can I even live in this village after she has another man's child? What kind of man would that make me? Even if the gossip stops when people meet me, what will I read lurking in their eyes?

And the child? How will he or she be regarded here? How will I *act around the child, knowing it isn't mine? . . .*

To save his own reputation, Yosef could have her hauled before the local Sanhedrin. There he'd denounce her. Since they were formally betrothed, the charge would be adultery. . . .

Then, so long as she didn't deny the charge, Yosef would be absolved from any wrong, completely justified in the matter. He was the wronged party, liable to receive smirking sympathy but publicly approved for his righteousness.

Of course, Mary's life would never be the same—not here, not in a village as small as Nazareth. She and her family would have to move away . . . to make up some story about the child's father being dead.

But would they go? What if Heli cast her out? What if he drove her away, as was his right? . . .

His view grew blurry with his tears.

If I don't denounce her to the council, what will they think of me? What will all my neighbors think? Will they take all their business somewhere else? How will I live? Will I have to leave here? Where will I go? Back to Yerushalayim?

But I love her.
Yahweh! Yosef's heart cried in anguish. *Help me!*
—pp. 90–92

Yosef . . . had no fears about Mary's character, but rather about his own. Was he worthy of this awesome task? Was he strong enough to do all that was required of him in such an undertaking? to rear the promised Son of David? to be the sort of father who could teach a prince to be the king of Israel?
—p. 221

Yosef clasped her hand and placed it over his heart. "I can wait for you. Love you always. Through everything. Anything. My life, that's what I offer you . . . and him. And if it means giving up my life . . . yes. Even then, it's yours."
—p. 203

ASK

How does Yosef move beyond his betrayal and anger to accepting not only Mary as his wife, but also his awesome responsibility to raise and nurture the Messiah?

____

____

____

Have you ever felt "not worthy" to do a great task? When? What was the result of your action or inaction?

____

____

____

READ

Chestnut hair tumbled over her shoulders. Oval face was framed by a pale blue shawl. Gold-flecked brown eyes locked onto Yosef's. Lips parted in a smile that seemed to say, *Well Yosef, I'm glad you've come. About time!*

She nodded to him. Welcoming. Forgiving his unbelief. Genuinely glad to see him.

He exhaled loudly, ashamed of the anger he had felt toward her and suddenly in awe at the love he saw in her eyes. . . .

Eyes shining, Anna confided, "Yosef . . . she always hoped you'd come. That you'd be here to witness this."

—p. 197

All the old feelings of tenderness—emotions nearly forgotten—awoke again. She was his. Pretty, bright, with a laugh like a song. Everyone liked her. And she was his!

She held her head erect, chin high, smiling, confident in herself. Yosef knew she would have been the same even if he had not come to Beth Karem. Even without him, even if he had broken off the engagement, Mary would not have seemed alone.

Highly favored. Her joy in that designation was not manifested by arrogance but rather by a kind word for everyone present, a pat on the shoulder, eyes that met another's gaze and connected.

And she is my own to love and protect, Yosef told himself as he noticed admiration in the expressions of other young men when they watched her move.

—pp. 197–198

[Mary] said, "It won't be easy."

"I want to take care of you."

"I think . . . there is some danger."

"I want to protect you . . . both of you."

"I don't know what it all means, Yosef. Herod. Those men at the Temple—the men Herod put in power. I'm not afraid of them, not now. But we'll have to be careful, you know?". . .

"I'll take care of you, Mary. I will."

"Everything must seem so . . . ordinary. Even though we both know the truth of it."

—p. 202

ASK

In what ways is Yosef's and Mary's reunion sweet?

Bittersweet?

WONDER . . .

"After so many years of praying, our prayers are answered."

Mama chuckled. "Only one thing a mother must always remember: All things are possible with Adonai."

—Conversation between Elisheba and Mama (p. 116)

"I still don't know why . . . me."

"Can't you see it? I saw it, always. But I didn't know what it meant . . . that I loved you so. Or how big it is. Or that God took notice of you too. I should have believed you."

"Little wonder that you doubted."

"I mean us, you and me. Ordinary, you know."

—Conversation between Mary and Yosef (p. 203)

Adonai uses ordinary men . . . and ordinary women . . . to accomplish His plans. . . . Believe His promise.

—p. 166

We are all so ordinary compared to the Almighty Adonai of the universe. And yet He uses us to accomplish His plans.

Dear reader, God takes notice of *you.* What mighty plans He may be accomplishing in your life at this very moment! All things are possible with Adonai!

5 PROPHECY REVEALED

> "Elijah. The one who is to come . . . to prepare the way for Messiah." The old man smiled. "So I will see him. I will see the One who will wear he crown!"
>
> —Simeon (p. 25)

If someone told your parents that their child (you!) would someday be a great leader and turn people's hearts toward good, what impact do you think that would make on how they raise you?

____

____

____

on the way you view yourself?

____

____

____

on the way you view others?

____

____

____

on the way you view the happenings in the entire world?

____

____

____

Do you ever tire of dealing with evil? of dealing with people who seem determined to do what's wrong and thwart what's right? of those who simply stand by and do nothing (from apathy or fear)? of fighting your own impulses that lead you to compromise or take the easy way out?

Nothing has changed much in the human condition since the first century, for that's how the people of Israel felt. But in the midst of terrible darkness, they also lived with the bright light of hope.

If you lived in Israel back then, you would have heard much about the Messiah—the Promised One who would deliver God's people. You would have heard bedtime stories of the prophecies that made your heart race with excitement and joy, knowing that someday there would be an end to the evil tyrants who rule over you.

But before this Messiah would arrive, prophecy stated that someone else would prepare the way. Who would this forerunner be? And how can we know if that forerunner ever arrived? What about Messiah Himself? Has He yet walked on the earth, as prophecied?

Scripture is filled with truths about Messiah's forerunner, the first arrival of the Messiah, the work of the Messiah, and the promise that someday He will return and establish a very different kingdom for those who believe in Him. Although we can only touch on a few of these prophecies here, we encourage you to carefully search Scripture for additional references.

READ

This is a record of the ancestors of Yeshua the Messiah, a descendant of King David and of Avraham.

Avraham was the father of Yitzchak, Yitzchak was the father of Ya'acov. . . . Ya'acov was the father of Yosef, the husband of Mary.

—p. 136

Thus there were fourteen generations in all from Abraham to David, fourteen from David to the exile to Babylon, and fourteen from the exile to the Christ.

—MATTHEW 1:17 (SEE VERSES 1-16 FOR THE CAREFUL LISTING OF GENERATIONS)

"Fourteen generations from Avraham to David? Fourteen from David to Exile? Thirteen from Exile to me? One more . . . and then? Fourteen is completed once again. The number of David's name. The number of the strong hand of the Lord. The fulfillment of prophecy. The establishment of David's eternal kingdom."

—YOSEF (p. 144)

Torah schoolboys learned to recite the list of Abraham's descendants through his son, Isaac, then Jacob, then Judah, till they finally arrived at King David.

Fourteen generations later. . . .

Many scholars could also recite the names of the royal offspring of David. Some were pronounced with spitting, or with the sign against the evil eye, since some of David's grandchildren had done great evil to Israel.

Still: fourteen again. From King David to the destruction of the Jewish nation by Nebuchadnezzar . . . fourteen layers of lives.

Onias paused to shift the light to a better angle on his reading.

How many generations had it been *since* the Exile?

The trail was not so clearly marked. Many of the records had been lost. Not all those who grew up in Babylon wanted to return to Israel. Families were divided; histories lost. Of those who did return, few preserved the accounts of their bloodlines. The old tribe and clan allegiances seemed unimportant to many. The kingship had been abolished. What did ancient history matter now, almost five hundred years later?

Many nights Onias had spent piecing the picture together from myriad books and fragments of scrolls. He stitched a patchwork quilt of ancestry: a bit here, a trace there, a letter reporting to a father left behind in Babylon that a new grandson had been born in Jerusalem. The work was all reference and cross-reference, painstakingly built up over many weary, bleary-eyed sessions. . . .

The conclusion he had reached just tonight lay in front of him: At least twelve generations of David's line had come and gone since the time of the Exile. More likely the thirteenth was grown to manhood.

The fourteenth lineal descendant of King David might already be alive, or at least must be born soon. The times were complete. Messiah would soon be revealed. Perhaps not today or tomorrow. Perhaps not for a number of years as yet.

But soon! Soon!

"Come soon, Lord Messiah," Onias spoke aloud. Such words in Herod's kingdom were treasonous.

Herod had reason to be concerned for his throne!

—pp. 69–70

ASK

Is the recounting of history important to you? Why or why not?

___

___

___

What have you learned about your own family history that may affect your present ? your future?

___

___

___

Why would the evil king Herod be so concerned about the fulfillment of prophecy in some ancient documents? Why would he bother to consult "the experts" to find out what it said?

___

___

___

Archaeological discoveries have proven repeatedly that Scripture contains historical truth. Yet many people today work hard to discredit these truths. Why do you think this is so?

READ

"I will send my messenger, who will prepare the way before me. Then suddenly the Lord you are seeking will come to his temple; the messenger of the covenant, whom you desire, will come," says the Lord Almighty.

—Malachi 3:1

"I will send you the prophet Elijah before that great and dreadful day of the LORD comes. He will turn the hearts of the fathers to their children, and the hearts of the children to their fathers."

—Malachi 4:5-6

Mary's heart sang out to the Lord: *My soul praises you, Adonai! Can it be that the longed-for baby old Elisheba carries in her womb is the same Elijah you promised would come before the birth of your Anointed, the Son of David? Like Samuel, who was miraculously born to Hannah, so this baby will be a miracle to Elisheba! As the prophet Samuel anointed David, the young shepherd of Bethlehem, king of Israel, will Elisheba's child anoint the son I carry as king of Israel? Will he mend broken homes, shattered families, and hopeless lives, and bring Israel back to you, O Adonai?*

—pp. 113–114

Mary . . . hurried to a town in the hill country of Judea, where she entered Zechariah's home and greeted Elizabeth. When Elizabeth heard Mary's greeting, the baby leaped in her womb, and Elizabeth was filled with the Holy Spirit. In a loud voice she exclaimed: "Blessed are you among women, and blessed is the child you will bear! But why am I so favored, that the mother of my Lord should come to me? As soon as the sound of your greeting reached my ears, the baby in my womb leaped for joy."

—Luke 1:39-44

In those days John the Baptist came, preaching in the Desert of Judea and saying, "Repent, for the kingdom of heaven is near." This is he who was spoken of through the prophet Isaiah [see Isaiah 40:3]:

"A voice of one calling in the desert,
'Prepare the way for the Lord,
make straight paths for him.'"

—MATTHEW 3:1-3

ASK

What life purpose(s) did God have in mind for the baby birthed by Elisheba (a Hebrew form of the name "Elizabeth")?

____

____

____

Why do you think God allowed this baby to be born to a couple like Elisheba and Zachariah?

____

____

____

READ

This is how the birth of Jesus Christ came about: His mother Mary was pledged to be married to Joseph, but before they came together, she was found to be with child through the Holy Spirit. Because Joseph her husband was a righteous man and did not want to expose her to public disgrace, he had in mind to divorce her quietly.

But after he considered this, an angel of the Lord appeared to him in a dream and said, "Joseph son of David, do not be afraid to take Mary home as your wife, because what is conceived in her is from the Holy Spirit. She will give birth to a son, and you are to give him the name Jesus, because he will save his people from their sins."

All this took place to fulfill what the Lord had said through the prophet [see Isaiah 7:14]: *"The virgin will be with child and will give birth to a son, and they will call him Immanuel"—which means, "God with us."*

When Joseph woke up, he did what the angel of the Lord had commanded him and took Mary home as his wife. But he had no union with her until she gave birth to a son. And he gave him the name Jesus.

—MATTHEW 1:18-25

Mary descends from the branch of David, through which the Great Shepherd, Immanu'el, God-with-us, will come. Pay attention! Nawzer *is the Hebrew word for baby.* Netzer *is the Hebrew word for branch. Baby and Branch, the child you name Yeshua, Salvation, will be Adonai, incarnate in human form. . . . But first you must carry Him on your shoulders. Yahweh declares this to you, Yosef, son of David! Do not be afraid! Hear the command of the Shema: "Hear, O Israel! The LORD our God is one LORD! You are to love the LORD with all your heart, mind, and strength!"*

To make the meaning of the commandment plain, the Lord enters the world first as a baby. What loving parent does not understand what it means to love his child? This, above all, makes it easy to understand and perform the first commandment to love the Lord. The Shema could be said, "Love this innocent baby as your own son! Love Him with all your heart, mind, and strength." With all the strength of your heart, mind, and body, cherish, guard, and protect the child from the powers of darkness who will seek to destroy Him while He is in your care. For this purpose you were born. Through love of a child you will understand the depth of God's love for you. From the beginning, before time, it was planned: The exiled heart longing for forgiveness will love and nurture and save the Firstborn Lamb of God, who will one day grow up and become his salvation! The plan is written plainly in Torah and will surely come to pass. . . .

Nothing is too hard for God.

—pp. 167–168

[Jesus] was the son, so it was thought, of Joseph.

—LUKE 3:23

Zachariah unrolled the scroll of the Judges and showed Mary the story of the angel of the Lord who brought word to Samson's parents that they who were childless would soon have a son. And when the couple asked the awesome messenger his name he replied, *"Why do you ask? For my name is Wonderful."*

Wonderful. The same Hebrew word used in Isaiah to proclaim the name of the Incarnate God who would one day rule upon David's throne [see Isaiah 9:6].

By Mary's serenity and joy, Zachariah knew that she understood her son would not be like any son ever born of woman. Her spirit understood all this, though Zachariah had no voice to explain to her.

He deliberately did not show her other verses: glimpses of suffering and rejection and even death for God's Anointed [see Isaiah 53:3-12]. Zachariah knew most of the atonement prophecies by heart. The scroll of Zechariah, the prophet whose name he bore, was planted thick in the sorrows promised for Mary's son [see Zechariah 12:10-11].

It was enough for now, Zachariah thought, that sweet Mary only knew her child's name was . . . Wonderful.

—p. 133

ASK

Historically, many have claimed to be the promised Messiah. What is so unique about the Messiah or the prophecies in Scripture? Why was He not like "any son ever born of woman"? Why is He not "a god," but "the God"?

___

___

___

How are the conception and birth of the Messiah different from the conception and birth of the forerunner of the Messiah? Why do you think this is?

___

___

___

Note: Luke 3:23-38 is a fascinating record of the lineage of Yeshua (the Hebrew word for "Jesus") all the way back to Adam and God Himself!

READ

Mary is also of the royal line of David. Through David's son Nathan. Her line is the lineage from which the Redeemer will be born.

"Mary? A woman?"

Carpenter. Do not miss the meaning of this writing.

"You are a dream. And I am a poor ignorant man dreaming you. Trying to understand. But I don't understand."

Both of you, Mary and Yosef, descendants of David but through different ancestors. Your ancestor King Jeconiah was cursed for turning from the Lord, and thus Messiah cannot come from your lineage. Mary's line back to David remains blessed. So each of you play a different role in redemption. She will bring forth the Redeemer. You are among those in David's lineage who will be redeemed.

—Conversation between Gabriel and Yosef (p. 141)

As Adonai promised to your fathers—and now swears to you—the babe soon to be born, this son of Mary, whose name means "bitter rebellion," is seed of woman. But, unlike Eve, this woman is no rebel. She is favored by the Lord above all women. He has searched her heart and found no bitterness there. She is found worthy. The seed of this woman is The One of whom it is written that one day He will crush the head of the serpent beneath His heel! And though His heel be bruised, He will break the bondage of sin and death over mankind once and forever! He who has spoken these things Was and Is and evermore Will Be!

—p. 143

Why do you think the Lord chose Mary as the mother of Yeshua? And Yosef as Yeshua's earthly father? What lineage and character qualities did they have?

___

___

___

What different roles do Mary and Yosef play in the promised plan of redemption? Why?

READ

There was a man in Jerusalem called Simeon, who was righteous and devout. He was waiting for the consolation of Israel, and the Holy Spirit was upon him. It had been revealed to him by the Holy Spirit that he would not die before he had seen the Lord's Christ. Moved by the Spirit, he went into the temple courts. When the parents brought in the child Jesus to do for him what the custom of the Law required, Simeon took him in his arms and praised God, saying:

"Sovereign Lord, as you have promised,
you now dismiss your servant in peace.
For my eyes have seen your salvation,
which you have prepared in the sight of all people,
a light for revelation to the Gentiles
and for glory to your people Israel."

The child's father and mother marveled at what was said about him. Then Simeon blessed them and said to Mary, his mother: "This child is destined to cause the falling and rising of many in Israel, and to be a sign that will be spoken against, so that the thoughts of many hearts will be revealed. And a sword will pierce your own soul too."

—LUKE 2:25-35

Simeon explained, "The *Ruach HaKodesh*, The Spirit of the Lord, has told me I will not die until I have seen The One about whom this is written. I heard his voice again in the Temple. The Lord has shown me. I know his name. What Messiah's name will be. It's written here. Plainly in Zechariah. Though this story was written about the high priest who presided here in the day of Zechariah, it reveals the name of The One who is coming to deliver his people."

—pp. 31–32

ASK

Of all the people who could respond to news about the Messiah, why do you think Scripture would record this old priest's response?

What is joyful about Simeon's vision from the Lord?

What is troubling about his vision and the few words he shares with Mary, the child's mother?

READ

For to us a child is born,
to us a son is given,
and the government will be on His shoulders.
And He will be called
Wonderful Counselor, Mighty God,
Everlasting Father, Prince of Peace.
Of the increase of His government and peace
there will be no end
He will reign on David's throne
and over His kingdom

establishing and holding it
with justice and righteousness
from that time on and forever.
—ISAIAH 9:6-7

"The days are coming," declares the LORD,
"when I will raise up to David
a righteous Branch,
a King who will reign wisely
and do what is just and right in the land.
In his days Judah will be saved
and Israel will live in safety.
This is the name by which he will be called:
The LORD Our Righteousness."
—JEREMIAH 23:5-6

Like a perfect lamb of sacrifice, He who is called Our Righteousness will make atonement for all unrighteousness! And as the Good Shepherd, He will lead the exiles home to safe pasture. Those who are lame He will carry on His shoulders.
—pp. 167–168

ASK

For what purposes is the righteous King coming? List as many as you can from the passages above.

____

____

____

What character qualities of Messiah can you gather from the prophecy in Isaiah 9:6-7?

____

____

____

How would the arrival of such a Messiah impact your life personally, were He to come to your home today?

READ

"I believe God alone is righteous."

Therefore believe . . . only God can atone for the unrighteousness of a man.

Pounding. Refining. Shaping. A pattern of timeless beauty emerged from unformed lumber.

"I know you are only a dream. But tell me, how would God do this for me?"

Yeshua means "salvation."

"Who can save me from my broken life? my loneliness?"

Yeshua alone can make a broken heart whole.

Both the timbre and the tempo of hammering changed. No longer removing obstructions but the softer tapping as perfect joints fitted together according to the plan of the master carpenter.

"Who is Yeshua?"

He is The Lord Our Righteousness.

"What must I do? Tell me? How can I free myself from the curse of a heritage which comes from the unrighteous branch of David's line?"

Free yourself? Yosef! Have you not learned? You can do nothing. It is not your righteousness but God's righteousness that will set you free. The Righteous Branch of David is very near.

"But not for me. I'm born from the branch that is cursed."

The Righteous Branch will not come from *you, Yosef. But He is coming* for *you. You are chosen because you are like all those who live under the curse of exile from the presence of God. You are like every lost lamb who longs to be found by God and forgiven and carried home in the arms of the Good Shepherd.*

"Oh, that he would carry me!"

First you will carry Him.

The smell of the unfamiliar incense intensified. Wood and blossom intermingled. Commonplace and holy entwined, inseparable.

"Me? How am I to carry one so great?"

In your arms. On your shoulders. Sometimes on your back. He will be very small for a while.

—Conversation between Gabriel and Yosef (pp. 166–167)

ASK

What does being "righteous" mean to you? Do you think someone can earn their way into heaven? Why or why not?

____

____

____

Would you expect the promised Messiah of the world to come in the form of a fragile baby? Why or why not?

____

____

____

Have you ever felt like a "lost lamb who longs to be found by God and forgiven and carried home"? When?

____

____

____

WONDER . . .

Have you not heard? What did the prophet Isaias write?

"A shoot will come up from the stump of Jesse;
From its roots a Branch will bear fruit.
The Ruach HaKodesh of Adonai will rest on him—
The Spirit of wisdom and of understanding—
The Spirit of counsel and of power,
The Spirit of knowledge and the fear of Adonai." [see Isaiah 11:1-2]
Tell me, Yosef, if you know, Of whom is the prophet speaking?

Yosef knew that answer readily enough. "Messiah, our Redeemer King, the Lord's Anointed, David's royal Son who is yet to come. He will be from the root of Jesse, David's father.

—p. 141

Who do you believe the Messiah of the world is? Do you believe He is "yet to come" or that He has already come, or both? Why?

6 SIGNS IN THE HEAVENS

> As the eternal plan quietly unfolded on earth, the heavens proclaimed the glory of God! Great wonders were transpiring above the nations. Yet except for a handful of men, no one on earth took note of the signs of the times.
>
> —p. 49

If a friend told you, "I think I saw a message in the stars," how would you respond?

____

____

____

When you see the stars or experience a lightning storm or a rushing wind, what do you think of? What emotions do you experience?

____

____

____

If you gaze into a starry sky, you cannot help but realize the awesome depth and breadth of the universe in which we live. You may also experience a stirring in your soul for a deeper, stronger connection with that universe . . . and the Creator of such a massive, complex world.

Throughout the Bible are fascinating glimpses of signs in the heavens. And even more amazing, they all point, like messengers, to one source: Almighty God, the Creator of the universe.

READ

God said, "Let there be lights in the expanse of the sky to separate the day from the night, and let them serve as signs to mark seasons and days and years, and let them be lights in the expanse of the sky to give light on the earth." And it was so. God made two great lights—the greater light to govern the day and the lesser light to govern the night. He also made the stars. God set them in the expanse of the sky to give light on the earth, to govern the day and the night, and to separate light from darkness. God saw that it was good. And there was evening, and there was morning—the fourth day.

—GENESIS 1:14-19

"Don't be afraid," said the Incarnate One who had by His word created the rising sun and the heavens and the earth.

—p. vii

The heavens declare the glory of God;
the skies proclaim the work of His hands.
Day after day they pour forth speech;
night after night they display knowledge.
There is no speech or language
where their voice is not heard.
Their voice goes out into all the earth,
their words to the ends of the world.

—PSALM 19:1-4

ASK

Imagine you have a front-row seat to watch the creation of the world. What would you see? Describe the story in your own words.

____

____

____

How would seeing the creation impact your view of:
whether or not God exists?

______

______

______

who God is?

______

______

______

what He accomplished at the beginning of the world?

______

______

______

what He could accomplish now in your life?

______

______

______

READ

What awesome power was locked inside Yeshua's ordinary seeming flesh.

Hidden behind hands and feet and a face and skin was the very One whose first word had commanded *LIGHT*!

His second word had been *GOOD*!

Too soon he had spoken the word *MAN*!

After the word *man*, things had become difficult and complicated because every man secretly wanted to be God. Every man wanted to give the orders.

—pp. x–xi [SEE ALSO GENESIS 1:3-4; 2:7]

[Yeshua] could have been every man's son.

Any man's brother.

The son of Mary.

The events of last night left no doubt that He was also the only Son of The One who had thundered from the cloud.

—p. viii

This is my Son, whom I love; with him I am well pleased. Listen to him!

—MATTHEW 17:5

Balthasar was excited by what he saw. He explained that Porrima, the star at the heart of The Virgin, is called in Hebrew The Star of Atonement. When Messiah comes, His purpose will be atonement for mankind, just as The Adam was very near The Atonement star tonight. I asked him what it meant that atonement dwelt beneath the virgin's heart, and he told me about a prophecy delivered by the renowned Isaias, in which the prophet says a virgin will conceive and bear a son and that this miraculous child will be the Messiah. Furthermore, there is an even more ancient prophecy, in the Book of Beginnings, *that the seed of the woman will conquer the serpent, the enemy of mankind.* [Genesis 3:14–15]

—p. 56

ASK

Why do you think the world became so complicated after man was created?

____

____

____

What do these passages say about:

who Yeshua is?

____

____

____

Yeshua's purpose?

____

____

____

READ

Skim the following passages from *Fourth Dawn* and Scripture for a quick journey through some of the nation of Israel's history:

Tonight [Zachariah] and Elisheba and Mary and Anna stood on the roof as he pointed out the wandering stars called The Righteous and The Sabbath as they spun around one another within the constellation of The Fish, which symbolized the vast multitude of Abraham's descendants. Zachariah remembered that such a sight had heralded the birth of the lawgiver Mosheh 1,365 years before. He remembered that these same stars had appeared in this exact way above Egypt. Then the frightened Egyptian astrologers had warned Pharaoh that every male Hebrew slave of two years and under must be killed.

Only the infant Mosheh had survived.

At what price was Israel's redemption paid? What would be the cost now?

—p. 132

With Your mighty arm You redeemed Your people,
The descendants of Ya'acov and Yosef.
Your thunder was heard in the whirlwind;

Your lightning lit up the world.
The earth trembled and quaked.
Your path led through the sea,
Your way through the mighty waters,
Though Your footprints were not seen.
You led Your people like a flock
By the hand of Moses and Aaron! [see Psalm 77:13-20]
Now You, Immanuel, come to dwell among men!
You will open Your mouth in parables!
You will utter hidden things,
Things from of old!
By Your own hand You will lead Your people
By Your own hand
Like a flock
You will lead their hearts back to God.
You are the Shepherd-King!
Son of Avraham, Son of David, Son of The Most High!
—pp. 143–144

Elijah was the prophet whose prayers shut up or loosened rain from the heavens.
—p. 46 (READ THE ENTIRE STORY IN 1 KINGS 17:1-7; 18:16-46)

"A menorah? In a cistern?" Onias asked curiously.

"Each of its seven branches represents one of the visible lights in the heavens and the seven eyes of the Eternal. Even here, where all is darkness, the radiance of the Lord's creation shines. The pagans have made false gods of what the One God has created, but here, in the stones of Yerushalayim, Truth will shine."

—CONVERSATION BETWEEN ONIAS AND SIMEON (p. 27)

I will send you the prophet Elijah before that great and dreadful day of the LORD *comes. He will turn the hearts of the fathers to their children, and the hearts of the children to their fathers; or else I will come and strike the land with a curse.*
—MALACHI 4:5-6

They were, Zachariah observed, almost the exact words the angel used to explain to him the purpose of his child's life. The immediate fulfillment of the final prophecy in Scripture had been announced to Zachariah in the Temple. Over four hundred years had passed since this ending prophecy had been recorded, yet to the angel it was as though no time had passed.

Gabriel proclaimed that God had remembered, and now Elijah was coming. The old blended seamlessly with that which was brand-new. The coming of the Lord was very near!

—pp. 47–48

"Can't help but wonder. Elisheba being fifty-six. Who ever heard of a woman giving birth at fifty-six? Has to mean . . . something good."

The old woman scowled. "Sarah was ninety. Aye. And it was indeed a portent of something mighty in the heavens."

—CONVERSATION BETWEEN TWO WOMEN WAITING FOR THE BIRTH OF YOCHANAN (HEBREW NAME FOR JOHN) (p. 184)

Zachariah spent his hours poring over the Scriptures, making notes, quietly studying the prophecies about the coming of the Son of David. On clear nights he climbed onto the roof and gazed into the heavens and saw the certain sign of Messiah as Mars, the star called The Adam in Hebrew, moved nearer and nearer to the constellation of The Virgin. The branch lifted high in her right hand, the shock of wheat in the other, the constellation of The Virgin told a story to anyone with eyes to see and a mind to ask the questions.

—p. 49

Between two and three hours later the event I have been hoping for occurred: The two bright lights in the sign representing the nation of Israel are once again heading toward a close conjunction. At midnight they stood due south of me.

United again, true Righteousness and true Sabbath rest for the Jews! It must be significant! It must! I can't wait to tell Balthasar and Esther. Something powerful is happening! The One God, whom I serve, is at last letting His plan unfold.

—p. 214

ASK

How has God used the signs of the heavens (stars, lightning, wind, etc.) to impact people throughout history (see the above quotes for hints)?

____

____

____

What do the signs of the heavens in these passages reveal about the Messiah?

____

____

____

What do you think old Simeon means when he says, "The pagans have made false gods of what the One God has created, but here, in the stones of Yerushalayim, Truth will shine"?

____

____

____

READ

Almost dawn. Everyone asleep but Zachariah, who searched the scrolls of the Isaias, Malachi, Dani'el, and Zechariah. His head ached. He was exhausted, but the fascination kept him riveted to his desk. So much he did not understand. So much. Layer by layer he examined the prophecies, inwardly rehearsing the words the angel had spoken to him.

He got up and stood at the window to watch as Mercury, The Messenger star, rose before the sun in the constellation of The Water Bearer. Were the heavens not filled with such signs in these last few months?

—pp. 46–47

ASK

What significance does the Hebrew name of each of these stars have? How do they point toward the Messiah? (See Melchior's observations on pp. 10–11, 45–46, 55–56, 146–147, 181–183, 213–214 and Zachariah's search of the scrolls on pp. 46–49.)

*Moon, Holy Spirit

*Mercury, Messenger Star

*Venus, Splendor

*Sun, Holy Fire

*Mars, The Adam

*Jupiter, Righteous

*Saturn, Sabbath

*Virgo, The Virgin

*Leo or Aryeh, "The Lion" (pp. 45–46—also the star, Regulus)

*The Water Bearer

*The Fish

*Cygnus, The Swan (and its brightest star, The Judge)

READ

Zachariah sang gently into the face of the little one who seemed to be earnestly listening to his father's every word—holding on, intent to hear it all:

"*And you, my child, will be called a prophet of the Most High;*
for you will go on before the Lord to prepare a way for Him,
to give His people the knowledge of salvation
through the forgiveness of their sins.
Because of the tender mercies of our God,
by which the rising sun, our dawn, will come to us from heaven
to shine on those living in darkness
and in the shadow of death,
to guide our feet into the path of peace." [see Luke 1:76-79]
—pp. 201–202

"Anything related to the comin' of Messiah makes Herod nervous . . . and anything makin' Herod nervous has twice that effect on Boethus!"

"It'll be hard to keep this under wraps." Eliyahu stared at the first stars popping out in the eastern heavens. "Old Simeon says he saw no angel, but he did hear a voice! It told him he'd not die before he saw the Lord's Messiah!"

"So, what's to be done?" Zadok inquired. "For our part, I mean?"

Onias shrugged. "We watch. We wait. We study. Zachariah stays with Old Simeon while here in Yerushalayim. I'll see what else I can learn from them. Meanwhile, you go back to your duties with the flocks, Eliyahu to his flock, and I to my students. And most of all, we pray." He gestured toward a bright star hovering over the Temple, directly above where the golden eagle carved into Agrippa's Gate was swallowed in deep blackness. *"A star will come out of Jacob,"* Onias said, quoting the prophecy in the book of Numbers [see Numbers 24:17]. "What if it happens in our lifetime? What if?"

—p. 21

ASK

According to these passages, why must the forerunner of the Lord come first?

___

___

___

What do Eliyahu, Onias, and Zadok decide to do as they wait for Messiah?

___

___

___

Why would the coming of the Messiah make Herod (or anyone else) nervous?

___

___

___

READ

Shout and be glad, O Daughter of Zion. For I am coming, and I will live among you," declares the LORD. "Many nations will be joined with the LORD in that day and will become My people. I will live among you and you will know that the LORD Almighty has sent Me to you. The LORD will inherit Judah as His portion in the holy land and will again choose Jerusalem. Be still before the LORD, all mankind, because He has roused Himself from His holy dwelling!

—ZECHARIAH 2:10-13

At midnight one of the brightest stars in the northern skies was directly overhead. It is the one called Vega and named by the Jews The Warrior Triumphant: He Shall Be Exalted. This star is found in the constellation that pictures a harp such as King David played. The constellation is called Lyre for that reason. It is said by the Jews that the celestial music is so enchanting that rivers stop flowing and that lions and lambs lie down together in perfect harmony.

So shall life be after the coming of Messiah.

—p. 147

A scroll of remembrance was written in His presence concerning those who feared the LORD and honored His name.

"They will be Mine," says the LORD Almighty, "in the day when I make up My treasured possession. I will spare them, just as in compassion a man spares his son who serves him. And you will again see the distinction between the righteous and the wicked, between those who serve God and those who do not."

—MALACHI 3:16-18

No one knows about that day or hour, not even the angels, nor the Son, but only the Father. As it was in the days of Noah, so it will be at the coming of the Son of Man. For in the days before the flood, people were eating and drinking, marrying and giving in marriage, up to the day Noah entered the ark; and they knew nothing about what would happen until the flood came and took them all away. That is how it will be at the coming of the Son of Man. Two men will be in the field; one will be taken and the other left. Two women will be grinding with a hand mill; one will be taken and the other left.

Therefore keep watch, because you do not know on what day your Lord will come.

—MATTHEW 24:36-42

ASK

What do these passages say will happen when the Messiah comes?

What clear distinction does the Lord make between the righteous and the wicked?

If Messiah were to come to earth today, which "camp" would you find yourself in? Why?

Scripture says that no one but God the Father knows when the Messiah will return. Do you find this disconcerting or exhilarating? Explain. How might you prepare for His coming?

WONDER . . .

For as lightning that comes from the east is visible even in the west, so will the coming of the Son of Man. . . .

The sun will be darkened,
and the moon will not give its light;
the stars will fall from the sky,
and the heavenly bodies will be shaken. [See also Isaiah 13:10; 34:4.]

At that time the sign of the Son of Man will appear in the sky, and all the nations of the earth will mourn. They will see the Son of Man coming on the clouds of the sky, with power and great glory. And He will send His angels with a loud trumpet call, and they will gather His elect from the four winds, from one end of the heavens to the other.

—MATTHEW 24:27-31

Onias turned his face toward the window. He wanted to tell them. Wanted them to understand what he believed.

The Light was coming! There—did they not see it? The bright morning star! Gleaming at dawn! The star, rising out of Jacob!

—p. 239

Scripture clearly states it's not a question of *if* but of *when* the Messiah will come to earth. If you knew Messiah was coming in your lifetime, how would your life change? Is there anything you need to do while you watch and wait?

The coming of Messiah is more real
than the earth beneath our feet.
—ZACHARIAH (p. 208)

Dear Reader,

You are so important to us. We have prayed for you as we wrote this book and also as we receive your letters and hear your soul cries. We hope that *Fourth Dawn* has encouraged you to go deeper. To get to know Yeshua better. To fill your soul hunger by examining Scripture's truths for yourself.

We are convinced that if you do so, you will find this promise true: *"If you seek Him, He will be found by you."* —1 CHRONICLES 28:9

Bodie & Brock Thoene

Scripture References

[1] Matt. 17:5
[2] Matt. 17:9
[3] Matt. 17:10
[4] Matt. 17:11-12
[5] Mal. 4:5-6
[6] Luke 7:28
[7] Luke 7:27
[8] Matt. 17:20
[9] Gen. 1:3
[10] Gen. 1:4
[11] Gen. 2:7
[12] Deut. 6:4-5
[13] Luke 1:11-16
[14] Luke 1:18
[15] Luke 1:19-20
[16] Luke 1:21-22
[17] Luke 1:16-17
[18] Mal. 4:5-6
[19] Luke 2:25-26
[20] Num. 24:17
[21] Jer. 3:16
[22] Deut. 6:4
[23] Deut. 6:4-6
[24] Deut. 6:7
[25] Zech. 2:10-13
[26] Zech. 3:6, 8
[27] Zech 3:9
[28] Zech. 4:6
[29] Zech. 6:9-14
[30] Matt. 2:23
[31] Isa. 48:6
[32] Zech. 6:12
[33] Late Winter, 7 BC, Purim
[34] Gen. 49:9-10
[35] Mal. 4:5-6
[36] 1 Kings 17:1-7; 18:16-46
[37] Mal. 3:1
[38] Luke 1:16-17
[39] Mal. 4:5-6
[40] Luke 1:18
[41] Luke 1:25
[42] Early Spring, 7 BC, Annunciation
[43] Isa. 7:14
[44] Gen. 3:14-15
[45] Luke 1:26-27
[46] Luke 1:28
[47] Matt. 1:17
[48] Ps. 118:1-2
[49] Ps. 118:4
[50] Ps. 118:6
[51] Luke 1:28
[52] Luke 1:30
[53] Luke 1:31-33
[54] Luke 1:34
[55] Luke 1:35
[56] Luke 1:36-37
[57] Luke 1:38
[58] Isa. 7:14
[59] Luke 1:38
[60] Dan. 9:25
[61] Gen. 49:10
[62] Luke 1:39-41
[63] Luke 1:31
[64] Mal. 4:5-6
[65] Mal. 4:2
[66] Mal. 3:17-18
[67] Luke 1:42
[68] Luke 1:46-47
[69] Luke 1:43
[70] Luke 1:48-49
[71] Luke 1:44
[72] Luke 1:50-55
[73] Mal. 2:13-16
[74] Mal. 3:17; 4:2
[75] Mal. 4:5
[76] Matt. 1:1-17
[77] Luke 1:8-25
[78] Isa. 9:1-2
[79] Isa. 9:6
[80] Judges 13:2-24
[81] Isa. 53:3-12
[82] Zech. 12:10-11
[83] Matt. 1:19
[84] Matt. 1:1-17
[85] Ps. 77:4-9
[86] Isa. 11:1
[87] Ps. 77:14-15
[88] Isa. 11:1
[89] Isa. 11:1-2
[90] Luke 3:31
[91] Ps. 77:10
[92] Gen. 3:15
[93] Ps. 77:13-15, 18-20
[94] Ps. 78:1-2
[95] Late Spring, 7 BC, First Conjunction
[96] Ps. 113:1-9
[97] Ps. 91:1

[98] Jer. 22:30
[99] Gen. 15:6
[100] Jer. 32:17
[101] Isa 53:6
[102] Jer. 23:5-6
[103] Matt. 1:20-23; Isa. 7:14
[104] Early Summer, 7 BC
[105] Isa. 9:6
[106] Ps. 139:13
[107] Luke 1:60-63
[108] Luke 1:68-75
[109] Luke 1:76-79
[110] Luke 1:20
[111] Joel 2:28
[112] Gen. 37; 39–47; 50
[113] Eph. 2:20
[114] Midsummer, 7 BC
[115] Song of Songs 4:9
[116] Song of Songs 4:10
[117] Song of Songs 4:12
[118] Song of Songs 4:15
[119] Gen. 29:2-11
[120] Ps. 29:6
[121] Num. 24:17
[122] Isa. 25:8
[123] Matt. 1:22
[124] Mal. 4:2

Authors' Note

The following sources have been helpful in our research for this book.

- *The Complete Jewish Bible.* Translated by David H. Stern. Baltimore, MD: Jewish New Testament Publications, Inc., 1998.
- *iLumina*, a digitally animated Bible and encyclopedia suite. Carol Stream, IL: Tyndale House Publishers, 2002.
- *The International Standard Bible Encyclopaedia.* George Bromiley, ed. 5 vols. Grand Rapids, MI: Eerdmans, 1979.
- *The Life and Times of Jesus the Messiah.* Alfred Edersheim. Peabody, MA: Hendrickson Publishers, Inc., 1995.
- Starry Night™ Enthusiast Version 5.0, published by Imaginova™ Corp.

About the Authors

BODIE AND BROCK THOENE (pronounced *Tay-nee)* have written over 50 works of historical fiction. That these best sellers have sold more than 10 million copies and won eight ECPA Gold Medallion Awards affirms what millions of readers have already discovered—the Thoenes are not only master stylists but experts at capturing readers' minds and hearts.

In their timeless classic series about Israel (The Zion Chronicles, The Zion Covenant, and The Zion Legacy), the Thoenes' love for both story and research shines.

With The Shiloh Legacy and *Shiloh Autumn* (poignant portrayals of the American Depression), The Galway Chronicles (dramatic stories of the 1840s famine in Ireland), and the Legends of the West (gripping tales of adventure and danger in a land without law), the Thoenes have made their mark in modern history.

In the A.D. Chronicles they step seamlessly into the world of Jerusalem and Rome, in the days when Yeshua walked the earth and transformed lives with His touch.

Bodie began her writing career as a teen journalist for her local newspaper. Eventually her byline appeared in prestigious periodicals such as *U.S. News and World Report*, *The American West*, and *The Saturday Evening Post.* She also worked for John Wayne's Batjac Productions (she's best known as author of *The Fall Guy)* and ABC Circle Films as a writer and researcher. John Wayne described her as "a writer with talent that captures the people and the times!" She has degrees in journalism and communications.

Brock has often been described by Bodie as "an essential half of this writing team." With degrees in both history and education, Brock has, in his role as researcher and story-line consultant, added the vital dimension of historical accuracy. Due to such careful research, the Zion Covenant and Zion Chronicles series are recognized by the American Library Association, as well as Zionist libraries around the world, as classic historical novels and are used to teach history in college classrooms.

Bodie and Brock have four grown children—Rachel, Jake, Luke, and Ellie—and seven grandchildren. Their children are carrying on the Thoene family talent as the next generation of writers, and Luke produces the Thoene audiobooks. Bodie and Brock divide their time between London and Nevada.

For more information visit:
www.thoenebooks.com
www.familyaudiolibrary.com

THOENE FAMILY CLASSICS™

✪ ✪ ✪

THOENE FAMILY CLASSIC HISTORICALS
by Bodie and Brock Thoene

*Gold Medallion Winners**

THE ZION COVENANT
*Vienna Prelude**
Prague Counterpoint
Munich Signature
Jerusalem Interlude
Danzig Passage
*Warsaw Requiem**
London Refrain
Paris Encore
Dunkirk Crescendo

THE ZION CHRONICLES
*The Gates of Zion**
A Daughter of Zion
The Return to Zion
A Light in Zion
*The Key to Zion**

THE ZION DIARIES
The Gathering Storm
Against the Wind
Their Finest Hour

THE SHILOH LEGACY
*In My Father's House**
A Thousand Shall Fall
Say to This Mountain

SHILOH AUTUMN

THE GALWAY CHRONICLES
*Only the River Runs Free**
Of Men and of Angels
*Ashes of Remembrance**
All Rivers to the Sea

THE ZION LEGACY
Jerusalem Vigil
Thunder from Jerusalem
Jerusalem's Heart
Jerusalem Scrolls
Stones of Jerusalem
Jerusalem's Hope

A.D. CHRONICLES
First Light
Second Touch
Third Watch
Fourth Dawn
Fifth Seal
Sixth Covenant
Seventh Day
Eighth Shepherd
Ninth Witness
Tenth Stone
Eleventh Guest
Twelfth Prophecy

CP0064

THOENE FAMILY CLASSICS™

✪ ✪ ✪

THOENE FAMILY CLASSIC AMERICAN LEGENDS

LEGENDS OF THE WEST
by Bodie and Brock Thoene

Legends of the West, Volume One
- *Sequoia Scout*
- *The Year of the Grizzly*
- *Shooting Star*

Legends of the West, Volume Two
- *Gold Rush Prodigal*
- *Delta Passage*
- *Hangtown Lawman*

Legends of the West, Volume Three
- *Hope Valley War*
- *The Legend of Storey County*
- *Cumberland Crossing*

Legends of the West, Volume Four
- *The Man from Shadow Ridge*
- *Cannons of the Comstock*
- *Riders of the Silver Rim*

LEGENDS OF VALOR
by Luke Thoene

Sons of Valor
Brothers of Valor
Fathers of Valor

✪ ✪ ✪

THOENE CLASSIC NONFICTION
by Bodie and Brock Thoene

Writer-to-Writer

THOENE FAMILY CLASSIC SUSPENSE
by Jake Thoene

CHAPTER 16 SERIES
Shaiton's Fire
Firefly Blue
Fuel the Fire

✪ ✪ ✪

THOENE FAMILY CLASSICS FOR KIDS

BAKER STREET DETECTIVES
by Jake and Luke Thoene

The Mystery of the Yellow Hands
The Giant Rat of Sumatra
The Jeweled Peacock of Persia
The Thundering Underground

LAST CHANCE DETECTIVES
by Jake and Luke Thoene

Mystery Lights of Navajo Mesa
Legend of the Desert Bigfoot

THE VASE OF MANY COLORS
by Rachel Thoene (Illustrations by Christian Cinder)

✪ ✪ ✪

THOENE FAMILY CLASSIC AUDIOBOOKS

Available from
www.thoenebooks.com or
www.familyaudiolibrary.com

CP0064